FOREBODING EXPERIENCES

A SUPERNATURAL SUSPENSE

Foreboding Experiences
by Shashank Jalan
Paperback Edition

First published in India in 2023 by

Inkfeathers Publishing
Vivek Vihar, New Delhi 110095
www.inkfeathers.com

ISBN 978-93-90882-92-2

FOREBODING EXPERIENCES

A SUPERNATURAL SUSPENSE

SHASHANK JALAN

Inkfeathers Publishing
www.inkfeathers.com

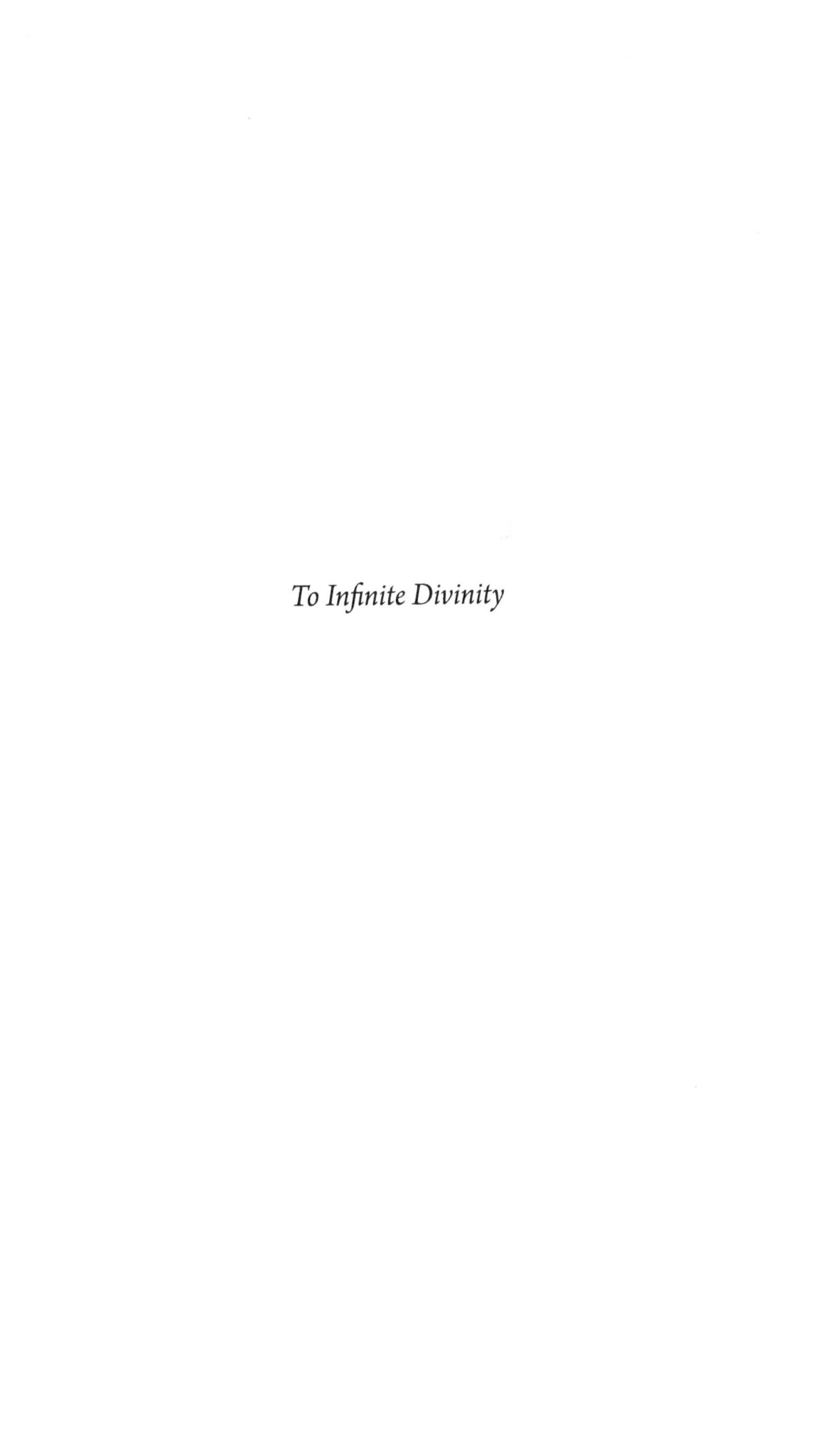

To Infinite Divinity

Contents

Preface

Have you ever explored the world of the mind? Yes, there are two worlds: one, the without, and one less explored, within. We recognize all the sensations and events of the outer world only in one place: the mind. So, actually, it is not the outer world but the inner world where experiences happen. I got an opportunity to explore the power where, solely, the mind can help in having various experiences of the outside world, which may be far from real reach. I got this opportunity during the pandemic lockdown, as I had the time to write freely.

I believe if the writing satisfies and pleases the author, readers with a similar mindset will also have a splendid chance of enjoying the experience. I am interested in various genres of fiction. This work is far from any actual events and there is no attempt to prove or disprove anything. The story is imaginary; however, it shows subtle realities of life. It's inspired a lot by natural landscapes.

I feel we should take stories as stories only and that fictional literature is creativity bursting out in language form, like the brushstrokes of imagination, which make the experience of a tangible life richer by intellectuality.

Ghost stories had once upon a time emerged as one of the most popular genres of literature because of many reasons. However, the most potent of all was the fact that fears in the olden days were very tangible, for example, wild animals, starvation, and isolation, and it was delightful and romantic to invent fears that would never come and get a person.

A particular kind of ghost story is dear to me. It doesn't concern itself much with today's techniques of crime and gore to create instant horror instead, slowly grasps the reader with a subtleness that transforms into profoundness. It focuses a lot on atmosphere—the mystery and the storyline are very important.

I like the style of various authors like Walter de la Mare, Emily Bronte, and M. R. James, to name a few; and that has inspired me to create a story in my style, which I would love. I believe that if the novel takes the readers somewhere, makes them think, and makes them feel even one-tenth of the ecstasy I felt while writing; it would fulfill my purpose of writing.

S.J.

Prologue

Two long hours had passed since we had dined, but still, no one had experienced a genuine terror. The plan was failing miserably. A strange stagnancy was in the air and the candles just showed enough to guess that each visitor grew desperate and uneasy.

There were eleven of us, five couples, and the host, sitting around a rectangular table in a closed room. The house was shaking, and the locked windows made queer noises as the winds struggled with them.

"We have discussed four stories and none of them were satisfying enough, I have to say..." a man said.

"Oh, yes! All were boring. How on earth are we going to spend three nights in this fashion if we still go by the plan?" It was a woman's voice this time.

"I thought none of us would be able to sleep because of the storm raging outside, so I suggested the idea of ghostly storytelling just to add some flavor to our already spoiled holiday in this part of the country... But what we need is something profound and real..." Another man uttered in a low voice, urging.

All the guests were confused and soon started a debate on the very idea of the existence of ghosts.

"I somewhat believe in these things. There is surely something there, which is inexplicable and though we can't see it, we can't deny it too...." A woman said.

The debate continued, and the last comment was,

"I don't believe in all this. I think it's just a psychological play… all in the mind…"

At this, the host, who was till this time silent like a saint, interrupted in a witty tone, "Oh, is it?"

Everyone was quiet for some seconds after this reaction.

"Gentlemen, I have myself experienced and known such things and thus want to be away from these topics. Yet, I must emphasize that forming any concrete view on such matters and expecting it to be correct is a mistake."

The silence of the other guests continued, and each expected the host to say more.

"Why don't you tell us your experience?" A man asked.

"Oh, yes! It would be a great idea. We need something real…" another voice supported.

"I wasn't directly involved…" he replied.

"No problem…" replied others in one voice.

"No… no…." the host hesitated but ultimately yielded and went on to tell the most intriguing story which I have ever heard.

The narrator read it aloud from an old manuscript, written in the most beautiful handwriting one can imagine. His elder cousin wrote it as a memoir, and she never wrote it to be read aloud. The narration stretched over three nights and left all the listeners with an experience that they would probably never forget.

I, as a man in the publishing business, felt an irresistible urge to solicit the manuscript for publication. The narrator, being a great friend of mine and a kind man, ultimately accepted my fervent requests.

Here is her manuscript in Chapter-wise form:

1

I HAD TURNED eighteen that day, an unforgettable day of my life, unforgettable as the commencement of a series of strange days filled with events which aren't near to general expectations. An unprecedented wave of inspiration has induced me to sit up in the middle of this rainy night and visit again, these territories which are far and deep. Initially, I felt that the dancing shades of yellow over my bedroom walls, caused by the bedtime candles, kindled in me such inspiration or passion. But now, as I have taken the pen in my hand, I feel it is something more and unfathomable. I have already put down some lines, but I have failed to find the correct word to describe the nature of those days, and now I move on by concluding that such rare feelings are even beyond the boundaries of the top dictionary words which are usually used in such contexts. Anyway, I assume the reader will understand what I mean, and I expect anyone who reads this is doing so solely out of his or her own free will, as I am sure I cannot be untrue to myself as I write and also that I have no answers for any question that may arise in the reader's mind.

Due to some socio-political tensions in my state, at least that's what I had been told then, I was sent to my uncle's house, which was far from home. My father, who was the chief editor of one of the prestigious dailies, looked extraordinarily occupied that day, and I still remember his expression. Despite my asking many times, he didn't tell me anything about the problem that was going on. He only told me that he was sending me to Uncle Vijay's place. I thought it would be best to follow my father without more cross-questioning. Strangely, I couldn't even find the newspaper in my house that morning. Everything was fast-paced, and at around three in the day, I was ready with all my things packed. My father gave a look filled with concern and bid goodbye to his only daughter.

"But… I don't know about Uncle Vijay much, and I have never been to that place..." I couldn't resist speaking these words at the end moment.

"I wrote to him about this before, I say, you need not worry at all..." was his only reply, and then a relaxed "bye" in conclusion which quite lightened the spirits.

My father's trusted staffer, Mr. Roy, was given the job of accompanying me and safely "depositing" me to the destination. The train journey seemed endless, as usual. A strange heaviness developed in my heart, as I couldn't still accept all that was happening, not even in my wildest dreams. I remember looking out of the window for hours with my attention captured by the bright blue sky and the small green hills as we traveled into the hilly regions of the state. Gradually, I could mark the crowded society fading away from sight.

"Do only a few people come to this part?" I asked, looking around and seeing nothing but vacant seats.

"Miss, it will rather charm you, the sight of the place in the wet season, and especially you will find a different lot of folks there." Mr. Roy, who made small remarks the whole of the journey, made this one with a uniqueness to stir the question:

"What is it about them?"

"You know, the last time I came here, years ago, the ticket collector wished me 'Good morning, Sir' and a 'Thank you.' Do you find it anywhere else? I had seen three schools in that thinly populated town. Three! Most of the people I found, and this is years ago, had courtesy and manners, which are not found normally. Rarely you may find any person untidy or ill-dressed." He spoke with excitement and amazement, which would make any person believe that what he said was only one-third of the actual uniqueness of the town. The conclusion I ultimately drew was that it was not 'just another place.'

Then, I only knew that my uncle was younger than my father, a very loving man whose wife had passed a long time back, and that by profession, he was a lawyer. I also knew that he had a son who was some three or four years older than me and was my only cousin, paradoxically, with whom I had only met in childhood. His name was Arun.

"Maybe I would enjoy his company." I thought.

Adding to my "vast" knowledge about my uncle, Mr. Roy remarked on the journey, "Ma'am, I have heard that your uncle has recently purchased an enormous mansion!"

"Is it?"

"Yes. I also know that, uh, what should I say? He is a lawyer by profession, and has earned good money by it but, and this is my feeling, he is a little thrifty kind. You get it.... Oh, but he is a gentleman."

This was all.

The outfit for the day was no different: light-colored top and skirt, socks, and shoes. I remember reading the English Book *Answers to Strange Questions of This World* curiously, but also leaving it completely when the chapter on paranormal questions came. Though I was a very inquisitive person, I had always bluntly avoided any conversation about ghosts throughout the eighteen years. I don't know why, but I didn't like it and wanted to be miles away from the topic. Then, I was unaware of what was coming to me in the future. The day passed slowly and when I opened my eyes the next morning; we had just reached our destination. I looked out of the window, as the train slowed and saw the bleak railway station, a gray-bricked platform amidst the tall, green grass. Mr. Roy took my heavy bag in his hand and kept on insisting on the other one too, but I smiled and carried it on my own. As soon as I jumped onto the station, I was filled with wonder. A natural smile emerged on my face as I had never been to such a gorgeous place. Cool winds were blowing, making my hair uncontrollable and my happiness too.

"Beautiful country!" I remarked on the countryside, slightly shading my eyes to look far.

The station was old-fashioned for sure. Unoccupied benches, a small building, and just a couple of men with hats, coats, and umbrellas. It was all. The platform being wet appeared not gray but black. Strangely, even with the sun in the sky, the vicinity was quite on the grayish side, and other than the noise of the train; the silence was nocturnal. Anyway, being there somehow eased any hint of discomfort from the sudden journey and the unease in the corner of my heart.

At the station I found my cousin, nay, to say the truth, my cousin found me.

"I am Vaanya..." I said as he approached with an expression conveying that he had recognized me.

He was quite tall, wearing a gray tucked shirt and black pants. His face which was quite wet just like his hair, probably as the clouds had been drizzling previously; expressed a man who occupies himself with a lot of thought. As he looked deep into my eyes and my face, I saw that a slight smile slowly emerged from the corner of his lip, apparently a smile of admiration.

"Hello! I am Arun. I was expecting you. You have grown taller since I saw you."

"When did we meet last? I mean, I don't much remember a meeting with you..." then I smilingly corrected, "Don't mind..."

He smiled back.

Mr. Roy left me when he was sure about whatever he wanted to confirm with Arun and then last, I remember him waving from a distance, which he had walked on, for the next train. As we walked out of the station, I saw a few horse carriages lined along the road, waiting for passengers. This was normal in one way as the terrain was high and low, but surely it was a thing to attract scrutiny by an ordinary person. Scrutiny because all the carriages were peculiar in the sense that they were high, black, and had covered "chamber" like structures for the passengers to sit. The wheels were enormous and there was a chief seat outside the chamber itself for the driver to sit and control the horses. Meanwhile, Arun called me to step up in one of them.

"This place has classical and fancy influences, I believe," I said as I climbed a couple of stairs to the high, curtained chamber.

I was finally successful in entering it. Well, not without the help of Arun.

“Yes… it may be…” he replied as he adjusted himself over the brown leathered seats and closed the gate.

As the carriage rolled, I tried to strike up a conversation with my cousin.

“Do you have any hint why I have been sent here?”

“If you don’t know, then I feel I am in a much worse position to answer... I believe you must forget all that. I believe all of it is destiny.”

The sun was shining beautifully over the expanded green cover. Over the left and on the right, low hills were covered in gray mists, suggesting that perhaps it was raining high up there. I fixed my glance at the countryside landscape. I was not at the leisure of seeing the sun for long, as it soon disappeared amidst the gray clouds which hovered in the sky. The sky had turned shades and against the background, a solitary big black bird was loosely drifting in the air, which also became invisible soon. Dense grayness had become the principal feature of the landscape. Occasionally, I caught the sight of some locals from my window. Greenery too was rather incomplete save the tall wet grasses which we had already passed. Now I could see low shrubs over wide fields which had a yellow-gray shade, shaking with the gusts. Breezes traveled in and out of the carriage, carrying with them the odor of rain and soaked soil, and though chilling, they were wonderful. The gusts were gentle and so freshening that I felt washed by the rain itself. This part of the country, I never knew it existed, was quite alien to me. A sense of gloom was there for sure. Loneliness had pervaded my spirit, but the incompleteness, the wet rawness, and all of it added to the mystical enchantment of the place. A strange nervousness, I know not why, gripped me, but still, the weather excited my nerves in a new way.

After a travel of another hour, we finally reached the house. The carriage entered it through a high, old, barred gate that was already wide open. The mansion: it was a structure of classical style which looked two-floored and very wide from the outside. I stepped down, failing to remove my eyes from it all the while, noticing that the sunlight was even weaker, probably obstructed and that the house was quite high. It was hard to even imagine such a house standing in such desolation and the deep of such countryside—almost remote. The ground was grassy and squelched underfoot. The atmosphere was mysteriously beautiful, and magical but also inexplicably silent—certainly more than what I had been seeing all this while, certainly more in all aspects. I could see no one all around, but outside, the concrete road which we had followed, trees on the sides of it, and inside here, the house. The breezes gave a chill as they passed between the legs.

I can't quite understand, why my eyes stuck to the house as soon as I saw it, maybe it was because of the odd shape and dimensions of it, probably because of its European influences, but I wasn't sure then and not even now. This structure, having shadows of grayness over it, stood strong and only a couple of dead trees surrounded it, the only ones in its large, uncared garden. The walls on the other part of the house must have been covered with moss I could distinctly imagine. Though the high winds seemed to have been hitting it for years, it didn't lose its grandness and still was a testimony of the rich taste of whoever got it built. I could see many windows; they were painted white. Most of them were closed save one which was drifting with the winds.

The environment inside the house was inexplicably calm. As soon as I entered the house, I became more conscious of the need for formality and waved back my hair as I expected to meet my uncle. Instead, a sweet little boy appeared out of one of the many rooms. He was wearing a buttoned brown jacket, half pants, and brown socks whose stretch just fell short of reaching his knees. It seemed like the fairness of his baby days hadn't left him, but his eyes were deep, gently roundish with deeper eyeballs, which shined like water was in them. His dark, lustrous hair was combed save some thick waves which sloped down his forehead in a gentle curvature, almost touching his eyebrows. He scrutinized me with eagerness and slowly and shyly came near me. His hands were behind his back. I asked with a smile who he was.

"I am Ajay, and I am eleven and I am in school..." He told in one shy and quick breath.

I turned to Arun in question, and he approached the little boy and told with his hands in his pockets, "Brother, take care of her. She is your sister."

It surprised me with laughter, as I wasn't at all aware of my second cousin. I drew him closer to me by his arms, slightly bent, and touched his cheek, which was perfectly childish, but also unnaturally cold as if rubbed with ice. I soon felt my cheeks, and the condition was the same. It was probably that the atmosphere within the mansion was on the colder side.

"So, this is my little brother… How are you?"

"Good," he giggled a bit, looking into my eyes, and then grabbed one of my fingers and led me slowly to the second floor, where a room was ready for me. We had stepped up the wooden stairs, which made heavy creaks, and after a narrow dark passage with small landscapes hanging on both walls, we reached a room. The doors were painted white, and the noise of the strong winds and loosely swaying glass windows echoed all over. On entering, I saw that the room had a high ceiling, two individual, magnificent beds covered with white sheets and each with a couple of cozy pillows, a small study table with a lamp on it which was before a big, open window. The room was clean, dimly lit by yellow bulbs held by small, black statues. Soon I realized that not only furniture, but the entire room could be categorized as antique. But the luxury of the room and the shine of the statues all looked faded; this room too was like the entire house, drenched in undisturbed solitude and having a story of its own. A light green carpet covered the vast floor. It was as big as one can imagine in such an old room.

I placed myself comfortably on the bed and felt relaxed as some time passed in silence.

"I have heard that you read many books." My cousin started.

"Just a few…" I smiled back.

The glitter in his eyes as he looked at me meant we were already friends.

"You know, I too have a story to tell. But I prefer telling it only at night. You know it's... It's real." I noticed an eagerness in his eyes, which the child didn't know how to suppress.

"Oh, that's nice... How many have listened to this real thing before me?"

"None. No one wants to listen... and no one would tell you this story," he replied.

I didn't understand him at that point. But didn't ask any further for the time being. My mind got occupied with the expectation of Arun to come with my other bag, which was with him still. Strangely, he didn't come up.

"Where is Arun and where is Uncle?"

"Father is out, and Arun has probably again gone to his study room... You know he spends most of his time there only..." he spoke the last line in a whisper, with his right hand vertically at the end of his lip as if it was a secret.

I had understood that Arun was a reserved person, and that was fine, but he didn't come to meet me upstairs, nor did he talk much, not that he wasn't gentle or lacked courtesy and cordiality, but still I found it untoward.

"What does he study?" I asked, stroking back the boy's hair.

"He never tells... Never allows anyone into his room."

This statement raised my curiosity to know what could be so special about the subject of his study. I thought he would reveal it to me, as I was older than Ajay, at least. I went down and saw that my bag was laid on the chair. Ajay followed me and told me that I was to eat the meal that was specially cooked for me. I had the meal, and it was different and nice. Then I came up again with my bag. My little cousin who was my only company all the while in that house, a house which looked to have been built to occupy at least twenty people, talked with me for some time but then asked me if I too wanted to go to the lane. I refused the offer for the time being but told him to go if he could go by himself or if it was his usual course. Seeing the child's willingness to go out but his hesitation to leave me alone, I asked him to carry out his leisure activity. He finally went out to play, telling me he would return soon. Till evening, I unpacked my bag and changed. I looked around my room and could see the usual moving shadows of long evenings around the room, taller than I had ever seen before. I slowly went out and saw another room on the floor, but apparently, it was locked. There was a large, glassed window in the passage from where I could see outside. My eyes were again filled with strange wonder seeing the captivating beauty from that height. The sun was setting; the cultivators were returning, and the streams were no longer shiny. Soon, the sun dropped and the infinite-looking gray-pink sky became dark and silent. It was all before my eyes, making me feel how magically and unnoticeably this happens. Nothing much was visible afterward, and I gradually felt slightly driven by the loneliness and the strange heaviness in my heart, which I figured was still alive from the journey. There was nobody around and such was the condition that I had to find and switch on the yellow bulbs myself. It was a peculiar solitude that had the power to instill mixed feelings of somberness and a pleasant excitement too, in anybody's mind.

The silence there had a noise of its own. I could hear the silence.

Then it struck to my mind, rather late, how sillily I had forgotten that I could find and go to Arun's room. I paced down and found my little cousin had returned and that he was now eating a piece of bread. He pointed towards his brother's room, intelligently interpreting the question in my eyes, and I knocked on the closed door.

"Who is it?" He exclaimed as if disturbed.

"It's I..."

Noises of closing a cupboard and moving of something heavy followed by falling of pens on the floor came and within a minute Arun emerged hurriedly—and closed the door behind him.

"Ajay, I told you to be with Vaanya... Well, did you enjoy the food and the view? Well, I had some work of extreme importance..." He said, half smiling.

"Yes, quite so. I understand. Can I come into your study and know what you research?" I spoke without thinking much.

On this question, his expression showed uneasiness. He replied at length that his study wouldn't excite me at all and instead told me that we could sit together and talk, or I could use this time to amuse myself in any way I wanted. The last line was true, and a realization overwhelmed me: I wouldn't find so much time as then, once I was back in the city and I could use it to read all that I had wanted. Arun sat with us on the sofas of the hall, but it appeared as a forced courtesy by him, as he still didn't join any conversation. I got absorbed in the book I had got and occasionally some talk was there. Time still passed slowly.

"Don't you have any visitors in the evening or so?" I asked at length.

"None. It's usual here. Maybe it's different in the city." My little cousin spoke.

Soon I heard the noise of the winds rioting. I could see nearby trees swinging with such force that it was scary. When I asked the boys about it, the elder one said that it was nothing new. The feeling of strange nervous excitement gripped me even more. I don't know why, but I would soon be well with my new situation and this I knew, surely. The air which was better than the industrial air of the city and, of course, the solitude; would both collectively prove marvelous, I thought, the former for heightening outward grace and the latter for inward.

Soon I took notice, and that was only once, that Arun was staring at his palms in an unbroken gaze, continuously, for some moments. I agree that I noticed ink stains between his fingers, but that only suggested that he could have been writing something previously, and that's all. I couldn't fathom what was he looking into, that intensely.

As the clock struck nine, we were about to eat, but the doorbell rang, splitting the silence. I opened the door and saw a tall man with a smile on his face. He was Uncle Vijay. It was a relief to see another human.

2

"Hello, my dear!" Uncle came in and embraced me with a smile of joy on his face.

Before I could even bow down to greet him, he held my cheeks gently with both hands and remarked, "You have surely grown up! But you are as lovely and winning as when you were a child." He then asked me about how I felt there.

Uncle didn't have a hair out of place. He didn't look aged at all. He was smooth-shaven, had well-defined features, and had he worn spectacles, he would have looked scholarly.

Ajay carried Uncle's bag, and I took the coat which was in his hand, and we sat at the dining table. Uncle's smile was the same even while he was sitting down. The three of us ate and a small conversation also began, but soon I realized that someone was missing. I couldn't see Arun anywhere—he had gone. I was wondering why he didn't dine with us, but I didn't care this time. Did he not like company at all? I still question myself.

"So, what do you study?" Uncle asked me while taking a sip of juice.

"I have just begun the study of psychology, Uncle, and that too not for a profession but as my interests lie in those areas... I want to know about the depths of the mind and actually, I understood that human psychology plays a significant role in problem-solving too..."

"That's great... You know I was a practicing lawyer and dealt with truths, so I would also love to know about your subject. I know that a question about why you have been sent here will arise in your mind, at least that I can say without knowing psychology; but I say that you don't worry about it. Ajay is here with you all the time and if you need anything, you can tell him. I am there too, after evenings." Uncle said in a go.

"So, Uncle, may I ask what you do now?"

"Business..." he didn't elaborate or specify, and I asked no more.

"Uncle, can I go out tomorrow as I want to see the little hills and the streams..." I asked at length.

Uncle paused a bit and rubbed his cheek in thought for a second, within which his eyebrows came together and parted. He answered: "I will try to return early tomorrow and then I, Ajay and you will go out. Is that fine?"

"But can't I go alone in the morning hours? I mean, I don't wish to impose a burden on you..."

"I insist on going with you and also because you are new in this place, the people in the town are not as friendly as they look." He answered and momentarily glanced at the other side.

I knew by then that I would have to endure the same isolation the next day, too. Uncle's unwillingness to talk about his work prevented me even from expressing my desire to go there the next day. In my heart, many questions had risen till the time I was alone in my room, resting on my bed, under the dim yellow light. Curiosity grew in my mind about my uncle's work and also about his psychology as a relatively young man without a wife. But I didn't have the information to make any conclusions. When the thoughts stopped, I started to feel the silence of the atmosphere influencing me once again. I was alone in the room. My reason forced me to question, I don't know why when I had spent not even a full day there, could there be something that burdened the very air, and which wasn't known to me. Also, Arun's behavior, which I thought to be cold, haunted my thoughts.

For a moment I turned back to the left as I felt seeing someone or something stirring. My heart skipped a beat. As I faced the direction, my back to the room door, I saw and rather laughed, that I had been mistaken by the unsettled dark curtains. I stepped towards the window to see if it was open. Suddenly, there was a noise. The room door opened behind me, and, with a start, I turned again, discovering none other than my little cousin who entered the room. I naturally was a bit surprised as I had expected him to have slept till that hour. On momentarily glancing back at the curtains, I was sure they weren't fluttering anymore. He slowly stepped up onto the high bed and sat beside me. He asked me whether I was reading something, and I replied with a no.

"So, do you want to hear the story?" He wittily asked.

"Yes, I would love to... But can you tell me what's it all about?"

"Oh, you want to hear it!" he excitedly said, made himself comfortable on the bed, and soon continued, "See, it's about a Mr. S—."

"Wait, let me first close the window," I said and advanced.

As I was in full sight of that corner of the room, and as I moved the curtains, I saw the strong window already locked.

I stood there for a moment, looking at it.

"Continue..." I walked back and sat on the bed near him, not thinking more of what I imagined then, was a short visual mistake of mine.

"I don't know his full name, only my father knows it. He was a very rich businessman in his time. He used to control the town's business related to liquor and soon became a powerful person in the entire region. They say that he didn't come from a good background and also that he had left two wives or that they had died, something like that. He used to be very tall and lean. His rise was sudden, within weeks, and this quite brought him into focus. It is said that he raised many followers and partners who helped him go about and expand his business. You know he also had a criminal mindset and gradually turned into a believer in negative energies, and some say he even practiced black arts. He had used things like magical roots to destroy other's businesses. Soon, people feared him and believed him to be someone otherworldly. No pedestrian dared to enter his house. He soon became more ambitious, took heavy loans, employed more men, and went more into those magical areas... Then... Yes, then! Soon his time went off, after government intervention in his business. Bankruptcy ate him. He didn't come out of his house for days and was mostly seen at the second floor's window peeping mysteriously as if trying to find someone down the hills. He remained missing for days. Then one day they found him hung..." he said it with extreme patience and care, and he even adopted different voices at different times along with appropriate suspenseful expressions. One moment his voice went low and the other, it blasted.

"Okay now, please stop!" I interrupted him and then calmly continued, "Boys of your age shouldn't think about or hear these tales... I know what you were going to say next, that his ghost wanders about. Isn't it?" I kept my hand softly on his chest to calm his heart, which was beating unusually fast.

"Yes! He hasn't left this place. After all, this is a fact... and not a tale." he clutched the pillow and almost crushed it. The narrator himself had become afraid of his narration.

I looked into his big innocent eyes and said "See ghosts are just, just a psychological play, mental phenomena of crazy thoughts... It may be mental imagery that arises when you are alone. "

"What is psychology? I have heard of it but..."

"Okay..." I sighed.

I had forgotten he was only a little boy.

"This story must be another folk tale but a modern version of it... So then why don't you tell me where this man lived in the town if he existed? See, I told you wouldn't be able...."

"Probably in this house..." He interrupted me.

He crafted words with such confidence that it would be rather hard to disbelieve him.

He kept on looking at me with his eyes full of meaning, as if saying "Don't put it away in such a manner, believe it."

For the first time, I experienced a chill run down my spine for a second, as I heard his statement.

"What do you mean?" was my reaction.

"But Papa disagrees and just says what you said."

He continued after breaking his gaze over me, "He dislikes my talking about it and gets angry. But I'll tell you something. I have seen him sometimes, lurking in the dark corners. Certainly, something stirs here at night, all about the hall, and comes in and out from the open doors. But do you know, the house has been renovated and some new furniture bought in too."

I looked at the dull ceiling, regaining myself. By Ajay's words and by the dim stillness of the room, I cannot deny a slight stimulation of fear in my nerves. The dim yellow bulb was flickering and everything else was silent in that house, a prolonged silence that was indifferent to night and day. The clock had struck one by this time, but a hint of sleep wasn't in my eyes. I knew I hated supernatural stories.

"Uncle is correct. You know I also got mistaken just sometime back. I thought I had seen something in that corner, but then it was only, yes, only the mighty curtain. This house is enormous, and you shifted recently, sometimes the eyes take time to adjust." I said what I thought, but then I saw something which solved my confusion for the time being.

"What's in your hand?" I asked him when I noticed Ajay was fidgeting with something. He handed it to me, and it was a magazine. I wondered why I couldn't see it in so much time. On opening, I found it was a graphic novel named *The Tall Shadow* or something like that, and also that it was not at all for kids. It was horror.

"So ... You read all this?" I said dramatically. I felt I had discovered the psychological reason behind his narration.

"No, actually ... You can take it, sister." He replied.

"Okay then, brother. This is going to remain with me for the time being and now go to sleep and forget about Mr. S—..."

I told him to forget all of it, but I couldn't. I stared at the ceiling with open eyes for hours. It's a general tendency in me that the first night in unknown places is quite sleepless and disturbing. I soon stood up and started walking around in my large bedroom. I thought deeply about the little boy with my arms crossed across my chest. He was a motherless child with such a strange brother. Maybe he felt better as I came, but what of the story? Children of that age make up such things and speak wrongly interpreting them. Though for a moment I giggled when his innocent, frightened expression came into my imagination again, but soon the feeling faded. I couldn't keep myself from thinking about the truth of the story.

I realized the clock had struck two already, and I felt exhaustion overwhelming me. I clicked the bulb off; Ajay had gone to his room by this time, wishing me goodnight, and I closed my eyes for some moments. What a relief it was.

But then I reopened them, and something shined into my eyes. It was, my eyes soon recognized, a small, circular, white glow that appeared as if dancing around the dark, high ceiling. I was terrified without a word. The light went all around the room with a wild speed and I, too terrified to utter anything, saw it from one corner. The source of the glow was the nearby window, which was wide open. I remembered opening it. It wasn't anything supernatural; I knew for sure, but still, my legs were shaking. I walked, gathering all my courage, and looked down through the window. What I saw was astonishing.

There stood someone down there, almost wrapped in the fog and quite invisible, but he was holding a torch and focusing it into my bedroom. If we assume it was a man, he couldn't be much differentiated from the background. My breaths became inconsistent. I was about to scream within which the figure switched off the torch and everything became invisible, as before.

I didn't wait and ran to inform someone. As I pushed myself down into the dimly lit hall, I could hear the dull noises of men. The noises grew to be alarming and as I reached the dining table, panting, they could be easily comprehended. I recognized two voices. The tone was of disagreement. These voices were of none other than Arun and Uncle. These shocking noises were coming from my uncle's bedroom. I couldn't help but hear and I heard some fragments. They were in there for a long time.

"You made the wrong decision—it was you, not I!" it was Arun's voice.

"Oh, so now you decide what is wrong and what is right?" Uncle replied calmly.

"Okay, so may I know the details of what you do, Father? And can you explain why you left the job of a lawyer?" There was no answer following this.

The conversation soon became silent, and I climbed upstairs once again. I couldn't speak to them. From the small part of the possible long debate that I had heard, there were some disagreements going on. From another display of Arun's cold behavior, I knew I was not the only one confused or concerned about my uncle's work. But soon, I thought my conduct too wasn't correct this time.

I felt I was in the middle of a new environment where there was grace, intelligence, and affection but also confusion, anger, a child's imagination, and horror. It was then that it struck me for the first time that all these were elements relating to the human mind. How could I forget this factor? After all, I was keen on psychology, then. I took out my notebook from my bag which I had kept aside but though I couldn't frame a research work out of it, those first-hand experiences, those details, which I jotted in that notebook are the source by which I write today in such exact detail, as to even the dialogues.

3

The next morning was a less bright one. I awoke somewhat late. On stepping down from the bed, the first thing I did after brushing was go to the window outside my room and look through it. I didn't want to peep down from my room's window, after the last night's incident. The view: I still remember it to be a perfect water painting of the gray, misty hills. The cloudy sky and its perfect reflection on small streams flowing here and there could be imagined as a complex interconnected chain of emotions and I could clearly see the silvery thunder cracking in the far face of the earth's horizon, which looked magnificent. I stretched myself a bit and enjoyed the fresh winds. But the window was open. I mean had been open since I had seen it last night. "Isn't this risky?" I thought as the window had no grills or bars, no windows in the house had them. Anyone could come up into the house from there, but I ignored this as the house was high and secondly wondered if it was another custom of town.

"Miss, Will you have some tea? It's down, perfectly waiting for you." It was a young man's voice, deep and unknown to me.

I turned back immediately.

"See, I only drink tea when I am nervous or anxious, but thank you..." I smilingly replied.

I didn't recognize the tall gentleman who was standing in front of me. He had a well-built frame over which he was wearing a white, collared t-shirt. His neatly combed hair was rather shining, and his clean-shaven face was on the serious side but with an intelligent, confident look. His features were sharp and strong. One would call him good-looking.

"I am Rajesh, Arun's friend. I hope I have not disturbed you."

This meant he was also perhaps of Arun's age, but what a difference there was in both their demeanors. I also introduced myself.

"But what about the tea?" I asked.

"Actually, Arun asked me to have tea till the time he returns from his room, and it was so much, I couldn't drink that alone."

"Oh…"

"Actually, well, I have just returned from the city where I study and came here to meet Arun, but ..." He spoke at length, while his hands were in his pockets.

"But what? You found out that Arun's behavior has become strange?"

"Exactly! How do you know?"

"Just because I feel something is disturbing him; I guess..." I slowed down.

"You know he wasn't like this before... Since he has shifted to this house, I think his behavior has changed a lot." His expression became serious, and his gaze was no longer in my eyes.

"Okay, I feel I will not take any more of your time. I live nearby. By the way, nice to meet you, and Good Morning!" He smiled a genuine smile and I did too. He walked down the stairs very athletically and within a minute, I could see him outside the house, on his bicycle. I don't know why I was left with a pleasant feeling, but soon I remembered the last night's incident, which didn't give way to any upcoming thoughts. I told the whole incident to Arun, as he was the first person I saw as I went down. He was drinking the tea alone. Patiently enough, he heard the complete story about the torchlight.

"So, others are after it too..." He murmured and then continued, "I suggest you should close the window and draw the curtains at night." I was studying his expressions, and they expressed deep thought once again.

"Yes... I never thought of it. Thanks for the suggestion." I stood up and paced towards the kitchen, quite vexed at his stupid "out of the box" suggestion. All the while, my mind suggested that the dark shadow might be an important part of this play. Arun had said that Uncle was out for work and Ajay was asleep and I climbed up to my room soon after. As I was climbing the stairs, I heard the banging of a room door. Probably Arun had left college, I thought. But then I let go of thoughts about him, thinking that sometimes people who do serious research get a bit lost. I spent some time studying my subject, specifically hallucinations.

It was noon when my little cousin came into my room. He sat beside me, and we talked about his friends. He said none of his friends lived near their current house, and it was no astonishment to me. I was sorry for the boy. He needed more friends and a change. He had to be out of the closed environment of that house and particularly away from his brother.

"You remember yesterday's story? I can show his face to you... I can draw it." He sprung up and then continued casually.

"You can draw it?" I was a bit confused but proceeded, "Show me then."

He drew the face in front of me slowly, carefully, and thoughtfully, as if turning back the pages of memory. He completed it soon. Yes, the drawing, to some extent, was a "child's drawing" but still it was such a face I had never seen. Drawn and shaded with a 4B, it was a face beyond any description, giving me a sense of uneasiness as I glanced at it. Describing it correctly, it was a thin face, firm jaws, and with gloomy, desperate eyes. The eyes were evil, enlarged, and roundish, the lids were only half open though. It was smiling, a bad grin, I must admit. It was as if of one who is sleepy or drunk; one can't imagine something like that. Strangely, I looked at it continuously without a word for minutes. But something was continuously knocking my mind while I fixed my gaze. From the grin, it looked like it had a cheerful expression, as if of achieving something, but from its eyes, it had a sad expression, as if of losing something as important as life. I looked even more closely, and I couldn't distinguish whether the face was a happy one or a sad one or even in a mood to laugh. Were these many expressions coming on the face because of the faulty sketching by the child, or was this the actual face? Such a horrible face it was, but still so captivating. I was eye to eye with the portrait. Soon I closed my eyes and breathed deeply. I knew I couldn't endure it anymore.

"You are too good at drawing... But if you have drawn this, then you might have seen this man. But..." I spoke, finally.

"I have seen him! Yes! In this house!" It shocked my nerves because according to the story Mr. S—was already dead. It was a moment of silence and after this, I asked him for an explanation. He had no answer to my question, but it didn't even make the slightest crack in the firm wall of his conviction.

As I sat expecting a reply, he uttered at last, "I had seen him in some room. I remember nothing more..."

I knew the child had raised the phantom from his thoughts, fueled by his readings, and knew in my heart that it was just an idle tale. Despite that, I was quite ill at ease. Had he been another boy, I would certainly raise the question of if something was wrong with him, but I couldn't even think of such a thing in the case of my little cousin. The shine in his eyes, his way of talking, his understanding of such a tale, and, of course, his reading tendency at that age were quite extraordinary. The story was hard to believe, as it resembled logic and reality in no manner. A question erupted in my mind: "Why had Uncle shifted to such a badly reputed house?" The little boy was indeed alone and as if he relished being alone. One more feature which I noticed was that Ajay was always very free. He roamed about the house all the time and I had never seen him with his academic books, or anything related to schoolwork.

When I asked him about his school, he replied that he had left it since it was very far from their new home and would join a new one in the next session, which was still months to go. Being alone and being absolutely free from any work or duty also disturbs the mind, and the person gets involved in unnecessary matters indulging in overthinking. In my little cousin's case, it could be all about overthinking some creepy story in his room and then making it a subject of his imagination, ultimately animating a completely new legend, and serving it to me. I hadn't completed my textbook and to be true; had not gone far with psychology till then, but still, I feared or imagined the next step for my cousin could be a hallucination if conditions were constant. I shook my head to stop my thoughts. Soon I remembered about Arun. He himself seems not doing anything. How could a person always, day and night, lock himself in his room for a study? I felt he was also subject to the same problem as his little brother, which was the void space caused by a lack of mainstream responsibility. For the first time, I was thinking so deeply and soon, soon I understood that this emptiness was the feature of that house in which I had been living and now I too had become a part of it. I too had nothing to do in that place; I feared being a victim of the psyche issue over which I had been thinking. My eye went to the study table in my room, on which I kept the drawing just before the open window. Ajay had gone out again, saying that he would return.

I went to have a second look at the drawing. As I was about to touch it, there was a powerful gust of wind coming in and as a result, the thin sheet flew out. I attempted to grab it, but I had no option but to watch the paper flying out, tossed by the air, far from my window into the gray sky.

"It would rain. I wish I could go out in such weather." I thought as I gazed over the hills.

I looked at the clock, which had struck four, and returned to my books. I took one of them, read the first page, flipped through the other pages, and left it; the same was the case with my favorite novel too. Something was strange. I couldn't focus. Soon I closed my eyes, which were quite paining, and something happened. The same face, the horrible face, came before me in darkness. My eyes opened immediately after. This vision appeared twice after also, and I was terrified as I couldn't get rid of it. I was sick of seeing the face again and again, forcefully coming over the film of my closed eyes. The face drawn by the child unnerved me until I reminded myself that I was a psychology student and that I could easily overcome such visions. The weather became even rainier. Darkness took over my room and in the silent atmosphere, everything looked shady. The passage out of my room was darker. Stormy winds burst into my room, the curtains were slapping wildly, and I sprang up to close the window. I could smell the moisture in the chilling air and soon in front of my eyes, the infinite clouds burst completely over the town, followed by shaking thunder. The people and even the birds were in havoc, hurrying to their places with the first thunder strike which appeared as an electric string hung in the sky. With my face already wet with droplets of rain, I moved to switch on the room's bulb. I switched it on, but nothing happened. I tried with the other switch too, but nothing happened, and I realized that the power was gone. My fingers slowly slipped down the board and I felt somewhat nervous, my heart was not beating but thumping. I called out loud, as nothing was visible; but no one responded. Soon, a fear came over me. I feared the house was empty. Blinded by the darkness, I carefully tiptoed towards the room door and when I had just reached it, I heard the horrible cry of my little cousin from the other room on the same floor. His screams were continuous. Strangely, at the same moment, I heard heavy footsteps as if, as if someone was walking in my very own bedroom. I turned my head even though I didn't want to and no; there was no one in my room, but how could, I be sure? Again, I got a very faint, shady glimpse of that very horrible face as a whitish impression hovering, against the black background of the walls. I closed my eyes in fright and stood still. After some seconds, on opening my eyes, a yellow glow was visible in the dark passage. I walked out of my room and saw my uncle holding a lantern standing there. He perhaps had come searching for us and soon we headed towards the other room from which the ear-piercing cries were still coming. Arun was not anywhere in the scene though he was in the same house. On entering, we saw Ajay trembling on his bed, wrapped up in the blanket, all hair scattered terribly over his forehead, with frightened eyes looking at the other wall and crying out in fear. With my shocked nerves causing my legs to tremble, I went to his bed as an immediate response. It was at this moment that the power returned as suddenly as it had gone. The rain was still rioting. We were all confused as to what had happened to each of us during the power cut, but first, we had to control the child who was in a state of shock. Everything was at last visible and ultimately entered Arun.

"Where were you? Why didn't you come up earlier to these kids? Were you scared yourself? Fortunately, I came from the office early as promised or else..." my uncle burst over Arun even before he entered the room completely.

"I was out of the house and came running when I realized the power cut." He replied, panting.

"No... No! I saw you with the torch roaming about in the garden but didn't waste time in calling you..." Uncle groaned and continued after something struck his mind, "Wait... Were you searching for something? Taking this opportunity?"

"First, look at him!" I exclaimed while I tightly hugged the boy, who was crying with his head over my shoulder. Slowly, he lifted his head, and with his teary, red eyes, looked around. I had recorded the total scene of the end part of the day in my diary, which I feel can better portray the conditions and so here is its excerpt:

"We all waited for Ajay to speak and finally he spoke, that too, in his weakest tone.

"'I saw it! When I looked towards the window, I saw some movement over there. It was a tall man, walking around my bed. The same Mister of the story. He was standing next to my bed when I was half asleep. The thunderstruck and I could see his face. I cried when he came towards me. He didn't speak a word and was still after me but continuously stared at me ...'

"From all this, nothing can be deduced now, but I must admit that something is wrong in this house. The boy is severely frightened by the incident in the dark, but it's also true that the atmosphere itself was very frightening today. Ajay is sleeping right beside me on my bed today and I have no issue because it is better not to be alone here. I am confused about the ghost, but I am left in a condition where I have looked around in my closed bedroom three times till now. I am skeptical about the incident, and I bet it was a dream that the boy saw. How does a child's psychology work? Amazing. Uncle and Arun are both in a bit of shock, but Uncle doesn't express it, which is good. When I told Arun about the 'torch incident', he murmured, 'Others are after it too' and I heard it, but after what? It is now midnight, the rains have stopped, my bulb is glowing, and I am comfortably sitting on a chair and writing the diary, despite that, I am not at ease. Even a banging of the door due to wind, or a flickering of the bulb for a second, gives a minor sensation down my spine. It's a strange psychological experience here. I wonder what the scene of the coming day would be like. I only hope for a good, dreamless sleep and for an outing tomorrow, in the town."

Then, I had the only option, yes, to forget about the face which I had stared at. This was the only way. I tried to do so by staring at other faces, in my books, and in the magazines of my cousin too, and strangely enough, nothing disturbed me the whole night during my sleep. No other face impacted my imagination. I didn't quite believe in ghosts, and I was proud of that.

"What do you feel about the ghost and why don't you tell me about the story of this house? Have you ever seen the ghost? Are you really indifferent to what happened yesterday?" I posed this question to Arun the next morning, while we had our breakfast.

"See, I do not know about ghosts, and I do not much care..." He replied, looking towards the stairs and I stared right at him. He surely looked under pressure, trying to overcome something, fidgeting with the tablecloth. He was trying to show that it did not affect him, but I knew it did. His expression and his eyes suggested he had not slept for days.

"You can share anything with me if you want and you know I would be glad to help. But I believe, you know, in your heart, that you are also afraid... Maybe you do not want me to know about anything personal, but don't forget that our fathers are brothers."

"They are and I know so, but you also know what kind of relationship they have had..."

"I do not know about the old matters as I was very young then, but I know this much that the relationship is towards betterment. Okay, promise me one thing at least. You are going to tell me the reason why I have been sent here before I return."

"Okay. Look, yesterday's incident is not new. . ." He passed on a cup of milk tea to me, and I didn't deny it this time.

"Why can't I go out alone, just because I am unknown to the locals? You know I am not a baby..."

"See, I promise we shall go out in the evening, yes on a drive and for now I have to study..." he abruptly ended, slowly stood, and went into his room. I was left alone with the tea on the dining table. By this time, after around two days of being rather gently locked up in the house, I decided that by any means I shall go out that day itself. I stood and walked to the window. "Sometimes being alone and having such a ginger milk tea was also good. . ." I thought as I sipped.

But gradually my mind became occupied with a lot of strange thoughts, and I soon understood something had to be done. I spent a lot of time reading, reading, and making notes on my subject. The house was certainly a heaven for anyone who wants some time for herself and her books, no disturbances, no constructions, no people, but only a deeper realization of the atmosphere. I relished doing my work, but after some hours, all my relish faded. Uncle was out at his work, Arun was in his room, and Ajay, yes, his company could be termed enjoyable. After spending an hour or more trying to explain my interested little cousin about my books, I saw his eyes had become drowsy. He, though, took one book to read and finally fell asleep on the bed before my eyes. I slightly pulled out the book that was left between the pillow and his cheeks and smiled or slightly laughed, seeing him whispering something while his eyes were closed. Looking at the sky, I realized I had spent most of the afternoon in this slow leisure. Suddenly, the extreme silence of the house broke.

It was a loud ringing at our main gate that echoed all up to my bedroom on the second floor.

"Who could it be? It can't be my uncle for sure." I thought and walked down.

4

It was exactly four by the clock. The doorbell rang a second time. Finally, I reached and opened the main door.

"May I?" Rajesh said after a "Hello!"

"Sure, I'll call Arun. You can sit on the sofa till then..." I replied, and he took steps into the house.

"I had told Ajay that I would come, but I can't see him…"

"Oh, he perhaps forgot to tell me. He is asleep now."

"Your friend has come. Come out, he is expecting you," I cried aloud at the face of the thick, closed door of Arun's room.

After some knocking on his door, a loud cry came from inside the room: "I am busy—you tell him to come next week or next month..."

I turned back. Rajesh was standing at a distance behind me, with a deep expression on his face and hands behind his back.

"I hope you didn't hear that..." I spoke.

"I fear I have." He sighed and headed towards the exit.

I didn't detect any stroke of anger or any other difference on his face, which quite astonished me, for it was an admirable level of patience.

"You can sit for a moment and have a cup of tea, maybe?" I insisted.

"Tea?" he replied laughingly and continued turning back.

"Will you make it?" he said in a gentle, witty tone.

"You know I drank tea today. You have come a long way and I am sorry that I can't do anything about your friend's blunt reply," I said and went to heat the evening tea which was still untouched.

"I quite remember that you..." he sipped the tea and continued, "… that you drink tea only when you are disturbed. So, is it anything that disturbs you now?"

"Oh... actually.… Wait, you remember that?" he must have studied my slightly amazed expression by then.

"Look, I have been a friend of Arun for years, he wasn't like this before... Okay, let alone all this." He paused a bit and continued, "I think you will tell me your worry whenever you are comfortable..."

"Yes, maybe, but I do not know about you much, I admit. So, what about your studies or yourself?"

"Well, I am studying law in the city; I love to read, and I also find myself somewhat attracted to paintings." He replied, sipped, and continued, "And what about you?"

"I have started the study of psychology and now I am here, enjoying the solitude. You know I like books a lot."

"That means we can discuss some of them?" he said smilingly, keeping his finished cup down.

"Yes. As it is, I am a bit bored..." I said, leaning back and exhaling.

"Why?" he asked instantly, somewhat amazed. "Haven't you visited the beautiful hills and various other sights over here? You know, people purposely come to these rare places to marvel at the beauty of nature."

"No—I am new to this place, but..."

"Do you want to come along? We can go towards the hills and the streams, and I can show you other places too... I mean if you wish." He charmingly asked as he stood and waited for a reply.

I contemplated the decision for some moments.

"No, it's not a problem to go with you. I do want to explore the outdoors but..." I said, still thinking.

"Come... it would be great for me to have such a cheerful and charming companion. This is the best way that I can thank you for the tea." He said heartily.

I decided and told him to wait for some moments. This time I thought little about going with Rajesh, as I found no other alternative at that point.

I went up to my bedroom, which was closed. As I opened it, a ball passed by and hit the wall hard. It was Ajay; it appeared he had woken up a long time back and now he was playing alone, inside the closed bedroom, hitting the ball on the walls and catching it—lazily. I didn't feel like asking him to go out and play with his friends, because I knew the reason—he didn't have any there. I informed him I was going out and draped a white shawl around my shoulders before moving down, as I knew my dress was flimsy for the wild winds there.

Rajesh stood waiting for me near the gate, looking around the complete house with extreme care and attention, as if scanning it, his sleeves rolled up and his hands in his pockets. His gaze turned to me as he saw me coming, and we moved. Shutting the gate behind me, I stepped on the wet grass outside. Amidst the tall trees stood Rajesh, calling me as he had moved ahead. The atmosphere was on the colder side, with winds rattling, flowing swiftly in the still, blue sky. While walking out of the area of the house, I looked upwards at the thin trees and couldn't sight a single bird or squirrel up there. I sat on the backseat of Rajesh's bicycle, which was a brown-painted one.

It was great to be out after a long time. The bicycle tore through the cool winds, freshening up my spirit.

I looked around the long lane as we were passing it; apart from the man-like trees, there was no trace of any human; the lane was dry this time and leaves had fallen all over it. The only noise was ours. With every gust in the gray sky above us, the leaves and soil particles on the lane started whirling and were set in a noisy motion; adding to the horrors of the lone lane which would appear to a person as unused, since it was built. On turning behind, the thick blanket of mists was seen, and in the sides were the brown and white tree trunks, other than the grayness. As the lane passed, Rajesh turned the bicycle towards the wet grassland. We drove, following the farms and towards the hills. Initially, few locals were to be seen, but gradually I realized we were going towards the area where people didn't live at all.

"Careful!" Rajesh exclaimed while I stepped down from the bicycle after he had stopped it in a muddy area under a tree.

"It's ok..." I said while I checked my white shoes and socks, "I do not have to keep them in a showcase after all..." I continued laughingly.

The place where we stood was lower than the rest of the town and a thin stream was flowing right in front of us, though at a distance. There was some strange but pleasant anxiety rising in me as I noticed the extraordinary beauty of the place. The fading sunlight filtered through the tree trunks as golden strips fell all around the stream, making it look divine. The chirping of different birds was pleasantly wild as it was evening and had an effect to make one believe the trees themselves made the shrilling noise. I looked up and saw little hills and a somewhat clear sky. It was fantastic to be out of the house finally and my mind was as calm and as free as the winds.

"This is the thing over here, away from people, away from synthetic—into the natural."

"Absolutely..." He paused for a couple of minutes and then suddenly asked, "May I ask you about the meaning of your name? You know it's an uncommon one, Vaanya. "

"Ah... my father is proficient in Sanskrit along with English; you know he is an English Daily's chief editor. So, he was the one who gave me this name. My name means the forest goddess; at least as far as I know."

"That's good..."

I bent down and plucked a couple of wet grass blades—in a slightly nostalgic remembrance.

"You said your father is a newspaper's chief editor. He must be an accomplished man and a learned man, too."

"Yes... yeah..." I said and sighed.

Rajesh was listening curiously and then told under his breath, "It's a tough time in the region and the press gets affected too in such situations..."

"Why? What's going on? I mean, it's funny to say that there is no newspaper coming to Uncle's house." I excitedly said as I thought that at last, I would get to know something about the situation.

"N-Nothing much. Nothing at all, leave all that. Nothing to worry..."

He said nothing more on this topic, and I didn't ask any further.

"Can you tell me something more about Arun's change and the family's shifting?" I asked casually, to shift my focus.

"Arun's condition is before you, but what I am noticing is an alteration in your uncle as well. Don't get me wrong, but his dress-up is a bit ... What should I say? It's somewhat old-fashioned. But no offense. Mr. Vijay, he was, after all, an accomplished lawyer..." He replied, his hands in his pocket looking at the faint sun and a look of deep remembrance came over him.

"Why? I didn't notice that." I was quite amazed and continued looking also toward the sun. "Maybe I haven't noticed him in that way..."

"I don't at all mean that he is ill-dressed but... but I feel he is always overdressed, or more formal than needed. You know this is also a sudden recent change in him. But don't…"

"It's okay, you are telling because I am asking. I won't feel bad." I uttered. In my mind, I knew that Rajesh's viewpoint could also be incorrect, to the same extent as mine could be.

"Good... Come, let's go towards the stream," Rajesh said and paced towards the flow.

"God is the best creator ..." emerged from my heart as I sipped the stream's cold water, held by my palms. The water flowed down my neck, giving a cold sensation to my chest.

"God is the best artist, you must say..." my listener replied.

The water was so clean that it somewhat even mirrored our faces. Rajesh kept on looking at the stream in an unbroken, tranquil gaze, somewhat diagonally too, and what I noticed was that he was rather smiling.

"Your face is very artistic…, especially your eyes and your hair…" he said at length, as he turned his gaze from the stream to me.

He momentarily looked deep into my eyes.

"That's a good expression by you... thank you." I replied after some moments.

"Now let's ride slightly up the hill. I know a place there." He soon said.

The place was a small grassy area at the end of a hill, which was higher.

Looking around which, I saw that it was filled with flowers. In the calm place, one could feel the mists and a strange sensation in the stomach as there was a huge void just in front. I could see nothing much of the other side save the hills and the profound infiniteness of the sky. We sat on bare grass, facing towards the infinity.

"Thanks a lot. You know I love all this, and I was waiting for a long time just to go outside my house. But it's because of you I could see the interiors of the town and be so near to places which are only read or heard about." I said seriously.

"You know this spot is a historic spot, too. Though it is dangerous and that's why we aren't exactly at the edge, the great artist Vishwakumar painted his first landscape here. He was seventy years old then," he said, looking at me.

"Oh?" I turned my face to him and continued, "I have also heard of him a bit. So, what did he do in his lifetime before landscapes?"

"Portraits; portraits of all kinds which sold in Lakhs..." he said as he gazed over the sky while combing his wet hair.

"Lakhs? That's great. He was very famous, I guess, and your knowledge about art is also good."

"You can say so." He slightly laughed and continued, "I will tell you about all this and you tell me some basics of psychology?".

"I will…"

We both discussed psychology, paintings, and the relationship between them for half an hour at that spot. We had a debate over the fact that paintings of artists are purposeful, forced, or deliver a message about their true psychological condition. My companion's knowledge was profound. How wonderful I felt and how merry I was... The evening was twice as long as in the city, as I thought then, and the slowness and calmness of the vicinity made it marvelous. An icy breeze passed us—and after that, there was a drastic change. The evening gradually turned colder and darker.

"Let's return as the sun is setting. You know people say that the grassy hillsides of here are eerie places after evenings and..." Rajesh said as he stood rubbing dirt off his pants.

"Wait! Is that our house? How can we see it from here?" I said, still sitting, pointing towards a similar structure at the other hill end. My eye caught it while I was observing the mists over the stream. It was a black spot in the scenery and quite unsettled me as I looked at it. It certainly looked older, gruesome, and bleak.

"No, no, this is not yours. This is... this is of a Mr. Shaitaan. No one lives there or goes there, and I do not much know about that place."

"Shaitaan? Was this his name?"

"At least people called him by that until his death eight months ago..."

"But... Mr. S—?" I uttered under my breath, looking at the house with confusion.

"But did he not live in our house before? I mean, this house also looks the same, but I have heard he was the actual owner of the mansion which Uncle has purchased." I stood up.

"Yes, it's a fact that many do not know; but I know. The fact is, Shaitaan or whom you are calling Mr. S—owned two houses, not one, and this is the identical, second, secret house that he was making for his second wife who also mysteriously died, and it was left unfinished owing to his bankruptcy in his last days. At least I've heard that it was left unfinished. Who knows? This is at a place where it can only be seen from this spot, and you have already seen how many come to this place. This house is known to few, and no one has ever gone there for long, it is very overgrown on that part. Who cares at last? Not enough people in town to occupy random, un-cared places." He said at his back as he turned towards his bicycle.

"Shaitaan means evil..." I murmured as I too turned away from the horrible house, leaving it again unnoticed as it had stood for years, in darkness and seclusion.

"You know this place is rather thinly populated and..." He was speaking, but I interrupted him.

"How do you know so much about this person?" I paused as something caught my eye and I remarked, "Something fell from your pocket!"

I picked the thin, black, leather-jacketed, tiny booklet from the grass. A couple of words were written in gold. "Investigation" was the only one which I could fathom, by the time within which Rajesh came searching in haste. I handed over the booklet to him and he slipped it into his pocket.

Sun had already set, and the yellow headlight guided the bicycle. The valley, the hills, and the grasslands looked quite unnerving, and the winds became mightier. The gaps between the hills and the voids down looked like mysterious black blots of shadow restricting vision. There were negligible streetlights. The cycle was carefully and skillfully driven in and out of the small woods and down the hill and up the other hill, where my uncle's house stood. I was clasping the back support and Rajesh was still answering my questions, not hinting at how tough it was for him to cycle at that hour. He seemed effortless and his tone was unchanged—happy. My heart eased only when we came to the lane from which Uncle's house was visible, at least.

"Wait!" I said and stepped down from the cycle as it halted on my demand.

"But why? I can't leave you here; I will leave you from where we came." He said with one leg over the paddle and the other supporting the cycle down the ground. His hands were still at the handles.

"It was great to be with you and I thank you a ton." I said smilingly and calmly, forwarding my hand for a handshake, and continued as we shook hands, "I can't bother you any further at this hour and you see the house is just there..." I told as we both looked at it.

"But it's dark and nothing in life, not even your house, is 'just there'; I have no problem cycling up the lane..."

"I insist. Please." I said, loosening my grip on his hand.

"Now... okay if you say...", only half satisfied.

"Thanks then… Bye... I'll follow the streetlight."

"I will come again to meet Arun in a few days... Bye, Miss," he said as he finally clicked the other paddle with his leg.

"Yes, sure, but I fear he won't meet you again…" I chuckled. His expression was no longer visible. He waved slightly and turned back, and I was sure no one was left there except for me.

Thoughts about Mr. Shaitaan again conquered my mind as I trudged up the dark lane. Uncanny noises of night animals followed, heard distinctively in the silence, and I knew the night was theirs, not mine. There was almost nothing to hinder the flow of winds and I tossed back my hair several times as and when it came over my forehead and eyes. I walked observing around, a bit recklessly calm was my speed. It was my conviction that I was walking alone. Perhaps my steps were not at the usual pace because of the extra caution that my mind felt secure in taking. Strangely, the house seemed more and more distant as I approached it, the lane, an endless tunnel of blackness, and the thin, fading, luminous and transparent blueness of the sky—still visible. Suddenly, as I was halfway, fatigue took over my whole body, and gradually each step felt heavier than the previous one. I felt an extreme gravitational pull on my legs, but I continued, though my speed was reduced by half.

It wasn't late when I realized I was becoming somewhat breathless; it had never happened to me before and I took a deep breath of the chilling air. Finally, I halted under a lamppost and released my breath, slowly. A rotten smell was all around the lamppost, forcing me to breathe through my mouth.

"Would I even reach the house?" That was my first thought from there.

"What a strange thought is this?" My second.

I rested one hand on the short, old lamppost, the other hand on my waist, and took consecutive deep breaths looking towards my shoes. At this moment, something strange came to my mind.

Slowly, I turned my head to check if anyone was following me.

"Excuse me?" I spoke.

No answer came. No one was there behind me but only the block of muteness and darkness which I had walked, stood. After a couple of minutes, I walked again with a strange anxiety burdening my spirit. I lifted my right leg, staring still toward the tip of my shoe. I saw something.

It was my shadow that I had seen the first time in this dark way, and I turned back, my eyes pursuing the ground, to look till where the shadow went. Under the golden, flickering streetlight I could not only see one shadow but a couple of them. The other one was taller and a bit more slanting to the other side. It suggested that someone was standing just behind me, standing still. I had got that innate feeling to the same effect. But, in the blink of an eye, the other shadow wasn't visible anymore. I realized my lifted foot was on the ground and I had already taken a couple of steps. I don't know what it was, but I stood still as a shudder of fear ran through me.

I thought if someone was following me, and who it could be? Or—or was this my shadow which took the form of two because of the positioning of the lamp dancing over my head? I slightly leaped and walked again. The feeling of being followed intensified as I walked. I had paced a distance from the lamppost and since then, I was sure someone was behind me. Walking and watching. I was reluctant to look back. I realized I was taking larger steps and faster ones and also that the one behind me was also at the same speed, still following.

My forehead was wet even though I was shivering from the chill. "This story of Shaitaan has really affected my mind," I said to myself as I felt a heaviness in my chest. I was choking with fear. The unpleasant odor was still in the air. I had walked to a spot from where the lamppost could only be seen, from the corner of my right eye, as a beaming star, and the light of it falling on the spot where I had stood before as a golden sliver, shaking.

"Ouch!" I cried in horror and strikingly forced my left arm away from my waist as I was feeling someone putting four fingers in and out of the gaps of mine. It could be cold air slipping between my fingers, I reasoned, but reasons probably don't satisfy in the darkness. It was a strange feeling in my stomach as I felt someone was enjoying all that. The slight grin of the same face, the face of Mr. Shaitaan, started to manifest in the dark, but before it could take its complete form, I closed my eyes and started rubbing them wildly. I didn't want to see it again at any cost.

Though my legs were trembling, I couldn't help but run this time, my whole body and mind in a paroxysm of panic.

"I will face my fears!" I affirmed, still in pace, slightly embarrassed, and abruptly turned back after I had run for a minute.

"Ahh..." I yelped as something wild, at excessive speed, crashed into me just as I had turned. I fell on my back on the grass at the edge of the lane.

"Who are you?" I cried with one hand over my head.

My head and heart throbbed hard, as someone offered a hand, held me strongly, and raised me.

5

A beam of torchlight was thrown right on my face while I tried to stand. My legs were feeble and one open palm was over my eyes, eyes which couldn't bear the strike of the light.

"Let go!" I cried and hit the tall figure somewhere under its chest.

He left his grip on me, and the torch fell. I somehow picked it. My head was still whirling, and my reasoning was frozen. The figure moved a little but didn't fall, and I knew that my hit, at last, wasn't hard enough.

"It's you?" I burst in amazement, in my still trembling voice, when I could finally focus the torch on the person's face.

The noise of night animals came forcefully from all over.

"Yes, me, Arun!" my cousin exclaimed as he pressed one of his hands over his stomach.

"Why? Why were you following me? Have you lost it? You know I could have suffered a heart attack!" I held one of his hands for momentary support of balance.

"Why did you hit me here..." he said, clutching his stomach still.

"Well, I am sorry for that. But if it's my hit, then it is not that hard... I'm hurt, too."

"You know what the time is? It is seven and have you not seen the darkness around? Where had you gone? You know it's not safe to wander in the valley after late evening and that too with Rajesh?" He angrily asked after we had both quite regained our balance and self.

“Why do you ask in such a way? You know, I am not like you and sorry I can’t keep myself always locked in the house, with nothing to do! You said we would go out, we would go out, but we never went... What is the problem if I go out with your old friend?” I angrily spoke and clarified, “I informed Ajay that I am going out nearby…”

“That is nearby? It was late, and I was anxious about you... I was searching for you!”

“Oh, very kind of you brother, but I had gone with your friend. He is your friend, isn’t he?”

“You...you are talking about him? You do not know him much. He lives in the city and comes only sometimes; he always thinks he is very smart. You know I–I was better than him always, in school, in sports, but-but now... he is, he is simply strange. My gut feeling is that he is up to something...He is planning something.” He said, still firmly strict as now he crossed his arms over his chest.

I replied on a calmer note, “You know him better, but I found him a good man and he was anxious about you. That’s why he comes to meet you... I feel you should talk to him once.”

“That’s the point, the whole point!” He said clapping his hands in a cross excitement, “He is excessively inquisitive and curious about me, and he wants to come and know about my study and my new room as you do...”

“Yes, but I know little—now please calm down.”

Finally, he regained his composure and spoke gently, “I am sorry that I didn’t...anyway, you know what can be done… Now let us return. Ajay is alone in the house.”

“Are you really hurt? I would hit no one, and of course not you if I would have known. Tell me, are you okay?” I asked, holding him by his arm.

No answer came and as I focused the light on his face, I saw him at me with the corner of his eye and half smiling.

“I knew you were fine!” I said, laughing slightly.

A gush of freezing wind blew over us. I crossed my arms around my chest, under the shawl, and rubbed my palms together.

“Does it always go so cold here?” I said, breathing out.

“N… Not really. After all, it is not winter, it's the rainy season. This night is colder than normal.” He said, tightly pulling his coat around his frame.

Black clouds were hanging in the sky, which was as if painted boldly over the moon, destroying its visibility. We silently began walking.

While walking, something struck my mind. Suddenly, the smell of rotting flesh was not there. It was gone. I was walking beside Arun, from whom a very light smell of perfume was coming instead. Was there something killed around there? I thought. But I left the thought soon as it only led to confusion—as Arun felt nothing.

“Hey!”

“Hey listen!”

We both sprang up and turned towards each other.

“First me!” I exclaimed. “So, well; I forgot to ask that in your successful attempt to petrify and stupefy me; how could you be so near to me?”

“What? I can’t get you.”

“Please don’t pretend, now. I know this path looks haunting. You were so near to my back that, that I could hear your icy breaths slip over my neck! I could feel it. And after all, why were you following me for so long? From the lamppost? You told me you came just to find me; you should have called my name.” I asked as suspicion regarding him grew in my mind.

“Wait a minute. First, I was never following you from the lamppost. It’s so far that I never even saw it tonight; I mean, I didn’t have to go that far. I saw you running; apparently from someone, when I was taking a turn from the other lane with my torch. I couldn’t quite understand who was behind you, as I was very far, but there was someone. So, I came running as only you were clearly and opaquely seen. I don’t know why, but then you stopped abruptly and...”

“What? I am confused. But I saw your shadow... under the lamppost,” the last words were not fully formed but came out as weak whispers, “So, whom did I see?”

“May I know who was following you? Did you talk with some locals?” He asked as we both halted.

"No, I wonder who was following me..." I thoughtfully said and asked, "Are the locals here beasts? Or kidnappers? Or murderers?"

There was no answer. Arun also had a similarly thoughtful, fearful expression on his face, twitching his chin, as in deep thought.

"So, are you okay? I mean not hurt or physical pain or something like that?... Of course, leaving our collision."

"No... not at all. Why do you ask? I am fine." I replied as we walked again and finally, the "just there" house was reached.

As I stepped into the house, I sighed in relief. The silence in the house wasn't much different from outside, but the difference was in the air's stagnancy. Nothing shined back in the yellow glow that had its rule over the house. But something did beam, the expression of my little cousin as he saw me enter.

"How was your day?" Ajay jumped from the chair where he had been sitting with some magazines and came to me.

The strange fear and anxiety hadn't left me completely. I didn't utter any word but just patted his shoulder in response and then shook my shoulders, which successfully made the shawl smoothly slip down to the floor, after which I sank fatigued into the already pulled-out wooden chair.

Uncle hadn't returned till that time and the clock had already struck seven-thirty.

I turned back to see Arun, who was with me all this while, but now he wasn't there. He was again in his room. Ajay walked towards the kitchen to bring a glass of water.

"Today's outing was good." I spoke when I finally could and continued, "Ajay, you know some strange things happened as I was on my way home. I am still baffled."

"What happened? Did someone follow you up the path or you saw something?" he asked from behind me, holding the glass of water.

"Now... you would tell that the ghost was following me as he aimlessly wanders in the lanes... But you know I am too tired for believing that a ghost is behind me..." I said bending my head onto my crossed forearms that were resting on the table and then closing my eyes.

After some moments, I felt something. Ajay was silent suddenly. I had heard him keeping the glass on the table. But then his abrupt silence and that too continuously for seconds, drew my attention, but still, I was reluctant to leave my position and open my eyes.

Soon there was a strange sensation on my back. I realized that Ajay had started rubbing one of his hands circularly over my back and down my spine and then near my waist. He was doing it extremely slowly, delicately, as if smoothening something. Naturally, it gave me an icy shiver of uneasiness.

I immediately rose and turned back, asking him what he was up to. He stood like a statue with fixed eyes and parted lips.

"W-What happened to you? Are you okay?" I asked, seeing his expression.

"I am okay, but you are not..." he spoke and slightly pointed. "See your back! Just see it..."

"What?" I was in a strange fear. Ajay's eyes looked very frightened, but they never moved.

I walked to my room in haste and alarm so to check what had happened, to check it in the bedroom mirror. Ajay followed me. There was a large mirror opposite the study table. I stood before it, watching my frightened expression, confronting my terrified self. I turned back in a half swirl and Ajay came in front of me with another mirror, raising it somehow up to my face.

"See! Who has done this to you?" he uttered, shaking with the burden of the mirror.

I lifted my heavy hair, and my back was completely visible in the mirror in front of me. What I saw unnerved me.

The top of the dress which I was wearing was ripped all over from the back portion. It was torn. It was slit. I touched my cloth. It was real; I could feel the badly torn fabric. It wouldn't appear to one as scratching, but it appeared to be a result of a wild pull from both sides. I had lost words. The slits were vertical and were seen in the mirror. Strands of fabric loosely hung from them down to my waist. The next moment, the heavy mirror, which Ajay could barely hold, fell on the carpet, and with its noise, the spell over me broke.

"H-How did this happen and when? I couldn't feel a thing!" I said in a trembling voice, glancing at my little brother.

"But how? Did someone hurt you or scratch you in the way or was this already tattered?" He asked.

I slowly and unconsciously walked towards the closed window and pressed my forehead against it—and then stood.

"This was a new dress, and it was totally fine when I left the house... I know nothing more," My heart was beating heavily, giving a pain.

I told Ajay to wait at the door till the time I changed. I was frightened when I was changing. I didn't like the moment when I was alone. My eyes were still on the destroyed dress that was spread on the bed.

Who could have done this and when? How? Why didn't I feel a thing? Rajesh didn't do it. Nor did Arun, and I am sure about that. Did someone do this while I walked up the lane? I immediately turned back again over the mirror and turned my head to check for any wounds or scratches on my body. My heart thumped again as I saw no sign of any scratch on my bare skin—down to my waist. Nothing hurt and my skin was the same to feel. Not a single proof of even a touch.

"Are you; Okay?" Ajay asked as he came in when I opened the door after changing.

"Yes, I am—fine. I don't know how and when. I never felt it..." I said as I fell, exhausted, onto the bed.

"But..."

"But what?" I asked.

"But your shawl is completely fine." He said as he raised the white shawl high which I had left downstairs.

"The cuts ... I remember I had rested against a tree trunk, but... tell me, Ajay, do you think it can even cause gentle slits in a top? Tell me..."

There was no answer from him.

"My hair openly hung down my shoulders, over the white shawl. My shawl certainly covered my back and its ends hung down from my shoulders. Under this was my dress. I never removed my shawl, I never lifted my hair, but then how is it possible that my top is torn?" I said in a fit of terror. "No... No, not at all. The winds can't certainly tear my cloth. I can't think! Or can they?" I said as I placed my hand on my forehead. It was warm, very warm.

"I think my top and skirt were too flimsy for the winds. Ahh, I fear I have caught a fever, too." I continued.

"You need to rest. Don't think about all that. It will scare you and even me. I—I am terrified... I will go down and bring your dinner plate up. Sadly, I—I fear that no doctor can be found at this hour..." He was in a state of gibbering terror.

He ran down as if wanted to return as fast as possible. I heard his steady footsteps down the shaking stairs.

At moments, a slight shiver ran down my legs and I remember staring at the tall ceiling. As usual, the bulb was flickering and only lightening around its circumference. The other parts of the room were very shady. The air felt so heavy and again there was no flow in it. I was filled with pride, as I could still overcome the thought of a ghost behind me. It would have been even intolerable if I would have succumbed to this.

In that day's diary, this was my explanation:

"I don't surely know how all this happened. It might have happened when I had unconsciously kept my shawl down when I rested against the tree trunk. The fabric was very thin, and I also remember the tree trunk to be rough. But I couldn't feel that my cloth had even for once stuck or scratched against anything. I had heard in my childhood that the sudden tearing of clothes is a very ill omen. I know little though."

I tossed and turned on my bed the whole night and never lost sight of the fluttering curtains. I had to keep the window open because of the very stagnant air. A day passed normally, and I didn't dare to complain about it being boring. Luckily, my fever was down completely after a warm bath. I sat on a chair with a book at the open window side, drinking ginger milk tea, as dazzling sunlight peeped in.

When the sun comes, the fear is gone. I didn't tell Arun or my uncle about the horrible incident as I believed they will fear my rambling and wandering, and I didn't enjoy restrictions. I was still enthusiastic about tramping in the lonely lands, which I planned to do when I would be well.

It was finally two pleasant nights after the incident and the clock was approaching nine of the night again. Only two of us were sitting out in the medium-sized wild garden where we had placed wooden crates. Wherever I could see, I saw that the garden was filled with weeds, creepers, and wild shrubs. The pale, dead plants in the garden were a very discomforting sight. I felt healthy in my mind after sitting in sunlight for a long time and now we were sitting in front of the fire.

"Ahh... Ultimately. This wet wood caught fire at last..." Ajay sighed over his triumph as he was the one who had lit the small fire around which we both sat, opposite each other.

"Great... Now put the heaps of paper into this." I said with a tranquil smile on my face.

Uncle had given Ajay a task to burn some of his confidential papers and notebooks and I sat beside him as he was feeling scared to go down to the garden alone. I sat with my elbows over my thighs, one leg over the other, in front of the fire and surrounded by two to three cartons heaped with old papers and books. None of it was a newspaper, I learned.

"This would take an hour... and I will do it fully on my own. You do not have to move, but please do not go and keep telling stories or anything you like, but just keep saying. Do not stop." Ajay said, as he somehow picked up a lot of papers in his hand and threw it into the fire.

We both were perspiring a little as the winds were calm that night. I stared at the burning fire. I was feeling it inside, a feeling of warmth germinating in me, as I gazed at the yellow, orange, red, and blue flames erupting and dancing. The smoke was filling the air above us. The ambiance was as peaceful as it was extraordinarily silent, only the crackling sounds of the flames were distinctively heard. Turning my head up, the lonely moon hanging in the infinite round sky, being almost submerged in the grayness of the sky, could be seen.

"Why didn't you tell Papa or Brother about the incident?" He asked, at length.

"It would be useless, I think. You know, I will try to solve it myself and find whatever is going on..."

There was silence for a few minutes as he didn't reply. I started checking the papers in one carton and, one by one, putting them into the flames.

"I feel we should keep out of all this. I mean, we two, as the spirit may be around. It may be moving around here and listening to us." He said, rubbing his left eye with his hand as his eyes were in a sensation of burning. I could notice the redness and moisture in his eyes. But he continued as if he wanted to finish the task as fast as he could.

"See, this book is about math... this one about law and the other one, too. We are burning very interesting books. Can't we keep them for you?" I said as I stood up.

"Can you tell me the meaning of this book?" He asked, handing me an old pocketbook.

It was titled, *Curiosity Kills the Cat.*

"What kind of book is this? This means... I don't like this saying much."

"What does it mean?"

"It means that being too inquisitive is dangerous for you..." I said as I disappointedly threw the book into the flames.

"Is this correct?"

"No, not always." I couldn't say any more. I fancied why I noticed only this book among hundreds over there.

"Why are there no people around this area? I mean, it is a strange feeling here. This house is so distant from any human existence. I am experiencing the nineteenth century..." I said as I rubbed my face with my hands. I was feeling strangely nervous again.

"You know, Father wanted to shift here. He said that he wanted a change and to be free from old memories. But I feel this house has seen even bad times and the walls over here hold even more memories. Look, don't you think that these dead trees appear as if dancing with the wind?" He said as his face looked like a combination of tints of red and orange. Maybe my one also looked the same.

"Your mind is very active, and your imagination is great... Was Arun in favor of this decision?"

"No, not at all. I feel he also sees the same image which I see many times."

"Why do you feel so?" My eyebrows rose.

"That's because I find him staring at something, something in the walls or the curtains or even sometimes the mirror. You know, he says he is going to get very, very rich soon. If this happens, I fear he will leave this place and go forever..."

"Very, very rich… Now, how's that going to be?"

There was no answer from him, but the conversation gained full momentum now.

"Have you ever seen a ghost, and are they real?" He asked me as he sat on the crate exhausted, breathing out a long breath.

"No! never seen and will never see. I think I can bet on that. It doesn't exist."

"Really? But some people and old books say that they are inhabitants of the other realm. They say that the ghosts come from the other side of the moon, on the darker side of the moon which is never seen." He said, rubbing his hands in front of the fire and making a low trembling hum. He perhaps was fearing to talk about all that, but still, he talked. I looked up at the moon above me and tried to notice the dark shadowy side which we always skip seeing.

Winds had begun flowing again and it somewhat suddenly became cold enough to be hair-raising; the crackling of the dead leaves could be heard behind, but the fire was somehow surviving.

"These books are not ultimate, and I know you are reading books that are not meant for children at all. Do you want to know the reality? What you are seeking and talking about is within you, in each one of us."

"What?" He stood immediately.

"Calm down. I mean, ghosts are nothing but thoughts or unfulfilled desires. Emotions like extreme sadness, anger, or unhappiness make a person very weak, and vulnerable. The sad soul in you, your mind and intellect, get affected deeply and think about in those directions. The thoughts battle with each other. At this point, a hint of a ghost story or tale or saying whatever activates your instincts in that direction; and your weakened mind feels things around. Yes, the mind needs healing after being hit hard and until then it works in strange directions, maybe abnormally, which you call indications or the intuition of ghosts. Being deeply affected, your brain thinks in that pattern, and you feel a dead one around. Ghosts' stories are stories, and you should instruct your brain to limit them to that point! It's the play of desires... of vulnerability to it. I don't believe much of it happens in modern, populated societies. At least I till now know and believe this." I preached at the boy sitting in front of me, innocently trying to grasp half of what I meant.

I knew I had preached a lot; but candidly speaking, my mind was also not fully free of doubt. It was only that I believed this, but a question mark had always existed. I started looking at the papers again, and Ajay resumed his work. There were a couple of pages pinned together and folded when I flipped over. I unfolded those yellow worn-out pages and saw something written. They looked like notes. Written in black ink, the letters were cursive and tiny, which were not properly formed, and expressed that they were written by a trembling hand. The first line wrote:

"Recent days have been very unsettling. I have written to the authorities for security."

It alarmed me. I stood up as I wanted to read the old notes only by myself. They excited me as they were about the house and its weirdness.

"What is in your hand?" Ajay asked as I expected.

"Nothing, just something I wanted to read about," I said as I faced away from the fire and clenched the papers.

Initially, Ajay was curious, but when I showed it to him, he obviously couldn't understand a thing and simply let it go. I had to wait for some more time in the garden and when the burning was finished, and the fire was safely extinguished; I was the one who ran up the stairs and locked myself in the room. My heart was beating because of the sudden run and excitement. As I read the papers, I knew it was worth all my excitement. It was:

"The house was deliberately constructed differently, following the design of one of the foreign houses. It had to be different at any cost, such house that would force the passer-by to stop and stare. But to my grave disappointment, the house couldn't be built exactly in the manner, which was desired, because of the unavailability of some materials. So, I suggested many changes. It was the biggest mistake to introduce strange changes in the construction model of the house. It was an unforeseen blunder. The corners were cut abruptly, the main gate's direction was faulty, the use of unmatching metals in construction, and the anti-clock circular stairs all were wrong, but not cared for. When the ill-fated house was constructed, there were more mirrors than usual. The unlucky construction brought distress soon. It will continue its only job to create distress for people living in it. I'll write why. Ill fate seized my business, life, and perhaps even beyond all that. Soon as the business started collapsing and everything seemed to end, the investigation began by hiring professionals. But it was already late when the full picture came into view. Though nothing could be found, I have some doubts relating to the land over which it is built. Who knows if it had a poor reputation in the past? I am trying to find out about it..."

Beyond this, the paper was burned. Somebody must have tried to destroy it, but somehow it was there right before my eyes. After reading the inexplicably strange paper, I only wished that I had never read it.

"Is this paper a message for others who would come to live in this house?" I thought, "I cannot understand this certainly and lousy businesses naturally come to an end."

I tore the paper and threw it, as I didn't want it to think much of it. It's not that I had got a correct explanation of the events that had followed me since the day I came here, but still, I wanted to know. I thought a lot. Those slumberless nights when I lay down on my bed, wandering alone in the lanes of my dim thoughts about the events I feared, but still wanted to know, a strange resilience it was.

The night didn't offer a pleasant sleep, as I wasn't accustomed to such intense mental occupation or pressure. I was still waiting for a breaker opportunity when I could inspect the house freely and particularly Arun's room and know about his secretiveness, but I knew there was no hope for that. The day came sooner than I expected, but that too after more incidents where the distinction could be made several times that they resulted from a mistake of eyes, and mind and were a play of shade. But the question was: *"Once okay, twice strange, but thrice? Or even more? Why do these never stop?"*- A line from my diary.

6

"Something is happening here for sure. What and why is the question. Support me as I find it. Will you?" I said, keeping down my book and looking at my sweet cousin who lay on the bed near me with eyes closed because of the morning sunlight, peeping in from the open window, over his forehead.

"But what can we do? I am not feeling well these days." He said as he stood rubbing his eyes and clutching his stomach.

I also noticed a gradual change in the expression and the energy of the boy, which only suggested that he was not fine. I feared the same was the case with me.

"I think we can get to know something from the locals around. That's what we can do now." I replied.

"Risky… But I will go with you... Maybe I can take you to the market, where we will find many people. Shouldn't we inform Father about it or take him with us?"

"It is not at all risky to go out in the market under the shining sun and second, I think we needn't inform anybody."

"Yes..." He said sleepily as he walked out of the room and down the stairs.

I followed him and ended up on the breakfast table, just somehow swallowing the breakfast with water. I put the bread onto Ajay's plate, forwarded it to him and at this moment I saw from the corner of my eyes, someone just came into the hall through the garden gate.

“Good morning, Uncle...” I said as I looked up at him and my eyebrows raised instantly.

Uncle was wearing a shiny, silvery blue colored night robe, under which were pajamas, which looked very expensive but appeared somewhat larger, anyway.

Oddly, my uncle replied in the regional language, which he usually never used at home and which I wasn’t able to speak but only able to understand faintly. This language sounded somewhat rough and raw, used in local transactions and only by the original locals in their homes. The words he said just meant a morning wish and nothing more. He walked imbalanced to a little extent and passed just like the wind from my side into his room with his head quite bent.

“Did he not sleep properly last night?” I whispered to my little cousin who was busy drinking the tasty cardamom milk, which I had prepared for us and he gave no remarkable answer.

I soon stepped out through the garden gate which I had discovered, just when my uncle came out from it. The ground squelched under my bare feet because of the night’s rain and they became muddy as I walked a few steps toward the fencing. The sun was pleasantly bright, just stuck between the withdrawing clouds in the grayish sky and the cool winds were still strong, fluttering my hair and night dress. It’s hard to imagine the mysterious gorgeousness that the enormous gray and cloudy sky holds and how it affects the nerve of a watcher from a lonely spot in an old town. I was pondering over the low fencing that looked old and unsafe when suddenly something dangerously fell on over my shoulder.

Instantly, I jerked my hand away and was taken aback, breathing loudly. It was a small branch. The branch was of a thin tree that had crookedly grown, wrapping itself over another dead tree, just like a serpent. I kept my eyes fixed for some moments on the branch, which lay dead and harmless on the grass—like a failed arrow.

I touched my forehead in amazement after seconds and a strange feeling struck me, a feeling that I was alone in someone else’s territory. It wasn’t something to be much frightened about, a dead branch falling over you when you are all alone, causing no harm though, but the silence of the vicinity, the soft movements of leaves in the undisturbed garden, offered no clue what was to come next. Everything in the garden was just lying down, nothing was awake or living, everything looked so harmless and so tender, the pointed branches, the small pits, the rough, scattered stones; but didn't these have enough potential to cause harm? If the energy of force is used? The feeling of being alone overwhelmed me and after some time I withdrew carefully into the mansion.

When the clock turned hours, at around one o'clock, I found the way to go out of the house as Uncle had left and Arun was again in his usual place, locked.

"Come Ajay. I have three cardigans here; you shall choose which I should wear."

"The light blue one, you'll be wonderful! But are we going somewhere?"

I nodded.

We unlocked the garden gate and squeezed ourselves out of it noiselessly. With an umbrella in hand and some cash stuffed in Ajay's pant pockets, we walked towards the marketplace, down the lane. The complexion of the clouds had somewhat improved. We passed several small ponds—created due to rain which gleamed with sunshine and the road dotted with dense trees and shrubs, the wet leaves of which were glazing too. We crossed the vast, beautiful plains, which looked baron as if no man visited them at all. At the farthest ends, it was difficult to say when the plains stopped, and the sky started.

We soon reached the market. Despite being an old-style market, it was immaculate. The road was of concrete, with trees on both sides with their branches almost covering the sky above; under which the small shops were dotted along. It thrilled me to see the bustling market filled with local customers, especially ladies, many of whom wore outfits tallying with the modern fashions. From the first look at the scene of the market, I got the hint that the old town was filled with wealthy people and scope.

We came across and halted at a roadside tea stall, sitting on one of its wooden benches. I thought that the place could be highly useful as there, I could have direct contact with the locals. Four men were seated on the other bench, and they were peculiar. One man raised his head suddenly and stared at the sky; his very careful stare longed for a minute and then he spoke about the color of the sky. The other man followed the same steps, and they started discussing the sky. I couldn't quite understand then, but later on, I understood they were contemplating the sky to gamble on the question of rain that day. I purchased biscuits from the seller so that some kind of conversation could start with those busy men, and it did.

"You look new over here, child. Where do you live?" An old gentleman sitting beside me with arms crossed over a stick asked when I made a gesture to help him with the teacup.

"We are new to this town; we live up the hill," I replied.

"Up the hill? You mean you live in that house?" Another man said as he kept down his cup and stared at me in a startlement.

There was a slight unexplainable chaos at the stall, among the men, and I link it with my words. No one answered any of my questions as they got engrossed in each other. Some kept on looking at me from the corner of their eyes and others left the stall one by one. The smell of the smoke of cigarettes was flowing in the air, surrounding the small stall.

"Sir, can you please tell me something about the house? We shifted here recently but since then..." I asked, ignoring the people.

"You should call the temple's priest, and have the house checked once maybe, only for safety." He said, sipping tea.

"Safety from what? What happened there?"

"Much shouldn't be told to you, but the house has a wildly lousy past, filled with crime. Many passers and land agents have had paranormal experiences over there. I will not ask who your guardian is or who has purchased the house, but if he is a resident of this town, then it can't be that he didn't have a hint of all this."

"That might be true... I have heard about a Mr. Shaitaan; can you tell me something about him?"

"Don't utter the name. The story of the secretive man has become a haunting legend of the town, all because of his mysterious death." He paused for a second, exhaled loudly, and then continued, "Listen, no one knows what he was up to as he spent his last days in perfect solitude, and none wished to visit him. He had been found dead in the early morning hours and by the time the town woke up, the news had spread that he was dead, and his body taken by the authorities. I know this, but I can direct you to a woman who may tell more because she lived nearby. I fear you have to check whether she is alive or already dead." He laughed a bit.

"Thank you, Sir! Please tell me where to go."

I noted the things that the old man had said and then proceeded to the lady's place. Fortunately, she was alive enough to speak and comprehend. I had a seat near the old lady in her house and asked her similar questions. She had similar prejudices about the man and she answered in an old trembling voice:

"Kids nowadays want to know everything... But I will tell you. I had seen that person many times as I lived nearby and that was around a year ago or so. You know, it is a fact that I have stayed at his place and worked there for a whole two days..."

"So, how was your experience there?"

"Very troublesome, as I remember. The days were unpleasant, and the nights were slumber less, I felt extremely weak and as if the strength in my feeble arms was gone. It was so cold in there! My health has fallen ever since I have come out of that horrible place. I had come out of the house as soon as I felt the owner was doing something which can be called the occult in his chamber. There were no such visitors to him, and even street dogs didn't roam around in that place..."

Of these words, it was no doubt anymore that something must have happened in that place.

"Can you please describe the man?" I asked.

"I must not do so. I will not remember him again. I will not; I must not!" she continued to murmur.

"I request you to please help me. You know we have bought that house and now problems are arising, so please give me some information." I said, coming nearer with the implore in my tone.

The lady gave a look at my cousin, who was sitting on the chair near me and was staring with wide eyes at the lady and listening.

"Okay..." she said as she sighed. "The man was tall; I could never properly see his face and he wore clothes that proved his wealth. He was particular about his clothes and dictated how to wash and press them. He boasted that most of them were imported from the West... always dull and dark colors, though shiny. Yes, shiny! He would kill any person who would even touch his clothes without his permission." She continued: "Something else too comes to my mind. Twice or thrice a day I had heard an extraordinary noise on the top floor as if something heavy was moved..." She stopped at this. After some time, we left the house thanking the woman.

The afternoon sun was shining heavily upon the head and the weather had become somewhat warm. I realized that this part of the town which was on the lower side was less windy than the place where I was living. After conversing with some other locals, I understood that there was nothing seriously abnormal about them, but mostly all of them had a superstitious blend of mind that was clear from their tone. It expressed their prejudices about Mr. S. Many of them simply avoided talking about Mr. S—and I also grasped that many of them truly had only a little material information to give on the man. Many accounts of small conversations with other people around, which I noted down, were just more perplexing. One said that Shaitaan's body was cremated in a particular spot, another said the authorities took the body, others said that his body wasn't found and many even believed that he wasn't dead! Another unsettling thing about this man, if these weren't enough; was that he was in his later days a severe alcoholic, a reclusive drinker.

While walking some distance, I saw an old-fashioned doctor's chamber, which was a small open room at the farthest end of the lane. The doctor was just returning home after his hours at the chamber, but as I requested; he became ready for a talk for some time. The gentleman sat on his mighty chair, one leg over the other, and a pipe twitched between his lips. He looked like an experienced and serious man in his forties who was wearing white kurta pajamas and thick black framed spectacles, with his hair combed back.

"So, I have understood your issue..." He said, taking the pipe out of his mouth and breathing out after he heard what story I had to say and continued, "I have a bit of knowledge of psychology and recently I am studying one book on the subject. But the thing is, I have never been to that house."

"Any bit of information, anything you remember? I mean, only a few people know about the man, and we have been walking about this place for over two hours." I said, with a childish disappointment on my face.

There was silence for a few minutes, during which the doctor looked engrossed in deep thought.

"Oh, yes, I–I have something for you. Wait!" He said, pointing with his pipe to his shelf, and stood up in a jerk of unusual excitement.

He sat again after a minute, flipping pages of an old register that he had picked out from his mighty shelf. After looking at the register continuously for minutes with extreme care; he said:

"Yeah; this one! Mr. Paul was his name."

"Now who is this, Doctor?"

"This person had visited me around seven months ago, as I see here. You know, he was a man in perfect health and structure as sound as a man could dream. He had an intelligent look on his face, but the strangest fact is that he complained of having inexplicable fears and horrific nightmares that he fancied were indications of a ghost. I figured out that there was no such mental issue with him when he visited me; his memory, vision, his ability to differentiate all were perfect."

"So, what's the link?" I said, making a gesture.

"The link is this, he was the first person to buy the house after the death of its owner... Yes. He had purchased the house about which you are talking, immediately after the death of its owner, and amazed everyone with his hurry. I guess that he might have monopolized the house with… I don't know. Leave. Further, I relate he came to visit me with his problems only a week after he had shifted to that house." The doctor said all this in a go and then paused, putting the pipe again between his lips.

"Then what, Doctor?" I eagerly said.

"Then what? gradually his condition deteriorated day by day. He would burst into tears sometimes, he complained of lack of sleep and frustration had become a part of his daily life. Once he behaved abnormally even in my chamber and all this time, he was under my close surveillance. His story also spread to many people and the general perception of the house was as a haunted, unholy place, with superstitious beliefs you know...

Ultimately, I strongly recommended him to leave that place as soon as possible—as it would affect his brain further." The doctor said with a slight sense of triumphant pride.

"So where is he now?" Ajay asked.

"Yes, Doctor, please say," I repeated in amazed excitement because at last I had got some very material information and did not know that someone else had also purchased and lodged in that place even before my uncle.

"He lives far from the market. But if you plan to see him, be careful, as he may have turned into a maniac. Yes, he isn't sane anymore, though he left the house in only a month... God knows what he saw there."

"Okay... Well thank you, Doctor, you have been extremely kind to attend to us." I said as I stood and continued, "Now we will not take any more of your time."

"Fine. You know one more thing. I have to admit that I appreciate you. Once I was also one of the few people who were inquisitive about the house up the hill and I am ready to offer help in this case you require it. Don't forget to tell me the outcomes..." He said as he stood and came out of the chamber with us.

I smiled at him and then looked up at the sun, and then my eye turned towards my cousin. He was standing, pressing his stomach, and I instantly understood that he was hungry for so long.

"Ajay, are you fine?"

"Yes.... I think not..." he could barely speak.

"Doctor, can you please tell me where I should go as we both are quite hungry? Is there any restaurant nearby?"

"Not exactly a restaurant, but a kind of small stall is there; a new owner has reopened it recently. Just turn the next lane, cross a few shops and you get there." He said, pointing towards the turned lane.

We walked over from the doctor's place to the lane and turned left. The road was not of concrete, but the soil was quite settled.

"If you feel a little better, I will talk to distract you from your stomach till we reach," I asked Ajay.

"Sure..."

"Why do you think that Mr. Paul purchased the house so hurriedly, I mean just after Mr. S—died?" I asked Ajay in a gossipy tone.

"You don't remember? The doctor said he wasn't right in the head. That is the reason he hurried. Simple." Ajay said, walking swifter than me.

"But..." Before I could say something more, we came in front of a shop.

"It is the place we were searching for. Come, let's have something." I said as I stepped up to the first step of three, which led to the main open gate of the stall.

The stall looked big from the outside and it was written "Food Cabin" or something like that, on its mighty signboard. We took our seats there. There, the ceiling was high, black fans hung from it, the furniture too was painted black, and the floor was made of black-and-white tiles. The table clothes were old-styled embroidered ones, the menu board hung in one corner with a tall pendulum clock and some decorative furniture was neatly placed at both corners of the room. All this gave a good look to the cabin, but still; it was as silent as a night, possessing some strange uneasiness in its very atmosphere. It was naturally illuminated, and all the glass windows that were closed offered a view of the outside lands and clouds as one turned head from one to another.

"Why are there no customers around? This is after all lunchtime." I said as I turned back and gave a proper look at the place. All that was seen were vacant chairs and tables, organized with care.

"Never been to this place before. Leave all this. Let's order something." Ajay said, looking lazily at the ceiling fan, which was also very slow.

"Excuse me, someone in here?" I asked, but there was no answer.

Then I shouted the second time and cried even louder the third time and it was after all this that I noticed a doorknob turning, a door it was at one quiet end. A man emerged from behind the closed door, which opened with a creak. He was a man who looked in his fifties, a tall, and very well-built, broad yet bent figure, which still looked strong though. He tottered to us, dragging one of his legs on the ground as if it was just a dead weight. Nothing was noteworthy about his appearance other than his heavily bearded face, which wasn't impressive because of several scars and marks; his eyes which appeared double a normal man's size, probably because of the thick glass spectacles which he wore over his quite disfigured nose, hypnotic in its way and above all, his expressionless "wooden" face itself. He didn't say a word but approached our chairs slowly, staring particularly at me without a blink. He initially did not attempt to break the dull silence.

"Sorry to disturb you..." erupted from my mouth as he stood in front of us with his odd concrete expression. "I mean; we thought we could order something here but... Is this shop closed?"

"Are you two new?" he asked in his plain, heavy voice.

A question instead of an answer to mine somewhat enraged me, but still, I replied, "I live up the hill and he is my brother, and we heard of your restaurant so..."

"Up the hill? Oh!" He said as if startled by my address and his amazement was someway even more strange than the others whom I had previously met that day.

"Wait; I think I can bring something for you. Sit; sit comfortably." He said in a soft tone as he turned and tottered back to the kitchen.

Was his voice like that?

He left behind a powerful scent of a very high-quality perfume, a type that I had never recognized before. The room became silent and solitary as before. I felt no longer the sensation of hunger in my empty stomach; it had completely died off and that too, unpleasantly.

We passed the next ten minutes dumbly staring at the closed door. The open front window, the only window that the man opened as he had come to us, showed that the gray shades of the rain drew nearer once again. Gradually the room turned darker and shadier, and its natural illumination and shine were going down.

Ajay soon said that he wasn't feeling nice over there and wanted to go, to which I agreed because, with every minute past, the heart-pressing anxiety only increased. As we were just about to stand, the door opened again and the man emerged, grinning with a giant tray in hand. As he approached nearer, a spicy aroma found its way to our childish senses.

"I am the owner of this place and the time for today is up... nevertheless, you can drink." He said as he kept the tray on the table.

"Thanks…" came out dryly from Ajay's mouth as the man looked at him for the first time.

My little cousin looked at me and I only saw doubt in his eyes; the same doubt which was in my mind about whether to drink the red-hot soup served before us. I knew that the man was looking constantly at me, smiling widely. I held a spoonful of the good-looking soup and reluctantly sipped it.

"Wow. This is perfect!" I remarked, looking into Ajay's eyes, which initiated him to sip too.

We told the stranger our true opinion of the soup. Till this time, the man had been standing silently looking at us from an arm's distance but no sooner than we remarked; he pulled out the third chair on the circular table and sat right there; next to me.

"I knew you would be delighted with this special soup… tomato, onion anyway... Now I want to talk to you about a matter."

"We too have to talk about something." Ajay interrupted.

"No sir, first you tell... and please also tell how much we have to pay," I demanded.

"Oh, leave the bill. I do not take money from lovely young people..." The strange smile reappeared on his face as he was eye-to-eye with me and asked very gently, "What's your name Miss? Never seen you here before."

"Vaanya and he is Ajay..." I introduced.

He strangely chuckled, but it never reached his lips. It collapsed in his throat itself.

"Lovely! You said you live up the hill... So, what do you want to know from me?" he removed his spectacles for a second as he spoke and soon put them on, but I had seen nothing but coldness in his eyeballs.

"I-I think we... we should not bother you; we have to leave also as we have to return before evening breaks..." I said as I meant it. I thought it would be the only responsible decision.

At this moment there was an ear-cracking sound outside and a string of current glazed the gray sky and glazed even the room, and I couldn't help but look at it—astounded. Not even a second had passed and the whole wooden structure was shaking due to the heavy water droplets that burst from the sky. It was again raining heavily, and my fixed eyes didn't move from the window until it was fully covered with water droplets, and nothing could be seen of the outside world anymore.

"Where will you go Miss, In this stormy weather?" He said, a tease in his tone particularly addressed to me.

My heart beat heavier than the wooden roof as I realized we had no option other than to stay in that place with that man until the crackling battles in the sky stopped.

"Nothing to worry about, nothing at all. I am simply called 'old uncle' by the kids, and I am going to serve both of you until the rain stops. You know we had to talk about something, isn't it...?"

"Yeah... Well... So, can you tell us about the owner of the house up the hill?" I asked.

"Yes! I mean, I can! He was called Shaitaan and liked to be called so; you know he named himself. He was a cunning yet intelligent fellow."

"How did he die, Sir?" Ajay asked.

"Oh, this boy is very curious... He had died as he killed himself."

"What? But this is a new thing we have heard." I couldn't resist speaking.

"New or old whatever... The truth is the truth. He jumped off from the window and fell into the deep void."

Ajay was going to say something again, but I indicated to him not to speak a word but just to listen. I knew what he wanted to say, the same thing in my mind because there was no void just down the terrace. There was another extension of bricked surface which was low enough and then some trees and beyond this, I didn't know.

"He fell into the deep void and died." He spoke with conviction.

"Was his body found, cremated, or?" I asked.

The man chose to remain silent at this question. His fingers smoothed his beard, and he put down his spectacles again. I observed that lately, his legs had started shaking. I think it was consciously done, but soon he started tapping the floor with his foot in a hasty motion.

"I do not know that much, dear. When he died, I was not there. I think your talk is over now and before my talk, we will have some tasty orange juice... Wait a second." He said with an enormous smile, showing his shining teeth as he stood up again and tottered to the kitchen.

"At last, the old man serves us orange juice... Isn't it great? This man looks good." Ajay asked, looking at me.

I looked at my wristwatch, which showed that it was four, but unfortunately, the rain hadn't stopped completely, though had certainly slowed a bit. I thought: Kids usually became happy with small things. Could this man be called jolly?

"Thanks for the juice... Please tell me what you want to know?" Ajay said after he drank, his expression showed that he relished it.

"For how many days have you been living in that house?" He asked, rubbing his palms as his gaze was fixed.

"Around six or seven months..."

"Who is your guardian?"

"His name is Mr. Vijay," I answered.

"Mr. Vijay! I know him. You know he often comes here to discuss business matters..."

"That's great," I replied without meaning it.

"How many rooms do you have, and have you opened all?"

"No... I mean, some rooms are closed, but ..." Ajay replied.

"Reply to me correctly now. So… have you found anything in that house? I mean something of antique value..." He said this in a low voice and, strangely enough, laughed as he came even closer.

"No, nothing much, but if there is something in our house, then we would be glad to know it, as it will be ours. Some things are messed up in cobwebs. But now we should leave. We have to return before it's dark," I spoke this time rather strongly.

"Oh ... Oh, okay..." He laughed again and continued, "See, there is a fresh fragrance in my old dull shop as you came; you and this young boy can come anytime here... Uh... Should I come to meet you and your uncle? And when should I?".

"If you know him, you may come on your own accord, but I'm sorry to say, our house is so high, it's a pressure even for us to walk up…"

We finally walked up to the door, and I turned to give him a last look for courtesy, he forwarded some lozenges to me and said slowly and heavily, with excessive, unrequired emphasis on these words: "It's sweet." with his same, direct gaze deep into my eyes.

Coming out of the restaurant; I took a deep breath of the fresh air and sighed hard. The drizzling hadn't ceased, and the temperature forced me to pull the cardigan closer.

"I hope you will tell what all you got to know when we return home..." Ajay said to me as he jumped over a puddle.

"Yes; but it's not over. I think I remember seeing a Police station on our path; we will halt there too."

"But why?" Ajay reacted in astonishment, "I never knew you wanted to be a detective... will anyone even attend to us there?"

I replied nothing as I wasn't sure whether I would go into it, but still, I wanted some information that could only be given to me by that source.

We walked the same path, watching the vast, empty fields, and the market, and finally reached the Police station, where I stood opposite, contemplating the decision. I finally took small steps. I had asked Ajay to stand out for some time and walked up to the porch, entering a small, unlit passage where there were rooms on either side. There were other people around in the small passage and one of the staff was sitting in the passage busy with others and his diary. Probably he didn't see us. I took this time to walk up to the end of the passage, where I noticed a hanging board. It was a board where photos of the Wanted were pinned. In the dull light, I figured out that there was only and only one big photo pinned; naturally, it caught my attention. It was of a man with a clean-shaven face, sunken, big hypnotic eyes who was holding a small board with his name, etc. I could quite read his name. It was "Neelnath," and it truly matched his menacing face, whose features were hard as stone.

"Hey, Miss. What do you want?" the Police staff called, while I was thinking about this criminal.

"I want to meet the Sir who is inside; to discuss an issue. I am from the newspaper..."

"Oh; he doesn't talk with news collectors like this. But you may wait for a minute outside. If he comes out after his meeting, then you may ask him."

I sat down quietly at one end of the wooden bench, which was at a distance from the closed gate, just following the same wall. Silently gazing at the other wall thinking what I would ask when I go inside, the gate opened. A young man came out, half smiling; I noticed him stuffing cash in his pocket, adjusting it, and then walking out of the station in just four steps with both hands in his pockets and his head down. By the glimpse of his clothes, his frame, his peculiar walk, and his shoes, I knew he could be none other than Arun. Fortunately, I just slipped a blunder as he didn't notice me in there. Instantly, I remembered I had left Ajay out and feared that it would again be a disaster if Arun saw Ajay in that place—everything would be out. I walked out of the Police station and before me, saw that Arun had already walked a distance. He was walking swiftly and had reached so far that he could no longer be clearly differentiated and was soon out of sight. I sighed a breath of relief as he had skipped Ajay, probably as he had taken the other lane, but it was very lucky for me.

"What did you get to know?" Ajay asked as he caught my glimpse.

"Hurry, we have to reach home before Arun does..."

Ajay followed me, matching my pace, but continuously threw amazed questions: "What happened? And Arun must be at home now..."

"No! I don't know what he is up to, but I saw him just now; inside the cabin of the inspector... Now he is heading home, and we have to reach before him." I said in breaking discontinuous words as I was walking even faster.

"But why? I mean, I or Papa no one knows he has ever gone to the Police station or the jail."

We followed the same path as it was the only one, we knew back to our place. Throughout the path, I was overcautious and looked at every man who passed by to avoid any kind of confrontation with Arun. The sun was setting slowly, admirably between the clouds, to which it gave an orange tinge. One moment we walked, the other we stood and the other we ran all in a splitting pressure to reach the house fast and in the first place avoiding him in the path.

We finally reached and luckily, before Arun's arrival. It was the same, wrapped in a fog of solitude. The same garden gate gave us the way into the house, and everything was dead dark inside.

We entered the house, almost falling into it in a hurry, panting, holding our stomachs but slightly giggling over our run. The trees in the garden cast peculiar shadows over the hall and the faint slivers of the distant moon were falling over the wall clock. We silently walked up, hearing our footsteps on the floor as the only sounds that echoed. Ajay switched on the bulbs and lamps, which were dim and yellow, casting more shadows all around the gigantic walls.

We sat on the sofas silently; facing each other blankly, as if we had forgotten all that had happened that day. As I entered the lonely house, again, the strange feeling of nervousness in my stomach was repulsive. But strangely, I felt I was getting used to it. It struck my mind at this point that I had not remembered my home in the city for even a day and such were the series of events; now I felt a little away or in a distant land. The feeling was strange. I stared around the walls, and the ceiling, and my vision got stuck only at the various black statues of little boys and girls with broadened, ball-less eyes; broadened as if staring at something in earnest amazement.

"Now—do you have any hint of why Arun went to the Police station?" I asked.

"No, it's a discovery for me... I thought he goes nowhere other than to his room..." Ajay replied, half lying down on the sofa.

"One thing is perplexing me..."

"What?" Ajay asked.

"I saw him putting cash in his pockets as he was stepping out of the inspector's cabin... Why? Was he putting it in, or could it be that he was putting it back?" I said, closing my eyes as the fancy of being watched was constantly overwhelming me.

"Hey! Is anybody there?" a sudden cry came out of my mouth.

I stood up, jerking my head towards the right.

"What? Who?" Ajay jumped up in amazement.

I walked up to the open garden gate and peeped out. There was nothing more than the dead, tall trees, and empty darkness with the sounds of breeze.

"Who is there? Uh..."

"No... No one." I said, still looking out.

My heart was pounding for no reason.

"I saw something, a strange, black movement from the corner of my eye; as if someone had just entered the house from the garden gate."

"Lock it!"

I locked the door.

There was a ring of the doorbell. Naturally, it was Arun. He came in as normal as he could be, and we talked normally. We sat for a while, had our dinner, and then again sat for a while in the hall. My little cousin and I had entered a casual gossip, but my mind was somewhere else. It was now not focused on Shaitaan, but it was on Arun. Yes, my mind was stuck on him. He thought that as he was silent; he was unnoticed, but it wasn't true anytime and not true at that moment too. I was watching him from the corner of my eye and his restlessness was clear. He looked up, down; right, and left shaking his both legs constantly. I wanted to ask him many questions but, how could I?

I thought about starting a conversation with him and thus turned to him. I saw him staring right at me. His eyes were blankly serious, and he didn't even blink as I turned to him in a jerk. It was as if he was not differentiating me at all but watching something else. I noticed his same wooden expression for half a minute and then checked right behind me. There was nothing but only the curtains, which were fluttering in slow motion.

"Hey..." I said to him, waving his hand in front of his face.

"I feel you have had no problem or any kind of difficulty..." He asked suddenly.

"Why do you ask?"

"No ... No actually, for a second, I thought someone was standing behind you..."

"What?" I was shocked.

"Oh, no, nothing, just the play of my shadow... Nothing at all." He said this but I could see his forehead wet and a silent horror on his face, which he was trying to suppress.

I looked back again, and this time also my eyes didn't detect anyone. Arun was murmuring something, slowly within himself; his lips barely opening. Was it a chant? But why?

"I feel we should talk about something... Break the silence." I spoke.

"Nothing about this house and this place and this town and especially not about my room..." He replied.

"Oh, no, not at all... But what... Okay, tell me something about yourself."

"Yes, tell us about your plan to be rich!" Ajay spoke, suddenly interrupting me.

"What? Have you told her also about all this?" He became furious.

"Oh, no... No. I mean, if you are going to be rich, then we all will be happy for you... That's it. I feel you can share your thoughts so that your burdened heart..."

"Until I am rich, I am in danger... the danger of life and maybe beyond that..." He said, getting excited and aroused.

There was again a long time of silence. I couldn't ask him about this anymore, the way he got excited and then sat with his eyes closed; I didn't dare to. The only thing in motion in that motionless silence was the arms of the clock. Time passed quickly but my uncle didn't turn up as usual.

"Do you keep the window closed at night?" Arun asked abruptly.

"No, sometimes I open it at night as it feels suffocating in the room..."

"Why do you do that? I told you to close it in any case..." He said as he stood up with a startled expression.

"B-But one thing. That the window in the passage outside my room is also open and that you have to check the garden gate too..." I spoke.

"Is it? It is not good... I'll go up and do with it right now..."

"I know you are correct. Isn't all this because of the man about whom I told you? The one who moves about the garden in the night and had focused torch lights into my room? It terrifies me to speak of it. Who could it be?"

"I do not know..."

"Surely he is a lunatic..." I remarked.

"The only lunatic in this town is Mr. Paul... that man..." he said in a way of frustration.

The name struck me.

"Why don't you complain to the authorities or grab the man by the hand at night?"

"Do you feel like going out at night in the garden? And who knows who the person is? He may also be armed, or who knows what it is?" He spoke.

"... Which means you also have seen him before, before I came..." I said, slightly pointing.

"What is all this about? Tell me, please." Ajay said anxiously.

"I can't take any risk. He could be a murderer; a burglar and I care for everyone's safety in this house and that is why I said to lock the window!" Arun spoke.

"Can he be the ghost?" Ajay suggested in a very low voice.

"Stop! Scaring the entire world out here..." Arun replied.

"Only locking the window will not help!" I exclaimed.

"I will leave this place soon and you even sooner than me. So don't worry." He said and stopped as the doorbell rang again.

It was my uncle.

The heated discussion between us stopped as my uncle came in. His experienced face was calm and aware, and the moment was as normal as if nothing had happened. He was wearing a checked brown coat under which he wore a white shirt and gray pants; a golden-chained watch shined over his wearing.

"Uncle, please, can you have some lights up there? It is a very dark passage even in the day and in the night, nothing is visible..." I said to him when he had changed and sat comfortably on the sofa, and I couldn't help childishly pointing towards the passage where my room was.

I looked around for a second and noticed that Arun was no longer there.

"Oh, yes. You could have told me before, child. Let's see what can be done for now..." He thought for a second and then said, "For tonight, I can hang another bulb there. Will it do?"

"Yes, uncle..."

The bulb was soon placed there, and I lit it. It made little difference, but at least another person's shadow could be differentiated. What struck my eye was that there was one more door in the passage. Why I hadn't seen it before, but it meant there was one more room and it was to be seen in the passage, in the dark corner. I looked at it for a second and wondered.

"Uncle, do you know of some Neelnath?"

"Neelnath?" He said with his eyes deep in mine "Oh, he was a violent criminal, had disappeared, and then one day the news came that he was dead and cremated in the nearby burning ground... Don't bother yourself with such talks; I hope Ajay might have told you all this. Forget it and have a sleep." He replied, quite concerned.

"Father, as you are early today, please, can we have something for the night?" Ajay said, catching his father's hand with an imploring in his eyes.

I initially thought they were talking about some bed hot chocolate or something, but it turned out something else.

"But I don't know any children's story and..." He said half laughing.

"Please... something..." Ajay insisted childishly.

"Anything would do..." I added.

"Okay..."

Half an hour passed in our room where in one corner a dreary lamp was flickering as the sole representative of light in the dark, casting monstrous shadows on the vast walls. I blinked my eye as I just saved myself from falling asleep. Uncle was still narrating, his eyes on his paper, and on the other side, Ajay had already slept with a wide-open mouth and one leg hanging down from the bed. Initially, he had narrated a wonderful tale, but then he had turned to his love poems. What a strange interest it was, and he looked very passionate about it and his poems were mostly melancholy.

"Uncle, can you tell me about the only food stall here and its owner?" I asked, rubbing one of my eyes.

"Oh, I thought you were listening to the poems. "

"They are truly lovely; I look up to here more but tomorrow."

"Yes... It's been late ..." He stood up, stretched a bit, and said, "That man is a nice old fellow. Had helped with one tiny problem once... Good night." He said and swayed to the sides while he walked out, leaving the door half open.

One shadow was reduced in the room and now only my one could be seen as an enormous erection on the walls, under the yellow glow.

Sleep again didn't come to me, and I was engaged in thinking.

"I didn't know Uncle was romantic at heart... he differs from his elder son in all ways. When I talk to him, I feel good. I wonder what the reason for his shifting to this house can be." I thought.

I adjusted my bed again and went towards the door to close it as it was swaying because of the wind. I walked to it and caught it, preventing a hard banging. As I was going to close the door, I heard some footsteps on my floor. I peeped out. The noise could be heard louder now. I closed the door behind me, leaving Ajay sleeping in the room, and silently came out. The noises were coming from the closed door, the one in the dark corner of the passage. My heart was beating uncontrollably. The passage window was open and strong winds came into, fluttering my hair. I walked, following the noise, slowly, reluctantly, and with a hurting chest. I soon realized that I was standing in the darkest corner of the passage and took a step back as if I was waking up from a dream.

Someone was coming out. It startled me. I walked back to my room and looked out from behind my door. A figure came out from the closed room and strode angrily down the stair, hitting the door hard. It was only when the sliver of the bulb light fell on the figure, I saw it was none other than my uncle.

"What? Why ..." I thought.

The figure walked halfway down and then again walked up. I closed the door. There was a loud knock on my room door within a second. I paused, my heart still paining without reason. After all, it was my uncle.

"Yes, Uncle. What happened?" I said, as I ultimately opened the door after the second knock.

He harshly said something in the native language, not to me for sure, as he looked around. I didn't understand it. But then he addressed me:

"Did anyone come here today or yesterday? In this house of ours?"

"No, not at all," I said, failing to suppress a yawn.

"Okay." He said, turned away, and walked down.

The notable thing about his expression was that he looked distressed, anxious, and angry at the same time, which made me feel startled because my uncle was usually calm.

I waited for some time as I wanted to be prepared for anything to happen further. I was left in a perplexed situation, not understanding anything. Loud noises were coming from down, they grew louder and more horrific as if Uncle and Arun were in a quarrel. Pondering over the quarrels was useless because till that time I had understood nothing. Ajay got up suddenly and started murmuring; his eyes were soaked in slumber. I still don't know the reason, but it must be normal; I hope.

"Ajay, tell me something about the room, the room at the end of the hall..." I asked, shaking his shoulders.

"It's just an unlit closed room, and I don't remember...it being open since we came here..." He uttered half-broken words and dozed off again.

"A dark, locked room..." I murmured as I forcibly closed my eyes.

7

I woke up the next day with a heavy head. Swaying from one side to the other, I walked down the stairs, still in my nightdress. I stepped into the garden again; maybe it was because the gate was open. I was careful in each step on the garden grass and continuously felt moisture-filled air. What a morning it was! Dull but beautiful. I looked at the sky and clouds appeared like a blanket over our place.

I closed my eyes and stretched my arms wide to experience more profoundly the solitary winds of that solitary part of the country. But, as soon as I moved my arms, my chest felt heavy. As I stretched them, there was striking pain in both, and I couldn't sway them. I experienced the same restriction in my thighs too as if something was clinging to me. Maybe I wasn't well. I strolled around in the garden with my arms crossed around my chest, looking around. I had no hint of the time and who was awake by then and who wasn't. While walking, I came to the other part of the garden, and something caught my eye. It was a window that was covered with black paper from the inside. I took a step back and grasped that the room was of Arun. The window, which was made of glass and wood, had a steel ring fixed to it, into which I inserted my finger and tried to pull. There was no result, as the window was locked from the inside. I knew it. After all, it was Arun's room.

"Vaanya! Where are you? Come in and have breakfast..." Arun's voice came faintly to my ears.

"Coming..." I cried and turned back.

A shrilling noise came from behind me as I took the first step. I halted for a moment. I turned back, but all I could see were some bushes. The noise came again, and this time, I fear, it was from the front. I forced my mind to take it to be wind or something and walked back as swiftly as possible.

Over there, Arun's expression was normal, which means that he was satisfied.

"So where is Uncle?" I said as I pulled out one chair and sat.

"I don't know where he goes..." was his only reply.

"You know I had seen a dream yesterday... it was appalling," I said, holding my head.

"A difficult dream..." He said with a changed expression, "What was it about?"

"I-I cannot quite remember. Yesterday's dream showed someone behind me and... My memory is getting a bit foggy... my head aches a little too..."

He said after taking a few swift breaths, "You know I don't have dreams. I have nightmares... yesterday, also I had one..."

"What!"

"For a few days, I see dreams like, like people running around in horror, clocks falling and cracking. . ."

"Oh, God!" I couldn't stop interrupting him.

"But yesterday's one was special," he continued, "a man standing behind me, patting my shoulders and I running and running, carrying a heavy bag on my back and–and then slipping down the hill..."

"Please do not say anymore." I interrupted again, "We had similar dreams the last night. What shall we do, and what do you think about these dreams?"

"First, drink this." He said as he poured coffee from the kettle into my cup. "And then, I focus on my work and you on your books or for a better change, a prayer book perhaps."

"Again... You do not want to solve things, I know."

"Do you not like what we cook over here?" He asked.

"No, it's not bad," I replied, keeping the cup down, "but as you asked; it's not fantastic either except the one on the first day. By the way, why did you ask?"

"That's only because you are looking feeble today. I don't know why but..."

"Maybe... I am feeling weakness all over, after last night and though I slept deeply, my head is throbbing..." I said, taking a sip, and then continued: "But I fear your dreams aren't normal. I mean, nightmares may come occasionally, but always. How is it possible? Dreams are not always something 'out of the box' but they are mostly an accumulation of thoughts and memories both of recent and of distant past."

"Ah... I do not take them seriously... And it's great that you are there or else if it would be some other person, she would have cooked up any linkage between the similarity of our dreams and..." He was catching up a light laughing tone but got interrupted, but not by me.

We were alarmed. It was the ear-piercing cry of Ajay, whom I had left sleeping alone in the closed bedroom. The sounds were so loud that they could be heard distinctively down to the dining table.

"This kid, crying again..." Ajay said as he stood up, a vexed expression on his face.

As we saw him, it was evident that the boy too had a bad dream, again.

"Now, what happened?" Arun asked, removing the blanket from over him.

For minutes, he pointed towards the window of the room. His cheeks were red and wet.

"What? What is over here?" I said as I unlocked the window and peeped down.

There was nothing but the baron garden.

"A man came in from here, patted me while I was asleep and, and went out, opening the door and then closing it. He-he walked out, turned left, and probably went into the other room of the passage..."

For moments, we stared at him and couldn't speak.

"The other room? Are you sure?" Arun spoke finally and as he did, so I noticed something.

His vexed and carefree expression had now transformed into one of an amazingly tensed man in no time.

"A man patted you also?" I addressed Ajay but looked kept looking at Arun, who took little notice of me.

"By the way, what is in the other room, Arun?" I asked.

He turned his head towards me, paused in speechlessness, and then said, "Nothing. Nothing for you to worry about..."

"Why yes! Last night I had seen Uncle going into that room and..."

"Uncle?! What did Father do there?" Arun asked in a manner that not the kid's cries, but my question had appalled him.

"How do I know?" I said and turned to Ajay, "Listen, you must have seen another dream. See, the window was all locked last night."

"I cannot see dreams with open eyes..." He spoke in a passion of horror.

"What was he like?" I asked.

"I do not remember his face at all..."

"It's so dark today, look outside... and you were sleepy too. Come down and have something and forget about all that." I tried again, holding him consolingly by his arm.

"Arun, isn't it strange that Ajay had also seen a similar nightmare yesterday?" I asked without turning back.

But there was no answer and when I turned back, I understood I and Ajay were set alone once again.

The rest part of the day was very usual and quite empty of any activity for me. Talking of being empty, most of my days at my uncle's place were not filled with any activity. Initially, I had liked that, I must admit, but as time passed by; I found my mind a bit more puzzled every day.

That day's diary entry shows how I had spent the long boring day in that ill-lit place:

"I will go out again in a day. I don't know why. I will go out in the open at any cost. Today I had a hard time choosing which book I should read during the long afternoon hours and also my mind couldn't be free from constant working. Who should I not suspect? Whenever I tried to have a nap to calm my mind; I couldn't succeed. It was as if my brain, which had nothing to concern itself with,

had been put on like a breakless express. I am only in search of an opportunity; an opportunity to advance some steps in finding and solving everything which I want to do. Why? I do not know. No matter how hard I try, I can't stay in this house and be away from all this."

A day passed by similarly and that night also, I couldn't quite sleep. Uncle wasn't in the house the whole day and I remember that when at night, I went down the stairs, under the light of a dreary lamp, it was my uncle whom I saw moving about in the hall. I watched him from a distance as he walked, then went out and came in again, with his head constantly down.

It was very early in the morning when my eyes opened the next day. They had opened suddenly, and I could just see the shady ceiling. The sun must not be properly up as sunlight didn't enter the room. I held my head and sat still for some minutes on my bed, in a paroxysm of irritation. This was because I realized I had again forgotten my dream, which had held my eyes together for the entire night. All I remember is that it was a very dreadful one and nothing more, simply lousy.

Then, something occurred.

I turned to my cousin, who was still wrapped in his deepest slumber and his blanket. I noticed his expressions. His closed eyes looked excessively strained; his brows were closer to each other as if in deep concentration; "He might be watching something," I thought.

He clutched the pillow tighter now and then, and moved somewhat strangely on his bed, kicking, and shaking his legs, but slowly. Probably he had done that all night, I suppose. I inspected him and what I saw was simply unsettling. His lips were moving. I wished I could understand what he was talking about and if, to whom was he talking, in the deepest layers of his dream.

A thought clung to me: "Was he watching the same dream which I had seen just now?"

"No, no; I am getting too imaginative now." While I was busy with this thought, with a sudden jerk, he opened his eyes.

It startled me as his expressions were unmovable; the widened eyes looked inhumanly regular, as if open but seeing nothing.

"What?" I whispered in confusion and leaped to switch on the yellow bulb.

The next moment I saw him slightly standing up, but so feebly that I had to support his back, or else he would have fallen on the ground right there. I looked at his eyes, and they shut again as if they hadn't opened at all. He took a couple of small, hurried steps, almost tripping; within which he reached the nearest wall, which was almost at the side of the bed where he was sleeping. I watched him wordlessly, doing nothing and making no forced attempt to grab him and wake him up. He soon started rubbing his right hand on the wall and then his fingers, as if he was writing something there. What was he doing? I wondered. It was not clear whether he was trying to write or draw. In a moment of hurried panic and confusion, I rushed for a pen and a piece of paper. I felt a pressing urge to know what was on his mind.

Within moments I hurried back with a pen and some loose sheets and, and held him by his back, after which turned him. The bulb had lately started to blink and flicker and soon it was in such a vibrating pace that one moment the room was dark and the other it was lit—light appeared to dance in the room horribly. Maybe the bulb was loose, but at such a time my heart had skipped a beat. I hadn't witnessed something like this. A feeling of being trapped in a play of sudden light and darkness seized me. Ajay turned, I couldn't see his face at first glance as it was dark, in the other moment what I saw was not only his face but a huge reflection, a dark shadow over his face, his body, and up to the pale wall. The next moment it was dark again, and I nervously turned to back and it was a moment of light again. My eyes started to pain, and words didn't come out. Someone was there. I wasn't sure about who or what. I saw it behind my back, but within a millisecond the almost falling bulb fell on the ground. It cracked. An ear-tearing sound followed as it turned to pieces and forced me to press my palms against my ears and everything became wrapped in sudden blackness and in-visibility. I was thrown back in a jerk, in a shudder of fear and panic as Ajay started screaming horribly; his screams coincided with the noise of the shattering bulb but surpassed it.

"Ah... Stop!" I cried, pressing my ears harder. I was on the other side of Ajay, with my back pressed against the furniture.

"What happened? Stop screaming!" I screamed.

Everything happened in only ten seconds and still what had happened cannot be rationalized.

"What are you doing?" I burst into horror, shaking Ajay by his shoulders.

No result. It was as if he was still in a dream, having no sense of what he had been doing for so long. I was the only witness. He had calmed down, and his head hung down again. I realized that the sudden events had set my body shivering as in my mind I thought: What was behind me? Who was behind me? What was Ajay drawing?

I lifted him and put him back on his bed again, and I must admit he was very light, his temperature was also high, and he sweated like one who is horribly exhausted. On my bed, I sighed. I couldn't stop my legs from shaking and my breathing was loud. The pieces of the broken bulb gleamed as the morning had perfectly broken and the brightest sun rays quite illuminated the room, though gradually. I calmed down at last. The fact that no one came to our room after so much noise baffled me, but I thought: "Maybe noises don't travel here".

I looked around the room in silence and there wasn't any phantom, only emptiness surrounding it. For a moment I thought about reporting all this to somebody, but then I thought: What would I tell? Maybe it was just a coincidence that the bulb loosened and fell at the same moment when I saw someone behind me. But how could I even say that I had seen someone because in that situation of light and darkness; I couldn't be sure.

I didn't know what to do. I left the boy sleeping along with the sheets and pen as they were and walked down hurriedly. My legs still trembled, and I had to take the support of the railing as I walked downstairs. Sleepwalking is a phenomenon, which I knew but this, which I saw; what could it be called? A thought came to me. I couldn't just ignore what was happening there. Maybe negative energies were flowing about. But I tried to brush off the thought as I didn't want fear enveloping my heart, which would freeze movement on the path of solving the problem, which had to be solved as soon as things didn't go wrong; terribly wrong.

I reached the dining hall and then walked up to the gate and then around the house; no one was to be seen. Most of the curtains were drawn over the windows and negligible light entered.

"Uncle?" I called, but there was my voice echoed.

I walked up to Arun's room. It was locked as I pressed the door handle, and the gate didn't move, and no objection came from inside. I went up to my uncle's room door. I knocked.

"Uncle, are you there, should I ...?"

"A...a... I... I am doing some important work..." his voice came from inside and it was surely not normal, full of hesitation.

The way it was told; I couldn't control my urge to know. It was rather wrong, but still, I had that as the sole option, looking through. I looked into the room from the keyhole of the door. The keyhole was on the lower side of the door. I knew this trick wouldn't work in a room that would be very dark, but still, I tried. What I saw was strange, baffling. From that small opening, I couldn't see anymore but a hand that was hanging down from the bed. I took a more concentrated look but couldn't precisely confirm if it was my uncle's hand, but I knew it could be no one else. It took me back in a moment. It appeared as if Uncle was lying upside down on the bed with his arms and legs hanging down as if he wasn't alive.

After this, I did nothing other than busy myself with some or the other activity. I was alone in the morning hours, and I knew I was breathing louder and also that I couldn't help it.

Apparently, not a single one was around me, and this made it even more difficult. No noise, no people, and nothing about me; but me sitting there with my eyes turning around to check the horrors of being stared at continuously.

The silence cracked soon when there was a sudden knock on the door. I stood up with a jerk. My look was at the main wooden gate that stood alone at the farthest end of the hall. I stood for moments without moving. The door was knocked again and then again—its tough wooden noise beating in the hose. I walked up to it, waited for a second, and then opened it.

"Good morning!"

I released my breath. It was not Arun, but Rajesh at the door.

"It's you—Good morning."

He was very fresh and cheerful in the morning and his ways quite lifted my spirit.

"B-But... I think you have to come again as..." I said to clarify that his friend was not there in the house and that if he wanted to find him, he would probably have to go to the Police station, but he interrupted.

"Okay, I get it... But how is he? I had a talk with him, which is of utmost importance to him."

"I do not know how he is. Eh, I am sorry, but ... I am a bit confused about where he goes at such hours." I couldn't help but speak this.

"Does he go somewhere? Never seen him on the path down to the town... Maybe he follows the path of the woods..."

"Woods... I didn't know there are something like woods here too. Well, is it something very important—what do you have to talk about with him? Because I can convey it to him."

"N-Not anything secretive but... don't mind, I would have to talk with him myself... Okay, no problem, leave that," he halted, took a closer look at me, and said, "You look exhausted. I hope I didn't disturb you. If you were busy, then ..."

"No yes, I am exhausted," I said thoughtfully, looking downwards; remembering what all happened today.

"What, what is it? I mean, are you not feeling well or something?" He said and sniffed.

"No one's there over here, so... being a bit bored is natural. But okay... I have got time to read, and that's what I am doing—"

"Oh! Yes, talking of your boredom's solution, I-I completely forgot something. I have a book for you; you know I wanted to give it to you..." He handed me a small pocketbook.

It was one of my interests and an old one.

"Thanks! I had been looking about for this book in the city..." I said as I flipped the pages.

"Okay then; I should leave now..." He said as he looked around and sniffed again.

"Oh see; you have been standing here for so long and I... Please come in... I assure you; this courtesy is not for the book." I said the last part laughingly.

He denied it initially, but eventually, he agreed. He came in and the loneliness in the house was now divided.

“There is a kind of damp smell over here, maybe because of the rain or...” He said sniffing again.

“Yes... Strange...” I also recognized it—it’s stronger since.

“Well, where is the little boy? You know he is very intelligent; I suppose...”

“Yes... But he is sleeping up for now. At least it’s good that he gets a sound sleep because I have experienced what happens when sleep just doesn’t come...”.

I was sitting on a chair in front of him, facing him, and we talked a bit. It was a pleasant change always. I narrated to him the whole incident that had happened that morning and even he couldn’t say much about it.

“I think you both must be sleepy, and Ajay might have some sleepwalking type problems... still I do not feel something right... I don’t know why, but I also feel you shouldn’t worry much... What else we can say? And you would not be much surprised about such things as, though I am not in psychology but there have been such incidents in the world, I feel.” He said in a serious tone.

“Yes, but as you said, I also feel something incorrect here...” I replied.

“Well, do you believe in ghosts—spirits?” I asked suddenly.

He halted momentarily, then laughed in slight amazement and said, “I do not have a true opinion on this, but I feel everyone is a frog in his small well, never comes out and believes that the universe is restricted to his well and know not anything beyond it.”

“That means you are on both sides...”

“I don’t believe in it for now, as I have no experience. But certainly, I get the reason for your worry. I feel you are battling over the thought of ghosts. Well, this place is classical and mighty, but you mustn’t think of spirits...”

“Well, yes, you got it. I don’t know how, but you exactly got it.”

“I feel going out on this windy day would work wonders... Am I correct?"

"Yes, you are ..." I replied.

I remembered the last time I went out with him; it was fun. But this also reminded me of the petrifying incident that had occurred while walking up. But I cared not much as it was day and not evening this time.

"The same place?" He asked.

"Yes, it is a quiet place, and the vicinity is gorgeous."

I didn't feel like knocking on my uncle's door again. About Ajay, I had completely forgotten. I shut the door and there was no reason to lock it as no one came to that place. At least that's what I had thought until then. We came out under the windy, open sky where it couldn't be confirmed that it was a shade of blue or gray. A strange coldness was floating, and the winds blew from time to time in a spray of raindrops. The grass was wet, and the vicinity looked wrapped in mists; filtered through the trees came streaks of sunlight—making the scene somewhat yellow at the same time. We walked out of the small encircling of trees and bushes and reached the lane. The wet lane had been set on a shining glaze by the sunlight falling on it, leaves were scattered here and there, and on both sides was deep greenery. The silence was such that our voices echoed and such that no one had ever walked that lane. A smell of moisture was in the air and water dropped from the tip of the leaves occasionally and if it fell on the skin, it was like ice.

"How much time could it take?" I asked as we walked over the lane.

"That depends on you..."

"Can we return in one hour?"

"As you wish..."

"Best... This part of the town always looks rainy, gray, and so, so gorgeous... Always like so much left to see." I said, looking up at the infinite sky, where the sun was resting between the clouds.

"Yes, see, you are better now." He said while he walked with his hands in his pocket.

We walked silently for some seconds.

"After half the lane, there is my cycle; you know; I had parked it behind the shrubs..." He spoke.

We reached a point where he told me to wait, and he went into the shrubs to bring out his cycle. I stood there alone, looking around. Minutes passed in the same manner, but he didn't come out.

I became somewhat anxious and stepped over into the bushes to see him. After passing through them and taking a couple of hard steps through the wet bushes, I came across a grassy area. Rajesh was standing there silently, facing the other side with hands wide apart, as if in amazement.

I came near to him and asked, "Where is your cycle?"

He turned to me and said, pointing down the slant of the terrain, "Look! Who did this?" His words were filled with emotions of anger, but more than anything else, amazement.

I looked carefully down the slant and there; the cycle was seen. It looked tiny, and it was upside down, completely broken. Whatever remained had been stuck between the stones. The scene was rather blurred due to the mists. I was left shocked and cold. It was damaged, quite unnaturally its handles had fallen apart, a seat had torn out and the wheel, which was seen from there, was still in slow motion, its strings breaking out. It looked like someone had just picked up and thrown the heavy cycle down. Down there it was wet, grassy, and not bright but dark; it seemed so tempting to go down the slant, so calling and so insecurely magical. Only subtle noises could be differentiated, though no one was to be seen.

"God! Did you not put the stand?" I asked.

"I remember I had parked it safely, against that tree, with the stands down..." He said breathing in and out continuously and then continued looking at it, with his eyebrows together, "Even if the stands weren't down, I wonder how the cycle can slip down in this manner on its own and how can it break apart like this?"

"I do not feel something good here... Let us go down and see..." I said, tossing my hair back.

"Hey, you!" Rajesh said loudly and leaped to the left.

He hurriedly walked, crossing me, and ran in a puzzled manner from side to side up to a tall tree. He looked all around the tree and stopped there, breathing out loudly.

"What happened?" I asked as I reached him—panting.

Among the noises of strange birds, he spoke "He is gone!"

"Who? Who has gone?" My voice half echoed.

"I saw someone here, standing silently behind this tree, watching us from that distance. I think because of the dark shadows of the trees, I couldn't quite see him properly, but he was rather dark." He said with his hands on his forehead.

"I never saw anyone standing there behind this tree... All here are trees and trees."

"How can he vanish in a second? I think he was the one who did all this..." He said again.

"There was no one there. Perhaps it was a mistake." I stopped at this and somehow a feeling came over me not to speak more.

"Yes, I think you are correct." He finally said, and we turned back.

"Now going down there for that cycle in pieces is worthless... Come on to the lane." He continued.

I felt a strange eeriness in the silent atmosphere and the whizzing winds added, occasionally, even giving shivers. Something was lingering, but was it in that place or the mind?

"I think you will be comfortable at home and pressing to this moment I feel we can go some other day… I still wonder how this happened, but losing a strong, new cycle hurts… I feel sorry." I said as we came into the lane again.

"I am sorry that we cannot go that far today... but..."

"Oh, it's nothing to be sad about. We can go some other day."

"I feel today we cannot have a cheer at far-off places, but we can have a stroll in the town areas..."

We walked a bit more, and I spoke at last.

"Is it completely fine? I mean..."

"Yes. These things happen; nothing can be done now—it's gone. Why should we ruin our plan completely? Don't feel bad." He spoke.

We walked—first slowly, with little talk. I was observing Rajesh's expressions when he wasn't directly looking at me and, to my relief, there was no such difference. He was not sad, not frightened too—but, to my slight amazement, a peculiar, extremely thoughtful anxiety and perplexity were seen on his face.

"Oh, I completely forgot to ask! Do you know of some Mr. Paul?" I asked when I thought would be appropriate.

He made a low humming sound, after which he replied,

"I hope you aren't talking about the insane man?"

"Well; I think yes. Do you know exactly his place?"

"Not exactly, but perhaps we can find out in the area where he lives. Only a few houses are there, and people don't quite visit him." He paused for seconds and then asked, "May I ask why you want to meet such a man?"

I told him many bits of what was going on and the reason for my curiosity to meet this man, though I knew he was not a man anyone would be keen to meet.

"I see—" he said, thought, and then said, "Okay then, come; we can walk up till there."

After half an hour's walk, we reached the place. No one was around and the house was a two-floored one but not huge. I knocked on the heavy door twice and waited. An old, feeble, and expressionless servant opened the door and directed us to the room where this man used to stay. The room was engulfed in nocturnal darkness and some faint light from unknown sources made walking possible. Dust particles could be seen floating in the air, under streaks of light, and there sat a man, strangely half-sprawled over his wooden chair, talking to himself. Not much of his face and body could have been seen under those conditions.

The servant closed the door behind us. As we were in and the room was silent again, dampness was its feature, with unpainted walls and some old furniture. The floor was of stones and was wet at places, lying uncleaned. Rajesh looked at me in confusion and then we sat wherever we could. The man took no notice of us and continued to look around and murmur in his manner.

"Excuse me!" I asked.

"Huh! Who are you and when did you come in?" He asked in a startled way in the strangest voice I had ever heard, shrill in starting but growing heavier in the end.

"We live nearby and came here to seek some help from you. I believe we haven't bothered you..." I replied again.

"You mustn't think that I am right here! In my head." He said, putting his finger into his ear, and then continued, "But still you came. You know you are before a madman, but you know I am half right in my head, too."

He stood and sat down once again, straightening his spine.

"Mr. Paul, we have come with high hope. We want some important information that only you can give us... Please answer some of our doubts as you were the only resident of the house of Shaitaan before we came in there." I asked, looking into his closed eyes.

"Ooo! You live in my house!" He jumped up slightly and then sat "It's a... it's not a good place, is it?"

"Yes, sir. Why? Why is it not a good place to live?"

"Why, why, why..." He looked puzzled but continued, "Have you seen this black snake over my shoulder's?"

He shook his shoulders as if shaking something off.

"What!" Rajesh spoke in amazement.

"Snake, what snake? Nothing is here." I couldn't help but say.

"No, no, this snake follows me from the day I entered that house; he never leaves me and roams about over me... See you want to hold it?" He said, making a gesture as if held something in his hand and raised his hand high.

"Vaanya, come! This man is crack-headed..." Rajesh said as he stood up in a jerk.

"Wait... Wait... I told you I am half right too; I forgot that this only I can see." He laughed again.

He was just as I had expected him to be, and that's what I knew; I made a gesture to Rajesh, asking him to sit. The man performed strange gestures and spoke irrelevant words. He turned his face many times and shook his head and again turned to us and I watched every bit of his movement.

"Why did you leave the house? I mean, what did you see there which forced you to meet the doctor?"

"Oh, you tell of the doctor! That man! He is ignorant and thinks he knows a lot..." He shook his head again and then continued, "What I saw there and what happened to me I have completely forgotten! Completely forgotten... Why I had gone there is a secret that I will never tell in front of even a mirror. But one thing I must warn you, there was someone behind me in that empty house!" He said, widening his eyes.

"Someone behind you?"

"Yes! One day, he attacked me and hit me hard in my head!"

"Then What?"

"I pretended to have fainted, but, but I stood up soon and hit him hard with a weapon on his leg. He ran out with a broken leg, and it got damaged completely!"

"What weapon? How did you get it?"

"Who remembers that?" He said, waving his hand in front of his nose in a jerk.

"I already told you; someone was behind me in that house... I was totally fine when I went there, but after coming out from there, they say I was in a hospital for days and then now I can see many things, many new people in this dim room of mine..." And he went on speaking irrelevantly in the same manner; stammering, shaking, and then stopped and closed his eyes again.

"Well, thanks..." I intoned. He took no notice of it, and we went out.

We walked around the lovely town a bit, strolled about the nearby alluring fields, and talked. Perhaps it had rained while we were inside, but then the sun had risen, bright among white clouds, though the ground squelched underfoot.

"This man is totally mad—snake, weapon, leg! What is he telling? I don't think we should pay any heed to what all he said." Rajesh said as he was walking, looking towards the glazing grass with his hands in his pocket.

"Poor man ..." I remarked, shaking some wet grass off my shoe.

"He didn't tell the reason he had shown such excitement and perseverance to jump into that infamous place... I still wonder what it is," Rajesh said.

"It's time. Should we return?"

"Sure." He replied.

We walked back in a leisurely fashion but reached the house soon. Extremely strong, rather stormy winds were rioting and could be heard distinctively.

"Well, yes, we have reached... Now I should bid you goodbye..." He smiled and said looking at me, while I looked at the shades around the place; he continued, "Why, you look sad..."

Probably I couldn't suppress my feeling under my face, the feeling of a strange nervousness, and a peculiar fear had started to seep slowly into my heart as I returned to the place, the place was in sharp contrast to the open nature from where I had returned.

"You got it again." I replied loudly, "I don't know why, but a strange nervousness, like something bad, would happen, is driving me... Perhaps it's, it's normal; I am totally fine."

"Yes... I get it. You will be fine, just have a pleasant conversation with somebody in there..." One hand into his hair, fluttering with the wind.

"I suggest you come in for once and—and have a cup of tea. We have been long in the cold. Probably Arun will also be there." I said, looking into his eyes.

A slow nod was the answer. We entered as the main gate wasn't locked. We entered the house where everything was still and silent as before. As suddenly as we entered, there was a noise loud enough to give a shock of panic and to shatter the silence into pieces. Some rustling and noises of footsteps moving hurriedly could be heard on the second floor. There was chaos. I stepped on the stairs as fast as I could, and Rajesh followed me.

"What is this?" It was a furious and loud cry from Arun that we heard still only halfway down the stairs.

"Reply! Why have you done this?" this time it was my uncle's voice in a tone of amazement.

All of it was happening in my bedroom whose door was closed, and noises still came from behind it. I leaped towards the door and opened it with a jerk, wondering what had happened.

"What is going on?" I asked as I opened the door.

All eyes went towards me as I emerged into the room. Uncle was standing at a bit of distance, near the wall; Arun was there, right in front of Ajay, who was looking downwards. This was not the end, or even a point to ponder, as the moment I looked around the room, I was left petrified and startled.

"W-What are all these?" I said while breathing in and out by my mouth and looking around.

Strange, terrifying sketches on paper were thrown all around. It looked as if there were tens of them filling the room. On the table, on the bed, over the window, all over the floor, they were lying down. The papers had strange sketches of a strange face and it was shuddering to look at them. I picked one, which was under my foot, a badly drawn, petrifying face it was, looking towards the left. It seemed as if drawn unconsciously, sort of scribbled as the lines weren't straight but as if made by a shaking hand. In one moment, it looked that the sketch resembled some human, but in another, it looked as if it was far from any man on earth. Everybody was silent for a moment, and everyone had some papers in their hands with their eyes glued in utter amazement and horror over the petrifying faces. I took hold of some other ones; they resembled each other as if of the same man but had different expressions and different views. But all were inhuman, otherworldly, and menacing equally. I knew that they were drawn by no one else but Ajay. Initially, my mind was confused but then I soon remembered the morning's incident, and also it struck my mind the fact that I had unknowingly left the papers and the pen near Ajay's bed, and this resulted from all of that. The same papers, the same ink.

"Ajay, what have you drawn? These horrible faces... where have you seen them?" I asked.

Ajay didn't reply. He stood facing the wall; pressing his head against it as if he didn't want to speak. The winds were beating hard against the windows.

"This isn't sane! Drawing such strange faces in the morning, for no reason, and throwing it all about the room? What does this mean?" Uncle said this time.

I suddenly noticed that even Rajesh was looking at the sketches, in a startled way, and a strange excitement was clear on his face, which was subtle.

Within minutes I had understood that it was not only me who was terribly unsettled at this inexplicable event, but Arun, Uncle, and Rajesh too looked somewhat the same, or even more intensely amazed.

It looked as if they were in deep thought as if relating something with these scattered drawings, reacting as a person who has encountered his old secrets and remembers them. At a point, I felt left out.

"But I had left you sleeping; is it what you saw in your dream?" I asked Ajay, but there wasn't any answer again.

"Where had you gone and when did he do all this?" Arun asked, who was moving around the room at a speed with widened eyes.

The next moment he turned to Ajay, who was frightened from before; grabbed him tightly by his arm, and in an angry tone said, "You will not be getting food today until you do not tell what all these are, where you saw it and what is your purpose behind drawing such things...."

"Wait! Why are you getting so angry with him? If we all create so much pressure, harassing him in such a way, he would probably never speak... If he never speaks about this incident, it will influence the way his thought processes work. At last, he is a kid!" I exclaimed.

"So why don't you tell us something, at last, he sleeps in your room, and all this happened when you went for a very long early morning 'stroll' with my dearest friend... and will my dearest friend who is the one most concerned about Vaanya also like to tell us something?" Arun said and he was the most hyper of all of us.

"Listen, Arun, I have come so many times to meet you, but you never meet me! I never see Uncle too and don't you feel that you should have first taken her around this beautiful place? But you didn't. You know I know something which you do not understand; people need to go outside the boundaries of their house, they need an outlook. I still say listen to what I have to say, it's for you, not for me..." Rajesh replied in the same way.

"No, I won't! You better understand it."

"Wait! Wait! I will tell you something." I said to calm down the heated argument and then I had to narrate the incident that took place in the morning.

Both Uncle and Arun, besides the general reaction of tense, didn't comment a word on it and soon the situation and chaos caused were calmed.

"Do you know this man?" Uncle slowly advanced toward Arun and asked him this question in a low secretive voice, holding his shoulders and looking deep into his eyes.

There was a long moment when Arun didn't reply. There was something deep and unexpected in his expressions, which were changing, and he was constantly looking towards the floor, moving his head. Something was happening between them.

"Oh, how can I know this hideous face? I have never seen it..." He said, at last, backed and strode out of the room.

Uncle also walked down after some minutes, continuously smoothing his dense hair back with his fingers. No one spoke for some minutes. But I knew in my mind that something, something wasn't correct; something was lingering for a long time, which had the power to influence and to affect the nerve of even the strongest ones. I sighed, I thought, and the one thing I got was that the most petrifying feeling of all is when you, yourself, slowly and gradually understand that you, yourself are getting petrified for a reason you don't know.

"Rajesh, what do you think about this?" I asked.

"I don't know but I feel that." He paused in deep thought and then said, "Probably he had seen this face somewhere in this house and then unconsciously drawn it. Maybe. But still, this is the most horrible thing to hear or see." He replied.

"Ajay, now everyone is gone. Believe me, I will not scold you, dear. Where have you seen this face? Did you draw all this purposely?" I asked.

"Yes, try to remember where you have seen this in the house; it's very important!" Rajesh said, and I quite observed his extraordinary interest in the affair.

"I don't remember..."

"You don't remember?" I uttered.

"I don't remember where I saw it and I don't remember when I drew it and also don't know why I have drawn such a horrible face. Look how scary it looks... I also do not remember any morning incident about which you are talking. What I can only tell is that I was seeing a nightmare and in it, I saw myself drawing someone all around the walls. The windows were shut, and curtains were drawn; only I was in the room, and it was as if everything was shaking and a storm bursting out. It was so real that I felt I was drawing something and then I saw some stranger sitting just there on that table. I do not remember when I woke up fully and how many dreams, I have seen last night; it is as if I have woken up after years of deep sleep. Just look at these drawings. Does it look like it has been drawn by me?"

We three gathered all the papers from the floor. On counting, there were seventeen of them and finally, I set them aside to be burned. I didn't feel like keeping such things around in the bedroom.

"Why do you think Ajay is seeing all this?" Rajesh asked.

"I want to tell you something…" I replied.

"What?"

"Ajay had previously too, shown me a drawing when I had arrived. I don't know why, but these have a striking similarity with that face."

He had nothing to reply to but breathed out loudly.

"We don't know if others are also witnessing something abnormal; we can never say until they admit it. But a child's psychology and mind are the most sensitive and vulnerable and imaginative; perhaps this is the reason."

Rajesh stood up to leave. He said that he was unsure that he would come again to talk to Arun because this time he had finally understood that it would be of no use. He talked little and told a slow goodbye, turned back, and went. The evening had drawn. Outside, the sky was orange, with red and purple. The sun was setting down and gleaming from behind the trees. Everything was silent within the room, where darkness was gradually walking in with mysterious shades and shadows.

I talked with Ajay for some time, as normally as possible, but nothing came out of it as he was himself, confused and frightened. If it was a psychological phenomenon, it was not under the boundaries of my knowledge. I thought it might need professional help and if it was anything else, then I didn't know; simply, I didn't want to characterize it as something else. I walked down within some minutes and when I reached the last step of the stair, I could see Uncle and Arun sitting at different places in the unlit hall, silently in deep thought. Uncle had his legs crossed and his chin supported by his hand, and Arun was gazing at the ceiling.

"It's still time if you tell something, something if you know," Uncle said to Arun.

"I know nothing." He changed his look towards me.

"Uncle, I feel we need a doctor and also Police because I didn't tell, but I have seen some unknown man moving about in the garden," I suggested.

"What we need is a priest!" Uncle exclaimed.

"Why a priest? I feel that perhaps someone is hiding in this old house of ours and from what Ajay did, it would be on the safe side to have some doctor, maybe it's just something simple like lack of sleep or something which has caused all this. It can be sorted." I said, hearing which my uncle sighed, slowly stood up, and walked around.

"We need no one! No priest, no Police, and no doctor; nothing! Coming here was a mistake!" Arun said harshly.

"I don't know how you have such an attitude. Go for some action first and then preach…" Uncle said half in the native language and in a fiery tone.

Arun stood, strode angrily into his room, and slammed the door. Uncle soon calmed down after sighing loudly.

"Uncle, can I tell you something? I feel that for Ajay, it would be best to send him to any of his friend's place for this weekend..."

"Yes, you are correct. I was also feeling so too. At least I don't want him to become like his elder brother."

So, the same evening, Ajay was sent to his friend's home in the interiors of the town so that he could play and have a change. Uncle's trusted staff was given this work, who was a local man; who worked nearby and also did the full cleaning of the house thrice a week in the early morning. (I had never known it before as he came from the other stairs, which was for the staff to come in through the balcony and did everything in the early morning and went.)

That night I was all alone on the dim, solitary second floor, on my bed in the room. All was silent and dead. It was difficult at the start. I felt as if I was waiting for something to happen. My heart pounded heavily for no reason, and my eyes were open to see anything extraordinarily horrific. But nothing happened. I soon realized that it was ludicrous to wait for something to happen. Nothing happened that night. Perhaps I was thinking so much so that the normal seemed abnormal. But my thoughts didn't influence the peaceful night.

The next day at the breakfast table, there was again a quarrel between Uncle and Arun, of which I heard little because I was late. Uncle looked as if he hadn't slept again. His eyes were quite red, hair all scatted down to his eyes, a sort of stammering in his speech; all this and the blackness under his eyes showed he was unwell. He looked sick and tired, but his dress up, and his clothes, suggested the opposite. They were as exquisite and shiny as before. The quarrel ultimately ended with Arun screaming out,

"I will not live in this haunted mansion a second more! There is a phantom in this house all bringing bad luck to me! I am going right now, and I will come soon to take my belongings from here!"

In a fit of boundless anger, he packed his belongings into a bag in which the chains were broken. He came out of his room with the bag in his hand. Uncle had already gone into his room, and I was the one in the hall. Some magazines, which were carelessly stuffed along with clothes into the bag, could be seen as they were half-pulping out. He didn't look back at all and walked out of the house in gigantic steps and leaps. I followed him to the lane where I stood silently, my hand over one tree; watching him walk at a distance until his appearance was reduced to a shadow in the lane. At the same moment, a deafening, loud, shrilling noise came to my ears that almost echoed in the valley for seconds. The same uneasy noise blasted twice more until when I finally recognized it as an unusual horn of a car. I looked closely down the bleak, foggy lane and within seconds, what I saw was a mighty black car. Though it couldn't be seen clearly, its build, its shine, and its loud and unique horn which was uncommonly heavy; were intimidating and doubtful. Adding to this mysterious effect of the black car, black curtains moreover covered it on its windows. Nothing much can be described, but a child could also differentiate it as somewhat of an antique car. Its rolling wheels soon stopped, and I saw Arun stepping up into the car from the gate, which someone had opened for him in a welcoming fashion. The car rustled past out into the mists towards the town and finally couldn't be singled out, leaving the lane noiseless once again. It left me wondering: "Who and why?" anyway, it was horse carriages that were more common than cars.

I returned to the house, which was emptier than before, and this was the turning point. I was free to investigate now. But how would I do this?

8

I decided not to do anything for some time and left things on their own. With no idea or hope for the day, I, again, was strolling in the dead garden with my thoughts and the evening shades nearer with a sort of twilight that had magically appeared in the sky. The winds sighed between the yellowed grasses and whistled from between the trees. While I was wondering, "Whether we need a doctor or a priest?" I came across the other side of the garden and the mighty locked window of Arun's room stood before me. I looked at it with my arms across my chest and it was the same; covered with black paper and locked, shivering with the gusts. It was so alone, so calling and so tempting that it again created an urge in me to put my fingers into its steel ring and to pull it open; to know the concealed world behind it. I sighed, as I believed it would be locked from the inside like the other day, and decided to pass by; but hope is such a strong feeling that clings. Just to give it a silly try, I pulled the wooden window with my force. It was so easily opened after a sudden jerk as if it was lubricated. Eagerness ran through my nerves. I managed to raise my foot high and with the support of my hands, I easily flung into the room, which was like a dark tunnel. Nothing much was visible inside it, and only old books, dust, and dampness could be smelled. I was finally in it.

I drove my palm, feeling the dusty wall, and, on finding the switchboard clicked one switch on. A dim red bulb glowed in one corner of the room. Things got visible under that glow. The room was a big one that was almost separated into two parts by an enormous curtain in the center, hanging from the ceiling. There was a table, a chair, a small bed, and, most striking of it all; a big bookshelf which was a bit dusty. Other features of the room were the same as the house; antique. But still, I was feeling a strangeness, and that was without even seeing anything yet. My heart was continuously questioning my conduct here, but I did what I thought then would be right.

I opened the cupboard of the study table and saw a bundle of sketch books-kind of thin booklets with black covers, stuffed in there, and they were tied together with a string. My eagerness increased to heights like the one of a student who is about to open her final exam results. I untied those booklets. I opened one of them and turned to the first page. My eyes widened, trying to gasp what was before them and my heart was beating faster. It took me seconds, perhaps even a minute, to understand that it was nothing else but a handprint. A real palm print of a man! The impression was neatly taken using black ink on the white sheet, which looked nothing but red under the light. I flipped through the whole booklet with my eyes fixed on it and found it filled with nothing but strange palm prints and small notes accompanying them. I really couldn't understand anything till then and wondered what he did with such appalling designs.

The other two books were also filled with the same horrible black prints with the strangest palm lines I had ever seen in my life. I noticed that the shapes of the palms weren't normal too. There might have been hundreds of such palm prints in the room as on opening the other cupboards I found other booklets as well.

I turned to the bookshelf, and everything got solved in a minute. Books like: *The Language of Palm, Advanced Palmistry,* and many others from both East and West of the world, were kept. It was unbelievable to me. This was an icebreaker, as I got to know that what Arun researched behind his closed doors was nothing else but this, but I still did not understand why he was so secretive about his obsession. Yes, looking at the stock of books and booklets, it looked like that of a man who was obsessed with "palms", but the worst part was yet to come. Once a bit calmed, I made myself comfortable on the chair at the table and couldn't resist myself to read and carefully visualize the latest booklet as they were all full of dates and kept chronologically.

As I ran my eyes through the notes that were written beside each palm print, I was shocked inside out. They were like:

"Name- ABC, jailed on- ... Charge-..." and it continued.

The case with the other prints was the same, and I ultimately realized that all the prints were of men who were pure criminals; charged with robbery, murder, and whatnot. Arun hadn't stopped just by giving the personal information of these villains, but also went to write the analysis of palm lines of each of the palm prints and ultimately concluded it by finding reasons for their nature. I shuddered and the booklet almost fell off my trembling hand when I noticed that some of the palm prints were also of people who were already dead in prison, till that date. I felt that all this was just unacceptably horrific.

"Really, a man who researches behind closed doors on palm prints of criminals and dead people with odd lives and studies arts like these will obviously lose his mind, like I am losing now." I thought.

I felt like cursing myself for opening such secrets of Arun and I wanted to forget them, but those palms, those life stories, that red light in the room all haunted and puzzled my brain.

A thought emerged in my mind that probably Arun would publish a book on such things which was still unbelievable, probably he had been following this research for a long, but the major question was that "How did he get hold of such people, selected violent criminals who are in the prison?"

Then I remembered an incident that had happened some days ago. I remembered I had spotted Arun at the Police station, and this perhaps was the answer itself. He probably would have some kind of informal relationship with somebody in there but I am sorry, I can't be sure. They would have found no harm in giving just the palm prints of criminals, but for me, it was the most preposterous thing that I could imagine happening.

I turned to other pages of the booklet to know more, though I didn't have a drop of knowledge on the subject. Accidentally, I came across a palm print that had the name Neelnath. The name looked similar to me at once and then it instantly struck my brain that this was the violent criminal whose poster was hanging in the Police station, and I also remembered my uncle saying that he was "dead" at that time. This was intriguing to some extent. I read the synopsis of the palm that was written next to it with cursive writing in black ink. It read:

"The most distinguishable of all is a big 'star' under the middle finger. Some squarish shapes are also seen in the middle of the hand. But the 'lifeline' is long and overall, it suggests that the subject will have a long life."

The above is an excerpt and not complete—but the only part relevant to the reader. I must say, I am only writing the facts of the peculiar case and I am not willing to make any impression or interpretation. The reader is free to choose his or her own opinion or even choose not to have any opinion. If I am asked, I say, I have no clear opinion on these subjects.

I really saw a mess of lines under the middle finger, which he was probably calling the star. It was enormous and distinguishable, but abnormally bad to look at, and also a couple of squares were seen on one of the lines.

"Huh… What he writes is weird." I murmured.

I couldn't understand much, but one thing from which I concluded then that his interpretations were all incorrect and silly was the prediction of "long life" because I knew Neelnath was already dead.

"So, this is Arun at his best." I jeered him in my mind.

I closed the books and kept them as neatly and carefully as they were to the extent till it looked like no one had ever come to that room. I sighed in relief, but still, I didn't like the idea of getting so very indulged in sciences or arts like these. But still, my heart was excited as before and it was unusual. I looked around the chamber and then the huge curtain that separated the other part of the room came right before my eyes.

"What's behind this?" I thought and drew off the heavy curtain.

With a loud noise that the rattling curtain rings made, another part of the room was opened to me. The sun had already set, and that's why the room was engulfed in darkness with the subtle evening noise floating around. The coldness was increasing in the air. The room was to be seen when I switched on a yellow light. I was looking around the ill-painted room, which had nothing but a bed and some furniture when I suddenly felt that I was being watched. I felt no longer alone. There was a pressuring feeling of being looked at from the left, and I turned to my left suddenly. Two cold, big, hideous white eyes were looking deep into mine as if piercing all my might and I was about to scream. But I stopped as I realized it was a painting; a painting that was hung on the wall was looking at me. I felt a rush of cold up my spine. I breathed out heavily and clutched my dress, pressing my heart, which was heavily throbbing. The room was quiet and still as before, but the presence of the frame and the strange-faced man in the black and white painting were so intense that I didn't feel alone there. So real was the painting, so strange, the white face on the black background and so disturbing its eyes; its nose; its mouth, and its ears; all crossing the boundaries of sinister and wretched faces of this world. It was still gazing at me, and it looked like it would just speak in seconds if I stood there in that way and all of it was enough to set my body in occasional shivers. In it, there was a man, with less hair, clean-shaven and looking straight, with a penetrating long gaze. I don't know why, but I stood face to face with the man there in the painting for minutes, I suppose, but then I don't know how my sense, fortunately, got back. I didn't feel like going a step ahead towards it, but still, it was so calling that I slowly stepped to it and found the name of the artist who had the skill to make that kind of face. With my widened eyes, I scanned the painting and at the bottom, it was written: "By-Vishwakumar".

"That's why great artists are great," I thought but I simultaneously also thought: "Why would Arun keep such a bad luck painting in his bedroom, right in front of him? How could he sleep at night alone with this thing hanging on the wall?"

I stepped a couple of steps back to get a total view of the painting. It could be carried by hand quite easily. I had never planned what I did next. I advanced again and pulled the painting out of the hook. It came into my hands, not very heavy but dusty. I didn't think of it at all, but I walked with the painting in my hand; and managed to come out of the chamber with the painting. Silently, I turned through the garden with the frame and entered the house. The hall was alone there, and I walked up the stairs making no noise; carefully carrying the painting. On the second floor, I stepped rapidly towards my bedroom gate, opened it with the kick of my leg and came in; and pushed the painting under my bed. Now, this painting was not in Arun's room, but in mine. I lied down on the bed exhausted and don't know when I fell asleep.

I do not know when, but my sleep broke with the call of my uncle; he was calling me down for the dinner and I walked down happily as I liked my uncle. It was as if breaking from a trance, breaking from a spell of hypnotism. I dumped the very thought of informing Uncle about Arun's weird hobbies as first my secret would be busted and second, silent observation is the key.

While at the dinner table, we talked a bit of psychology and it was a very calm talk, and I was the one who mostly spoke; but still, I didn't feel something right in that silent, dim vicinity where we both sat opposite each other. For some moments, I must admit, it was not like I was before my uncle. His words, his accent, his tone, and his very way of uttering seemed to fluctuate between the real Uncle and a strange, violent man. Nothing was significantly unusual other than his noticeable feeble trembling grip on the plates or on the spoon; I must add and that's why I blew the thought as a misleading instinct, and it only seemed that I was the one who was wrongly noticing such things because whatever he talked reflected his knowledge and his deep understanding of things which was unique and adorable.

"Uncle, is something disturbing you? I mean, I am not in any position to guide a learned man like you, but still, I feel sharing a heavy heart helps," I asked, wiping my mouth with a handkerchief.

"Oh! Do you feel so?" He giggled slightly and then said, "You can say that I am not feeling very well today..."

He sighed and continued, "I know you have nothing to do with it, but have you seen a lost book of mine?"

"What's it about, uncle?" I interrupted.

"It's about a famous artist, Vishwakumar, and his paintings... You know it was a magazine-like catalog, of importance to me in a business matter. I can't find it for some weeks, and it was just a couple of days ago that I noticed the book was missing."

"Sorry uncle, I have never seen it," I replied.

"Uncle, have you ever thought of opening Arun's room?" I asked as we were washing our hands after dinner.

"No—I don't care what he does, and you see, I am not the type of person who will break into my son's room, it would just be foolish, and I feel it would be a show of desperateness and nothing else." He spoke.

After this, I went on to close the garden gate, which was banging because a sort of mini storm had started to blow outside.

A voice suddenly came from my back in the native language and I turned back immediately. It meant: "I hope you will be fine sleeping alone up there?" I could only roughly understand it.

It was unbelievable that my uncle had spoken and for a second, I wondered about his change of language and finally to which I replied, "Yes."

I walked up the dim stairs after the clock had struck nine and my uncle retired to his room in front of my eyes. I stepped slowly and carefully onto the second floor, which was empty and looked hollow in the dark. The only window in the small passage was banging with the winds outside and the whistling noise of the wind passed touching my ears. I locked my room door after entering, changed my clothes, and then relaxingly sat in front of the open window, watching the deep purple sky, the vast hills that looked black, and the visibly swaying trees around the house. The old country. There was no way to see the town from there. The cold gusts blew in and out of the open window at that height and there was no passer-by around; only the purest form of nature, which was mysteriously adorable, like I was not in the twentieth but in the early nineteenth century.

It was I and my uncle who were probably the only humans living in this huge, isolated area with no sign of inhabitation all around. Everything seemed like sleeping or in a dream state from that height, but soon I had to close the window because the winds were now being accompanied by thick raindrops. I sat on my bed, still without the bulb on, and thought about many things in the silent dark room with the knocking noise of the winds and the rain on the window; because of which it also seemed to tremble.

I thought, "This house is now uncle's home but not original, it had been constructed by a man who is very mysterious and a villain in the town and we are living in his house..." I thought deeply, "He used to live in this house, he used to walk up and down these stairs, and he might have also used this room and this very bed! The antiques here, the designs, and even the bricks of this house used to be his when he was alive. If that wretched man would be alive, would he like someone to live in his house? But he also considered this house a mistake, an ill-fated house, and it's also true that when he came to this spot, he got nothing but ill luck. It's even hard to imagine how that personality dwelled here for years and God knows what all hideous crimes have been performed here. These walls, these antique statues all have seen and heard only bad things, only wretched and violent incidents, the cries of people, and the laugh of this man. Ajay said that he had also practiced black arts, and I have heard terrible, bloody, and unholy things about it, so is it true that these things were practiced in this very house? The vibrations itself of this place seem to echo the unimaginable incidents that might have occurred here. We are quite simple and regular people and I feel it's not correct to live in such a house. I don't believe in the typical ghosts but still, the empty vacant rooms, the dead garden, the shaking windows, and the storms that rage outside and above alone being alone here are affecting my nerves in the same way as the real hauntings do. Then what's the difference if there is a ghost when the harm is of the same magnitude?" I kept on imagining the past incidents of this house and the fact of Paul losing his mind after an experience in this house.

"What Paul could have seen here that he cannot even relate to the world?" was a pressing question.

Soon I understood that thinking in this manner was increasing my painful nervousness about something unknown, and I stood up in a jerk.

"Overthinking is as bad as no thinking." I decided and soon something clicked in my mind.

I remembered I had kept the strange painting under my bed and pulled it out, deciding to have a clear look at it. After switching on the dreary bulb, I placed the framed painting carefully on a wooden wardrobe that was opposite the table and the window. I sat on a chair at a distance from the painting to get a broader view.

I looked at it, crossing my arms across my bosom and one leg over the other. What a wretched face it was, and how magnetic it looked on the black background cannot be written. It gave a pressing feeling that he was really there. I gazed at it until my eyes pained and became red, but still, it was as if I couldn't help it. I realized I was really trying very hard to understand the expression on that face. One moment it looked as if it was laughing, but then the other side of the lip suggested that he wasn't. The hair was less and eyebrows thick and at another moment his eyes suggested he wasn't happy or sad but angry and when I looked even more carefully, his deep waterless eyes looked half open as if he was gloomy; and then suddenly my trance broke as there was a terrible thunder noise outside and a string of current hung in the sky for a second. A shudder of fear ran down my nerves and I jumped up thinking that what silly thing was I doing, sitting in such a way in front of such a face and looking deep into it. If somebody would just gaze at a back menacing painting at midnight behind a locked room like I did, I thought I would really call him crazy. I left the thing as it was and switched off the light. I lay down on the bed and covered my hurting eyes with my palms. The usual black film came over my eyes, but I felt a bit uneasy. After minutes of this uneasiness in my eyes, I opened them again. I opened my mouth in horror as it was the same face that I could see in front of my eyes as if hanging from the ceiling. Wherever I took my eyes, in whichever direction, the face's white impression was seen clearly over the completely dark ceiling. I shut my eyes again with my palms in horror and the face started to disappear between the strange green and purple patterns that emerged on the film of my pressed eyes. I was down with a shock of horror. I didn't open my uneasy eyes the whole night, but my mind still ran uncontrollably.

"This face was perhaps similar to the face that Ajay had shown me initially. There also I saw a similar mixture of expressions... but the sketch flew off and the recent ones drawn by Ajay were burned by us. But how is it possible that Ajay had drawn a similar face, having no chance of seeing this painting because of Arun? Ajay had told that what he drew was Shaitaan himself and then, then can it be true that he had seen him wandering about in the house?"

Somehow, sleep came over me and the next day I woke up again the same way. The first thing I saw in front of my dry eyes was that painting staring at me differently from the night, or maybe even different. I shook my head away from it and then started the normal course of the day. Uncle was sick. I realized it by the way of his walking and confirmed the fact with him. He was still dressed in his glazing robe, though other features like his slumber-less eyes and his scatted hair subtracted the elegance from his overall look.

"I am not very well today." He said, pressing his head, and continued, "I will not go out for business today..."

He continued as a person who is in fever but tries to present himself as normal as possible.

"Uncle, whenever you need me, please call me," I said to him as he lay down half on the sofa in the hall.

The weather was shining and dry, but the coldness of the last night's storm blew with the very air. Hours passed by in trivial work and it was when the evening was coming nearer that I was completely jaded with no important activity to do. The idea of trying to reach the top terrace to see or try to find the spot from where Shaitaan had fallen down forever as per the "old uncle" came to my mind. This very idea made me slightly uncomfortable. But the sun was still on and Uncle was somewhere in his room; this would be the best opportunity, so I resolved to act upon it. The direct way to the terrace was sealed, and that's why I had to go from the stairs that were on the outer part of the building. Trees surrounded the stairs and pierced their growth through the bricks of the building itself, and I had to walk up cautiously. Any right and left of my step on that feeble stair with a feeble handle would throw me down. I sighed after I ultimately reached the terrace. Though the speed of the high winds was incredibly strong, almost pushing me the terrace was dry and dilapidated. The boundary walls were very small and tripping down was a risk, but I walked on around it. I got mesmerized by the incredibly infinite view from that spot which showed only green hills, streams, and woods till the farthest end; the horizon where the sun was mixing with the dark greenery, casting the day's last tinges of red all around. The sky was getting gray. At the far ends, some birds were seen returning, and I turned myself to the other side of the terrace. Moisture soon filled the air, and the gusts suggested an approaching storm. I went on and slightly bent my back over the small boundary wall to see that if a person falls, could he die? Down there was an extension of the building at the level of the first floor. On the other side also, the scene was not different; falling down from there and getting killed seemed not a chance. But then why did that "old uncle" say that Mr. S— fell from there was the question and especially his remarkable confidence in relating the incident (which wasn't in any of the other narrators) was such that he had witnessed it. I looked at the far end towards the west of the house, where there were several hills. Something on the hill and amidst the deep woods caught my eye. It was very far, and it looked like it was almost covered in by nature; trees had grown through it and all around it were wrapped in creepers. From the small portion of the terrace and bit of the walls that was the only part uncovered by trees; it was an old building where no one could go or live. It stood alone like ours and there was no such human habitat all around that side but only voids and streams and hills. The sky's red tinge was shifting to blue and the faint light of the vanishing sun made the view look blue and black and increased its terrible solitude. Suddenly I saw someone, a tall dark figure, moving about on the terrace of that structure. It looked not like a man but more like a shadow of a man, but it was moving, taking long steps. It suddenly stopped as a person who is disturbed when doing something private. I was petrified without a word but when the darkness increased, there was a heavy gust that covered my eyes with waves of my hair, and by the time I hurriedly struggled to remove them, with my fingers, it had gone. I couldn't believe it. It looked like he had fallen from the edge, but who could he be, was the question, and how could he possibly get there? I was nervous, and it felt like I would fall from the edge, fainting. Being alone in such places is a terrible experience, and I knew that. I regained myself and ran and then somehow walked down before it was nocturnal dark. When I reached down safely, my heart was pounding heavily, and looking up again; everything was black. The structure which I had seen there was nothing else but the other construction of this man, "Mr. S—" or "Shaitaan" and this made everything even more startling—which I had seen before when I was with Rajesh.

I saw Uncle moving about in the garden and I could only see his back.

"Uncle, are you searching for something?"

He turned towards me, a shovel was in his hand, and he looked a bit bent. I noticed he had dug at many places in the garden as the soil was scattered all around.

"No, nothing." He said mournfully, sighing in deep exhaustion.

We backed into the house and locked the garden gate and had our dinner, after which I again went up to my solitary room, passing the third night in complete isolation.

I changed and then sat on the rocking chair, and the dreaded portrait again eyed me. I was left in a dither about what to do with that painting as keeping it in Arun's room again would be very tiring and I was also thinking about what all this meant and why had I bought this thing in my room in the first place. But then I calmed down.

Soon my mind was so silent; as never, not even in my sleep. Nothing bothered me anymore. My vision got frozen towards the painting and so was my mind. This time the noise of the silent night also didn't affect me, and the pain caused to my eyes because of the dim yellow glow also didn't have a difference in my glued view of the wretched portrait.

"Is this full of expressions or totally with no expression? I see nothing in his face." I thought.

I lay on the chair in a sunken way, and my legs were almost on the floor as if I was slipping from the wooden seat. Within some more minutes, I knew I was shivering, feeling uncomfortably nervous, and wanting to close my eyes and move; but I simply couldn't. I kept watching, failing to remove my vision from it, failing to resist seeing that white impression grinning. It was again the trance of that painting and I felt restless to move my eye from it. It was magnetic, it was hypnotic; it was petrifying and soon, step by step, the face looked bigger, as if I was getting nearer and nearer to it. I simply couldn't bear it anymore. Water dropped from my eyes, but still, I looked deeper into those expressions, which were twisted and cynical. A horrifying conviction grew in my mind that the painting was inflicted by a soul. It was a spirit, but logic brushed it off in a moment. The face was nearer and nearer and bigger and bigger and soon the wall and the room looked dark like the painting; and only the voice of that man was left to be heard.

Just then, the rocking chair turned upside down in a jerk and I landed on the floor completely, which pulled my thighs and strained my legs.

"Ahh," I cried as I pressed my waist with my hand and turned back as if I would sight someone who had pulled me down.

My head was dizzy and my vision through my hurting eyes, which were covered by the strands of my hair down my forehead, showed me I wasn't alone. A tall man was standing right there, the same as the painting. His face and the rest of his body were indifferent in darkness, but the neck very slightly reflected the light and was the only visible part. The entire room seemed whirling like a moving discus and the fading dark impression bent down to me. The room was locked from the inside and even if I would scream, my voice wouldn't reach down. I hung my head down and pressingly shut my eyes, still clutching my waist for seconds. I was about to faint in a paroxysm of horror. Slowly I regained myself and, taking the support of the bed, I somehow stood in an imbalanced, feeble way.

"Who's there?" I somehow spoke with one hand over the bed.

But by the time I cracked my eyes open, no one was in my room.

"Is anyone there?" I spoke again, but there was no reply.

Suddenly then, what I saw still shakes my spirit. Behind the closed glass window, out of which, faint light falling from my bulb created a slight visibility; I saw a hand swaying from side to side for support. Then it grabbed something, after which the other hand also got hold of the support, and gradually a head emerged. Trembling in horror, I saw a whole heavy figure that was wildly trying to climb up to my floor and possibly enter my room through the window. I couldn't speak. Half of the man's body loosely hung over my mighty window from the grabbed support. It was dark and stormy outside and I couldn't see the dark impression's face. I was about to cry loud for help before late, but suddenly, when the figure was face to face with me, its wild struggle to climb stopped. The climber stood still, looking at me, or probably behind me. In those moments of pressing anxiety, one cannot reason much and so I cannot deny a feeling that I perhaps heard a sigh behind me. I was breathless with a freezing sensation running through my very nerves as if my blood itself was frozen. I looked behind my shoulders, but I couldn't find anyone standing behind me. Slightly high up too, there was nothing but the painting—staring down. The climbing man left his grip immediately from the support and started to slip down from my window in a hurried manner. I clutched my night dress at my chest with my uncontrollably shaking hand and walked up to the window; opened it and peeped down. I didn't know what was happening, and I didn't know what I was doing. The dark figure almost tripped on the ground of the garden and started running in horror. It appeared as if one of his legs was damaged and attached to him like a dead weight, which certainly reminded me of what Mr. Paul had said. He hurriedly walked up to the fence and crossed it; nothing could be seen anymore. Possibly he had come up by the drainage pipe and was the same man who had thrown a torchlight into my room previously.

"Uncle—" I spoke, but words came out like a squeak.

After some minutes of organizing my shaking legs, I rushed down the stairs to meet my uncle. The hall was dark, and some dreary lamp was glowing in one corner, casting massive shadows of all the antique things present in the hall. I came to Uncle's door but before knocking pressed my left ear against the door. I was forced to pull my ear away as strange, unnatural noises were coming from inside the room. These spell-like noises were disturbing, but I knocked on the door hard.

"Uncle! Please come out once." I exclaimed and knocked again.

My tall uncle came out and stood before me, but his face couldn't be seen in the almost unlit hall.

"Uncle, there is a thief in the house, and he is trying to climb up to my room!" I said as I saw him.

"What! A thief?" He said in a shocked way and continued, "If anyone else would tell this I wouldn't have believed but if you tell so I will check, certainly."

All this while he went on speaking in the native language with no reason at all—a rough language. He opened the garden gate, and a lantern light was all over, but there was nothing but rain and mud.

"See, there is nothing, sweetie. It must be a bad dream; many see the worst dreams of their lives in this house." He sighed mournfully, shifting again from the native language.

"But I am sure that it wasn't a dream. This has happened earlier too, and I had told this Arun, but he also told me to ignore it."

"I will inspect tomorrow again, my dear. Tonight, I will be with you, and you could sleep or talk, whatever you want. I feel sleeping alone on the second floor is not good." He said as he walked with me back to the hall and continued, "You know; now I too believe that purchasing this mansion was a blunder and the purpose also failed. The locals said the truth; the reflections of strangely violent past incidents are witnessed here. I never believed that this place is haunted, but..."

"Uncle, you were correct and do not believe in things like ghosts or that something paranormal goes on here. There are many strange incidents that I too have witnessed, but I still think that we are missing some point. We are mistaken." I wanted to say as I did normally, but this time I just couldn't.

The incidents that were taking place spared me no chance of saying that I wasn't afraid. I still didn't want to believe in paranormal phenomena, but there was a terrible feeling in my heart that something was wrong. Perhaps not a ghost, but something even horrific could be going on.

All this while, I hadn't seen his face properly, and nor did he see mine. I was still confused about the strange noises from his room, but it was also impossible to even think that these noises were made by my uncle. It was a rare blessing that the rest of the night granted me a normal sleep. The next morning, my eyes opened in the hall where I had spent my night sleeping on the sofa. The morning was not a bright one, and the hall was quite the same, not bright. It was as if it needed bulbs in the morning hours, too. Uncle was also up and preparing his morning tea, and I went up to help him.

"Ajay will also be called from his friend's place today; he will be back in the afternoon," Uncle said.

On the dining table with tea and bread, where I was sitting face to face with my uncle, I noticed that his expression expressed extreme exhaustion and his voice confirmed all this. His face looked more faded than the last day and very different from the day I had first seen him.

"Uncle, are you okay today? Are you not well?" I asked, putting my bread down from my hand.

He sipped from his cup and said, "I think I have a fever, but I won't need a doctor. Some rest is what I need."

"Can I feel your forehead?" I asked.

His temperature suggested that he had a fever. I told him to rest on the sofa and he did so, though walking swaying from one side to the other. His condition worsened within an hour. I was sitting just beside him, and he lay there with one hand covering his eyes.

After some more minutes, he spoke, "Can you please bring a tablet from the bottle that is kept in the first cupboard of my mirror table?" He said feebly, with his finger pointing towards his room.

When I turned back and advanced towards his room, he again said, "Do not bother yourself with the other things kept in the room."

"Okay, uncle," I said and advanced.

While approaching towards uncle's closed door, a relevant thought struck my mind that similar to Arun's room, I had till now not been in my uncle's room at once. It was also an unexplored corner for me in this house and thinking this, there was a strange excitement in my stomach. I looked back to Uncle who was a still in the same position and entered his room by opening the door.

A larger, well-organized room opened before me. It was quite dark inside and strips of sunlight peeped in through the corners of the drawn windows, which gave a sufficient impression of where things were in the room. Suspending dust particles of the air could be seen under the sunlight. I looked around a bit of the room and what appeared was a bed, a big mirror table, a wooden wardrobe, and four mighty bookshelves aligned side by side on the farthest wall and a table. I went up to the bookshelves, which were locked. They were full of law books but were covered in visible dust, which suggested that my uncle didn't use them anymore. I looked around again and apparently, nothing exciting was in the room. I went up to the mirror table and opened the cupboard to take out the tablets. At first, I couldn't find the bottle, but I could see a medium-sized wooden box as the only thing in the cupboard. I moved my hand about in the cupboard and soon the tablet bottle was found. Now that my work was done, I had to go, but before going I thought to have a look at the wooden box. I opened it and there I was quite startled to see that it was filled with strips of medicines. I had never thought that my uncle needed so many medicines and this forced me to look at them.

Among many unknown strips of allopathic medicines, I recognized some were for sleep, headache, and calming the nerves. I am not sure at all, but I feel that others were also related to the mind because I had read about some of them and remembered vaguely. It was hard to even think that my uncle used high doses of such medicines. I kept them again as they were, took the tablets, and came out as soon as possible. But one more thing which I did was to jam the door from locking by the stopper. He took a tablet from the box and then told that he would rest for some time on the sofa. Slowly, I came back into his room. All this didn't seem correct, but I had to do it to understand what was going on in that place.

I opened the window for more light to come in and then I looked around. A sudden gust of wind followed through the window, into the room, which made the heavy curtains flutter, and a thin creek was heard behind me. I turned back immediately. The wind caused the left door of the wooden wardrobe to open, leaving it in a loose swaying position. I advanced towards it.

"Should I look into Uncle's wardrobe?" I thought but at the same second another thought came over me "It is not correct."

With more wind coming in, the door swayed from right to left in a constant motion, and it had to be closed. My heartbeat increased for no reason as I took slow steps toward the wardrobe. I sighed in difficult excitement before looking in—and this decision left me amazed.

Such an unusual collection of exquisite clothes was in the wardrobe that it appeared no less than a display wardrobe of a shop. Shiny coats, shirts, and night robes hung from hangers in the wardrobe. In the first two cupboards, there were pants of various colors and even various fabrics which were each different to touch and feel; all kept carefully. I had expected beautiful clothes but such a bunch, I hadn't thought of. I ran my fingers through those hanging coats to just feel their extraordinarily apparent smoothness and texture.

"Uncle really is a man of fashion, but these clothes somewhat do not have the latest fashion feel." I was thinking.

Controlling my attention from the clothes, I started to think about the match between my uncle and that collection. Uncle was a tall man, but not very tall, and his shoulders weren't also so broad., rather they were a bit rounded. But those coats looked way bigger. Silence still prevailed in the empty room, and the window kept swaying from side to side. I stretched myself over my toes and managed to pull out a brown coat.

I have no reason for what I did, but I slipped my arms into the coat and adjusted it over my shoulders. Now I was in that coat. I started walking towards the mirror. While walking, I started to feel a strange sensation gripping my body. By the time I was face to face with the mirror, it will not be an exaggeration that I was shaking. The sunlight had declined, perhaps because of the clouds, and the room was turning to a grayish shade. I looked at myself in the mirror. I was impressed as I looked good in that shiny coat, but its shoulders hung down almost to my elbows, and its ends hung down at my knees. I looked at the mirror for minutes and I saw myself and the ash-gray background behind me.

"Great…" came out of my mouth almost un-intentionally and it was also the first word that burst out of me in the native language.

For a moment I felt like it wasn't me wearing the coat, but I brushed the thought. The unnatural sensation that had come as I wore this coat kept on increasing and clouding my mind and in a matter of seconds, the marvelous feeling took a turn towards an awfully nervous feeling. I still looked deep into the mirror with dizziness when suddenly a fearful apprehension was all over me. Just then, the loose coat slipped down my shoulders and arms and sprawled on the floor. I was startled and felt so light like a heavy burden came off me; fortunately, I didn't fall or something like that. I turned behind and looked at the coat on the floor and then lifted it up. Perhaps it had come off because of its heaviness, but at that moment I was simply left without thought.

"How could such an oversized and costly coat be of uncle? And if not, then whose is it?" This thought thrilled me.

The dizziness of mine had also begun subsiding, and the same was with the sensation. I checked the inside of the coat. Some words were stitched in there; the brand of the coat was written and below it was written: London. When I looked at the bottom, a big "S" was written with a thick red fiber. There was a sudden lighting strike outside, which illuminated the room momentarily like a silvery blaze, and the menacing growl of the thunder followed. I dropped the coat and stepped a step back in a paroxysm of fear.

"This coat, these coats, shirts, pants do not belong to uncle! They are not his; they are of Shaitaan!" I wanted to speak, but it didn't come out.

All the clothes that were in the wardrobe had the same stitched "S" and all my doubts were cleared.

"I should have never slipped into a coat that was once worn by such a hateful man." I thought.

Shaitaan; such a horrific man, an evil soul, and slipping into his clothes for even once was such an awkward and insane idea. I was strangely anxious after this revelation that my uncle sometimes wore these clothes—even though they didn't look used much. It shook me up. I came out of the room after making things of the room normal.

I stood speechless in front of my sleeping uncle, looking at him for minutes. He was still wearing one of those exquisite clothes. I mounted the solitary stairs and again ended up in my bed, behind the closed door. Outside, the clouds had burst again, but the thunder was striking right in my heart. The horrors of last night, my uncle in the garden, Arun's mysterious run from home, the paranormal incidents, and the above all, the strange painting that was again not letting me alone in the room crowded my mind. I grew slightly melancholy. This time I was cautious and covered the painting with an old cloth that was in the wardrobe. Then I fell asleep on the bed. Perhaps a cool rainy day helps with sleep.

My eyes opened after an hour because my bedroom door had opened. Ajay came in and stood right there. He was drenched in rain and muddy were his clothes.

"You stay there, don't move," I said and gave him a towel. After changing his clothes and having something, I sat face to face with him on my bed, hearing what all he had done at his friend's place.

"You know I related the same story to my friend, about the man and he was terrified..." He spoke with childish excitement.

"Did you not have your strange dreams at your friend's place, too?" I asked.

"No. But we slept scarcely as it is," he answered.

There was a knock on the door, and Uncle entered the room. He gave a look to Ajay, as if thinking about his childishness, and then looked at me.

"Do you know what you have done there?" he said, looking towards Ajay and continuing "I have been informed by your friend's parents that for the past two nights, you had been scaring your friend with stories. Then they said that you started speaking in your dreams and, ultimately, they had to put on the lights the whole night."

"No, I just told him the story because he wanted to hear it and I remember nothing after I was asleep."

"How can he..." I uttered.

Uncle went down again, and we were left alone in the bedroom. I lay down again, blessing myself for covering that painting. Time passed by and I kept hearing the noise of water droplets cracking at my window.

"What a sleep. Refreshing." I said as I woke up, stretching myself.

I ran my eyes around the room, but the only moving thing was the slow ceiling fan; Ajay was not in the room. I looked at the clock that had struck four thirty of the ashy evening. I opened the door and came out into the cool passage.

"What lovely weather," I said, looking outside the passage window.

The blue-gray sky was as before, a bit of the sun was seen between the black clouds and the wet grasses in the vast fields were swaying towards the left in a fast vibration. The landscape looked magical and melancholy. I kept looking at the vast, wet, and lonely countryside when some loud voices started coming to my ears. It backed and walked up to the stair railing. It was heard as if two people were talking in the hall and I carefully heard. One was surely my uncle and the other voice was somewhere heard of, but I couldn't recognize it. I walked down the stairs, holding the railing; thinking about who could be there in the hall with my uncle. Faces of those strangers started coming to my mind, whom I had met in the town.

"Who could it be? I pray he is not him." I thought.

As I came down inquisitively, the noises grew and the man I saw sitting with my uncle shattered my mood. My fears came true. It was him.

9

"Come here Vaanya, meet Mr. Candy!" Uncle said as I got visible in the hall—standing on the last step of the stair.

I walked down; his eyes were looking at me constantly all this time and when he was about to speak something, I instantly made a gesture by shaking my head indicating to him not to speak. I didn't want my uncle to know about my secret wanderings in the town.

"Hello!" he said and continued in his same, awkward, giggling tone, "Mr. Vijay I prefer to be called 'old uncle' by young people,"

"Come have a seat!" Uncle said in a cheerful tone—he was in a good mood. The reason was this man's arrival.

I had unconsciously slowed down and reluctantly advanced without a word. I took my seat next to Ajay who had a chocolate bar in his hand, giggling in front of that Mr. Candy or "old uncle", of the Food Cabin, whatever you wish to call him.

The chocolate had been gifted to Ajay by the same man.

I simply avoided looking into his eyes, behind his spectacles, but I somehow felt he was constantly staring at me. I had never expected this man would come up to our house to meet. His big, scarred face, mostly covered by his rough, gray beard and his mighty, thick spectacles under which I suppose he hid his cold eyes from the world, may seem jolly to some but it kindled such a peculiar discomfort in my mind that I instantly hated sitting in front of him.

My uncle introduced me again to him and he said, "overwhelmed to meet you…" and "again" would be the last word that he didn't speak, luckily.

"You know, he is a man who had helped some days ago. He has a food cabin in the town." Uncle said, looking at me, and then turned to him and continued, "I hope you do not mind yourself being called a newcomer in this town?"

"Mr. Vijay, I am a newcomer, but this town seems like it's now no less near to me than the town where I was born. Here I see the hills, the fields, the sky, and, above all, lovely young people." He told in a laughing tone, and everyone laughed other than me.

"You know Mr. Vijay," he said with his growling voice, coming out battling from his rough throat, and continued "These days I am quite a person of archaeology too, perhaps it is one of the many things that have bought me to this lonely town in the deep foggy valleys."

"So, tell us something about your research..." Uncle said.

Suddenly the only glowing bulb stopped, which startled all of us, and most startled of all was Mr. Candy.

"Nothing to worry about; only the current is out. This keeps on happening because of rains and storms," Uncle said as he lit a mighty candle that was on top of the head of a child's statue.

"Please continue, Mr. Candy," he said, blowing out the matchstick.

"I have not much to say till now, but you know Mr. Vijay, the same study has brought me to your house too," he said.

He turned towards me, put down his spectacles to wipe them, and at that moment, I saw the candle flame gleaming into his cold blue eyes like a terrifying burning fire blaze with which he gave a hideous glance and again turned on his glasses. I was taken aback at seeing this and shut my eyes momentarily.

"Mr. Candy, by research I mean something else..." Uncle said in a low tone, sounding funny.

Tinges of red and gold fell on the depressions of both faces and other features were invisible in the dark. Mr. Candy's thick frames and beard gleamed and were the only sign of him being present in one corner of the dark hall.

"Not in front of kids..." Mr. Candy replied in the same tone and they both started to sort of laugh.

Ajay also broke into laughter, but I wasn't feeling good and looked towards the dancing flame in the corner.

"Vaanya, it looks like something disturbs you. What is it?" Uncle asked, looking at me.

"I am fine, Uncle."

Uncle turned his head to Mr. Candy and asked, "Well, what we can do for you?"

"Oh, very kind of you," he said laughingly and continued, "I wanted to say..."

"Wait, a second!" Uncle interrupted him and then said, "You have come such a long way in the rainy, chilly atmosphere throughout the valley and I haven't asked you for tea or coffee."

"That's unnecessary. I will not stay longer."

"Where will you go out when there is a thick fog all around and clouds up in the sky? Ajay, please give Mr. Candy some hot coffee." Uncle said and gave me a look, too.

I also followed Ajay up to the kitchen with a candle in my hand.

"Dear girl, don't put a lot of sugar in mine; as it is, I have had a lot of sweetness recently." Mr. Candy said behind me and burst as if he had cracked a joke, but I didn't find any humor in it if not anything else.

"Be careful, do not trip," I told to Ajay.

While we were in the kitchen making coffee, I could hear Uncle and that man discussing something and I knew that would be the thing about which Uncle wanted to talk. When three cups of coffee were done, I rushed out of the kitchen so that I could hear even a word.

I remember grasping only two words: "A setting in liquor" spoken by Mr. Candy and a pressurized "I don't know, I have to think" by my uncle.

They both stopped the moment I was visible, and I advanced to give one cup to Mr. Candy. He forwarded his open hand towards me to get hold of the tray when I was very near, but there I instantly paused.

The lines were the same; the palm was the same! It took me a step back, and the man withdrew his hand in a moment.

"Any problem?" Uncle asked, seeing me at pause and mum.

"Oh, nothing I-I was just thinking..." I said and handed over the cup to Mr. Candy, saying nothing.

My mind was puzzled, shocked, and whirling, confused from the glimpse which I had gotten under the flame; I sat down in my chair again.

"Lovely coffee, Miss. The sweetness, though, is too much for me," he remarked while sipping the boiling hot coffee from the cup.

He had no uneasiness in drinking it that hot.

My cup was in my hand with its vapor still coming out visibly. The windowpanes were shaking, making wild noises and the wind occasionally flew around the ears, humming. I sat there with Mr. Candy's bombast words going into my ears but not appealing to my understanding; I was just engaged in one thought: How could this possibly happen?

Soon his words didn't come to my ears anymore, and I looked up again. Mr. Candy had halted and was looking at one end of the hall where no one was standing, only the faint light made an old chair visible. Ajay and I exchanged looks in confusion.

"Mr. Vijay, I cannot stay any longer so..." He sipped the coffee again and paused, drops of anxiety had wetted his forehead.

"Uncle, I am having a terrible headache, so can I be in my room with my coffee?" I said before Mr. Candy said anything.

"Okay. I feel it's cold in your head. Perhaps a light sleep would help." Uncle replied.

I stood up immediately and advanced towards the stairs, taking the other candle with me. While walking up the stairs, I was thinking only one thing: "Perhaps I am wrong; but how can it be? Everything was the same!"

I reached the second floor and hurriedly entered my room, closing the door behind me, after which I took a long breath. I momentarily sat on the rocking armchair after opening the mighty window.

I wanted to scream, "How can this be?"

When Mr. Candy had forwarded his palm to me for the tray, I had seen an unusual star-like sign on his palm under the middle finger and I had also faintly recognized the same odd, square shapes in the middle of his palm; all under the yellow candlelight falling on his palm. Soon my memory gradually matched other points. I couldn't drink the coffee cup anymore. The very thought that Mr. Candy's palm exactly matched the palm print of Neelnath, which I had seen in Arun's booklets, burdened my mind intensely.

"My mind is gone; what am I doing?" I whispered to myself because Neelnath was already dead a long time ago and there could be no other chance of any possibility beyond that.

There are some thoughts that you cannot believe and don't want to, but they stick to your mind inseparably. I couldn't brush off this thought, as I believed in my eyes, sense, and memory, but common sense was totally against it. It couldn't be a coincidence.

"Then who this man is?" I asked myself in a paroxysm of horror and confusion while the cool air with a spray of raindrops wetted my face and hair. I stood up and advanced towards the gate when I heard some noises coming down. It was footsteps. They were a couple of footsteps approaching the second floor or probably my room!

I walked back from the door. I immediately pulled down the heavy photo frame and pushed it under my bed. I don't know why exactly I did that, but I did it. The footsteps were very close to the room, and the people were moving around on the second floor.

"What could they be doing?" I thought and remained silent.

Suddenly there was a shocking, heavy noise outside as if someone heavy had fallen over something. Following it came screams. The floor shook in vibration till my room, and I came out in the dark passage to see what had happened.

"Oh, God! Pick him up! Mr. Candy, are you fine?" It was my uncle's voice that cried in the dark.

"Oh! This leg of mine!" Mr. Candy uttered in horror.

I held the candle high to see what had happened in the dark passage. I was in a state of terrible shock.

"Keep the candle down and pull him!" Uncle burst out. I ran towards the falling Mr. Candy, who was hanging half over the staircase railing dangerously.

"Hold him!" I cried to Ajay, who came up running, and I tried to pull his heavy figure over.

Our vision was no better than blindness and what a terrible situation it was! It took all strength, cries, and might of all three of us to pull up the heavy guest of ours from the railing and to save him from falling from the high second floor. After a couple of moments, we could pull this man up, though it felt like the whole earth itself was pulling him down into the dark void.

I was left panting and totally out of breath, with my hand clutching over my heart to calm it. Mr. Candy was wordless for minutes and he looked like a huge man under the candlelight with a monstrous shadow, sprawled over the floor trying to recover from the horror of death.

"Mr. Candy..." Uncle spoke in a speech of prolonged pauses. "I feel you are fine"

"I-I ..." Mr. Candy could hardly speak. "You have saved me, or else I-I,"

"But how did your leg suddenly get stuck under the gap of the railing in such a twisted way? You were walking fine." Uncle said as he tried to stand up.

There wasn't any reply from the shaking Mr. Candy. He stood up after some minutes and said in a whisper, "So you stay in this room...". He said, slightly pointing to my room.

I feel it was so slow that others who were a hand away paid little heed, but I heard it quite clearly. It seemed wrong. He was faintly sneering. I failed to think why.

"Papa! I saw someone there..." Ajay spoke suddenly in a startled way as I took the candle in my hand again, but he was interrupted by my uncle.

I looked in the direction where he was pointing, but only a blurred reflection of the flame was seen other than the blackness.

"Don't start your stories again! This isn't the time, it's only Mr. Candy standing there!" Uncle replied.

He didn't speak anymore.

"Mr. Vijay, I have to leave now; I will come to your place again." Mr.

Candy said, as Uncle and he walked down the stairs.

The silver blaze and the explosive sound of the thunder which followed notified the storm's presence. The lights were still out, and the wind still made a noise in the ears.

"But it doesn't seem that the storm will be fine tonight, and it is pitch dark out..." I heard Uncle say.

"No, Mr. Vijay; thank you. But I have to leave with my umbrella."

"But you told me you had plans to stay tonight with us... Rough weather too, it would be muddy..."

"I have to change that," he said hurriedly and continued "I have a long experience in walking alone in these foggy deep dark valleys... I have an appointment, so I have to go. Thank you."

Mr. Candy raised his head and gave a last look to me and my room, and then opened the main gate. With the opening of the gate came a gust of winds which made things fall here and there on the second floor, but Mr. Candy walked out, pushing through the gusts. The gate was pushed and locked by my uncle after the "old uncle" had gone and silence once again grew to its peak, as before.

We talked a little after that, and Uncle retired to his room saying, "God knows what made Mr. Candy run in such a way..."

I mounted the stairs again and went up to my room, where I sat on the bed with puzzling questions that intrigued me more and more, even though nothing was understandable. The night had grown colder, and my room was lit only by a candle.

What can I say about how I was feeling after witnessing such an unnatural experience in a series? But the jolly Mr. Candy's presence had unsettled me more than the horrors in that place. I drew the curtains of the window remembering the last night and locked the passage's window too. I changed into my light, white nightdress and after I had done, Ajay entered the room.

He sniffed the air and said in a confused manner, "Are you getting a strange smell?"

I breathed deeply and said with little attention, "Yes... But isn't it normal over here? It's sometimes in the lane, too."

"Wait, seriously, I am also marking it now." I paused and couldn't help but remark, "I can feel this old, damp, dusty smell... it makes me somewhat nervous..."

Ajay looked around the room, but there was nothing uncommon and I brushed the thought away because that smell was always in the rooms of the mansion—sometimes even in the hall or the stairs, always traveling.

When he was about to speak, I interrupted him, "What do you think of Mr. Candy?"

"Oh! What to think of? He is a jolly old man who loves company. Initially, he looked scary, but I was wrong."

He paused and then said, "Leave all this, have-have you seen Shaitaan when you were alone in here? How could you sleep alone in the night?"

I leaned my back over the armchair and said, "I do not know what's going on. Last night, a man tried to come up to my room. I couldn't see his face in the darkness, but all I remember is that his leg was damaged. Who could it be? And then some other things also happened, but..."

Ajay's expression ran out soon. All he said was, "I am not liking this; I don't feel good..."

He slipped under the blanket and how could I explain to him the terror which terrorized me? The nocturnal darkness grew in that remote area, and in our room, it was special. I insisted Ajay play the game of shadows and he agreed. Our room was the best place to play such a weird and childish game where we made signs of various animals with our hands before the candle flame, which cast enormous shadows over the wall. Soon we had made all kinds of strange gestures, after which we left the game—it was certainly a peculiar enjoyment. After minutes, I could see that Ajay had already dozed off under his cozy blanket.

As sleep didn't come to me, rather stubbornly; I decided to be with my diary for some time. The stillness in the room, which was in the initial days, capital, was now affecting my heart as a discomforting burden. The candle flame was like a tongue of orange in the thick darkness of the room and writing under it gave me a feeling that was already present there, a feeling of the previous centuries. I couldn't write much. My eyes pained and as I closed my eyes, the film, which I saw, was bright orange, as if the flame was still burning inside. As I lay there on my table in a rather fatigued manner;

the only candle suddenly blew off, leading the room in a flood of black. I was quite startled, but not much because within seconds I re-lit it. I don't know from where that blow came. As I blew off the matchstick, a thought came into my mind. I pulled out the photo frame again.

Why I did so is a question that I am as less inclined to answer as the question was, "Why was I doing all this at all?" The first glimpse of the face as the streak of light fell on it was terrifying. It looked a different expression to me this time, like questioning me with a big 'Why!'. I kept the painting on my table, and it was visible as the candle was near it. Then perhaps I must have wanted to find something unknown in the depths of that painting. Maybe I had a hope of finding something unknown. But mind it, this time I was more cautious as till then I had understood that there was "something" in that face.

I gave a gentle slap to my cheek as I noted that exactly eight long minutes (by the table clock) had passed and I was again lost in the hideous white face. I stood up in horror, whispering: "This painting captures me!"

I knew what I had to do next, though I feared this part the most. I pressed my eyes shut with trembling hands and—it happened the same way I had thought. After several seconds, the same white impression danced before my closed eyes and the same happened even after opening them. I could, and I mean it; see a full-figure glimpse of a man standing still right there near the painting. It was like a dark impression gaining itself. The face was almost the same as that of the painting and as white as it was in the painting. He was silent as if the portrait itself had come out from the frame. The stories that I had heard of Shaitaan were beating in my ears and by this time the readers must have understood that the painting which I was carrying with me, keeping in my room, and looking at continuously was of Shaitaan himself. His dress wasn't seen, but the impression of it was the same as the painting: exquisite.

I clenched my fists tight and pressed my feet on the ground in a try to not fall with a fit of fear as I had decided this time to endure whatever was before my eyes and look at it till the end. I felt as if I was just waiting for it to speak up. But it stood still, facing me with a drunk look, and soon I knew I wouldn't be able to resist anymore. A person shouldn't talk about his fear much if he was ready and expecting to witness it. My head started whirling again and if I wouldn't fall from fear, out of dizziness, I would certainly fall.

The apparition reduced its details in a containing manner as I pressed my eyes shut and fell on the bed, somewhat deliberately and consciously, with my head over the pillow. It was a time when I had forgotten words. Gradually it was completely gone, lastly seen by my shut eyes as a silvery blue impression. It rather got merged into the other shapes that came over the film of my closed eyes—into red, purple, and blue.

Though shaking, I stood up after minutes with my hand over my mouth, which was wide open, giving me the true feeling that I could somewhat now understand what was going on with me.

"Whenever I see this painting, which is just not more than a white impression; and then when I close my eyes or look at a dark corner, the same face comes over my eye film. But not in the rest part of the days; this happens only when I am alone..." I thought and then figured out more "I have always seen this painting in very dim or dreary light when my mind was occupied by nervousness and then this figure comes before me but never speaks..."

I thought for more time when my mind went deep into the psychological knowledge which I had learned from research papers, and I sprung up with a thought: "This is just a hallucination! Yes! I feel that this white impression is a simple trick or mischief by the painter because its odd expression stays within even after minutes of closing the eyes and reflects itself whenever I look at a dark corner..."

I thought it was a very simple type of visual hallucination that occurs under dim light and kept the painting under the bed again, after which I also slipped under the blanket. The sense of achievement, that of gaining the surety that the apparition was not a ghost but just a play of my eye's biology, was rather short-lived. Thought I had written this as a reason for all the experiences at that place, in my diary; it wasn't so convincing after minutes as I lay on the bed thinking.

"Do hallucinations happen in such a way? And do they occur to people who do not have any disorders?" I stood up once again.

The flame was burning as before, and I thought: "Then-then what type of hallucination was last night's incident and how can so many people hallucinate with the same subject?". I was now convinced that all of it wasn't just a hallucination. But this doesn't mean that I lost my grip on the fact that leaving other incidents the painting's incidents that were recently described as a very tiny kind of visual impact which was, though inexplicable, not out of scientific thought.

A sense came over me that some part of all this could be explained in a way of psychology and biology, but on a whole, the experiences couldn't be explained as totally natural, probably. I thought the entire night about that and something unknown remained unconvincing.

"But what about the unknown man who tries to climb up my room now and then?" was my last thought, after which sleep took over my mind.

10

It was half-past eight when I woke up the next morning, but Ajay was still asleep on the other bed and nothing else was uncommon about the morning. The storm was over, and the electricity probably had returned.

"Now I will not look at the painting at all and will put it back again whenever possible." I thought while on the bed.

I had my breakfast alone, strolled in the garden alone, and enjoyed alone; the chilly winds where the tiny raindrops whirled in the air. I had so much in my mind, so many strange facts and questions that there was a pressing desire in me to discuss them with someone; but who could I find in this part of the town? The pressing feeling of being alone was burdening me when a thought came over me that I should probably have a general talk with my uncle and ask him to write to my father too; so, I walked into the hall. I hadn't seen him that morning and called out "Uncle? Can we have a stroll in the town and buy some flowers or seeds for our garden?"

There wasn't any reply from Uncle's room. I touched the door slightly, and it opened wide with a noise. I must clarify here that I hadn't done it purposely.

I stood in front of the door in a moment of amazement and horror. What lay at a distance from the door was a horrible sight, which pushed me a step back from it. Two big brooms were kept crossed over each other right in front of the door and suggesting nothing, but that my uncle had kept them in those angles deliberately.

What was it? I heard some footsteps behind me. Perhaps it was Uncle. I closed the door as before and walked back—as I knew Uncle wouldn't have wanted me to see whatever it was. When I was at a distance from where I wouldn't be seen easily; I saw my uncle open the door. I watched. The door didn't close behind him and what I saw was this: Uncle looked at the brooms for a minute or so and then kicked it off from its place—as if denying a proposal in his mind. Then he picked them up and dumped them in a corner of the room. I wasn't feeling that everything going on was correct when my uncle called out my name loudly. But probably he was just cleaning the room and kept them, just like that—coincidently, I rationalized again.

"Yes, uncle," I replied as I walked normally up to him, though his sudden call had raised the poundings in my heart.

He looked quite exhausted, and his sigh was of despair.

"I think I should go up and be with Ajay or else I fear something would happen again..." He spoke.

"That would be good, uncle." I replied and continued, "But I had something to ask."

"What?"

"I feel that we have a suitable space over here in the garden, so..." I was a bit hesitant to demand, "Can I go up to the town's market and buy some..."

After seconds of pause, Uncle said, "It's a good idea, but there is no one here to care for such gardens; only if there would be another woman..."

"I can look after it till I am here and then Ajay can certainly do it if you are busy. I feel the vast flowerless garden doesn't look good."

"You are correct, as it is everything is lost now..." I didn't know what he meant. He continued: "But I shall also come with you and tell Ajay to be ready too. We will seek the blessings on the way."

"Blessings? What do you mean, uncle?"

"There is a temple on the way and there is a new priest in that temple..."

A blissful smile must have appeared on my face because we were going out.

"So, what happened to the old priest?" I asked as we were walking down the lane to the town.

The path was illuminated at places wherever the shines of the bright morning sun broke down on it through the gaps of the high, man-like trees that were half-bent all over the lane, rooted deep in the sides of it. The shiny day perhaps had lifted both my and uncle's spirits as he had lately started a small conversation with us after a refreshing cold breeze breathed between us. He seemed a wonderful companion very many times. The gusts were as before; strong.

After a deep breath, he sighed and started, "The old temple priest was a great man; he was a kind of mentor for me when I was a child and then he would be not more than forty or something." He continued in the glory of the old priest and with his words, it was clear that whoever he was, he had been playing a deep, supportive role for my uncle.

While talking about the old priest, his scholarly, serious expression was relaxed, and bliss was floating on his face as he remembered his childhood incidents. He went from the day of his class eleventh when he didn't pass in math to the sad day when my aunt passed away and how this old priest had consoled him all along these years.

"He seems to be a great man. So, are we going to meet him?" I asked as excitement erupted on my lips.

Uncle sighed and said, "My dear, these are old days; they are like dreams—vanished forever. If only the old priest would be alive; he died because of ... Oh, leave that."

I was left speechless as after such talks; I was feeling unfortunate for not getting an opportunity to see this man.

"If only he would be there then I would go to him as a child and he would sort out all my–all my problems that ..." he didn't continue, probably because he didn't want to share his problems.

"So, there must be a new priest out there? We could meet him." I asked.

"Oh, no… no. The new priest is naïve. A young man of twenty-nine probably becoming the supreme priest of such an old temple is dissatisfactory."

"But..." I got interrupted.

"He looks boyish. I do not talk to him much. He can simply not meet the glory of the previous ones in the temple. And I am elder than him. How can he give me preaching and suggestions?" He went on, "I do not think him capable and so I haven't even gone to the temple since, though. I've heard that he has been to foreign countries to preach religion there—but he looks like a stage actor instead."

"The old priest had always told him since childhood 'You have an excessive love for money, control it; control it' and this was so true. I couldn't control it..."

"We have come to the town," Ajay spoke, interrupting my uncle; proving his existence with us all this time on the path.

"He was certainly not interested in these talks." I thought laughingly.

Uncle soon forgot about the old stories and the new stories, but they stayed with me.

My mind was completely biased about the new priest till the time we entered the old temple and that was after we had done with buying seeds. There weren't people around at that time. After some minutes, I could see a tall and slender figure, dressed in a brown robe, approaching us from the other side of the temple. As he became visible, I noticed his slender but strong frame and broad shoulders. His complexion was slightly brown, and his black hair was so neatly combed that not even a strand disturbed his bare forehead; even though it was so windy. He wore round glass spectacles which gave a boost to his learned and calm look, which he had on his clean-shaven face. He had nothing in his hand or round his neck and was barefoot. Seeing his face and ways of dressing up, he could be best called a young professor of philosophy.

While I was wondering who this gentleman was, my uncle spoke out, addressing him as the priest.

I turned my head in amazement at the man.

"This is the priest?" I questioned myself because actually, he didn't look like one conventionally. The man came nearer to us, and Uncle talked with him about some general matters of the town, but unwillingness to talk was seen on both sides. While talking, the priest moved his head towards me so suddenly that my eyes automatically turned to the swaying grass. He kept his vision deep into my eyes with an expression so serious, as if he was studying a book. He turned his head again in a jerk and sniffed, after which he rubbed his palms vigorously together. I realized that the sun had almost hidden behind the clouds and coolness increased in the winds. No one was around other than fog, trees, and a couple of cows, which looked more restless than normal.

"Papa! I forgot to get the change from the shop!" Ajay said suddenly while counting the coins.

"Oh!" Uncle paused in dismay and thought, after which he said, "Vaanya wait here while we come in some minutes... Remain in the temple garden—don't go anywhere."

Within seconds Uncle and Ajay walked back to the market, leaving me alone with the priest, who stood right behind me, and the winds which became even stronger. I didn't turn back for seconds and looked around as there was no garden but only vast, deserted grassy fields wherever the eyes could reach. I was feeling the presence of the tall priest just behind me, but I didn't turn to him; maybe because his presence was so, so serious or I was nervous. I kept looking at the infinite sky, which was turning a deep blue, and gray clouds hung low, resulting in making the vision of the fields and the whole area dimmer and bleaker. The odor of moisture floated in the very air and the presence of the priest behind me was heavier and more impactful.

I turned back with a jerk, thinking that my act could be misunderstood as arrogance. But there was no one standing behind me. The priest couldn't be seen anywhere in the gray atmosphere and as I stood there awestruck, a powerful gust came with a spray of cool raindrops. In seconds, other gusts followed, which bought rain. It was amazingly pleasant initially, but within seconds, I got fully drenched in the rain, which was growing wilder. The winds gave me shivers, and the grounds squelched loosely under my feet. My dress was heavy with water and my arms were crossed against my chest. The swaying grass looked black and blue. Soon, the raindrops didn't let me see anything, and I feared a horrendous storm, where I stood as the only human under the open, cloudy sky.

I tried hard to walk but realized that another blind step would lead to a slip into the muddy grass. The noise of the winds and the rains was as if the ground itself was rumbling. Thinking about what to do, I saw, from somewhere in the thick black mists; a man approaching me hurriedly. A shudder of fear ran down my shivering back as I was alone and a man seeing me and running towards me in such weather was overly unexpected. But I stood there, shivering, and soon the black figure could be seen.

"Be under this!"

It was the priest. He held a mighty umbrella high and the beating of the rain over me stopped. I was breathless for a few seconds, but after this, I looked up to the priest who was with me in the umbrella and said: "Thank-Thank you."

"It's god's wish... Thank God, I remembered you when the storm broke."

Everything was dark, and only the priest's voice indicated that he was nearby.

"Come; walk." He said, and I followed.

We both walked, beating against the mighty gusts and rain with steps heavy and hard to take. After a walk, we reached the room in the temple where he lived.

After entering the warm room, I sighed in relief. The room was lit by a lamp, which made it yellow and black. The priest gave me a towel. After using the towel to the most possible extent, I thanked him again as he sat at his table at a distance from where I sat. He sat there silently, and I couldn't see whether his eyes were open or closed. It was evident that he was a very calm and reserved man who talked little.

"Was Uncle correct about him?" I thought.

At last, he spoke "I-I must say that." he paused in deep thought after which he continued "I would like to talk to you and inform you about a very-very important thing which I have noticed... I feel the urge to guide you out or else..."

He told this looking at me and I asked, "Please tell me what it is?"

So, went on a long conversation with him, which was crucial, giving me shudders of fear and bliss of realization at the same time. Curiosity in one's mind might grow to know what he told me, but I feel certain secrets should remain secrets until the correct opportunity comes when there is no other chance than them to get revealed.

Time passed, the rain stopped, and the priest and I came out into the fields where the cool winds still gave quivers.

"You have helped me a lot with your observations and experience—but can you sort out one more query which I have?" I asked him, looking towards the vast hills above which the sun seemed to beam beautifully from through the screening of gray clouds that were fading away like vapor.

Before I asked my doubt, the priest started, still looking towards the sun, "Have you ever experienced, and if not don't hang this in your mind for now; but sudden slits or tearing of clothes?"

The question left me silent and spellbound for seconds, after which he continued, "A bad omen it is," he sighed loud and continued, "It happens as smoothly as a broken flower shrinks overnight; you never know when it happens… A very ill omen… If you ever experience this dark phenomenon…"

"It has—happened once," I said in a low voice after a couple of pauses.

Again, here I am just presenting the happenings or facts of the case.

The priest turned towards me in a moment and said, looking deep into my eyes with extreme caution, "This confirms what I have told."

Seeing my natural uneasiness which I failed to hide, he said, "Always remember, all powerful is the soul within you, much more mighty than any confused spirit wandering in this realm…"

He intended to lead me to our place, but Uncle and Ajay came hastily up to the place where we were. They had an expression of worry.

Seeing that now the time of departure had come, I asked, "Would you come…"

"When the time comes…" He answered even before I posed the question in full.

After concerned and almost paternal know-how, when Uncle was satisfied that I had got a shade under the storm; he exclaimed, "It's strange, —there is horrible news circulating in the town..."

"Horrible news? What horrible news?" I spoke, perplexed.

"The milk supplier has seen something last night when he was returning after delivery. He saw a bulky figure of a man coming out from the woods in the east at night. He naturally couldn't see his face in the darkness with the rainstorm whirling, but still, he followed him alone from a distance. They passed hills and fields. The figure finally stopped in the woods around our house. Then the supplier realized he had come up to our lane. He last saw the figure going into our house..."

"Into our house? From the east? Isn't it the direction in which…?" I was interrupted soon by Uncle.

"Yes; people say that in that place stands the second house of—Shaitaan. But you might not know about him. Leave all this."

"Papa let's go home before it rains again. He is the ghost who is coming to our place at night. Now the whole town believes it!" Ajay said imploringly, giving a slight pull to Uncle's pants.

His legs were trembling because of the winds. I was also left petrified as it was I; who had witnessed these scenes alone—with my own eyes. At that moment, even the look of the very sky, the clouds, and the baron-ness all around seemed to affect all present there.

"We have to return to the house, and all have to be safe. Perhaps it may be another gossip of the superstitious ones of the town. You never know. The milkman himself could be in dizziness in the night when he himself didn't know where he was going in the woods—probably he was lost. People suspect he is a drunkard too..." Uncle said, and I knew he was changing his original stance or sort of maneuvering himself.

"Was Uncle thinking everything as child's play and taking it lightly?", I thought.

We walked back, lifting our legs high in between the tall grass, with Ajay almost clinging to me by my side.

"Now what will happen?" Ajay asked me, but I had no answer.

I looked back at the priest, who was still standing there. I noticed he nodded his head slightly, looking at me, confirming my understanding of what he had told, and I replied with a nod.

"Let's see," I replied to Ajay at length.

We reached our house, and the rest of the day was spent, apparently in a normal way. But everything still looked abnormal to me; perhaps because everyone was trying to behave normally and not behaving naturally.

After the dinner, we sat together for some time in the hall where Uncle told twice the same thing to himself mournfully, "Now it's lost, it's gone..."

"What is lost? What is gone?" I questioned myself whenever Uncle spoke the above words.

Soon Uncle told other incidents that had happened before I had come to this place. He told things like: "Plants are worthless in the garden as they never grew, or if they grow, never survive," and then he continued with another topic, "Ajay had once created such great chaos and tension in the house when we were new; he screamed at our first night here, that someone was standing in one unlit corner of my room and what we saw when the lights were on, was just a hanging coat. It was just a coat hanging on the hook of the wall and due to the shades of the candlelight he thought that a man was standing there!" Uncle laughed at this continuously, which somehow made the little boy embarrassed.

"Uncle," I asked, "how did the milk supplier describe the figure that he had seen in the dark valley?"

"You are stuck on that? Well, I remember he told the person walked slowly and was imbalanced but what I think is that the milkman himself was imbalanced..."

I was silent in thought after hearing this imbalanced walking thing. I thought I had heard this before from somebody else.

"Uncle, can I ask you something? What is that room in the hall's corner? I have always seen it closed..." I asked after some time, as my eyes had detected the previously unnoticed.

"There are many dark unlit rooms in this huge house of ours—when I opened it once, it was kind of trivial, dirty storeroom where old newspapers were stuffed which weren't ours..."

I looked at the room again, which was dark, and I decided in my mind that I would look once there—however trivial it may appear. We stopped for some time and when I got the opportunity I questioned, "Uncle, can I tell you something about my friend?"

"Yes, sure..."

I wasn't sure that the project which I had embarked on by my words, was the correct thing to do, as I knew I was very less experienced and couldn't match my uncle's intelligence in any way—but still, I tried.

"This is a story of the past year. One of our common friends who was fashionable and broad-hearted had gifted this friend of mine her own loveliest dress on her birthday."

"Yes; so?"

"So, this friend of mine accepted the lovely pink frock with which she was gifted, and she was very excited about it—it was really expensive and imported, too. But then the friend who had gifted her dress became ill in some days—the undiagnosed fever kept her on her bed for a week after which she abruptly left the world."

"Oh, that's so sad..." Ajay said.

"So, this friend of mine who had got the gift of the dress was also terribly sad, like me. But after four months she came to my house where we both had decided to meet. She was looking lovely that day, with a strange glamor on her face and the same scent of that dress. Yes, she came wearing the same lovely skirt in remembrance of our friend, and we found nothing uncommon in that."

I could see Uncle's expression changing.

"We spent time, and she went home. The day was very warm and there was not a gray cloud in the sky. But when she went home; news came the following day that she had fallen on the path back to her home because of dizziness. After which she was suffering a terrible fever where her temperature was as high as 104. I visited her immediately because of a fever in that warm weather and that too suddenly had startled me."

"Then?" Ajay asked, leaning forward.

"Then I told her mother about her lovely pink dress and to whom it originally belonged. After which, her mother took the dress away from her immediately. She probably returned it or discarded it. This move startled my friend, but she got a good scolding when she told me that the dress was very much attached to her now. Uncle, you tell me why did Aunty do so? What a lovely dress it was, how well it suited both my friends... a dress that every girl would be happy to own and wear. What auntie did was correct?" I asked, looking deep into the eyes of my uncle.

He was speechless for seconds and the expression in his eyes ran off.

He pressed his forehead with his hands and with the other was feeling the lovely, lined texture of his pant.

“Probably she didn’t like her daughter wearing the cloth of a friend who had passed, in such a painful way. Is this true and what happened to your friend after that? Did she recover?”

“Yes...” I said, looking at my uncle.

“Her mother knows better,” Uncle said, stood, and walked into his room.

He told us to sleep in the hall that night. The night offered a sweet sleep to me, but only after midnight hit. In the starting hours, I laid down on my bed, but my eyes were open; running about the vast, dark hall, which was engulfed by darkness and, at various ends, blackness. The thought which didn’t let me sleep was: “I am missing something.” But I didn’t know what I was missing.

At a moment I was very near to that, but then I kept on thinking and consciously realized in my sleep that I was already asleep. Not much time had passed when suddenly my eyes opened wide. A disturbing echo had caused this awakening. It was vibrating in my ears. It stopped the other moment, but only to rise again. Heavy and just heavy. I recognized it as a horn, a peculiar horn. I sat up on the sofa. Perhaps I could be asleep and in my dreams. Looking at the clock, it was past midnight. I thought and relieved myself, as I would soon be awakening. I rubbed my eyes hard and pinched my cheek. I passed that test and to my dread; it was not a dream. I sat up and looked around. Ajay was fast asleep beside my sofa and apparently, no one else was in the hall. It looked frightful at such an hour. As I reluctantly pulled off the cozy blanket and stood on the floor; a chill ran over my feet, which gave me a shiver. The room was chilly as if ice itself was whirling in the air. I carefully took another step with my trembling feet and the horn echoed again. All my senses weren’t as awake till then and in confused haste, I reached the closed window and opened it.

“Who on earth would drive in this part of the town at such an hour of cold darkness?” my thoughts added to my shiver.

From the large window, nothing could be seen in the countryside's darkness but hints of trees and, of course, the purple sky. Suddenly, among the distant trees in one corner of the vast valleys, there was a strike of yellow light. It was as forceful as a bolt of lightning and disappeared as suddenly as it came into view. The view was left as dark as it was, again. There was certainly a car in that corner of the valley, near the other hill. Probably I knew which car was it, it was certainly the same car that picked Arun up from the lane! That black car, the rioting horn, was the same, and I recognized it. I stared down for minutes and not a single man was seen.

"Probably I am wrong..." I thought and drowsiness pained my forehead—I didn't wish to overtax my brain anymore.

I shut the window, as looking at the valley at this hour was very disturbing. Then walked up to my sofa, involuntarily swaying from side to side. It was as if I fell on it and slept, forgetting everything. In my cozy sleep probably I had smiled like I used to do previously as I could realize that I was asleep very, very well.

"Wake—wake up!" Ajay was shaking my shoulders wildly.

My eyes opened slowly. It was early morning, and the hall was quite illuminated.

"What happened?" I asked Ajay, who stood right next to my sofa.

"There has been an assault in the valley last night! A-a murderous assault."

"What? No…" I stood in amazement.

"Yes! Don't you remember the ghost sightings of the previous night? I said there was a ghost. Oh, I—I am fearing to say..." He was visibly trembling and telling unnecessary words in fear and hurry, "I believe it's the horrible spirit that moves around, who has done this..."

I caught him by his shoulders but failed to stop his shivering.

The memory of my risky lone walk through the lane after dark came to my mind as a first thought and instantly increased my heartbeat.

"Where is uncle?" my second question.

The hall was still and most of the time being completely alone is horrifying itself.

"You remember Rajesh, the friend of Arun?" he said.

"Yes, so?"

"He is the one who has been hit!"

For a moment, it was as if I couldn't understand his words.

"What? How did he come into this scene?" I spoke in shock, not believing him and at the same time knowing he couldn't speak such a piece of misinformation.

To my further questions like, "What was he doing in the woods last night?" Ajay's answer, which came out unclearly from his trembling lips, was: "I don't know."

Worry and an inexplicable nervousness drenched me like the rain. Every incident which had occurred to me started coming to my memory, and I was feeling it and questioning all the existence of supernatural elements in this vast world of us. From my further movements in unsurety, I knew terror had gripped me.

"Tell where we have to go?" I asked after I was fresh and ready.

"Do not panic. We are going to the doctor's chamber. Come, the carriage is standing." Uncle said to us as he came in from the main door, as calm as a man could be.

We sat in the carriage that was driven by a couple of strong brown horses.

"It mustn't take over twenty minutes..." Uncle said.

He was settled on the front seat and didn't speak more, more reserved. The carriage drove fast into the thick fog that floated all over the lonely lane. Ajay was sitting with his head downwards and pressing one of his palms over his eyes, perhaps to escape from the darkness of the carriage and the scene outside. His ways made me feel the striking coldness in the air even more. The lonely black carriage rattled through and through the endless lane. To look outside, vast blocks of empty, muddy fields and the boundless light gray sky could be seen. On the other side, the hills could be viewed, covered with films of mists and rain clouds, till the farthest corner which seemed as the unreachable, heightened realm of heaven. The cool air filled with moisture came in and the silent carriage rolled into darkness. Soon came into view the bleak woods in the farthest corner and a pond whose water was lusterless and still. Not a man was seen all along the road, but the bumpy carriage still carried us on. The sky grew darker and dimmer and so did my frozen imagination, and so my anxiety and so fear grew perhaps heavier than the rain-filled clouds that were gravitating toward our carriage. Only one word was lingering in my mind: spirit. That was the word that I had heard since the morning and came after. It was only a bleak, melancholy thought of fright and tragedy as well. Looking from the back glass was the road which we had followed, its wetness shining blue, appearing as if not men, but fog took human forms and walked there, keeping its undisturbed mysterious gloom and menacing silence as undisturbed as it had been for centuries. Soon, an alarming thunder was heard cracking among the bundles of clouds in the farthest left corner of the sky. The horses sniffed, and the carriage rolled even faster into the middle of nowhere. Suddenly, when I had already clutched my dress at my chest when the grayness was turning indifferent to me, and sighting a dark spirit on the path didn't seem a fancy thought; a terrible noise echoed in my brain. It made my head and heart ring. A heavy, growling sound came into my memory, not to my ears; the same horn of the black car I had seen last night and the same car in which Arun had gone. This car's horn, as heavy as the foghorn of an old lighthouse, disturbed me by its ceaseless motion. It kept on bumping slowly and slowly filling my conscious memory with the last night's scene.

"The black car, it was the same black car with the same horn, and I had seen it last night during the same time within which the assault on Rajesh happened... So, is there any connection?" I thought.

The black car, Arun, the spirit wandering around in the dark, the assault; all these things showed a meaning, leaving me pressurized with thought. Soon, certain houses of the town started coming into view one by one, and within minutes, the foggy veil left the sky. We had, at last, entered the town and people started coming into view. The horse carriage stopped and we, one by one, stepped down.

"Mr. Rajesh has been sent to the city just half an hour ago. You know we do not have facilities here right now." The doctor said to us as we were in the doctor's chamber.

Some people were still around the chamber, showing that a crowd had perhaps gathered there before.

"Is-is anything that serious?" I asked the doctor as he gave me a look.

"No, nothing to be that worried about…" he said to me. "I just wanted to have a check of any spine injury. The hit was from the front, and he perhaps fell by his back. But may I ask, do you know Rajesh?" The doctor asked me, he had probably remembered me.

"Yes not exactly but…" I replied when I got interrupted by my uncle.

"Yes, I know him; we came here to meet him but doctor, now that he's not here, can you please tell me about what happened?"

"Mr. Vijay, I do not know properly, but he was brought to my chamber early morning by a passer-by who found him lying down unconscious in the middle of the fields around the hill." The doctor said, sitting on his chair and putting the pipe between his teeth.

"That's the place where the car was!" I thought but didn't speak.

"A strange case it is. He had been pushed into the darkness of the foggy night, probably suddenly and rather aggressively, but the biggest question is, what was he doing there?" The doctor stopped and smoked out into the air and made a gesture for Uncle to sit.

"Yes! The biggest question is, what was the young fellow doing at night in a place where people fear going in the day?" Uncle said as he sat in another chair.

"People are saying that there was an evil spirit sighted in that area in previous days…" the doctor said in a low voice, crossing one of his legs over the other.

"People say that the place around there is haunted by an evil spirit, but they do not know who it is…" he continued as he kept on looking at his table.

"Do you—" Uncle asked, looking deep into the eyes of the doctor "also believe in such things doctor?" anxious and tensed was his very speech.

"I have been a doctor for twenty-five years, but I have been hearing such stories for nearly half a century…" The doctor said, "I shouldn't tell that it is a ghost but, in my mind, I pray it is not. But I don't think I believe in ghosts."

Uncle was taken aback for a moment.

"The question is also that who was the other one who dared to be there? We haven't heard of any wild animals there too." The doctor said.

"Yes, who can tell what has happened in the darkness," Uncle said.

"Can we return? I am not feeling quite good." Ajay addressed my uncle slowly, his childish expression showed uneasiness.

So was my condition.

"If it is not a spirit, then it is probably something else and maybe the young chap was purposely involved in it."

"What can it be? Doctor?" Uncle asked.

"What can it be? Another case of smuggling or some burglar group. Rajesh seemed an intelligent and noble-looking man though…"

The thought of Rajesh being involved in any criminal camp and roaming about for mysterious purposes at night was unbelievable to me. I don't know why, but it grieved me.

"When will he be well, doctor?" I asked again.

He stopped and looked at me. "If there's no back injury; then he will be fine; do not worry so much. He looks strong."

"No money was stolen from his pockets, though he carried a lot; God knows from where he got so much of it." the doctor said.

"This is becoming even stranger…. It means that the attacker didn't want money." Uncle said.

"What happened at night? We do not know; the authorities are behind it." The doctor said, looking at Ajay.

"Police?" it came out of my mouth.

A thought came over me about Arun, puzzled I was as it is.

"A couple of men from the city came and had a long talk with him in the chamber and then they went with him in the ambulance." The doctor said.

"But who were they?" I asked but was interrupted by my little cousin.

"Those valleys, those trees, the hills are all very scary and very otherworldly at night…." Ajay said and implored once again to return to our place.

"Yes… yes, come child... Do not worry dear boy." Uncle said.

I couldn't ask what I wanted to, as I couldn't plan my questions into an appropriate sentence at that moment.

Uncle stood up.

"Mr. Vijay; stay careful." The doctor said in a confident whisper to Uncle while we were leaving.

One's house seems comfortable in a time of fear, but to me, the town, though likely the most thinly populated one, looked safer to me than those mystical, foggy hills where our building was.

As all of us came out, the weather and the sky were one which could lift anyone's spirit. The sun shined brightly, and footsteps of people and horses could be heard on the wet street on which the sunlight glazed. The sky was blue in one corner and even more adorable in the far-left corner where a shy pinkish tint was spreading. A fresh flowery aroma was floating in the air and we walked around for some time.

"We probably have to walk up to the near station. We will have a carriage there. Come along." Uncle said.

He said not a word more, exhausted in deep thought. One fact that was alarming about my uncle was his unusual silence and his tendency suddenly getting to speak words in the native language—mostly to himself; words which were incomplete as far as I believe. I remember that when I had come to the place, he never spoke in the native language in this unorderly, inexplicable, and chaotic way.

But Ajay looked charming again, jumping over the tiny pits on the road that had gotten filled with rainwater; such is the nature of kids.

"Tell me," Ajay asked me, "Is Rajesh a friend of yours too?"

"Such innocent questions—Is he not a friend of yours?"

"Yes, you can say so, but for me, he is a normal friend. I didn't get my answer yet." He asked me again and suddenly a sort of fun appeared on his face.

"Okay, leave this." He said after my gentle denial reply, "What did the priest say to you?"

"He said that he saw someone with us, something following us; a dark, tall figure, as translucent as mist. Many things more…" I stopped before saying any more.

Ajay's expression had already run off, and I realized saying this wasn't necessary.

"Oh—Oh, I was just making fun… forget; look, there is such a funny horse," I spoke, instantly realizing my mistake.

"Someone's following us?" He asked in a voice in which I sensed a slim tremble.

"Oh, I was just making fun… I am sorry. I was joking with you; did you not get it?" I replied.

He didn't speak anymore and looked behind his back several times while we walked along.

We walked up to the station, after which we returned to our place with no new adventure on the same path. On the way, in the carriage sat an unknown gentleman in a sharing, who, by all ways was a gossiper. He kept on talking in a way about rather irrelevant issues, to which no one replied, but only benefit; the haunting silence couldn't grip any of us. I remember my uncle showed an expression of irritation during his talk, but I understood by his words that he was a knowledgeable man; and one thing which he told highly intrigued me. He talked of a strange smuggling scandal relating to locally made, banned liquor across the deserted valleys. On further asking, he said that these were a series of scandals that happened, leading to murders and other crimes; all of it had happened a year ago and had completely terrorized the town. I wanted to ask further about this chain of criminal cases but somehow didn't.

When we were down from the carriage, when we walked over the solitary lane, when we walked across the muddy garden around our house; my intrigue about this scandal was heightened to incredible heights. Such that I decided at the door of our place that I would try to find more of it.

Then when I sat after some time of rest after our shaky carriage ride; my eyes ran across to the closed room in the hall's corner that was wrapped in a thick dark veil. I was alone in the hall and walked towards it. Uncle had earlier told me that there were old papers or something in there, and I wanted exactly that; old newspapers is what I mean. The door was jammed, probably not opened for years, and I pushed it with force. It suddenly opened, and I fell as if I was thrown into it.

"I will need a candle flame for this." I thought.

11

I was certainly back in the room with a candle in my hand. But I feared to enter. I must admit; a fear of the unknown, perhaps it was. However, I entered it, feeling the thick dust layer that lay on the floor of the room, which probably wasn't lighted or opened for such a long time.

I walked into it; a strange smell was in the air.

"I got it!" came out of my mouth as a whisper when I saw bundles of old newspapers dumped in the right corner of the room, against the wall.

After shutting the door behind me, I dragged the heavy bundle to the center of the room where I had kept the candle. The strange smell kept on floating and was like affecting my nerve with a unique uneasiness. I untied the bundle and separated the various newspapers; fantastically enough, they were dated years back, all recording the incidents that took place around the town even before my birth. I looked over the rotten papers under the yellow tinge. Luckily, there were papers from the previous year on the top, which probably suggested that no one had bought papers in the house since.

One headline read: "Another case of missing in the valley" and this was dated 17th August.

I rubbed my right ear with my fingers.

The next headline read, "Another death in the valley, a returning guard" This was dated 21st August.

I brushed off the hair that fell on my other ear and then shook it slightly.

Then I turned to some other newspapers, randomly.

"Town shook by nonstop 'night crimes' in the valley"- dated 15th September.

I ran my eyes across the article. I put both my palms over both my ears and rubbed them, ignoring why.

30th September: "Police suspect Smuggling"

17th October: "Smuggling group link from town"

"Who's there?" turned back instantly.

My heart was beating very hard, and I could hear only my loud breaths. I ran my eyes across the darkness behind me, but there was no one. I calmed down my breath. Sighs that came from behind me were unsettling. They were continuous but still, my eyes showed me no one there and how could anyone be there? I turned back to the newspapers.

I was suddenly feeling sickly, and it seemed that suddenly the room was colder than ever.

"Smuggling of banned, hazardous liquor"—dated 22nd October.

I was breathing even harder and a strong feeling of being watched seized me along with the sudden coldness, but I didn't look back and kept scrutinizing the newspapers. The winds might be coming from some corner of any broken window, I thought as the low and disturbing sighs continued.

I lifted this newspaper high and read the headline:

13th November: "Shaitaan suspected but denies involvement in liquor smuggling"

A strange uneasiness was in my chest, which may be called cold nervousness or excitement because I was getting nearer to it.

"The whole town against Shaitaan"—a line from an article- dated 21st November.

"What is this going on?" I uttered as still the whole incidents were not understandable, but there was certainly a connection between the murders at the night in the valley, the scandal, and… Shaitaan.

The candle flame got extinguished suddenly. Luckily, I got hold of the matchstick and relit it. Under the fresh flame, I caught hold of newspapers from previous dates within the same year.

19th August: "Town shows gratitude as Shaitaan funds for hospital"

29th August: "Shaitaan to employ a hundred youngsters in town"

These two headlines shocked me a bit. "Was Shaitaan doing all this to hide something and improve his public image?" I thought.

I suddenly turned back again as I was very startled due to the reason that the candle tongue was extinguished again.

"Is this someone trying to communicate? Certainly not… These sighs are just the air playing tricks," I said to myself, though it was not a conviction.

"God… am I shaking?".

I looked about me unreasonably, took an audible breath, and, after lighting the candle for the third time, continued with the papers.

I turned to many newspapers that had trivial information, but afterward, one headline intrigued me very much. I almost jumped.

"Shaitaan and Neelnath join for a business deal"- dated 3rd September.

These two names I knew and two sinister names in one line struck me, and I was stunned by the fact that Shaitaan and Neelnath had had some kind of connection.

"But what was the deal about?" I thought.

I stopped for a second as something came to my mind while I fixed my eyes on the red candle flame.

"Probably there is some connection between the murders in the valley and this deal, but what is it exactly? It is probably possible that Shaitaan had the newspapers of the town under his control…" I thought.

Noises were echoing in the room, which suggested raindrops beating against our house, shaking that room too. I looked at the papers again. Suddenly there was a sharp silver lighting in the sky, glazing up the room, which somehow got reflected and pierced into my eyes like an arrow. It was probably the glass that reflected the sudden shine, but by this I got leaned back, supporting my body with my hand. I pressed my eyes with my palm in reaction to the pain caused deep in my eyes. The rolling thunder noise followed.

I couldn't see anything but bright silver light, even under closed eyes like a blind rippling sensation. I kept my eyes covered for seconds, after which I painfully opened them though blinking wildly. In these moments of white vision, it was a face. It started to take form in my vision at a distance. Among the first few things that were bleakly visible to me was another gate, and a wretched face that had almost taken its form. Yes, it was the same face-the face in Shaitan's painting. It was clear. For a moment, when my eyes were almost shut, it looked like a real man stood there in the room's corner. A chill ran down my spine and I stood up to walk out. I rubbed my eyes vigorously and stood motionless, though my feet were trembling. I wanted to go out, but at the same time, I was reluctant. But the apparition was as momentary as the pain and loss of vision. Though my eyes were watery after the incident, I could see as normal. The gate at the end was probably again hidden in the darkness and I raised the candle high to confirm another room in there, which was strangely calling. I stood up, leaving the newspapers, and walked towards that door.

Suddenly, amidst the cracking of another thunder, the room's main door behind me opened in a jerk.

"Who-who's there?" a gibbering voice echoed in the room.

I turned back.

"You... you stupefied me..." I replied to Ajay, who had opened the gate.

"I-I'll not come in, but you have to come out..."

"How many hours have passed?" I asked.

"Evening has turned in and—and first you please come out..." he raised his head and stretched over his toes, to peep.

"Wait..." I called out as I walked over the newspapers and a hundred trivial things.

Finally, I came out of that room and asked after sighing, "What's the matter?"

The noise of raindrops was still audible, and a couple of yellow bulbs were on.

"Father is nowhere to be seen," Ajay said, and a shiver ran over him.

"What...?"

"Yes, I have been finding you and him for hours and I thought I was completely alone… he should be in the house because it is terrible weather out."

This clicked in my mind, and I thought just the opposite. I swiftly mounted the stairs and Ajay came along, sliding his palm over the railing. The open windows and doors were banging wildly as we reached the second floor, and I peered down from the window of our bedroom.

The gray-black fog was like a veil over the entire sky, making visibility slim, and showers of rain noisily danced with the winds like a spray. It was too wild and rough for a mortal. The hills of the far weren't seen anymore and under those conditions, two men could be seen just at the fence of our garden—not very far from basic visibility.

"Don't open the window—I would freeze," Ajay called from the back.

"Who-who's there..." I pointed at the otherwise deserted site.

Both the men were standing facing each other, wearing black jackets or something of that sort, bleakly visible, and apparently talking. They were gripping the fence and their clothes were visible in the direction of the gusts, though the rain had drenched them completely and, in the mists, they looked like phantoms. They didn't move, none of them had an umbrella. One was a rather big man and the other, who was shorter, who was swaying more and had his other palm over his head, was Uncle, though I wasn't completely sure. The upper part of the other man wasn't visible due to his height and the obstruction of the swaying dead tree, but he looked probably calmer and more composed.

"Who are they?" Ajay cried.

"How can I know? But the right one… is he not Uncle Vijay?"

"Why is he out there and who is with him?" Ajay jabbered again.

"Look!" I spoke.

Suddenly the unknown distant figure raised his opposite hand in which I discovered he was carrying a-a bottle. He pushed it in front of Uncle. The figure which I assumed Uncle looked reluctant, slightly gestured in denial but the other one held the bottle almost to Uncle's chest, and then finally Uncle grabbed it. They talked more, and the weather was wilder.

After passing a few minutes, Uncle headed back to the house and the big impression walked in the other side. They both didn't forget to have a handshake—and I mean a good one. Soon there was the noise of opening the main door of our house and we knew Uncle was in once again.

"What is this going on?" Ajay spoke, annoyed.

"Don't ask, just wait and watch...."

We peeped down through the staircase's railing bars, watching Uncle coming in with the strange glass bottle in his hand, looking at it with extreme care for a minute, and then going into his room.

Ajay said the same thing which was revolving in my mind "Probably the other man could be Mr. Candy... the way he walked made me feel so and bedsides this no one has ever come here to meet father..."

"Yes, I assume so too. But that bottle... and what can be so important that they were discussing?"

I knew what the bottle contained.... I had heard them talking about liquor previously.

"Mr. Candy is always laughing... Do you think he is up to something?" Ajay asked.

"You don't know who he is." I turned back.

"Who is he? Is Mr. Candy, whom we call old uncle too? Not Mr. Candy and somebody else?"

"How can I explain when I myself do not know properly about what I am getting nearer to?" I told him or probably to myself, looking at the other side.

A strange anxiety and confusion were on our faces as we stood there with the damp smell in the cold air and radiating yellowness of the hall. The thunder growling followed.

After moments of silence, I told Ajay, "You know; I know many truths that you can't even think of, but the point is I am not sure about them..."

"Why? What's that?"

"Don't you think something is wrong with Rajesh wandering at midnight on the path to our home? Have you not heard the loud car horns on the same night? The stranger who tried to mount up to my bedroom twice, yes, this happened too... And of all, uncle, and Mr. Candy..."

His expression suggested he couldn't assemble all these facts at the moment.

"What of it? This is confusing…"

"I don't know about the ghost, but something is horribly wrong…." And then I asked,

"Do you want to come to that room where I was?"

My little cousin denied it in fear, saying that he had read of negative energies dwelling in such closed, unlit rooms.

I felt a strange heaviness all over my body and my weakness that was growing day by day became more unbearable as if I had lost all my strength—but on the outside, I was as fine as I could be.

"Wait, I too have something to tell which you do not know…" he called from behind as I held the doorknob.

"You know why I called you? I was reading a book on the dining table and suddenly when my eyes ran to the ceiling and then turned to the second floor, for a moment I saw someone slipping into the other room…. I thought it was you, but when I went to the second floor and then again to the first, I couldn't find anyone in the entire house…"

I stood in front of him, listening and awestruck.

"I-I… think that someone is up there."

"In the room which is generally closed? Oh, I had seen Uncle going there one night…"

"But Father is down in his room!"

I looked up to the high and pale ceiling and then around the dark and dim second floor. It was noiseless up there. We both reluctantly walked up the stairs to find out who was hiding there beyond the shades. Ajay switched the bulb swiftly and, though lighted, no one was in that passage till the end. The second room was at the end where much yellow light didn't reach. I looked there for seconds and then stepped slowly and slowly until I was at the door. A sensation was in my bosom, which continuously resisted me by opening the jammed doorknob. I held it and discovered that it was loose, and the lock was smashed. I breathed out and looked at Ajay, who stood at a distance looking at the door with frightened wide eyes, his chest visibly moving up and down. I shut my eyes and pushed the door open. Thunder grumbled, followed by a creak of the heavy door which was pushed back. Only darkness was there. We waited for some time and when no one came out; I took my first steps into it. I searched for the switchboard on the wall and lit it. Apart from my palm, which was almost black because of the dusty wall, the first sighting was a medium-sized room.

"See! There is no one…" I looked at Ajay.

He came nearer and looked in. "B-But then I-I saw someone going in and closing the door behind."

"But no one is here…. Oh, again this smell of rotting and dampness…" I went more into it and Ajay followed, walking feebly.

The room looked like it had been long used as a storeroom suggested by some furniture that was covered by white sheets. The walls and the floor were covered with dust and cobwebs were easy to sight.

"I don't know why, but this room looks like I have seen it somewhere, but…" Ajay uttered as he looked about.

Apart from the fact that there was not a single window in the room, On the left wall something peculiar struck me. A big rectangular shape was seen as separated from dust that was all over the wall. It was a medium-sized impression as if something was over the wall at the spot for a long time. The boundaries that separated the dust were clear and at the top, as my instincts came true; there were two nails into the wall. Clearly, it was a portrait or a frame that might have hung there. I contemplated the impression for some time, and I feel I knew what was there; exactly. While I looked at it, the silence was heightened so much that I turned back to find Ajay. He was standing there, right behind me, but his eyes were closed, his chin high and arms lose at the sides as if he was mulling over something. He remained there for a minute and then I couldn't wait anymore.

"What happened?" I shook his shoulders. "What are you doing right now?"

"I-I am remembering something…" he said, pressing his eyes tighter.

"This room, these white sheets, all are revolving in my head as if I have been to this place sometime…. B-But I cannot remember."

"Try! What is it?"

"Something else is also coming to mind... Ahh... I can't remember." He became quite impatient.

"Okay... leave open your eyes! Open your eyes!" I shouted.

I shook him again after which he screamed loud: "I remember! I remember!"

"What?"

"I had seen the ghost of Shaitaan over here... the... his face is coming to my mind constantly," He opened his eyes and looked about him in a startled way.

"You saw Shaitaan first in this place? But you said that you had never been to this room..."

"Yes. I have never been here, it seems..." I looked deep into his eyes over his confusing statements. "I mean... I don't remember coming here. That's all." He corrected and then we finally went out.

While walking down the stairs, one incident of the previous night occurring at that place reminded me I had seen my uncle going into that room, I had heard his heavy footsteps in the room and then he had come back to my room with a look of deep anxiety asking: "Had anybody come to our house while I wasn't there?" In continuation of this incident, he uttered words like, "As it is, all is lost now...".

All these things clicked in my mind as I walked.

"Is it something related to the portrait which I have got under my bed?" I thought and there was scope to think more, but as I landed on the last step of the stairs, came a terrifying noise, as if the sky itself was ripped in two.

"What kind of thunder is that?" Ajay turned to me with a jerk.

"Not thunder. That seems like breaking of glass..." I replied in the same startled tone.

The noise had probably come from outside and was distinct even after the winds and the rain. We came into the garden.

"Something's there!" He pointed towards a big stone.

Tiny puddles had been created around that stone filled with a liquid that didn't look like rainwater with the color of reddish brown.

Walking under the showers and over the mud struggling with the puddles, we walked to that stone where the reason for the noise was. We stared at the big pieces of glass and then noticed that tiny pieces, too, were scattered all around the rock.

"Stay there!" I said as I moved forward carefully and picked up one of the bigger pieces.

Rainwater slid over the piece, washing it.

"What's it? Well, be careful with the glass..." he called from the back.

"Nothing's written on it..." I called back as I carefully looked at it. "Looks like a glass bottle which had been smashed here..." I said as I walked back with the piece in my hand.

"This glass smells..." Ajay said as he kept the piece on the table after we had come in and changed our wet clothes.

"I feel I know what it is.... It seems the same bottle which Mr. Candy gave to Uncle—and which he carried back to the house."

"Oh, yes!" He stood up. "I remember."

Certainly, it was a bottle of liquor and the smell of the liquid in the puddles confirmed the fact.

"But why has Mr. Candy given this to Papa and why has he smashed it down from his room's window?" Ajay asked.

I breathed in and said, "Uncle didn't drink it at last..."

I continued, "He didn't drink the contents of the bottle exactly as I was assuming.... And probably to avoid an uncontrollable urge of drinking the alcoholic liquid which this bottle contained, he threw it out of his window in a jerk...."

"What are you thinking?" Ajay asked as he looked deep into my eyes after minutes of silence.

"Isn't it true that Shaitaan was also a drinker in his last days? In his last days?" I said, looking at Ajay.

12

I stood up, turned away in a jerk, and swiftly walked towards the room which contained the papers.

"What am I supposed to do?" Ajay called from behind.

"Study your textbooks, you'll soon have to go to school again and that's my word..." I called as I closed the door behind me.

I lit the candle again, sat on the floor, and here I was looking into the yellow papers again.

"Something... Something is yet to be found..." I must have murmured.

I knew I had left on the verge of discovering something, lastly; I had left at the point where there was some deal between Shaitaan and Neelnath—the dead criminal as we all know or believe and drawing a linkage between this and the crimes in the valleys seemed natural to me too. Shaitaan must have been quite a man in this town, and his deals, especially this one must have something to do with the town, I supposed as the newspapers were filled with such headlines but the most unfortunate part of it as we all know are in case of many newspaper articles; the information in was trivial and mostly stories that weren't worth remembering.

The most stunning and jaw-dropping one was the headline that hit me first...

29th November: "Deal canceled and Neelnath in Police custody"

I took a deep breath in, sighed, stopped, and pondered, looking at the other side as this statement had raised many questions.

Intrigued, I was, though, thinking this headline as the end of the story, but the other one came as a thunderbolt...

31st November: "Neelnath breaks out! Town in Fear!"

The answer to the question that why Neelnath was arrested; in the first place would only be in the deal and what was it related to. Searching for the details of the actual deal in the newspapers was worthless—but this increased my intrigue even more. Yes, about the actual contents of the deal.

2nd December: "Authorities still in search of Neelnath"

"If Neelnath was in jail and then he fled from there, why wasn't Shaitaan in jail if there was something sinister with this big deal? And Shaitaan had denied any hand in the crimes, so if we draw a parallel between both, the chances are high that Shaitaan had halted the deal. But what was in it? Why?" I sat thinking. I wanted to see the deal at any cost, I thought, but laughed at the other moment, as this wasn't possible.

Suddenly I almost leaped towards the candle flame, guarding it by my hand and it got saved, fortunately; though its size had by this time almost reduced to the size of a thumb. A tiny drop from my eye fell on the newspaper and when I closed them together, I knew they were watery, and no sooner, there was a kind of weakness which I felt. I slightly stretched my legs and sat back with my hand smoothing my hair.

"It must have been a long time here..." I thought and suddenly a strange feeling came over me.

I could no longer sit straight. I felt as if I should lie down just at the moment, yes, on that dusty floor; my hand dropped from my forehead, and I had to support my body with my arms. Came after this was a series of deep breaths and sighs, which continued till I felt everything draining out of me. I wanted to stand, but when I couldn't, I was left in a state of anxiety. I remembered I was all alone in that room. No one other than Ajay knew I was there and suddenly I imagined the chances of being trapped in there for the entire night. I didn't care for the time till now. Perhaps it would be an hour of me being in this room; and with this thought, I raised my arm to look at my wristwatch.

"It's dark," I thought and paralleled my arm with the candle; and the time was a quarter past twelve.

Stupefied; I started tapping my wristwatch and shaking my arm in jerks and now, the hour hand turned to one and then to three, and then both the arms of my wristwatch hung loosely dead as arms of a broken magnetic compass; further shaking was worthless. A chill ran through my whole back following this phenomenon, as a sudden current and I felt feverishly cold from inside; such was the intensity that I had to clutch my shoulders to control the shivering of my nerves. I still couldn't stand but only looked at the candle flame. If the last time shown on my watch was correct, then not only uncle, Ajay, but the whole town would be asleep, and what if I couldn't make it to the door somehow?

Adding to the sudden soak of energy, my emotions became chaotic. I felt sad, and sully; all sensations that were perfectly new to my nature, and being as if my mood was not mine but some stranger's, and the only emotion that I felt known of was that I wanted to cry loud.

"Where am I? What is this room? Who's was it?" a strange question emerged in my mind.

On turning back, I could just see the hint of the massive door that was closed behind me at a distance.

I sniffed and then sneezed; there was a smell in the air. Something like burning paper, or a cigar, or maybe something… it was uneasy and bizarre, going to my forehead. No, it was not the smell of the burning candle; I was sure it wasn't as I took a deep breath and sneezed out again.

"Probably someone is burning something; maybe Ajay or the house staff is burning another set of uncle's papers!" and by this hopeful thought of having another human presence around me, I stood up on my shivering feet at last.

"Yes!" I thought and after picking up the candle, moved forward, taking large steps.

I was walking to the perpetually dark ends of the room. Cobwebs were hanging high with just a candle in my hand. Soon my steps weren't large anymore. Finally, I stopped in the middle of the large room and called out in strange security, "Is… anybody there?".

I saw someone standing, leaning with his back over the other door, which had recently made a noise of opening and closing; probably this person who was causing the bonfire outside had come into this storeroom from the other gate and with this, I walked towards it. I came very near when I almost sunk into the floor with fear as I realized it was still raining outside, and no bonfire could be made. I was till this time very far from the gate and even if I would run back, I wouldn't reach it. No one stood there, nothing leaned against the other door; absolutely nothing.

I kept the candle down as I couldn't handle it anymore; a cold sensation was spreading through my back nerves. I turned left, for there was a small window, but it was locked too.

I had always pondered about the observation that how, in most cases, people just turn back miraculously, when they are constantly being looked at from behind; probably this is what we call sixth sense or instinct, but now I; was feeling it. I gradually realized that there was this uncanny, dominating feeling of being eyed constantly, as if someone was over my head, sitting somewhere over the shelves; my childish imagination reached to suggesting me not a way out but that the room could be the place where Shaitaan had his enemies killed; but this notion was proved to be wrong. I comforted myself, saying to myself that I was completely alone in this room, turned, and took my first step towards the candle.

"Ah..." I cried loud in horror as I tripped over something and landed on the floor. Nothing more came through my mouth, and I thought I had fainted.

There was a dangerous wooden noise that echoed in the room following my cry and followed by an even harsh thunder setting the entire floor through vibration. The rain's noise followed and as I could still hear it, I knew I hadn't fainted. I had got hurt but a little and after taking the support of a doorknob; I stood up. Wait; a doorknob it was, which means that there was a door and as I held the knob; the door was opened slightly after my fall over it. I lifted the candle again and with the first contact between my finger; the door opened wide. A creak followed. Another room was there and in the profound darkness, I couldn't figure out anything in there. Shivering in the same manner, I had no other option than to fulfill my wild desire to enter this unknown room—I thought it was the best thing to do.

The noise of dropping water vibrated in the room, coming to my ears distinguishably. Thinking there couldn't be a source of light in this room; not opened for years by any man, I entered cutting through the heavy dark veil, pressing my chest with one hand and holding the candle with the other. And suddenly something tremendously unnerving happened.

When I was just in the room, it lit up suddenly as fire. I turned back immediately, and the unknown light was gone. I kept on breathing, but it was as if I had a block in my chest and soon the room lit up again, followed by darkness again. It was a bulb hanging at one end, which was the author of this strange event; though I was left utterly shocked, I reasoned that this might be because of the switch left on a long time back—leaving fire in this bulb intact-unnoticed.

"This looks like an abandoned study room!" I thought, seeing the almirah, shelves, and the old table out there, all casting mighty shadows after intervals of darkness. After settling the candle on the desk, I went up to the almirah. Probably it was a hope that I shouldn't lose this opportunity to find more facts. I started to pull the almirah that was there feverishly. In one word, it was jammed; a piece of a museum, it was, surely. The dust and the odor made breathing difficult and uneasy, though my terror was rounding, subsided by curiosity taking over; the uncanny sense of being watched gripped my ringing heart. At last, I pressed my head against the small upper door of the wooden structure; succumbing to fatigue and despair, realizing that pulling wouldn't be of any help when the breakthrough happened. It opened not form pulling but from pushing the other way into it. Too stupefied to question its design, I pushed it even into and with my candle peeped in. A heavy black thing fell over me as soon as I looked and I reacted in overwhelmed fright, turning it off over me to the floor. I sighed heavily in relief when I saw it was nothing else than a black leathered bag. I lifted the dusty thing, inverted it, and let all its trivial contents fall over the table. A heap of papers came out of it, and I inspected them reluctantly as they had nothing uncommon than the common paperwork at offices, still wondering about on who's chair and table was I sitting; I came over to this extraordinarily large and differently textured lot of paper. I understood nothing written there but was sure it was not just a paper but a document, as what was typed was in serials. I soon realized that there were several other papers with the same dimensions in the lot and when I arranged them in order, what came was this: a deal it was. What was written in bullets and numbers were the terms and conditions of the deal and my heart must have stopped for a moment when I understood what it was; though partly. I turned my head to the candle flame which was dancing; and looked about me in a way of not understanding a thing—so shocked I was. At the end of the last page, two distinguished and large signatures were visible, and after it came blankness and void. For clarification, under the signatures, the names were typed, and these were the names of SHAITAAN and NEELNATH.

"This, this is the very deal!" I thought and now I didn't want to call these papers trivial.

Nothing uncommon was in Shaitaan's signature—bad handwriting, it was for sure. But what captured my attention was the "N" in the signature of Neelnath; the N's head was turned right as a straight line, like a long square root roofing the other seven alphabets of his name.

My breaths were occasionally disturbing the candle flame, the air still smelled heavy and suddenly I halted looking into the yellow sheets.

"Did I hear something?" I asked myself.

It was a long whisper, "Yes…" that came out of my mouth as an answer. I drew in a large one and held my breath to hear this something more profoundly. It sounded like footsteps walking around, as an invigilator walks around the examinee—very low yet audible. Not a word came out of my mouth as if the movement of someone around me was accepted indifferently by my brain—but still not by my heart and I wished I hadn't entered this room. By this time, I had understood that I was in the very room that Shaitaan had been using before his death as his office, the room had been left unnoticed by any of the residents of the place probably due to its location and now I had in my hand the very partnership papers which had stirred such cyclones in the town.

"Oh, god!" I wondered "Why can't I understand this!" forgetting everything that would terrify a normal person in such situations.

A sudden bursting sound behind me shook all my spirits, making me realize that the bleak bulb had fused off, leaving me to the mercy of the tiny candle tongue which was the only thing visible. In a panic about where I could go, and the cold gripping me by my very throat, I stood up with my eyes open wide than ever; staring at the white wall before me and a hundred disturbing and fierce sighs bombed my ears—I had never even thought of all this. A dominating feeling came over me that I was standing in front of someone and on turning back I would see it. I don't quite remember what I saw that night which proves its intensiveness and here I turned my head to the left—something moved swiftly like a black flash followed by a shot-like noise over the wooden shelves behind me. In a tremendous fear of nightmare, I ran and ran blindly until I bumped into something and fell by my chest-out of my senses completely.

The noise of water dropping grew even more intense and alarming as I slowly gained my lost senses, realizing that something liquid was sweeping into my mouth, eyes, and nose. I spitted out as I stood, my feet deeper into the mud, my face and body being washed by fountains of rainwater that whirled around me—I was finally out. A gate was swaying behind me as I looked back, and this was the very gate against which I bumped and landed on the garden ground. I sighed—my breaths were now normalizing and now I walked under the stormy sky, in the unmanned muddy garden, up to the gate of our mighty house, having no strength for thought.

I reached the room door, quite breathless.

"Oh! You are wet all over..." Ajay said in a startled way, as he stood on his bed itself.

Strengthless to speak, I did the needful, and after minutes of rigorous wiping, cleaning, and then changing into my nightdress, I fell on the bed, spiritless. My mind was still troubled with thoughts racing, with the speed of the terrible winds outside and gradually my eyes closed down before the amazed face of my brother who still stood on his bed, resigning from his dreams and looking at me like he could see my nightmares.

13

Time slipped at a strange speed, subtly, and the old, gray, red evening was drawing nearer-four thirty it was by the clock, and I was sitting by my bedroom's window; simply sitting with Ajay near me scribbling things in his notebook. What a wuthering evening it was, blasts of cool air came in, flushing my face wonderfully and my eyes were stuck to the most distant ends of the terrain where a mysterious veil of mist floated in the darkness of woods and the all-silent hills, large tracts of unmanned lands stood still sharing their solitary and suspenseful nature when I saw someone—some traveler walking in between the distant trees. I stood up and peered down with an unknown nervousness. Who was he?

I turned to Ajay, perhaps to ask him too, to have a look outside, but to my surprise, he was not there, not anywhere in the room. When I turned my eye again to the landscape, the walker was to be seen; in such a small interval he had walked a distance and was now entering our house's main door; unlocking the latches. The next moment, I heard at least ten knocks at the mighty wooden door echoing in our house. I rushed down—no one was seen in the hall too, so I was the one who opened the door after three more hurried knocks which had followed.

It was Rajesh at the door and though his extraordinarily rapid recovery ringed my rationality, his stunning appearance, the fresh shine in his eyes, his subtle smile, and the intelligence of his look radiated such confidence, such elegance that it dominated all rising questions—as if he was expected already; filling me with a strange excitement to see him again. It was also no time to ponder over his attire, formal and quite uncommon, though it was.

The next moment we had walked quite a distance, he was walking swiftly with his hands in his pockets, and I was quite behind him as I didn't leave my ways of walking calmly while observing around the lonely vicinity—pure, washed, and misty. In no time, we had crossed the long lane and now we headed towards the wooded regions of the valley. The lane was bleak as before and I was astonished to see more streetlamps than ever as if I was in the city; but it was no difference to the grayness because all of them spread dim yellow lights, flickering and dancing with the winds. A chilling, rather unsettling breeze slid through the moss-covered trees such that I was forced to look at the sky. The sun was no longer to be seen. Pale black and gray clouds had flooded the sky. More icy gusts followed, freezing my legs, and when I lowered my vision—I could see everything about me enveloped in a strange shadowy shade of blue. The tall grasses looked nothing but black and so looked the far sights of the woods with a screening of silvery mists that mysteriously floated as if engulfing the whole of the woods. Even though I had hastened my steps from the normal relaxation as the darkness grew behind me but still, I failed to match Rajesh's speed, who was considerably in front, and he didn't once turn back. The odor of wet soil and rain floated heavily in the air and thought the dense old woods and the bleak visibility were unsettling, my nerves were rather set in a strange excitement as if "something" was going to happen. As we rushed even faster, the sky growled, and the uneven terrain rumbled, and it was ultimately followed by drizzles.

Now any other corner of the woods wasn't visible. No sooner there was a silvery blaze in the sky which momentarily lighted the whole area and the soft drizzles turned into heavy, cold drops. The visibility turned into blindness, and I was shivering to my bone, but still, I continued as if I was alone. Perhaps Rajesh was in front of me or beside me or behind me, I thought and tore through the fog and rain more swiftly and more dangerously.

Finally, when the showers had stopped and visibility normalized, I opened my eyes and after shaking my wet hair; I looked about me. All I saw was swaying grass around me and above me, the dark sky, and not a single human being. Where was Rajesh? a question arose in my mind, but my washed eyes again confirmed the fact, heightening my anxiety; that I was completely alone in the middle of nowhere.

I walked all alone through the infinite grasslands, with an increasingly beating heart, leaving behind a couple of bare trees as the last signs of the misty woods. I didn't know the way back; I didn't know the way front and in such a situation; I continued my walk.

The open sky above me was still ashy as if the rain had just stopped for me and the whirling breezes embraced me from time to time, keeping my spirits burdenless and drying up my rain-drenched self until I had reached a strange spot—a sort of garden. Yes, a garden in the middle of nowhere it was guarded by an incomplete encircling of brick walls which were covered heavily by moss and creepers. A smell of fresh flowers floated in the air and intrigued as I was, I followed, took a couple of twists and turns according to the way, and reached a place that couldn't be called a perfect garden but yet a wonderful one with bushes and pink flowers. Though it didn't look quite maintained the variety of flowers didn't let it lose its charm and I could even clearly see drops of recent rain dropping slowly from the branches and bushes. I turned around to my right to capture the fuller view, but instead, a lonely building that stood there caught my eye. It must have been someone's living place, I thought and stepped towards the grand building. It had a look of fresh and it resembled something, but I couldn't remember then. As I stood at the mighty gate of this structure, a strange sense of fear gripped me, probably because of the profound, silence there which made the vicinity eerie and even unsettling it was to see that the building's gate was locked, suggesting no "happy family" lived in there. After observing the building, I turned and was a little surprised to see a man standing at a distance and looking after me.

I should have been filled with wonderful merriness to have found another human, but instead, what overwhelmed me was the emotion of slight terror. The man looked at me from there in an unbreakable, mute gaze, screened by mists he was and all I could see was his exceptionally tall figure and his broad frame over which he wore an uncommon attire: it looked like a long black cloak, over black coat and the lower part was quite invisible. His complexion appeared on the darker side and what I could make out of his face were only his eyes, fixed upon me. A desire kindled in me to go to him, but a strange resistance restrained me from stepping towards the man, not because of his frame, or his attire but because it was something so uncanny about his silence that exaggerated my cold shivers and to my utter surprise the solitary man too didn't make any move towards me. Time passed in this silently and motionless paly where I stood frozen and alone with this creature, looking at me in a perpetual gaze as if I wasn't there at all, as if he were staring only at the building. Soon, there was a drastic change. The man started to walk, with his hands crossed behind his back, spine bent, and glance to the earth as if engrossed in thoughts, dreadful thoughts. His pace increased and soon the walk became a spiral. His pace suggested that he was not old, but his clothes were antique and as I stood wondering about my next move; the winds hurled once again, but this time it was so frightening and so violent that even the leaves along with the loose earth of the garden started to float in the air spirally. I screened my eyes with my palm and at this moment my eyes captured a hint that the man had started running. He ran, reaching one corner of the house, becoming invisible momentarily and the next moment he was seen at the very edge of the terrace. Here I caught a glimpse of another man, who emerged suddenly behind this cloaked man. By this time, the rains restarted, and the cloaked man was standing at the very edge of the terrace, leaning over the low wall. What I saw after this shook me; the other man crept noiselessly and advanced towards the cloaked man, with his hands widened in such a way as if he was about to catch a bird. I was alarmed, but not the cloaked man who didn't have the slightest hint of who was behind him, and, within a moment, a tremendous noise followed. I immediately shut my eyes and when I reopened them; I saw the cloaked man fallen on the ground by the side of his back, arms widely sprawled and eyes still and enlarged. I was left speechlessly horrified seeing this appalling sight and shakingly I looked up and down—the cloaked man was dead and was thrown in front of my eyes. This realization shook all my spirits and filling my eyes with water and leaving a block in my heart. Now the criminal, the murderer, came slowly to the edge and looked down at me in a malevolent way and a loud cry came out from me instantly. I had seen a murder!

My loud cries grew to heights, and I started to run, cutting through the fog and rain, and finally, it led to a tremendous fall.

After falling, my whole body was burdened with pain, and I was shaking wildly as if there was an earthquake—the terror of a nightmare took over me, and at last my eyes opened.

The trauma finally stopped, leaving me taking in just wild breaths, but as my consciousness recovered, I was more than astonished; stunned to see myself on the carpeted ground. A general yellow tinge was all around me. At last, my eyes were open.

Ajay's panicked calls came from behind and grew louder. "You terrified me! You were yelling and restless the whole time and now you fell off your bed!"

I lay there a couple of minutes regaining myself and from that floor perspective I caught notice of a gentleman in the room, standing just in front and looking down at me; perhaps it was Uncle who had come up hearing my yells. The light was bleak, the vision blurred and as I stood up slowly and embarrassed at my frenzy I said "Please… Stop shaking me, Ajay…".

"What is happening?" Ajay asked as I gathered myself on the bed again, covering myself with the warm blanket.

I supported my head with my fist and sat silently; after which I spoke looking about me "where is Uncle? He was in the room, right?"

"Uncle?" he looked clueless. "You have just awakened from a nightmare! I was asleep just next to you and Father is down; why would he come up at two in the night?" This was his answer.

The man whom I thought was my uncle wasn't anywhere in the room. Was he similar to the man in my dream? I can't remember though, but at that hour, I took it only as a fragment of my imagination, just after the troubled nightmare. I sighed in relief and drank some water. But the rest part of the night was sleepless for me. I have never, ever believed in the powers of dreams though.

"Which was the place that I had come across? Who were those two men? And was what I had seen a part of the sleepy imagination of the subconscious mind, or was it something even dreadful? a real incident of the past?" I kept on thinking and only the next morning's early tea aided my brain to rest. As the soothing sun came over gorgeously, and the darkness gone, I was convinced that it was just a nightmare.

The morning was cold but pleasant and I and Ajay spent the early hours talking about the world and other general, kid's talks which I thought we had missed since the day I had come and of course, goes without saying that he, though being a child was a good company while drinking tea. Uncle didn't join us and was very late that morning; I wanted but didn't think it correct to discuss my dream with him too as he was in his general tendency of morning dizziness and swaying.

Ajay kept on talking and I kept on replying because I had to, probably I was trying to keep myself away from something, and talking is the best thing to do at these times and the only other thing to be heard was the loose window behind us.

Suddenly I got up in creative enthusiasm and told him all about my early visit to Europe with my parents and as I had expected he was always very cheered up and interested to talk on these matters, though I had not more than a couple of incidents to relate, one of which was about my interesting meeting with a friend of my father who was a psychology professor, which can be called a root of my interests.

I looked outside momentarily, perhaps the window's noise attracted my attention and said "How gorgeous it is here! Just a few people around, cool winds, mists, hills… all we need is a pleasant garden with blossoming flowers, well what happened about the ones which we planted?"

"Not a sign of growing… This garden!" he laughed. "Nothing grows here… I have tried before…"

It was quite fun to talk to this sweet cousin of mine who was most charming whenever we talked.

"Is your tea done?" He asked.

"Yes..." I said sipping the last sip as we talked of tea, I was reminded of something, and I kept on speaking looking into my cup "You know one early morning I woke up and Arun's friend asked me for tea that morning and I replied a no to his offer…" I chuckled a bit, raised my eyes again to Ajay, and asked "Well, I completely forgot! What about him? Is he better and has he returned to his parents' house in the town?"

"Parents' house?" his reaction was confused, astonished, and even as if I had been completely mistaken. "Who said his parents live here?"

"What do you mean?"

"Huh! His parents lived here; not live here. They shifted to the city some years ago… after his shifting there to study."

"What!" my confusion knew no bounds, "But I thought Rajesh had come here to meet his parents… and now that's the reason I didn't see any family member in the hospital… But why did he come here? And who were the people who were with him in the hospital?"

"Well, he used to play with me too… that's what I know all about him and that he is good."

I didn't know what to reply, but Ajay kept on speaking, but now I had lost all interest, but probably my apathy wasn't seen on my face.

"So…" he was saying something, but suddenly a mighty gust blew in, rustling in violently through the loose window.

The curtain fluttered and many things in the room started falling here and there and this chaos; I stood up, as I remembered something-something where my mind was sticking still after the dream but unreachable. I ran and hastily mounted the stairs, ultimately reaching my room. I pulled out the portrait from under my bed, and after wiping off the dust from over it what I saw ringed my head and heart and now, now I remembered the face had an exact resemblance with the cloaked man whom I had seen in my dream. I kept on looking at it and reminding myself of the scenes of my nightmare, which I hadn't forgotten yet; I was left in such a position where for the first time when I realized I was alone in the room; I was nervous about staying.

At such times, what we call our silly intuition starts suggesting to us the most expected superstition and so was mine; that last night's dream was special, I must have seen something related to the past truth, a real incident that's memory got somehow superimposed over mine in the troubled dream, and the biggest strike was that I remembered it scene by scene till that moment.

I pushed the hideous painting away from my sight and sat down on the bed, with my eyes fixed on the bare wall in front. I desired to run down and say to Ajay that he was probably right; that probably now I believed that something dreadful happened here and that a fiend could be around.

As I normalized soon, I believed these thoughts to be superstitions and the nightmare to have occurred probably because of troubled thoughts of the past days that hung in my head. Additionally, also because of changing my head's direction before sleeping. But though these reasons may be partly correct, can they be called perfect?

14

"Ajay... where is Uncle?" I asked as I came down the stairs soon.

"Father was in his room, but he went out just now..." he answered.

"Perfect..."

"Wait, are you going to that dusty old room again?" He asked as he stood up and followed me.

"Yes, but this time I will not close the door behind—"

"But I forgot to ask, what did you find there? And what happened last night when you were there..."

I resented and denied permission, but Ajay accompanied me inside the room this time, where I remember I had some more papers left to look at. The room happened to be more illuminated as the sun rays peeped through the glass windows, but still, last night's incidents were enough to make it seem eerie even if a hundred bulbs lit there. The newspapers were still scattered as I had left last, and as I sat down; Ajay also did the same.

"See what I got!" he startled me with his sudden call.

I took hold of the paper and the mighty headline on the first page itself left me stupefied and appalled.

5th December: "Shaitaan, a renowned businessman of town; found dead in front of his house gate"

The article's writer surely didn't have any other clue about what had happened, as only a few other important things could be derived from the article.

"What does it tell?" Ajay asked in excitement as I ran my eyes through it.

"Nothing much..." as I read the starting lines, "the news journalist labels it as an accident and has no clue about it, according to me. According to this article, Shaitaan's fallen body was seen by a passerby wood cutter and after checking that he wasn't alive they all ran to find people but as they returned after some minutes after failing to find anyone around the farmlands, the body had vanished."

"What? The body vanished into mists?" He said and his last words trembled.

"Let's read more…" I said and looked into the very next day's paper.

"Oh, my God! Now what's this?" came out of my mouth.

"Neelnath reported dead and cremated in burning ground" dated -6th December.

"It even says that this was reported to the Police by the keeper of the burning ground and was also confirmed by the records… But still, aren't you finding things very strange?" I asked.

"Very strange, beyond imagination..."

My curiosity and eagerness were almost exploding to see what was written in further newspapers as it was my conviction that the print media would have published further investigations on this heated topic, but I was disheartened completely as I saw the further newspapers of December.

7th December: "Massive Earthquake Shakes the State"

And the headlines of papers of subsequent dates were:

"Rescue operation in town"

"Ninety dead and nearly 137 reported missing"

"Seeing at further newspapers is worthless, this massive calamity thing is over the news for months… No article about the further Police investigation on Neelnath's death." I said as I flipped through the papers, ultimately dropping them wholly in a saddened way.

Now I had understood that somehow, after the unfortunate

earthquake, retiring to normalcy would have taken a long time for the town and authorities and somehow the case of Neelnath and his finding was dropped after assuming his death according to the news and case had finally dropped because Neelnath wasn't seen again.

"So finally, this person; Neelnath died, and everything got over…" Ajay asked.

"Yes, it appears…" I pitied him. He couldn't see the wide horizon, but I pitied myself too as I had no one to discuss such matters and if I had to go, I go till the end alone.

The liquor conspiracy part, Rajesh, Uncle, Arun, and the painting, were all whirling in my head and I found it silly at that time but strangers and outsiders like Mr. Candy and even Vishwakumar were also parts of the cyclone which didn't let the thought of returning home come into my mind for the following days.

"Can you hear footsteps?" Ajay asked, holding his ear with his fingers.

"Yes! Probably it's Uncle, coming..."

Alarmed by this fact and believing our hearing sense at least, we both came out of the room and were relieved only after we had locked it as before and had reached the chairs at the dining table.

"Doing good, eh?" Uncle called in the "native language" to me, smilingly, and passed by without waiting for any answer by me. He walked with large steps and hurriedly passed out from the garden gate.

We both exchanged confused glances over my uncle's haste and, of course, the bit of charm of new enthusiasm which had reappeared on his face didn't go unnoticeable. I made a halting gesture to Ajay, who was on the verge of standing and followed my uncle into the garden. It was cold there. The topmost branches of the bare, thin trees were visibly vibrating, and I saw the sky as blue but with a tinge of red between the growling clouds. I turned with the circular garden and found Uncle talking to a man. I stood at a distance where the tree could screen me and saw them both talking but couldn't make out a word. The man's face was unfamiliar to me. I could make out that their words were fast, and the other man was certainly in haste. Their talk lasted only for some time and after that, the stranger made a thankful gesture and walked back, but Uncle waited there looking after him. The stranger came back in seconds with two other men who appeared to me as the workers. They carried two heavy wooden crates on their head, supported by their hands, and went in, guided by my uncle, through a gate. The heavy sound of dumping came to my ears, and after coming out, the two men followed another round of the same procedure with two similar crates. I was left more than curious about what was going on; after the three men left and Uncle closed the heavy door of the place where the crates had been dumped; which I thought was a spare storeroom.

Seeing Uncle coming to my side, I rushed back and reached the house timely; unnoticed. The rest part of the day, uncle, already in fine clothes, looked finer and genial. There were no more rains that day and when the evening broke peacefully, finer than ever, I and Ajay went out to the lane to plant the left seeds in the soil that was on the sides of the lane. The sun shined, spreading its red beams all over the blue sky and from between the clouds that had almost dispersed freely. Cold breezes blew, no doubt about that, but something was exceptionally charming about that evening, which was realized by me, especially when I was standing at the little grassy slant that was beside the lane, from where the expanse of tall leafy trees started. The place was silent, and a bit lower than the lane, the mud could be smelled, and I had already kneeled to caress the tiny pink and white flowers that were dancing, filling the air with a fresh scent and shining due to the fresh drops that had accumulated at the ends.

"Shall I come down? Nothing to worry, I have been born here…" Ajay called from the lane, bending on his and peering down.

I looked at him as his speech had kindled a laugh in my mind, "Not required kiddie…" I said, "I am going to enjoy this place myself." I answered.

After doing the task, I looked about me again, and sat down for a moment where I was, hearing quietly the noise that a thousand birds must have been making in the trees high above me, the general noise that birds make in evenings: pleasantly shrilling and peculiar. Seeing above; the sky had turned ashy; the clouds had gathered again, and birds were seen returning, a sight which looked so new to me after this long while. The farthest end of the sky was red, like a huge fire in the horizon of the earth, and the sun which had almost retreated, cast its most powerful red rays as its day's mark which by the time of falling on the tall and slender trees, shined them like sparkling gold. The enormous tree trunk looked almost white and cast vast blackness over the grasses, down where I was sitting and the whole vicinity; gray as well as gold looked so ancient, so true, so unknown and so magical that I realized a tear of bliss and nostalgia at the edge of my lashes. But as I wiped my eyes, I saw everything gradually. The burning horizon turned soothing pink and everything around me turned dark, like the soil. The mists were visible in the ends and now, as I stood up, still facing the slant, a dominating feeling of being watched seized my instinct. It was at the instant when sounds of nocturnal animals started to come to my ears; as if they had awakened from a deep slumber, that it struck to my mind the fact that Ajay had also been with me all this while but, why was he so silent? By the time I figured out that perhaps there was something wrong about this exceptional patience shown by my little cousin, I could feel myself shivering form cold, and what I could see as the most distinguishable thing in the blackness that was gradually enveloping the vicinity was foggy exhalation out of my mouth.

I stood up immediately, re-buttoning my long brown coat, and then looked up for Ajay. When I couldn't see any hint of him, I walked a bit forward and stepped up finally, which I thought would be best in response to the eeriness of the slant.

"Ajay… Is anything there?" I called from back and re-called, stepping forward. "Ajay! Who's there?"

I continued walking slowly with my skeptical gaze fixed on him, as he didn't answer me the second time too. He was standing, with his feet together, facing his left; silently as if looking at someone or perhaps something.

Sensing something wrong, I took hasty steps towards him but, when I had reached only a short distance, it didn't go unnoticeable that he was trembling; if not by his back but surely by his legs, he was.

Perhaps my footsteps came to his ears as he turned to me in a sudden jerk as I reached him.

"There… who is he?" he said in an equally frightened voice, pointing towards the left.

My glances jumped in this direction, and I said after carefully checking "There is… there is nothing there… Only some tree perhaps…"

"No! Look carefully, amidst the fog-there is someone standing! So sleepily and loosely, can't you see?" his voice and his expression expressed dissatisfaction over me, along with a strange fear.

"There is no one! Maybe you saw a dead tree…" I said after checking again and then forcefully turned him to my side.

"We are not alone here! "He said, "I can see him, standing…" it appeared his hasty and trembling words were stifling him.

Though these words made me feel uncomfortable, I asked, "Ajay, what book did you read last night?"

By this time, he had turned again in that particular direction and answered, "Fifty Real Stories of…"

"Of, of what?" I asked and continued without his reply, "Ajay; was it Fifty Real Stories of Supernatural? The old book? I bet it was! I told you; children shouldn't read so much horror… Now come… It's your imagination of the stories…" I called.

A strange fear crept over me too and I didn't look in that dark direction anymore. Suddenly following a cool gust of wind, a yellowed leaf lingered about in the air and finally dropped over Ajay, and he, tremendously terrified as he hadn't seen it, jerked it off.

The winds grew stronger, resulting in more dry leaves raining over us. Finally, I walked forward and grabbed Ajay by his arm and lovingly pulled him; so easy it was, that I enjoyed it. We started to walk hastily as I suspected a rough storm. The gusts floated with the smell of rain; and all this while Ajay still had his head turned in that direction, constantly looking behind to "what" I do not know.

"It's misty and dark. I am sure it was a crooked dead tree that you saw," I said laughingly to Ajay.

"Yes… I think you are correct…" he replied finally with a bit of a giggle and turned his head, probably convinced by my words, and walked on.

But within a couple of steps, he stopped abruptly, giving me a pull by his grip.

"Now what was that?" He asked, looking at me, terrified.

I heard it too, a sudden, heavy noise it was. It echoed, splitting the silence of the deserted atmosphere, ultimately piercing through the ears, and ringing the heart.

"I told you something was wrong! There is someone around us!" Ajay's voice was abnormally low.

Not even a minute passed, but the sound, rather sounds, came again. The source of these hard and appalling sounds was unknown, but surely it was coming from our front, from the other side of the lane.

"It's better we walk on from this place..." I said and we crossed the lane.

Though the noise wasn't consistent and very soon dropped completely, suggesting that no one was approaching or beating against something hard, the fact that we heard it in a situation where there could be no man for miles but only, solitary tracts of lands and hills; was more chilling than the icy gusts. I think at the moment I was, as an elder sister, only acting to be courageous. As we reached the main iron gate of our plot, it became a confirmed fact that the disturbing noises had not come from anywhere else but from our very own garden.

I slightly pushed the mighty gate and entered slowly. Our garden and house were cast into a play of shadows and glows; caused due to the flickering lamps that were set on windows after evenings as usual. I turned with the garden, cautiously enough, guarding myself by the walls and dead trunks lest I be seen by whom I wanted to see, and by the time I had turned twice I reached the same place, where I saw the author of such noises. It was uncle, his hands in his pockets and looking down at the same crates which he had pulled out-the act which had caused the noise. With the indication of an eye, I showed him this and then turned my eyes again to Uncle who had by this time considerably bent over and was now peering into the crate.

My heart skipped a beat when suddenly it struck to my mind that perhaps there could be a chance that I knew what the contents of this crate were; but though the idea looked convincing, it was a gamble because if it were true the, the series of uncanny events that were rallying in my mind since they had occurred—would turn out to be absolutely true.

I knew Ajay couldn't fathom a drop of what were possibly the freezing realties, and this was quite evident from his expressions—his dropped jaw as he stared at his father's actions.

"Can my dotty and imaginative interpretations be seriously true?" I questioned myself, "But I have to tell something to Ajay, or he would start judging Uncle's mental soundness if he stays unaware any further."

Now, Uncle put both his hands in the crate and started lifting something; a bolt of lightning flashed behind, followed by a loud grumble and Uncle probably became aware that someone was in the corner. Within a moment, he turned slightly to our side, and what after that—Ajay and I walked back swiftly and carefully, lest we got seen.

"What was Papa doing? I'll ask him what is in the crates…" An earnest determination was in his eyes.

By this time, we both were sitting face to face in our bedroom, and Ajay, as soon as he posted this question, stood up and started to walk around the room.

"No; you shouldn't ask in that way," I answered, catching him by his hand to stop his restless motions.

"Then how will we know? What is going on?" he sat down on the bed exhausted.

"How do you intend to explain? Will you say that we both kept a watch over Uncle from behind? We both will not get good words then…"

He didn't answer this and stared at the ceiling, as if in deep thought. I had never seen him staring so intensely and expressionlessly any time before. Everything was silent, apart from the occasional blasts of winds. There was no such rain, and, in those moments, I finally combined *one and one* of my theories.

"Wait," I stood as soon as Ajay stood up and peeped under his bed.

"Ajay… What's lurking under the bed?" I said playfully, in a way not to upset him.

"I was going to show you this…" he said, raising his head for once.

I took the lamp in my hand and pushed it through the floor, under the bed. In the whole area which got lighted, I saw lots of scattered books which I one by one pulled out in intrigue.

"You got a good collection… where did you get these?" I said as I looked at them one by one.

"Ah… here goes one," I said, separating one horror book. "Here goes the second and… here the third!"

“I haven’t read all of them…” was his only reply, as if he guessed what I would say and expected the same.

“But they all look so old….” I said as I clapped my hands to spark off the dust. “Where did you get these? I am stunned… and how do you understand these now?”

The publication dates of a couple of books that I checked were about four decades ago.

“Eh… I got these books from papa’s library, I do this often… he doesn’t go there anymore, and I bought books by seeing their covers. Aren’t these the best cover drawings?” he pointed to one book.

“Library… Why didn’t you tell me before that there is also a library? Oh, we could read books and discuss, and time would pass wonderfully, but now tell where is it. I will also tell you something, then.”

We landed on the stairs and turned in the other direction of the kitchen, ultimately reaching a small room that could be called a library, and what I found there was fuel to my theories. The room was thin and had no windows; it was just squeezed in between two rooms and the shelf was only one, but large. The books which I searched for were old, very old rather but somehow even after spending much time over there I couldn’t find books of my interest.

“I think you have taken out all the fiction books from here already,” I said to Ajay and as soon as I took steps to withdraw myself; ‘it’ struck my eyes. A large-sized book it was, hardbound and with a peculiarly artistic cover; kept like a photo frame over the shelf—all alone. It caught my attention, and a question arose in my mind as to why it was kept aloof from other books. Finally, I stepped over the chair and got it.

Mind and times of Vishwakumar was its heading and as I rubbed the dust further, I was much surprised and tensed by seeing the appalling effect that the cover portrait made, at my first glance.

I opened the book in curiosity and my uncle’s name was written on the blank: “This book belongs to…”

“Come, we will have this book in our room, and I’ll tell you what I find in it. It seems interesting,” I said to Ajay, and we directly headed to the dining table.

By the time we three started with the dinner, the expected rains had burst outside; late, but in frantic fury. We ate without much informal talk, and I didn't miss glancing at Uncle each time he dropped his eyes to the plate; though this was seldom as most of the time he was either looking up or at the window. In these limited moments that I got to look at my uncle directly, it didn't go beyond notice that he was lost in deep thought. His expression was rather of a man who is troubled by something and constantly trying to battle with his mind. He didn't eat much, even after my repeated persuasions. He couldn't concentrate on his plate for a long time, the same way he turned his glances up and down within tiny intervals. The rain had turned into a chaotic storm and following the third and the most shakingly unnerving thunder strike; the load shedding happened as expected. Under the unstable lantern flame, our only protector from blackness for the time being uncle's face looked ghastly. His face appeared completely yellow due to the tinges of the flame, and whenever he raised his hand, either to stroke his hair or to adjust his long sleeves, his tremendous shadow behind him looked monstrous, with its broad palm and long fingers not only reaching the white ceiling but covering it and catching it. He surely appeared more distressed after the load sheading and the coolness in the hall, the silence, and darkness at the corners, with all the giant shadows staring at us, together; were disturbing for me too.

"Did you see father's shadow?" Ajay said as we were mounting the stairs after the dinner, "It looked like a ten times large man sat behind Papa... didn't it seem blacker and larger than our shadows?"

"Oh, you are making me scared with your imagination." I could say only this as a reply, but in my mind, I was quite surprised because my imagination was matching the same.

"Leave Uncle alone for some time, elder people have a lot to think.... But why are you... are you not feeling good, Ajay?" I said as we stood now at the door of our bedroom.

I bent down on my knees in front of Ajay as I saw him brushing something off his cheek. I knew the child was deeply disturbed.

"Everything is okay," I said, gently stroking the hair back from his forehead.

He slightly smiled at this, wiped his eyes again, and threw his arms around my neck.

"I can't carry you. You have become a strong man now," I said as I carried him in my arms, though lifting him was not tough.

I remember making a joke, but what exactly was the humor in it which made him laugh? I can't put it in words now. He started laughing at this joke, exactly as I wanted. A long sigh escaped from my mouth after I finally landed him on the bed. Before asking anything, he started on his own.

"We'll not switch off the lights this night…" he said with a look of a deepened sense of fright, which was so peculiar that it couldn't be observed from the conventional perspective; it didn't result in any shivering, nor tears, but it could be observed as a strange and profound seriousness in his eyes, as if the supernatural was not super, but accepted; which was even more uncanny.

"I don't want to sleep… can we not just talk?" he spoke again, this time leaning back over the wall, "is sleeping necessary? Can't we do without it till the mornings? And then continue this…"

"What!" was my first reaction to his question. "Ajay, tell me if you are feeling unwell in any way; something is surely incorrect. Of course, every human has to sleep! And you very well know it…. Why, what's the problem with sleeping? You sleep fine… I see you sleeping.", my tone became gentler as Ajay's questions made me worried for him—as it is, I was not in my relaxed state.

"It looks like I sleep fine. But for some nights…"

"But for some nights, what?" I said as I observed that he was exerting a lot of force over his feet, pressing the floor, evidently trying to suppress a slight shiver, and trying to prevent it from heightening.

"Strange thoughts relay in my mind as soon as I keep my head on the pillow, the same story which I had told you, always comes to my mind and I imagine strange incidents that might have occurred here, where we are sleeping now. I don't like nights, especially cold ones. In the middle of last night, half asleep, I thought I heard some noises outside, then they became hideous as if someone was running up and down the stairs. I tried to call you, but this is not the only thing. I also have strange dreams and one thing which is the most dangerous which I had forgotten in the day but now it comes to my mind again is that, as I lied two nights back, looking at the high ceiling and this door of ours was left slightly open and a sliver of the moonlight came through to our room, visible clearly both on the floor and on the ceiling to a certain extent; I saw in that impression of white light something black for an instant. The door was intact, the room silently, and within a second, I saw something like a shadow move past, cast over the tiny impression of white light on the ceiling. Surely someone was moving in the passage at night, near our very door, with his shadow entering our room… He walked fast, as I saw, then I pressed my eyes and took God's name… my shivering slowly stopped, I started feeling the warmth and I don't remember when I fell asleep. I am not fearful, I am brave…. At least I think so…"

His words had left me not in a good state of mind, certainly. I took a moment to imagine what he might have seen, and if it were real, how would it look? After that, I didn't know how to respond maturely or correctly anymore.

"Of course, you are brave and that's why you are a sweet boy…. Don't think a lot about such things. It will come into your mind in such circumstances, in any mind; but take it as involuntary imagination which happens when you feel very cold and cannot sleep. It was, after all, a shadow in the night. Every child sees such impressions when sleep doesn't come. It's common. We two sleep together and I will be quite awake this night and keep a watch. If anything happens, I am here. The incident which you saw must also be a dream. You don't know when you're in the bed in the middle of the night; what is a dream and what is not, it's all mixed up. In my case also, strange thoughts and overthinking lead to ill-formed dreams which were senseless. And if anything is there, which I still am confused about, you aren't alone, I and Uncle are there. Wait, I will settle you between pillows in such a cozy way, you would be forced to fall asleep; even my father slept well in this way once and it was so unusual…"

I knew in my mind that his fears were not completely baseless, yes most of it could be because of this atmosphere, child psychology, repetition of legends, void of responsibilities, and general child fear of ghosts, but could it be all this? And nothing else?

"Please talk for some time. You are the sweetest. I want to hear you till I get to sleep and promise me you will wake me up if I…"

"Yes, of course, and for now I'll not off the bulb too…" I said as I started arranging my bed "You know, I like nights, don't you feel that it is calm and beautiful, cold and serene and especially rainy nights… Too beautiful."

"Yes…" came his answer, which was better than before.

In my mind the general question arose again, why had Uncle purchased such a house and it came as an angry thought against uncle, I couldn't even directly talk with him about this, and Arun's conduct of disappearing, leaving away everything in this manner was very wrong and expressed the lousiness of his character, I thought, but then I also thought that without reasons I could be totally misjudging everyone—and true it became soon.

"But I haven't told you one thing yet…" he said after I had tried my best to divert his attention from his supernatural thoughts, engaging myself for not less than an hour by the clock for the same and ultimately getting exhausted and also exhausting the whole stock of my bed-time stories too.

By that time, dominating fatigue was over me. I wanted to sleep, but still, I asked from my bed, "What is it after all?"

Then he started, ducked under the blanket, replying slowly and with the utmost care, which didn't allow me to shut my eyes, "Don't you remember the day you had come? And near about that I had told you the story of Mr. S—, and that day or a day after… yes! It was the next morning. Those days I didn't sleep in your room, but all alone-feeling isolated and lonely. That night, I had a good sleep for sure, but only till I started hearing noises. Believe me, I heard dreadful noises which were real, not the usual low un-understandable voices that books accuse of being supernatural. I was in a deep sleep, but the noises woke me up. They were so near as if shaking my bed with vibrations. Initially, as I opened my eyes, I thought it would be some animal somewhere out; but the very next moment I realized that it was not far; just down. It surely suggested as if somebody heavy was wildly shaking the fence of our garden, trying to jump in. But the time for which the noises were heard was unusually more than the time a fit man would take to jump through the fence. Anyhow, I was petrified and looked around; my room was quite blue, and its features weren't much visible. In another moment, the noise stopped. The man had jumped in by this time, probably. I lay down in my bed, with my face buried in the pillows, speechless. I was and couldn't sleep until morning…"

His story made me sit up on my bed and I tried to fathom any hidden similarity. "Then what?" I spoke.

"I locked this whole thing in my heart, partly because I brushed it off in the morning as a nightmare and partly because I enjoyed playing for some time in the garden with Rajesh, who had come that morning."

"Rajesh had come.... Now I remember!" I thought to myself.

"But then when I was leaving the garden, I saw it!"

"What?"

"Real; distinguishable footprints... yes, on the muddy ground and at the exact spot around the fence. Now, what can you say about this?"

I was in deep thought and was regaining my memory to which this revelation paralleled. But before I spoke anything; he started again suggesting that he was also in the same process as me, digging into his memory, but his expression showed he was forcing himself hard.

"I bent; and observed the footprints when I was alone... and can you think what I found? In short, clearly, one foot's print was deep and full like a shoe's sole, but the other foot's print looked somewhat smaller and half—roundish throughout the three-four impressions that remained. Now I don't know if it means anything silly on my part, but..."

"Silly? It's great..." I said, "If I am not wrong, this suggests that the person was walking on his heals with one leg..."

"I am fearing to discuss this now.... At night-time, who entered our place? Who could he be?" he hid his face under the blanket and rolled the tip of his feet in too, which was previously out.

"I didn't know you see so many things," I said as I stood up and went nearer to him. All my fatigue was drowning.

"And now are you ready for a shock? What if I say that you are absolutely right? Yes, there was someone who had come!"

"You never told me this...." He said as his voice exploded, and he raised his head out of his blanket.

"Now I tell you...." I said as I seated myself beside him, "He also had a light, probably a torch-which he focused into my room; this room, through that window at the hour of darkness."

Ajay turned to the window, which was now closed, and kept on looking at it.

"I said nothing to you because I thought… eh… because somehow I just didn't."

"You should have told! He might be a criminal… But why does he come here?" He turned to me with an expression of horror and confusion in parts.

The coldness in the air and the blank dullness of the beautifully furnished room gave me a sudden irresistible shudder as I spoke of such things, especially because I believed the man mustn't be a ghost. But is the idea of a criminal any better? And as I related the other day's incident too, that is, when I had somehow caught a hazy sight of two men, not one and if I believe, which I did, that it was not just a trick of drowsy imagination—who was the other one?

I briefed him about all the incidents that were unknown and also how Paul's (the previous resident) words of seeing a figure appearing in darkness; whose leg he had injured matched with this stranger's incident and there was surely something behind it.

"All is seriously strange," Ajay said after a while, "But still I can't say that this stranger is playing the ghost…"

"I agree…" was my response, "I have a very different kind of feeling in my mind, over this place, something inexplicable in words—as if something is trying to get in my thoughts, probably some truth which lies unexplored and I am sorry, I don't feel I can completely deny anything horribly abnormal going on here, around this place."

I said this hard, with words breaking out slowly as if rising from the deepest side of my mind.

I tried hard to avoid thoughts over this subject altogether but ducked into my blanket; with my eyes open wide for most of the night, I somehow couldn't let go. Whenever something else tried to get into my mind, an unprecedented nervousness crept over me-as if I was ignoring a danger or a surprise by simply not giving it a thought and my mind again rambled in the plains of thoughts about the original owner of the place. In the deep of night, I felt a strange burden of responsibility, but about what I didn't know. It was followed by a beautiful wave of love in my heart; where I didn't imagine anyone but still it was over me like pink waves in the ocean of my feelings—of such dynamic magnitude that I had never felt, forcing me to smile and also make my eyes watery with drops of ecstasy, filling my heart with a strange thrilling and lovely excitement. Soon as time passed, the feeling of love (which was beyond my handling power) turned to a low and rainy melancholy; though highly romanticized, it choked my throat-giving me a feeling of nausea and again I do not know why. I placed my hand over my forehead and then on my neck, trying to control the strange experiences of my heart physically, as it was now tiresome and was affecting my sleep. It miraculously worked. My forehead and neck were very warm and as I closed my eyes again—the concluding feeling in my heart, which was left calm at last—was that I had to know the truth because I felt it.

The night passed and morning came, misty and cloudy. I woke up early and saw Ajay still stretching and turning in his bed. Before going to bathe and carry on some morning chores, I opened the outwardly opening glass window of our room for some sunlight to come for the sake of my little cousin. As I went to the breakfast table, fresh and washed; I saw Uncle sitting there already and talking with the morning house worker. He wished me back at my morning wish and asked me to sit.

"Vaanya," he commenced. "So, I hope, my dear, that you had a nice time at our place; if not a delightful time; you see if your aunt would be there, things would be even better but…"

"But Uncle, what's the matter?" came out of my mouth as I was confused by his statement because I hadn't complained about anything.

The house worker, a man of about forty; stood like a statue behind uncle's chair-hands back and mum. There was no other noise, apart from the occasional blasts of wind coming through the window-making the mighty curtains flutter.

He replied, "No… I mean that there is news for you."

"News? What?"

"Your father wrote to me, which I got yesternight. Apart from the general thanks and wishes, he wrote that after four days; hence, you will return to the city…"

This sudden news surprised me to the extent that I couldn't much speak; a hundred thoughts, both happy and sad, ran through my mind.

"I must say you being here, I and Ajay felt very nice, and I am sure we will call you again very soon."

"Uncle," I started at last, "do not tell Ajay this now; he would be very sad… I too hadn't expected this news…"

"Right, yes, you have only one cousin, the kiddie. The other one is of no use…" he said mournfully.

By this time, the servant disappeared into the kitchen and had returned with the breakfast. As we had breakfast, though, it looked good; it was very hard for me to eat. I had such less time in that place; I thought over and over. The servant took his position again as a statue beside Uncle.

Uncle said after taking a bite, the act of eating looked equally hard for him "Dear girl, give anything you want for pressing before you leave to our person. He will deliver it to the presser in the town and bring it back in an hour or so…"

After glancing at the servant, I replied, "Okay."

After breakfast, Uncle went into his room, and I was left with the servant.

"Why don't you come every morning to serve breakfast?" I asked the housekeeper, who never looked in my eye; "It's so good to be served by you—so neatly and smoothly, it would be even better if you stay here throughout the evening and serve uncle…"

"I am sorry…." he said a bit stupefied at my unexpected question, "I cannot stay longer here—only four hours in the morning and I do everything in the house…"

His words were breaking and, as in the native language, they were confusing for me, but I asked, "Why?"

He had no answer for it and I, after telling him to wait; mounted the stairs to my room.

My mind was heavy with thoughts as I walked up. The work was undone, I thought, and I didn't want to leave it undone. This feeling also filled me with haste. Ajay still slept and I, without disturbing him; started to take out clothes from the wardrobe. This act took me some time and by the time I opened my suitcase; a feeling that I had left the man standing and waiting down came over me, which forced me to haste even more. Without looking at every cloth, I picked up three or four randomly. I left the now half-emptied suitcase open in the middle of the floor and went down—ultimately handing over the heap to the man. He tied them into another cloth and advanced, and I walked back up.

As I opened the door of my room, I saw my big suitcase wide open right at my step and as I bent on my knee to close it and corner it; I saw something in it.

"Ah… this I had completely forgotten!" I spoke as I held it in my hands.

Now as the clothes were out of the suitcase, I saw the book which I had bought, which was a kind of travel book about that town in particular. I bought it for some reference for movement as it had a very detailed map of the town, and I was delighted to discover it. I jumped directly to the map page; at the end and held it high.

Probably I had the desire to find something related to our house; I don't know, but I really found something else too. I figured out the hill over which we had our house; and all around its name; were grassy plains on one side and slight woods on the eastern side, as I already knew. Then there was the heart of the town, a bit far, but still visible on the map. But as my eyes ran in the east direction, there was another hill, and following it was something completely unexpected for me. A sit was very far from both the town and the hill I wondered why it was on the map. A wavy line of a river flowed around it and it was at the banks; yes, a crematorium it was. Probably the only one for the remote town. It was nameless, but I don't know why; it provoked an odd thought in me, and I turned to further pages where I expected to find about the mediums of transport in the area-and I got it. Unexpectedly enough, reaching the burning ground was faster than reaching the town itself from our place, as the book stated. It further added that the service of horse carts was there for going to the burning grounds, which could take the fastest routes and shortcuts through the plains and hills.

"Wait;" I thought, "doesn't this confirm the fact that Shaitaan's dead body was transported to the burning ground so soon that nobody got a look at it?"

"And it would be even faster if it were traveled from this hill." Another thought dominated my mind as I pointed towards the hill beyond the woods in the east.

I grew a bit anxious as I turned my memory very fast to find anything matching what the hints played and again that feeling of losing something very valuable in the darkness of memory seized me and I kept the book down.

"I have; to go the..." I spoke involuntarily and Ajay counter-questioned me on this before it even came out properly.

I saw him rubbing his eyes with one hand and still clutching the pillow with another; his legs on the floor and a cluttered mess of blankets and bed sheets over the bed, which resembled exactly the way of his hair, which came to his eyes.

"When did you wake up?"

"Where are you going?"

"Oh, nothing... You first be ready and then have your breakfast... you are late today as it is."

He replied with a drowsy nod and went out of the stairs. And soon I heard him walking down the stairs. I was left alone in the room; I walked to the glass windows and pressed my forehead over it. It opened wide and sweet but mighty winds came in. The curtains were disturbed, and some noises were heard behind my back-probably the wind had caused the candle holder to fall, but I didn't care. I was controlled by my thoughts then. The sky was gray, misty and from there I could see the silent plains, pebbled paths, and at the end the woods mixing with the heavy veil of mists of the eastern horizon. The soft winds didn't allow me to move from the window and I pondered if I would be there in the misty woods. How grand it would be; wait, it probably rained there too. How ideal it would be to be in the open plains alone with sheets of mist revolving visibly, and how ideal it would be to be alone in the woods with the shadowy, moss-covered trees and drafts of rain rioting over. How far it appeared, but why did I feel it so near as if I was there? Like an experience it was, and then I remembered my nightmare. Could it be that the woods where I was; in the nightmare, resembled or was exactly these woods of the east?

"Ajay; don't trip over my suitcase... it's near the door," I uttered, still looking out as I heard some noises of the door opening behind me.

I heard the bedroom door open and close behind me; Ajay had come in. Suddenly, I got startled by the heavy noise of the suitcase falling on the floor and I turned back immediately uttering, "Ajay, did you get hurt?"

But to my utter shock, there was no one in the room. Ajay hadn't come up, and the door was closed. My standing suitcase lay fallen, wide open on the floor and the book of the town had its thin pages turning wildly with the wind. The room was shady and silent as before and despite my heart beating faster; I realized how alone I was in the room. I closed back the window, not romanticizing more with graceful gusts, which I believed must have caused the suitcase to fall. I was then sure of this, but as I see it in retrospect; I am unsure because the suitcase might have not been so light.

Ajay came up soon and cheerfully said,

"Father has called both of us down…"

I wondered what might be so cheerful about this fact, but as I came down, Uncle said that he wanted a good outing for both of us—apparently, because it was one of my last days of that trip.

"I will leave you both in the carriage till the riverbank… Ajay's friend's mother has invited Ajay as the two friends had planned to race at the banks someday in the morning. Ajay had forgotten this, but his friend still insists" Ajay blushed half in excitement and a half due to his forgetfulness and Uncle continued "And so his mother, asked if you could also come along… She is a good woman and you both might sit and talk at the banks. The weather is good and at the streamside, it is the best."

I looked at Ajay and then at Uncle and then I agreed too. By the word "bank", the thin, riverside line of the map came into my mind, and then somehow, oddly, the next thing which came into my mind was the burning ground which lay very close, then about the carriage services. I thought "it" only as an option if things would somehow give me an opportunity, but the "it" itself wasn't much defined.

Ajay's cheeks were chubbier as he smiled and cheered up—all the time until he reached his friend. My clothes were still out and now it was more than an hour, but still, I tried to forget about it, thinking the servant would keep them in my bedroom once he came; but this wasn't very pleasing.

"Hurry… We will leave in ten minutes…" Uncle called.

"Yes..." I called as I walked down. Ajay followed.

"Oh... the skies..." Uncle sighed, looking at the sky above.

It was drizzling and thunder strokes were being heard in the backdrop. It looked as if it could start raining in some time. Uncle turned around, looked, and then said that he wanted to once check the storeroom's gates lest the muddy water seeped in and I quite knew why he was so careful about the storeroom. He walked swiftly towards it, telling us to get into the carriage that stood not too far. I told Ajay to quickly get up into the carriage lest he caught a cold out in the rain and that I would follow him in once Uncle came. I was left alone in the profoundly silent and perpetually bleak vicinity as Ajay finally disappeared. Everything was calm save the barred iron gate, which was making a shrilling noise, swaying with the winds and cracking against stones scattered among the grass. I stepped forward and grabbed it in time; and it was at this moment of satisfaction I thought that I, with the left corner of my eye, noticed something stir in the darkness. The region engulfed in blackness didn't offer any clear vision as I immediately peeped out of the gate. I was not amazed to see only motionless trees. A sense of being deluded seized over a sense of unknown fright and I now accounted this delusion to the bleak shades and loneliness of the place. The drizzles had grown intense meanwhile, and I didn't feel it correct to stay there longer, though I still compelled myself that I was nothing but alone.

I ultimately sat in the carriage, but after that, too, kept on looking through the back glass. By this time, I completely dismissed whatever I thought I had seen, unaffected by any forebodings. Uncle followed within minutes and as soon as the carriage rolled; I was utterly shocked to see a figure emerging from within the darkness. All I had seen was not a delusion at last. It was unnerving. The unknown figure, invisible in its features, stood far behind the trees where it must have been hiding all that long—and it was real. It had emerged clearly on the lane then and soon it was walking towards the iron gates. He held the bars and made such appalling motions within those seconds, suggesting ceaselessly that he was trying to steer in or even break in. His manly head rose to the windows and then he walked a bit to get a right-arm view into our garden as if trying to detect someone. He was of an unnatural build; very tall, broad, sturdy, and looked holder of power beyond a normal man. I turned my vision purposely to his legs, but both his legs were totally fine. He surely didn't resemble any person I had seen in the town and, mind it, not even the climber to my window.

I resumed my seat next to Uncle after losing the final sight of this stranger to darkness and drizzles. Before I could decide whether I should say anything or not, we had traveled a long distance, with the carriage roaring at high speed. A question gradually dominated all other thoughts: Why didn't Uncle see him or it? Probably the only answer I got then was that I had been mistaken, misunderstanding the man as there was a high possibility that he was one of the workers who had come to Uncle carrying that heavy boxes and maybe he had stopped to smoke or something. This somehow satisfied me.

I stood silently, watching the shades of gray, blue, yellow, and green as the carriage rolled down the lane. When we were probably halfway, my uncle commenced talking, which shifted my focus from the window to him.

"Children don't go too far. There are some dark woods around, so be careful, be with auntie… and when you are called, come back."

"But why are you not coming to pick us up? Please…" Ajay implored.

"Eh… I have a meeting with Mr. Candy. He wanted to discuss more …." He spoke with quite a hesitation, stopped, and continued, "This carriage driver will only pick you up again…"

After this, he called the carriage driver by his name, and he replied in a genial way. Uncle instructed him to be around and pick up the children within some time and he agreed most responsibly and respectfully as if he had known my uncle for years. He must be faithful and loyal to Uncle.

At reaching the place, Ajay was the first one to jump down into the carriage, waving of hands had started between the two friends from the carriage itself: his friend waiting for him at the bank already. Soft breezes started to play between my legs, with my first step on the grass. My skin up to the knees was already a little wet. The august winds were mightier on the riverside and profoundly cooler too, heightened in all ideal qualities by the baron tree-less grounds all around. In the first glimpse from where I stood, not a single passer-by was in sight, but only silence reigned. The ends were very far and mysterious, as if in the middle of nowhere. The land was covered by thick bushes and grass which appeared of colors not only green but yellowish and I must say, blackish too. Everything seemed to be swaying and under the control of the gusts. I never knew when I turned around while looking at the huge sky above as if to find where it ended, opaqued by the masses of black clouds, it traveled from one side of the horizon where it was visibly lit by white sun rays to the other where it was veiled by mists tuning with the darker hills beyond-almost invisible: at the same time. The air smelled of wet soil and rain and I do not know why but from the very first look at that place I was realizing currents of excitement down my back. The bewildering silence and the mystical enchantment; picturesqueness of this cold, gloomy, rough, and rainy landscape, I still don't know why it had something so sensitively peculiar as to kindle a pleasing sense of nervousness in my bosom. Uncle had gone with the carriage by this time and, seeing that Ajay had proceeded far too, I commenced walking. I walked carefully, looking down at the puddles of mud, the black rocks all around, and at the same time up at the woman, supposedly the mother of Ajay's friend who also stood alone, near the river looking after me.

The woman was as glad as me to have a companion on that solitary end and on further talking I got to know that she was a regular walker over there, almost every evening with her boy, and also that she had been bored walking alone. I struck up a good friendship with her, and we sat for a long time on one of the rocks at the shore while both friends ran wildly along the river. Her deep brown eyes had a pleasant calmness, and a wise expression was shown on her face, which was so rich that it could be nothing but natural. She looked no more than ten years older than me, and her very words expressed her education and knowledge of which she soon revealed that she had a college degree; which strictly suggested not of a superstitious rural woman. My eyes discovered her carriage standing at a considerable distance, with the driver lazily stretching his hands and back. For the case, I'll refer to her as Mrs. A—.

We started our talks with general issues, but soon we became more open with one another, and I understood that she had good knowledge about most of the town's matters, probably as she was born and raised there.

"The river generally overflows in the rainy season…" she said in her slow-paced way, slightly swinging her legs over the grass while looking at the river whose subtle sound was heard clearly in the whole vicinity.

"Yes…" I replied looking at the sky and opening my hands on the face of the sky "I hope it doesn't rain now, the drizzles have commenced again… oh, it's nice and icy-lovely."

She laughed slightly at this, remarked "Rough weather" looking at the sky, and asked, "Are you on a holiday here?"

"Yes… kind of but an involuntary one..." I said laughingly and questioned her, in the hope that it was the correct moment in which I could ask something un-casual "Well, can I ask you something, something related to this place?"

"Of course, probably I can answer you. What is it?"

"Have you heard the name of Shaitaan?" I asked, dominating my hesitations and thoughts otherwise.

The expressions on her rain-flushed face changed visibly for deeper thought; she didn't reply immediately but her fingers involuntarily commenced twitching with the blades of the tall grass from which raindrops were dropping ceaselessly.

"Not heard… It was something more" she commenced, halted for a deep breath, exhaled, and then recommenced "I should not say this, and pardon me if you already know or don't like, but the villagers have superstitions about the place which Mr. Vijay has chosen."

She gave me a look with the corner of her eyes, and she stopped speaking for a while as if waiting for a reply to which I said, "Oh, it's completely fine, I won't feel anything bad if you tell me. Please, can you tell me something more?"

"You know, when we were little, we used to go to that hill and play hide and seek on the sides of the lane. But now nobody goes there, especially not women because again, superstitions of the people bind everyone… Locals believe that hideous crimes have been committed there, but no one knows exactly what. Once it was the most beautiful hill, but now, it lies eerie and man-less." She paused for a while and stroked off a broken blade of grass that had on her hair following a rough gust.

She recommenced "People believe that the area is haunted and that some even claim to see a lonely specter. But these are what people believe, not me, yes, the area looks ghostly now with everything growing wild, but I believe you have been living there for so many days and must have a clear mind that all these are just rural superstitions, folklore and you may completely defy them on the face. That's the best thing. Mr. Vijay must have thought something and bought that house."

I had neither a yes nor a no for her words, but I marked the brightness of her face had gone down as she spoke, her breaths were deep, and expelling them from her mouth resulted in a contraction of her shoulders. Her expressions and occasional smiles perhaps tried to hide something deep within, something fearful perhaps, probably something in her mind left forgotten, buried in a territory where she had not gone for long.

A sudden drift of gusts passed us violently. It was not of a normal speed as its effect was an add-on to the burdened expression of the woman. A sudden grayness, as I saw, had shadowed over her face, and not only her face but all over wherever her skin was being seen, but till now she hadn't spoken. I looked at the sky where I saw the heavenly authors of such grayness which I later understood had befallen the whole vicinity, including me and not only the woman; it was the black clouds that had gathered like a heavy mass, hovering above our heads. The sky was still visible as light blue in the corners. There was no other movement around the featureless expanse.

She glanced for a moment at the children, wiping her face because now the winds were with a spray of raindrops and checking that they were the least concerned about the dark and rough sky still running about, probably waiting for the so dreaded rain itself; she glanced at me again.

"Is it something you want to tell?" I asked her genially, pulling my cardigan tighter.

My implore made her speak, "Yes… I-I remember something related to this but was never comfortable to say so and it got locked up in my heart for years." She paused, looked at the sky, and said, "It was a bright day then like spring and the evenings were pink…"

In the unnatural noises that the wet winds had started playing, knocking, shaking, piercing, and howling; which were enough to make the horses uneasy and grass to hurl with the dust; she continued her tale and ended with a subtle, tiny smile but not unnoticeable for me.

"I can't tell much because this is an old incident. I was probably ten then. In those days we would go playing freely and always searching for new places like inquisitive children always tend to do. One day we reached this hill about which I am talking and came across this house where you now live. The place was mystically mysterious, and its silence—I don't know why—could be called somewhat eerie, candidly speaking, 'unbearable' for us. There were no people around but tall and beautiful trees and high winds, so high to blow your hair in the summers. Then we kids didn't have any bias or prejudice, or not even the slightest information about who lived in that silent mansion that stood proudly strong. We played there for some time that day, four or five of us. But there was something unusual about our play. Everyone played, but a strange resistance dominated probably each of us. No one laughed or cried as we used to do while playing and at the end of the day after playing only half the time we did; no one was willing to return to this beautiful corner of the world again. And from that day we somehow decided that it would be better not to play for some days, the reason as I now remember was supposedly the hot weather, but now I think it was something in the back of our minds as all the kids agreed to this idea unanimously and instantly, which was rare between us.

"Some days later, when the summer was retreating, we resumed our play and on the first day we decided on Hide and Seek. After being caught thrice, my childish anger and frustration were at heights and this time I didn't want to lose. An idea struck me. I decided to hide behind the trees of this particular hill, thinking I would be the winner till last. So, with this in my mind, I walked alone up the lane. The silence was the same, dead in itself. I reached a high situation where I could see numerous trees. I had two minds in going that far, and under the trees, which though looked calling but there was, I mean, probably something in the air or in the silence which was hard for me to cope with. Ultimately, I decided to walk on fast so that I do not see much of the surroundings and on reaching the spot, I bent behind one of the trees. Time passed very slowly, and I started getting nervous bit by bit and ultimately reached a point where I stood wishing someone to catch me. But no one came. I was there all alone and now I started fearing that everyone must have returned home, leaving me. I started looking around, trying to fathom what to do. There was still some sharp golden sun ray falling over the ground and the lane was visible, and I was still in a safe position to run back. As I took my first steps, it struck me because of the foot noises that someone was walking. I couldn't see anyone till that moment amidst the tall grass and trees, but the noises were clear that someone was very near, walking somewhere, crushing the grass and dead leaves by his feet. Within a moment, I turned back, and my heart seemed to explode as someone stood behind me. He was at a slight distance. I noticed him, probably triple my height then. He was standing just blocking the fading sun and the bleak golden rays that hit him from the back and screened by the tall, lean trees scattered all around him, making his face invisible. His face wasn't much seen other than the structure of his strong jaws; as a shadow, he stood there and only what I could figure out then of this mighty figure was his eyes and that he was holding something circular and big in his hand. My heart was beating fast, and no words came out of my mouth. It felt dry. I felt like crying. When understanding that I was failing miserably to make a rapid move, I burst into tears. The man slowly approached me, and my crying became louder. Probably no one could listen to them, anyway. He came very near to me and touched my head once, gently though, and spoke something, and then what he did still amazed me. Whatever this man was carrying in his hands, he raised it and placed it over my head. It was a bit loose but fitted somehow over my ears, that I had realized at least, but I was shocked with terror, not knowing what this thing put over my little head was. Then this figure lifted me like a feather and carried me to the middle of the lane, after which he put me down gently. Now was the opportunity. I was out of the tall grass, and without looking anywhere, I started to run in a frenzy of terror. It had been too much for me. I remember nothing more of him but only remember that somehow my friends found me on the way, and I landed home safely. Now comes the main part. My friends and mother when they saw me told me the same thing: that I was looking cute. When my tears were wiped and I calmed down, I was amazed to see that the circular thing put over my head was nothing but a band of flowers. I then bleakly remember he had more of such bands or flower crowns in his hands and probably he had come that way collecting some flowers. Later on, I understood or got to know that he was Shaitaan who had become a businessman later on. This is my faint memory of this person. Now I am feeling lighter."

"I understand such experiences lead to a profound horror in those moments…" I said after hearing this "But this personality making flower bands… this feels strange. He was bad, I have heard… I don't… know…"

"I know this town has old superstitions about places, though education level is pretty good. But never mind, these are just memories…"

"Well do you think that these stories of ghosts are real?" My words must have come out with pauses.

"I can't much agree or disagree. The old ones say if the last rites aren't done properly, or the corpse is left un-cared…. you know. But I sometimes imagine, maybe living in old towns makes you imagine; that it must be like a twilight zone between complete life and death, being stranded between both. That's what I…"

I was seized by deep thought over this "twilight" statement and instead, my glance dropped over both my palms, which had become rather black. It surprised me, but it was because, as I realized, due to the wet and mossy rock on which we had been resting.

"Why does this town not have any photographs of this Shaitaan? I mean, he was rich and clicking is in fashion."

"No. How did you think of this question?" She replied, "As far as I know, there is not a single picture clicked of him. Nothing even came in the newspapers, and few remember how he looked in real."

"Strange enough… the dead are soon forgotten,"

"Yes…. You know, some people or collectors wish to give anything to have a look at him, even after his death. But there is no evidence." She continued.

"But why?"

"Ah..." she smiled. "Should we go so deep into the stories of the town? Okay… It's what some people believe that he had a phobia. Yes, I don't know if I should say but it's believed that he had a phobia of being clicked; he couldn't jar with the technology of reels and photographs as he…"

"As he might have an unknown undertone of the superstition of being captured by the click; captured in the camera or the reel forever. Offering no escape even after life?"

"Yes, that's what is said. He found something occult in it. In the click." She replied in a low voice.

"Oh, my god…" I replied in an even low voice. I couldn't help it, so astounded I was left.

An involuntary tremble ran over me for a second, and I pressed my palms over the rock. Probably noticing this, the woman spoke again. "Oh! Why do you dive into these? I am sorry. Ah… tell me something else, about your city or your study. These superstitions are bound to make people feel eerie… As it is, we are sitting at a place where people do not come much often."

"Oh, I am good, just as I could hear the sound of the winds and it's grumbling around here," I replied.

"Yes… the winds are stronger than ever. I think we have to get going before it's late."

Within moments I was compelled to say, "It's unbearable, let's stand up…"

We both stood up instantly as a reaction to the absolute riot that the winds had started making. Probably it was late. Even after covering my eyes with one hand and brushing back my hair continuously with the other, I couldn't see a thing other than the raging, slanting drops and the wildly swaying grass all around. In a moment of panic, I called out loud in a random direction, "Where are the kids? Where are you?"

"I am ahead of you! Run fast to the opposite side and you will find my carriage!" Her voice was faintly coming to my ears, jammed by the rough noise of the winds, but with whatever I understood, I tried to obey.

"Got both the kids! I am walking towards your carriage! It's here-I have found it! You walk towards mine! It's just there, fast!" Her last cry gave me a sense of relief.

With no second thought, I started walking swiftly, following my instinct, hoping not to fall or crash into something and to reach the horse carriage as soon as possible. The gelid winds almost cut through me, with their appalling shrills beating in my ears. Gradually and luckily enough, I could see at least what was coming in front of me and by the time I had reached the spot where I had remembered seeing the carriage, it horrified me as I couldn't find it there. Only half-bent trees and dropping branches were seen. I didn't stop and ran faster and faster; as I could bleakly see a concrete road in front of me, though abandoned it was.

I was shivering with cold, but I continued to run until I could hear the horses neighing wildly, though I failed to catch sight of them. The neighing of horses became louder and ultimately my rain-flushed eyes could see a secluded, black structure-a carriage. I ran to it with a feeling of "alas" and stepped into it through its loose gate. I threw myself over the seat and closed behind. I had to hold my chest for minutes, and it took some more time for me to control my horrified breaths and the vision of my rain-flushed eyes. By the time I became calm and, in a state, to understand who was the driver; the first thing I realized was that the carriage was already racing like the winds. It was shaking me up and down. Nothing was visible in the dark chamber, and I had to hold on to the seats lest I fall over the opposite one. The road was severely jerky and the bumps it gave because of maddened horses, are too terrible to contemplate now.

Unaware of where the carriage was taking me, with no instructions from me, soon I thought, "What if I was not in Mrs. A—'s carriage at all but any other carriage?"

"Excuse me! Where are you going? Hello!" I somehow called and when no answer came, I started knocking over the small glass window which separated the driver from the passenger.

After repeated hits over the fogged glass; a man's loud and astonished cry came to my ears. This was the driver's bewildered cry, responding to the knocks and calls which I made from inside. He was unknowing of my stepping in, and he seemed appalled even more than I.

"Hello! No need to worry, I live nearby… Let me in till the storm slows!" I cried with all my might, but still, there was no response other than a puzzled "Huh!"

I had very well realized that I had been completely mistaken and had ended up in an unknown carriage with a horrified driver who was just giving his life to control the horses. I clutched the handle with all my might and sat concentrating all my strength on my back and legs to stay in the seat; with my eyes closed tightly. At one moment, it felt like the carriage was falling, and at the other, it felt like it was flying, but still, I didn't open my eyes. Everything was pitch dark. How much time had passed I do not know, but this never-ending horror ultimately ceased when the horses gradually slowed down; finally leading the carriage to an ultimate halt. I sighed hard and stepped down, almost falling. My head was whirling after the rioting journey and my legs didn't stand in place. By the time I held my head and balanced myself holding the muddy wheel; the driver jumped down. He hurriedly turned towards me to see who was in his carriage for so long and he was quite expressionless and speechless and breathing loudly like myself. I took a look around; the clouds had faded, but the sky was gray still, but lighter. The ground squelched and the unknown area was only a baron field until I realized that on the other side, there was a tiny structure, the riverbank, and some logs scattered and piled over one another.

"Where am I?" I asked the driver.

15

"Let me see where we are, but who are you and how...?" The driver turned and looked.

I informed him briefly about how all that had happened and who I was. He gradually got my point, and I assured him that if he would take me back, I would pay him double fare; I had to make this offer, as he was returning home with his horses and became bound by me.

"See there, the burning ground of the town..." He pointed toward the logs, and I instantly remembered the map.

Something struck my mind as I kept looking at the corpse-burning ground, which was as silent and gloomy as the unknown place.

"Wait a minute, who is that man there?" I asked as I saw someone coming out of the structure and then going in again.

"Oh!" the driver said, looking there with narrowed eyes. "He is the main and the only person here, the old fellow, the caretaker of the burning ground. Greedy wretch!"

"Can you wait for some time over here? I will come back in a moment and then will you take me back for..."

"Eh... where will you go from here? I'll have to take you back, anyway. Waiting here; return really quick, the horses need rest too..." the driver said and walked towards his horses.

I walked to the burning ground, the desolate area with certain old and broken trees, leaves, and logs scattered around; wrapped in total silence. A smoky smell was floating around, and smog was visible to the naked eye. The rains had stopped and the tempest too. On entering this small, cabin-like structure, which appeared as the office of the caretaker of the place, I saw him, an old languid man—with stern and wretched eyes sitting on the chair with his back bent. He lifted his eyes to me and asked in a torn voice as soon as I entered, "What is the matter? Where is the corpse?"

"No, actually no one has died, and no corpse has to be burned," I replied in the fear of being misunderstood.

"Then what is it? We do not sell any flowers here!"

By this time, I had entered the chamber with some tasks in my mind, with the risk taken, but I had also realized that the man was not a very cooperative one.

"I am from the paper! The town's newspaper and I want to get some information from here. Are you the one who checks the death certificates and sanctions all the corpses to be burned?" I asked.

He stood, but his looks suggested he couldn't believe I was a reporter from the newspaper.

"Nothing happens here without death certificates." He replied instantly and without my even asking this, "No one has till now come here, and this place is not for reporters to gather information. I am the only one here for years!"

"I have come here to ask something. Will you help me?"

"What is it? Ask fast…" he replied and sat down.

"Where is the burning done?"

"There." he pointed out towards the riverbank.

"Nothing without death certificates? No chance?"

"Obviously not!" he frowned.

"Okay. So, do you do the rites of the corpses in case someone has unknowingly left it, or someone comes with an unknown corpse and deposits it here?"

"Rites? Rituals? I am not a priest. Whatever anyone wants to do, he does himself. If in any other case, I just put the thing on fire."

I was shocked by his words and some dots got connected—it was the only corpse-burning place there, so it was implied every dead body came there only and whatever he said were his own words.

"Alright. Can you…"

"No, nothing more can be done. By this time, I would have gotten the tip for burning three corpses. From the paper, huh?" He replied sarcastically.

By this time, I started feeling languid. This feeling of cold, feverish uneasiness wasn't unexpected, as I had been wet for so long.

"I am not asking for free…" I looked into his eyes. "I know how this news collection business is done. You know I want some information, and I can pay for it. Can I see your register once? The record of the corpses and all…."

He denied it at that moment sternly. I asked him twice and assured him it was only for once, but nothing happened until I offered him cash. With whatever I gave, I don't know if it was very high as I didn't have the faintest idea about how all those things were done, don't know whether I was right or wrong, but he agreed.

He bought an enormous pile of rotten registers from the shelves and dumped them before me.

"See fast and go. This isn't legal." He said without facing me.

In accordance with the dates of Neelnath's death declaration, I figured out ultimately which register was it. I started flipping the pages in a hurry and the man got busy burning the lantern in the dark, damp room.

This was the register of the past year, and as I jumped to the page, I found it blank, except for one entry for the night, the time being seven-thirty. It used to be dark till that time. On reading this entry, I saw the dead man's name was entered, Neelnath. But the signature of the person who supposedly deposited the corpse at the cremation ground was some strange spelling written in a strange handwriting, which I couldn't fathom at that time. The letters were un-understandable; I concluded soon, either written by a person who didn't know how to write or written in that manner purposely. Every letter seemed in a different style of writing and coping with the pressure that I had to hurry or lose a chance of getting anything; one letter which I understood and am sure about was the capital

"N". It struck me instantly, and I recognized it, an N whose right top end roofs the whole word like a big square root.

"Now it's high time!" The man turned to me again and spoke words with a feeling of hurry and vexation.

"I am done…" I closed the register and pushed it towards him over the table.

"Hurry, miss!" The carriage man called as he saw me coming out.

I hurried towards the carriage and embarked.

"Take me again to the riverside… please, fast."

The horses neighed loudly, and the carriage rolled again with a heavy jerk. I gave a last look at the cremation ground, the ground where dead ones are burned and, and where I had gotten the lesson that truly, things could be done with money in the world. As I fixed my thought again on what I had derived, the peculiar letter "N" on the signature, was implying simply that the person signing the depositor's column was the Neelnath who was himself the corpse who had been deposited to be cremated. The signature of Neelnath, as I connected with what I had found in the house's storeroom, on the papers of the deal showed that peculiar "N" which exactly, exactly matched the one in this signature and I was sure that the signature was false, the name of the dead man was false and not Neelnath but in his name, some other person had been burned in the dead of night. Yes. I was also sure that the way the "N" was written, no two people could even think of writing it in a similar way. Neelnath was not burned on that day, and the person who signed the deposition was himself Neelnath signing with a fake name, declaring himself to be dead and probably there wasn't any need to, to get a doctor's certificate if one had big sums of money to spend in this town. I also thought I knew who had been burned there, in Neelnath's name, and I feel it's needless to say for the readers, too.

With my thinking frozen, I settled near the window and gazed out, being satisfied that truths of that nature no longer disturb me as much as they would have done a week before. I thought I could now cope with such facts that were beyond contemplation. I couldn't think much more, and I am wondering now about this; as the depth of this piece of information which I had derived would open the jams of the whole thing, but still, the questions arising in my mind were far less than what it should have been.

Just the silence before the storm. I know now; it was. The carriage was now calm. I noticed I could see the white particles of the atmosphere hovering in the air, in the black backgrounds—hundreds they were. I maintained my composure and serenity to such an extent that it was very unlikely, though; I felt lethargic, and tiredness forced me into an unplanned slumber. Maybe this heaven-like sleep, lasted for some minutes and I had no intention of opening my eyes until I had reached the destination, only if my consciousness had control over opening and closing them, but I am not sure about such control in that situation. But soon, in my deep sleep, I grew uncomfortable and within moments of realizing this, started a series of rapid sneezing, which I failed to control. It forced me awake suddenly. The reason for these sneezes was none other than the dust particles whirling around me—their numbers visibly more and settling all over the leathered seats and my garments. As soon as my sleep broke, I leaned forward to open the window for fresh air to come in, to control my sneezes and what I saw was strange. The blasts of cold winds overwhelmed me as I forwarded my head out for a minute or so and within this, I saw a massive old structure, covered in mists, towards which the carriage was rolling faster. It appeared bigger and bigger as we neared it and when I faced it; I was terribly surprised to, to recognize it the same as what I had seen in my disturbing dream the previous night. I had been there before; I had been through this place in my dreams. The neglected structure looked older than what it was in my dream, but it was just the same, it was the building that I had seen so closely only and only in my dream. It was covered with shadows and moss and rain had faced off all the paint from the walls. I pushed forward a bit more and as we had already crossed the house and I was turning back my head, in the last glimpses of this, I saw a wild garden, trees, and the terrace. Soon we passed it completely, and it became invisible again. It was just a matter of seconds. If, if I would have not woken that minute, and not opened the window immediately because of my sneezing, which had now ceased, I would have completely missed seeing this structure.

I settled back into my seat and closed the window, breathing hard. A peculiar, innate sense it was which overwhelmed me, as if the atmosphere in the closed carriage had got congested as if the limited space in it got reduced suddenly and my freeness of being the sole passenger of the carriage hindered. The psychological feeling and discomfort were the same, as what one feels when two or three people sit in the small carriage. But here; I was completely alone. Gradually, the carriage grew colder and colder than ever, though I am sure the windows were locked. I was still wet and now I was shivering. In such lone moments, one can't reason anymore, and I sat wishing that the ride be over faster. Enduring the ride made me feel sick. It was after some time had passed from my waking up and spotting this structure, that I realized, the feeling of not being the only passenger was fading, the air was becoming less heavy, almost as before and the cold also had reduced as instantly as it had heightened. It's how I felt.

"We are near!" called the driver loudly.

My heart started beating heavily with a thought. The structure which I had seen in my nightmare, I still feel hard to cope with this fact. I had just now seen it from my carriage, and it was existing! The scenes of falling of a man who had been pushed to death by another from the terrace of the same building came to my mind and could it be that what I had earlier laughed off as just a discomforting dream was a vision of some real incident of the past? If the structure existed, then what was the big deal that the incident also happened in reality? So, this suggested that I had seen an actual murder that had occurred sometime in the past, in my nightmare. But how could all this be true? I had known nothing like this in psychology, at least with the very little I know. Then who was the man who I glimpsed standing in front of me and whom I had mistaken as Uncle for the time being, as I had landed on the floor-which ultimately broke my nightmare? I somehow coped with all this in the little more time in the carriage, remembering God's name, and finally, when I stepped down once reached, I contemplated that the crime had really taken place. That I had seen something from the past and that it had happened on that building's terrace some years ago and that one had pushed the other.

"I don't care how I am getting all this. I am sure nothing of this sort has happened to me before and I do not care, as I feel it is 'induced'. My finding of the map, seeing this dream, my findings of old papers in the storeroom which even an investigator would fail to find easily, and my waking up at the same instant when we crossed this structure, all can be induced by something or probably someone," This was my apparent thought as I stepped down,

written in my diary for that day.

I was indeed shaken, and it is also true that as I stepped down and saw the open sky and the pleasant sunshine, I concluded the above thought again as a fragment of imagination. But now I feel it was true. I knew I hadn't overcome the fear of ghosts entirely and that my previous satisfaction was premature. I also commit that I haven't experienced such phenomena ever since.

16

I was calmed and a blast of relief came over me as I saw Uncle, Ajay and Mrs. A—standing amid the expanse. I approached them and they approached me.

"I stepped into the wrong carriage… but I am fine…" I began and said whatever had happened, subtracting the part of the cremation ground, as I felt it would be a disaster to reveal it.

"Oh, you are okay, oh, God! I was cursing myself for somehow failing to get you safely with us and dreadful thoughts smothered me…." The woman said, wiping my wet face with whatever she had got.

"You are drenched all over—I pray you do not catch a cold or fever." Uncle exclaimed, felt my forehead with his hand and continued "We'll be back home soon my dear—I hope everything is fine, we'll manage the fever but tell me are you hurt?"

"No Uncle please don't worry; I am just wet…" I barely spoke, for the winds were still not warm.

The affectionate woman, now with a calm and pleasant expression, kept on rubbing and wiping my wet hair as one does for a child, for all the long, and I felt warmer. Suddenly, it struck like a thunderbolt. It would be a catastrophe if Uncle got informed about where I had gone. But things were already out of my control because, as I turned back, I saw my uncle had already reached the carriage driver who was still waiting there. One moment I thought of walking towards them, but the next, I knew it was too late. Uncle had already gone off talking with the driver and probably he asked everything, and the driver revealed everything; the most unwanted of the revelations being my stopping at the cremation ground.

I thanked the woman and bid her goodbye and as Uncle returned; we embarked on our carriage to return to the house. I didn't speak even once in the carriage and nor did my uncle. I sat all the time with my eyes closed, and supporting my chin with my fist, with my elbow over the knee.

The silence of the house was broken by the noise the gate made as we opened it and retreating sunbeams entered with us into the dark hall.

"Vaanya and Ajay, first take a proper bath with hot water, change off your wet clothes and I am preparing tea. All have it lest all be sick tomorrow." The words of Uncle seemed benign, but I must say, his accent was sterner than ever.

I was prepared. We sat on the sofas and chairs facing each other once we had done what was instructed and were now sipping the strongest tea that I had ever had. Uncle didn't look into my eye all this while but looked down. He was still quiet.

Uncle sat with one leg over the other, arms crossed, and head angled down with his eyes shut. He sat like this for some time within which none of us spoke and then finally he broke the silence, asking a minor question.

"Vaanya, where did you go alone in the carriage?" He neither lifted his head nor opened his eyes.

"Uncle..." was my only initial response, but I continued seeing him still waiting for my reply, "I think—I think you know it, Uncle."

I replied in a low voice, showing that I didn't have an answer and that I was sorry, but he didn't reply and questioned again.

"Why?"

I sat there silently; I knew I had to avoid answering the question but, how could I? My hands instead went towards my sleeves, and I started folding them up as I felt a sudden warmth or unease.

Uncle finally raised his head to me and looked into my eye. His arms were crossed still. He then stood up and walked towards the window. He was more unpredictable now than ever, and I gestured to Ajay if he was getting all this.

"He is furious..." He whispered.

Immediately, I stood with my apologies and was ready to give the complete account whatever the results would be. I couldn't bear to tell lies and create misconceptions in my mind about my uncle.

But he began before me, "You ordered the carriage to the corpses' burning ground. There must be a good reason to go to such a place. It's not a beautiful sight, I suppose, or is it?" He said without facing me, but his words didn't express a hint of anger or roughness.

"What!" Ajay whispered, looking at me in a confused way.

"Uncle... I can..."

"Do you think it's safe? The driver was unknown, and the place was so far. No one goes to such places, and you went there without notifying, without informing, and above all, with no reason. How can you risk yourself? What if you got lost there? Or fall off or get hurt? I wouldn't be able to find you there at all. No one could. It's not a play. People get lost in the woods and—and what could I have told your father?"

He still didn't face me and coping with this was tough.

"Uncle, I will explain everything. I believe you will listen. Mr. Candy or whatever; is not a good man... He is certainly not who you think he is, he is someone else! I say this to you."

"Mr. Candy? Where did he come amid this? What's the deal with Mr. Candy? And old retired man!" he thundered at last.

"I had told you previously also about this strange man who had tried to enter my room through the window, but you ignored.... I again say to you, things aren't right! It is not as you see it..."

"You have known enough, I suppose.... Do you really, really remember anyone coming up the window? How can one? Are you sure? Do you remember his face or any other proof? Can't it be a misconception with some-some mongoose or other animal at night?"

"I-I don't know—I can't provide any evidence for now," I replied, somewhat affected by his way of speaking.

The way he spoke, I started doubting my conviction.

"That's the whole point-it was a misconception, and I also had a similar misconception when I came here—it is certainly some animal moving over the walls. Now say why did you go there?"

"Uncle, I still suspect the man can come up again. I believe you shouldn't ignore this." I replied.

"Ahh..." he made vexed noise, "It's my mistake, I should have given you a room on the ground floor—you wouldn't have heard any such noises of animals."

I thought for once of speaking about the previous resident, Paul, the madman who had also told of somebody coming there—but I stopped. At last, it was a testimony of a madman! How could I believe what a lunatic of that sort said?

"Uncle, why are you so cross today? I am sorry and I am upset because of my conduct, and I do not want you to be cross. It is not your nature; you are not looking today like you usually do. You have broken so many times in the native language, though you know I don't know it well. Why? Why are you, unlike other days?"

"What! Unlike other days?" he turned back to me now. "Yes, I am angry dear…"

A thought came to me. I shouldn't have told you that, but now there was no return. I had to continue.

"Why do you think I am unlike other days?" he walked nearer and held the chair with his hand.

"Uncle, I feel you are different today. I have accepted that my conduct was reckless and dangerous, already…" I didn't move.

"Can it do? No. But why do you think I am different today?" he finally sunk exhausted into the chair but leaned forward, his elbows over his thighs and a look deep into my eyes.

I shuddered with his look—his eyes; they didn't look like his and his tone; I was certain it was not of my uncle.

"Why?" he asked at length with a grave and grumbling voice and sat in that position as if his body wouldn't move without my answer.

I sighed loudly, and a feeling of pressing stress overwhelmed me. But he kept on looking into my eyes, with no expression on his face, and I couldn't bear to look into his.

"Uncle, be yourself, please! None can stand this way." I was compelled to speak.

"Father...." The only word came out of Ajay's mouth, who sat appalled and expressionless.

"I have never seen you like this..." he spoke again, but it was so meek that probably didn't reach Uncle's ears. Uncle was still staring at me with his arms crossed again.

"I am very, very interested in your story, dear girl. I am sitting; answer." He said, nodding his head twice.

His precise talking would crash, and silence regained every time.

Finally, I spoke rubbing my cheek with my hand "Uncle I believe you are not behaving yourself because-because..." I shut my eyes and spoke, "You are wearing the coat of Shaitaan."

Finally, I told it and there began a series of harder and faster beats in my heart, "I strongly feel you shouldn't wear his clothes and also that you should meet a doctor for your lack of sleep and headaches and hard health rather taking medicines of all kinds on your own."

I kept my eyes closed, my fingers patting my hand softly, and I sat waiting for a consequence of what I had said—which I had never imagined of speaking.

"This is worse than eavesdropping!"

Also, came a coinciding yell of amazement by Ajay.

"Now I understand!" he burst into a strange expression of laughter and anger. "Your 'story' about your friend and all... Oh, yes... Huh!"

He breathed out loudly, leaned back into his chair, and, after releasing a peculiar laugh in the air, looked back again.

"You know, I never knew you believed in these superstitions. It is unexpected and alarming! Your condition is poorer than the folks in the town."

"Uncle, you can detest my thoughts but can't justify your conduct! He was a bad man, a bad personality!" I answered.

"I do not detest you or your thoughts—dear girl," he said and kept his hand softly over my shoulder.

Another change in his attitude!

He regained his previous composure and for seconds rubbed his face, particularly his eyes, with his hands and answered then "You don't know the rules in the town, I suppose. I have paid for this!" he said, pointing towards his heavy and magnificent brown coat.

"In the town, you can purchase idle houses with all the things present in them and they are yours if the seller agrees! I have purchased this house with all its belongings as they are—the curtains, the tables, the bed. Many things are the ones that he may have used. What about it? I couldn't have bought all new things for the house in such a short period. How could you believe your friend's story? I knew it was false, or some other filth, that the dead's energy keeps on receding for some months or years from his clothes and all. The seller told me that these were almost unused by that man—he would only stock them and used them little. And after all, I have paid a high price for these! Really, I paid a very high amount—almost the actual amount this collection might have cost!"

We both sat with jaws dropped. Uncle had already started again in the local language.

A thought captured my mind. "Really, Uncle is right. How could I believe this theory? How could I; I believe that my uncle's clothes are influencing his mood and psychology. As it is, there is no proof of the dead's aura being tied to their clothes for a time after death. Oh, silly me! I have created this chaos and offended him and disturbed my mind with these philosophies. Maybe uncle's mood is generally like this, maybe he has these mood changes naturally. I have not known him for long. Maybe, maybe he is not having any swings, but I am taking extra notice of it. Oh, how could I? I was never like this before! Or was I?"

I sat there thinking, while he recommenced at full speed, "You know you are telling of Mr. Candy; I do not know what all you are imagining in your mind, but he is a gentleman. An old man, problematic with his leg, walks and works around, is genial and runs an outstanding restaurant, cares for children, and has had created not a single complaint of dissatisfaction among his neighbors for the past eight months he has come to this town." Uncle started to walk around.

"People believe this house is haunted--that's true that they believe, but not Mr. Candy. He has helped me, and we are now friends. Do you know how many times he inquired about the well-being of you kids? Do you know he also gave me some new cookies from his restaurant for you all? But you doubt him! Has he ever misbehaved? Has he ever behaved wrongly?"

It struck me hard. I was wrong! Uncle's words appeared to me as true every inch! How clearly he spoke! It can be that I was judging Mr. Candy wrongly. Maybe I was taking too much of the old man's notice and above all, it is true he never behaved wrongly, save some strange questions. The reasons why I was skeptical about him vanished suddenly—and it surprised me to a large extent how I mistook the old Mr. Candy.

"Uncle, I certainly didn't know of his conduct, that he asked for us."

"Yes! Obviously, he asked…" Uncle looked satisfied. "He is a gentleman…" he said again, pressing harder on the "is".

"You know, I am living here only by ignoring the tales of the folks and you should learn to ignore them, and I didn't also want the kids of my house to know such tales and that's why I restricted at least you to go out in between the locals—I am sorry if my conduct was stern. You know this situation is the best in the whole town which I have secured at a good price and as now the barrier of someone living in this house has broken, others who missed this opportunity because of their prejudices envy me."

I held my uncle's hand, apologized, and sat back, almost sinking into the sofa with a feeling of an embarrassed little child who realizes her mistake after a long time.

He breathed out loud. Now he was looking for my uncle. The strange fire in his eyes had subsided, and he looked cool. Another cup of tea was prepared and this time, by me, and my uncle and I loved it.

"It's just magnificent and sweet, as it is made by you," Uncle remarked.

"Yes, Uncle—its rainy and cold. That's why it is even better—the effect of good weather on good tea and good taste."

"Please do not be upset—I was stern today just because I am concerned about you—a lot. You are dear to me. Don't mind me." he said.

I felt a sense of calmness after the thundered debate, as the ginger tea smoothed along my throat. But at the same time, I kept on asking myself, how could I be so terribly mistaken? Why did I take Mr. Candy like that?

"Yes, it's drizzling." Uncle looked out the window.

The room was as it is on the darker side and yellow bulbs had to be lit. The drops made a clear tune as they beat gently against the window glasses and inside all was silent in the enclosed hall.

It was at this time that I put another question, rather innocently, "Uncle, do you know Vishwakumar? And his visit to the town, Rajesh, told me about this."

"Uncle, take another biscuit...."

"What did you just say?" he continued. "Not the biscuit; before that. What did you say?"

I saw his hand go up to his shirt's collar, and he started to unbutton wildly.

"Oh, I just wanted to know about Vishwakumar, don't mind Uncle, it's not important..." I replied.

"How do you know about him? What do you know about it?"

"Nothing much, Uncle," I replied, this time with caution.

"Do you know about it? Dear girl, I ask do you know about it?"

I didn't reply. I couldn't fathom what was he asking. What was this "it"? I completely failed to understand.

"What Uncle? What are you talking about?"

"How do you know? Rajesh—he must have told you such things.... I suspect him quite. He is after it, perhaps!"

"After what?"

Uncle's tone had changed, and his demeanor altered to restlessness.

He stood, leaving his tea, rubbed both his hands, and put them into his pocket, trying to regain his composure.

"Do you know where has Arun disappeared? I hope you know—I am sure you know. You know a great deal."

"No, Uncle, surely if I would have known, I would certainly tell you."

"There is certainly something going on here. How has it vanished?" at least I could comprehend these rapid whispers or murmurs which he posed to himself, with his head down with thought.

"What… What do you think? What are you asking for?" he asked me in a cross-tone.

"I don't know what is this 'it' and I am very confused Uncle, I—I just think that there could be some other reasons also for you buying this property." Here was my risk, and I realized I had offended Uncle again.

My words surely shocked Uncle for some time and when he regained his speech he said, "So now you also think exactly like your elder cousin? Unimaginable!"

I regretted my slip of the tongue and sat motionless. On Uncle's demand, I had to tell him about Arun's secret study of palmistry and who were his subjects; to my surprise, he didn't have any hint of where his son was going and what he was engrossed in. He simply didn't care for it before, but now he broke open the door and asked me to show all that was in there. The books, the prints. He grew uneasy, like me in that room, and Ajay was not allowed to enter. He was quite shaken, yes.

Not a word came out of his mouth all the time and when he had examined the room, he pushed off the curtain to see the other part of the room. This part of the room was suffocating and dusty, filled with a strangely rotten odor.

Remarkably, I noticed he halted in front of the wall of this part of the room. He stood almost frozen and kept on his gaze concentrated on the wall. I held my hand over my chest, as it was exactly the place from where I had taken off the portrait and kept it in my room. It had left a deep mark on the dusty wall and Uncle noticed it—it really was similar to the impression on the second floor's closed room.

He went out of the room without uttering a word and I, too, before leaving, looked over the wall. From where Arun had got this painting and why had he kept it locked in his room was the question, but if what I thought was true; Arun would be returning. Returning soon.

17

Before I made a move out of the room, the noise of the heavy main gate slamming came so hard that it halted me for a moment. I swiftly walked out and saw Ajay struggling hard to pull the gate open. I joined him, but it was futile. Within one moment we were across the hall, peeping through the wet window glass, but my uncle was nowhere to be seen. The main gate of the house was jammed.

"How did this happen?"

"Papa left angrily, slamming the gate behind him and it's the rainy season, probably it is stuck from outside!" he said chaotically.

I stepped back in a wave of confusion and tension. For the next ten minutes, we both tried all the means to open the door, but again, without luck. Two of us felt trapped and probably my uncle or anyone else didn't know about this. The sky was darker and the rains, which were drizzling, would be soon in for harder drops. The thunder growled and we could do nothing but observe the riot created in the wild skies. Darkness wrapped around the hall, and the current went off. The windows also didn't offer any vision of the outside world, save the impression of the wild dance of the dead trees. We were reduced to the mercy of candle souls.

"What should we do now?" Ajay asked.

"I am more concerned about Uncle! It's raging outside. He would be blown off or fall somewhere...."

I at length took a seat, on the sofa hopelessly looking at the clock which had struck six thirty and night would soon break in-it would be harder for Uncle to find the way. Ajay paced up and down the floor, pressing his hands against his ears-struggling with the piercing cries that the window glass made.

"It's my fault. I shouldn't have told those words to Uncle—he was okay, but then I spoke and…." I sighed.

"What did I speak that angered him? I can't remember exactly." I exclaimed "I never knew that it would vex him so much—I wish he comes back fast! I pray!"

I finally stood up and paced towards the window in a fit of passion and as soon as I recklessly opened it, a huge blast of furious, rainy wind soaked me, somewhat pushing me steps behind. By the time I gained balance again, Ajay had shut the window in the face of the lightning, which growled even more violently.

"Don't even think of going out to find father!" Ajay exclaimed with teary eyes and a terrified rage, "I hope he will come fast."

The last words were as if he would cry and I went up to him, embracing him and saying that I wouldn't do such a mistake for sure.

We both didn't have dinner and sat for a long time in our beds on the second floor-quitting the lonely, dreary hall. It was uneasy to be in that mighty block of darkness and dimness, all alone.

In the bedroom, we could just see the old and gloomy walls staring back at us, and the small view that the open door offered; a view of the whole house almost, shadowy and expanded to unimaginable lengths, was enough to stir fear. There were so many rooms, blasting was their old windows and uncountable open doors banging wildly in the unknown corners of the mighty house-and none could have the courage to step out to find these old things and lock them. The storm cleared in about half an hour or so, evident as the noises were less; but it was for the worse. We lay on our beds, and the boy didn't lose grip on my hand, even across the bed. Finally, it became quite silent, and amidst the drizzling noise, I can't remember when sleep conquered me. The last thing I saw was Ajay, who also was immovable over his blanket, his hand hanging down the bed, probably the child was asleep too.

But I didn't have the leisure to sleep for over three hours. My eyes opened on the bed itself. I soon realized that hard sounds, as if someone was banging something in a fit, had awakened me. By the time I stood up, alarmed, Ajay had also awakened, and the noises came ceaselessly, echoing all over the empty house; until I understood the hits were not mad, but violent. Initially, we exchanged confused glances and thought it was Uncle, who had returned and was struggling to open the gate, but the next moment we were sure it was not coming from down. Not a knock it was, but a savage attempt to break in, and the direction of it was tough to fathom. Now it was with both hands, certainly beating against our window glass.

In a moment, I was taken aback towards the corner of the wall and Ajay sat sunken, in a state of shaking on the other side. I'd do anything against allowing this unknown creature to touch any of us—the idea of it coming near me was intolerable. The tempest was striking with full fury again, and visibility, though it existed, was poor. It struck as a thunderbolt had fallen in the middle of us; the last hit on the glass had broken the lock. My body refused to move an inch and I just blankly stared in terrified perplexity at what had entered our room. It was big, bulky, and black. It bumped over the floor from the window, making a heavy noise, and started to walk around. It seemed to feel about it in the dimness as if it was searching for something—it soon became conscious of us at the corners and darted towards Ajay in a way that made me shudder. I still couldn't well see it, implying that he couldn't see us too, save our impressions in the darkness. I dashed forward, but before I could even reach him, yes, there were the legs of a human; it, fortunately, changed its direction and started feeling the wardrobe and the chairs. His vision was certainly poorer than mine and I managed to come nearer to Ajay who, to my genuine fears, had already fainted, for his body laid loosely. With quickness, it moved to the middle of the room and what I saw it do, removed any questions. It bent down, down under the beds, and pulled out the big, mighty portrait of Shaitaan which I had put under there. It held it high and then its eyes met mine. He saw me. What a flame in his eyes. Its expression I fail to put in words. It walked towards us, and I sunk more and more into the corner, covering and clenching my fainted cousin tightly, with his head over my shoulder and my back towards the climber with the corner of my eyes fixed on his every move. In a horrified and very horrified confusion and chaos which my mind was in, I thought I would faint there and then too. His rough hand touched my back and finally, cries of horror and repugnance came out of my mouth ceaselessly at the highest pitch enough to awaken even the dead animals. In a moment he walked back at a terribly fast pace, certainly not because of my cries, but as if, as if he had recognized that it couldn't waste its time anymore. It reached the window in one bound, with the painting under his arm, and within the last second, it climbed over it, and he was gone. Gone with the frame. My body acted immediately, and I leaped towards the window, with my legs still trembling, and saw this demonic climber slipping down the pipe. The storm was furious and biting winds and rain showered through the uncontrollable windows and the floor under me was wet. I stayed at a distance, safe enough to protect myself from the slight part of the rain that was coming in. It wasn't over yet; I knew.

It managed to slip down, and it was lost out of sight. Suddenly I noticed something stir in our garden and it was him. He would certainly jump over the low fencing, and he would certainly escape. I cried with force, but it neither reached my lips nor my ears. What dark scenes I witnessed in that rattling storm's night still give me nightmares, and can't be braved. Just when the figure reached the fence, I saw with my hurting heart—paining with wild poundings. Another figure stirred somewhere around and within a blink of eyes, I saw it jump with full fury over this one. They struggled in the mud and the crackling current in the sky occasionally showed them. Soon one figure overcame the other, kicked him, which appeared very merciless, again gained balance, and started to run out, leaving the other rather dead. It was, I noticed, the demon with the painting who had overcome the other. I started pacing from one window to the other on the floor to catch glimpses of terror and madness. It was as if a hundred shadows were lurking and waiting for this creature, to stop it, because another figure emerged from behind the dark trees, stronger than this one for sure, and came between him and the fences. I watched it like a nightmare. My eyes stopped blinking. The stronger one struck down the climber, and the climber struck back. It was a battle for minutes and at this point as if everything, enough to kill me there; a loud horn vibrated in the lane. Flashes of light could be seen, and I remembered that this grumbling lighthouse siren was of the car which had come some days previously there. I shut my ears and eyes in a frenzy of fright, but when I was compelled to free them again; I saw now not two but three figures struggling. My frozen reason fathomed minutes after that. They were trying to block and hold back the climber. Madness, madness I perceived it was, how could I endure it? I wished I too had fallen unconscious than seeing this. The two figures would surely overcome this, I thought, but no—it was the inverse. To my frantic horror, it was never more than when I saw the climber overcome one by one both the other figures over it; struck the feeble one first and then the stronger one, too. All three fell on the ground, moving and struggling wildly, but only one stood up again and it was the climber at my window. This creature had overcome three men and was now still running in a frantic hurry towards the fence, with the portrait of Shaitaan still with him.

The thunder grumbled furiously, and, in the light, I saw three figures stranded over the ground like corpses.

"What is this happening? Who are they?" I sobbed.

But when I lifted my wet eyes again, the climber was gone. I made a last attempt; I took large steps and went out of the room immediately and pushed open the wide window of the passage. The enormous view that it offered was obscured by fog at the ends, but my eyes immediately saw the climber who had leaped over the fence and was now running in an unknown direction. No-the direction wasn't unknown to me. Probably he had been mistaken. He was running in the direction of the cliff edge. As I watched it; it still takes me all my courage and faith to write about this. I must write, that I felt a sensation over or under my right ear. Like someone breathed out very, very close to me. My palms, my neck, and my back felt chilled. In those moments of anxiety, I thought this time I heard a sigh. Before I could think of turning, I felt someone near me, beside me, and not only standing but also peeping down from the window like me. It was at this moment when it became unbearable and if I would turn my head right, I fear, I would have seen another face. I know not how, but for the first and last time, I felt, if the reader could imagine, a sense of both terrible fright and terrible anger. Anger seeing the climber who was running mad with the painting, such, and anger that I couldn't handle it; leave the question of it being mine. My grip on the windowpane was loosening as my trembling hands couldn't hold it and in such a moment a mighty, and terribly forceful gust, to my horror, from behind me passed from over my shoulders with full fury out of the window. It left me unharmed and set my hair flying, but a cracking noise suggested that the window glass was cracked. It didn't bother me much then as it was stormy, but it bothers me very much now. How could it come from behind me? That is the question. From this moment, I felt that all energy from my body was soaked out.

Here on turning as I found nothing behind me in the labyrinth of blackness, I turned again to the climber who had still been running. When I realized everything was over, something, to my astonishment, made the demonic figure stop. Apparently, something had blocked his way, but this time there was no shadow, no black figure, animal, or tree, but still, there was something. I wouldn't write in detail, as a peculiar unease is overwhelming me, but I must briefly describe it. It was as if the fog had taken form. It appeared from a distance as a luminous, smoky figure standing before this demonic climber. It was scarcely visible to me but to the climber, he must be clear as the climber stretched his hand forward as if pointing at the figure in fearful recognition as if saying, "You?"

The figure was feeble and taller than all the figures who had previously tried to stop this man but seeing this one, the climber was set in a maddening terror as he didn't confront it but instead started running, making the most terrifying noise ever heard by me. Whatever it was, it followed this climber rapidly and effortlessly. Its manner of movement I cannot or rather would not write.

The climber probably was driven to the edge of the cliff by "it" because he had now stopped to confront it. He screamed something loudly which came to my ears but so faintly that I could understand only three words: "I", "kill", "again". I had no breath left in my body by this time, and I didn't know whether I was even alive. Horror gripped my neck. Could it be that the three words meant "I will kill you again"?

The climber ran, didn't lose his grip on the painting, but held his hand high as if it was a weapon. Within a blink of an eye, the foggy figure, probably, to my unimaginable horror I had recognized whom it resembled, glided with an inhuman pace and faced the climber eyeball to eyeball. It moved in a way that made my blood curdle. It almost overwhelmed the climber. A horribly terrified cry with a terribly torn voice, as if of a man being stabbed ceaselessly, grumbled, and echoed all over, setting hundreds of birds mad in their respective hidings. The cries kept on coming for minutes, and my head whirled. It held my head but futile it was, my balance was lost.

18

A smoky smell, the smell of a lit pipe, stirred my senses again. I opened my eyes in the local doctor's chamber with him beside me, smoking with one hand and with the other feeling my forehead. I was glad that I was alive and also glad that as I rapidly checked my reason; I got that it was also rather unharmed and sound like before.

My waking up was certainly not smooth, questions like "Where am I?", "Uncle?", "The burglar", "Who's dead and who's alive?" came out of my mouth.

"Dear girl, calm down," the doctor said and laid me again on the bed, "your uncle has just broken his left hand, your elder cousin has broken the right one and the junior secret service agent, the strongest of them all, has broken both arms and one leg. Only you and I are fine and sound over here."

"God..." I could only say.

The nurse was continuously rubbing my hand and bare feet with her palms, and it felt good.

He lifted his spectacles for a moment, bent and looked at me closely, and passed the last judgment most casually, "Oh, she's fine."

"She's healthy and hearty!" spoke the nurse.

The doctor left, and I moved my body, simultaneously moving my view curiously all over it, and was more than satisfied to find only one bandage wrapped over my right arm. A white blanket was over me. The most satisfying realization was that my face was unharmed and also that I had somehow not fallen off the window.

"Don't move miss, only a bandage and no serious damage—I assure you, only a fever out of a cold, you will be fine in a day or two." The nurse said and asked, "Would you like some tea?"

"Ya, yes…" I could rise by myself, and so I did.

"Sister, could you tell me about Ajay and…"

"Oh, he is at his home, looked after by his friend's mother. He had just fainted last night but regained consciousness after the doctor was called… I think you will be released by today too…"

She helped me drink, and I asked another question after thanking her, "If I heard the doctor correctly, he said a junior agent or something, now who is this?"

"I know not much, a dark young and sturdy fellow he is…. See, rest. Do not ask much or burden your mind or you could be further detained. I am not to disturb you much, as the doctor said."

I remember that I was allowed a walk in the small clinic's passage and though I urged continuously that I was fine, the doctor didn't leave me before two o'clock in the day. As I ventured around, I saw a person from the Police walking around, and a couple of suited men sitting with crossed legs over the chairs proudly, who I thought looked exhausted. Maybe they had just finished their interview with the Police. I instantly recognized one of the faces, without even thinking about why they were there. The white-suited elderly man was the same person whom I had seen in Vishwakumar's book which was in my uncle's library and there he was put in a list of the famous painting and antique collectors of the country. The other one, a middle-aged man, was certainly his secretary who was arranging some papers. Both men were in the newspaper. I had seen them before. When one nurse came out, the door cracked, and I looked in. I saw Uncle, Arun, and one another man on the beds. This other person wasn't Rajesh for sure.

I failed to understand anything in the beginning, but soon things were clear, and I would clear it for the reader too, certainly. I asked some other people and also the doctor as he came my way, what had happened and certainly all the questions that the reader might have in his mind, but it was futile, everyone conscious of what happened had gotten to know me and avoided telling anything and it came to some point where a strange, unaccountable nervousness gathered me. I was one by now. They were surely hiding something from me. I became quite confused that whatever happened last night was in reality or if I had fainted halfway and what further I saw were my nightmares.

But after the last check-ups, when the doctor released me and I was escorted to be left home with one of the nurses accompanying me, I was calmed down to see the same black car, classic design, parked in front of the clinic. The sun was shining brightly over its tough black body, and it was glaring back. It was the car in which Arun had gone; it was the car that rang its siren-like horn last night and it was the car that authored flashes of light in the wooded lane. What I saw last night wasn't a nightmare. It was true.

I reached the house in half an hour and now stood contemplating the sight of the building. I felt as if my eyes moved to catch any change in it. I knew the idea was innocent. The house was the same: strong, serene, proud; with all the bold shades of shadows wrapping over it and moving as they appeared to me—surely because of the flickering branches around.

I went in thinking about something else. I had seen a gathering of local folks on my way to the house. It was certainly at a distance from our house, but surely, I would get a clear view of it from my passage's window. As I went in, I saw Ajay comfortably sleeping on the sofa, a blanket over him, and he bore the expression of an exhausted child. The nurse left me to the gentlewoman, the mother of Ajay's friend, who smiled pleasantly and received me. She let me know that she, on her own accord, had decided to remain there for a couple of days. I knew the importance of this exceptional conduct bearing in mind her childhood experiences, which she had told me previously, which all suggested that she had a slight psychological aversion to the place.

Ajay woke up as we stirred around, and his face showed excitement at seeing me, but I was resolute and I expressed to him that I wouldn't be discussing anything about the past night.

I sat on one sofa, and henceforth we engaged ourselves in a conversation. As I talked, I became more tranquil. Everything else was also calm that afternoon. The breezes were gentle and natural in the sense that they squeezed in and out through the windows, which were for the first time opened all at once. It was not only this which was quite new but as I couldn't stop looking around the hall as I spoke; I observed some subtle changes in it. It looked grand. It looked somewhat brighter, neater, and as if it had received back its previous composure, which had been lost for years. It must be the sunlight coming in, I thought, no; though it was brighter, there was still something about the house which made me feel rather charmed.

How hard it is to talk when all the speakers know they are actively avoiding something, I realized it that day.

"I am coming from my bedroom once, excuse me," I said at length and walked up after receiving a "Sure," from the woman.

Ultimately, after such a wait, I was standing before the window of the second-floor passage, the same window which had shown me sights of fantastic terrors the night before. From here I could see the cliff and not over seven or eight people standing there. It appeared they were gossiping, and some were moving around in a scrutinizing way. My immediate next move was to express a desire to be granted permission of having a walk in the garden and I got it more easily than I thought but with the word "the garden only".

In a casual stroll, I am rather sorry to say about my conduct here. I walked past the garden and within minutes reached the site. This place was rather remote and also certainly a colder place relative to where I was, on the comforting sofa as the sun here was filtered by tall trees standing intermingled with each other, covering most of the ground. I carefully navigated over the wet rocks and grass and as soon as I reached the middle of the crowd, I got information about the things just as I had expected.

I asked an elderly woman near me, and she replied, "Oh… it's such a terrible sight!"

She talked in excited anxiety and while this the grayness which I observed was again set to overshadow the bright sun-rather unsettled me. What she spoke may unsettle the reader, too. Here's the gist of it:

It was that last night some laborers returning home had heard dangerous cries echoing in that part of the town and as they reached the site, it was already over. What was over? As I asked about that, she said that they went mad at what they saw. They immediately left off to call for help, leaving the oldest of them all to keep an eye and when they returned with others, they were shocked too. What they saw on that rainy night was nothing but a bulky body of a man, stranded dangerously over the rocks, his legs stuck between branches of deep trees, and the body upside down. It was lying down the mighty cliff in a lost balance, and it didn't stir a limb. Not until morning broke were they able to see the actual condition of it in the void. Forget the question of going there and picking it up. Its hands were apart and so were its legs, way apart. It was wearing deep black clothes and was surely not alive. She also told that it still lay in the same from the morning and the locals were waiting for the authorities to bring it up. No one dared to go that deep.

She further told a peculiar thing, that the old fellow who was left there says that he had had some visions. He had seen a peculiar, luminous, visible fog; almost as if a man it was; overwhelming and moving around the body, which was, till that time, stirring. The next moment the old fellow thought he was mistaken as it lost its physicality like vapor spreads in the air and soon became one with the darkness. She also added that the old man who had seen such things had fainted a couple of times after that and was terribly unwell.

"Oh, it must be the rain and thunder—any mortal in that cold weather at three in the night would surely be ill to death. What do you think?" These were her concluding words, and I was not in a mind to reply.

I walked silently to the end, and for once caught the glimpse of the thing lying there. After that I, I swiftly paced back home; I had never seen a dead body before and till now never after.

As I returned, I didn't speak of it, and fortunately, no one noticed, Mrs. A and my cousin was rather engaged in lovely amazement, and for the first time I too; saw a pretty bird at our place, innocently peeping in through the window. Had birds started coming to our place? Especially Ajay was the most excited of all to see it. Soon the evening drew nearer, and the bulbs were switched on one by one. They lit the house well, and it too looked quite new to me, but as the darkness gradually enveloped the whole house and Uncle or anyone didn't return, a reflection of uneasiness gathered on my face which was noticed by my older companion.

"It though feels lovely here, such a mighty house," she spoke in a rather nervous way as she looked around the ceiling and the second floor "but tonight we are and we can surely have a good time—see, I have lit all the lamps and lights here."

She spoke her last lines smilingly and succeeded in lifting my spirits too. She was calm, aware, and confident in a pleasant way which didn't make me feel the horrors of being alone like the previous night, wherever there were circles of light, it was golden and chrome but as one's glance slid forward and backward, the shades and occasional shadows over the walls didn't go beyond notice. Silence in such a house with twelve or thirteen rooms and a hall with only three people sitting in the middle of it is a sort of peculiar and strangely burdening. It followed and overwhelmed us for minutes to such an extent that when my cousin crammed his fingers; it was heard distinctively. But we didn't allow it to conquer us as we were alarmed to see that the little boy was lately showing signs of nervousness by his directionless and purposeless fidgeting and bodily movements over the sofa, which also suggested that he was becoming rather restless.

We recommenced our talks with various fascinating incidents, and it traveled through the various folk stories of the town, it grew engaging and was at its peak, when I was reading to my two companions, from the pages of a book on my favorite subject.

"It's rather interesting to know about such fascinating cases from different parts of the world and I wonder how specialists in this field interpret things by this subject..." she remarked when I was done.

"Oh, yes, these stories are interesting," Ajay remarked, too.

"Is it? That's good to know." I answered my little cousin, waving back his dark brown hair from his forehead and eyes, and then felt his forehead. He was surely in better spirits than before.

"But…" I thoughtfully spoke to her "I now feel that there are there are things which can't be explained by studies like these too—I think humans' anticipation to one day know everything is a myth."

"Can I see the book?" She asked.

"Sure."

I handed the red-jacketed book to her and relaxingly leaned my head and arms on the table and kept looking at her through my drowsy eyes. She started flipping the pages and at one moment halted suddenly. She took a closer and more careful view of that page, which I perceived was at the last of the book. Her glance momentarily jumped to me in gentle, inquisitive scrutiny, while she still held that page. She returned the book and when it no longer hindered the view of her face; I was just a little surprised to notice a sort of sharp smile that had broken over her lips, which she perhaps didn't want to express openly. It kindled a smile on my part too as I grew inquisitive about what she had seen.

"I am keeping the plates for dinner," she said, stood, turned, and walked.

"I am coming…." I replied regarding setting the dinner table, while I still sat there, taking this opportunity to look at that page.

"Oh…." A realization struck me as I saw "Rajesh" written there.

I soon remembered that it was the book that he had gifted me, and this certainly reminded me of him as a person who remembers someone who she had met decades ago, like a faint memory. I was not holding any wrong thoughts for him, but I was quite in doubt related to him as he probably didn't turn out to be as he suggested. He was rather "unknown" to me still.

I walked into the kitchen and we both busied ourselves. The rattling of even a few utensils made a loud noise.

"This book, which I am reading, was gifted to me by my elder cousin's friend…" I said to clarify; I don't know what.

"Nice…" was her only reply.

"It's rather unimaginable to be here alone. I am very thankful to you for being with us… Your presence is absolutely…. I mean, I do not have words." I told her at this good opportunity.

"Oh, not a problem…" she replied gently.

When we had our dinner, the peak of our conversation was already over, and we sat rather silently. Our voices occasionally echoed, but every time silence re-conquered. A look of exhaustion was in the eyes of my companions, but now it was nowhere in me. I didn't want to go to bed anymore. I didn't want the conversation to be over. The idea of the deep night re-approaching and, after an hour I would be the only one awake with all other voices silent, ran through me as an uneasy sensation. A sensation that I had experienced only as a child.

"Time's passing rather slowly, I feel—look, it's just eight of night, but it looks like it's twelve," Ajay spoke, breaking the silence, but momentarily.

As I glanced around, the corners of the house looked even far and even somber.

The imagination of the dreary night in that house that was awaiting me, reflected before my eyes in a way that made me dread. The solitude, on the other hand, no one now had the energy to crack its veil again. As I was about to rise from the table, a momentary knock at our garden gate startled me. Perhaps normal sounds in prolonged silence can inspire.

"Who is it?" I asked and looked at my cousin who, as I knew, was looking at me with a question in his eyes.

Some seconds passed; no answer came from the other side. The clock had already struck nine, and the knock wasn't repeated. None was to come to us at that time and that too never from the garden gate. Mrs. A—stood up and walked towards the gate and I, freeing my hand gently from my cousin who had clutched it tightly; also walked. It was a dilemma and a risk. I halted at a distance and could see her figure in that unlit corner near the gate. She glanced momentarily at me and then finally her hands twisted the knob slowly, which made a creaking noise, and at this moment, another couple of louder knocks came. This time it was from the house's main gate. She was taken aback. Surely no one could turn from the garden gate to the main gate in seconds.

I felt quite choked with fright this time. Mrs. A's tensed eyes questioned me, but I had no answer. Soon the knock came for the third time, and there was no option of waiting anymore. Mrs. A—paced towards it and asked in a tone that expressed confidence which I knew all of us lacked at that point.

"It's me! Me! I have come here with Ma'am's pressed clothes."

I sighed hard. It was just the worker at the house.

It was opened. He entered.

"Miss, this is the third time I have come for this purpose—I found no one previously. Your clothes are ironed and as you would return, I thought I should return them to you."

I thanked him for coming at that hour. Mrs. A—locked the gate again. The man, after keeping the clothes, started on his own accord to organize and clean the dinner table. He did the cleaning of the utensils too and we were overwhelmed with gratitude, as none had the energy to do the pending task. He even, on our request, organized and prepared a room on the ground floor which had three beds, for our night stay. Without this, we would have to manage in the dreadful hall all night. After work, I asked him to have dinner at our place. He readily agreed. The clock had struck ten by this time. I got to know that he certainly spoke more when the master of the house wasn't there and his conversation with us, which we had initiated as he sat down to eat, once again killed the silence. It was naturally good. He ate in the kitchen, and I stood leaning at the door, listening with arms crossed against my chest. Mrs. A—washed her hands with the kitchen tap and walked out, telling me she would return soon after changing for the night. Meanwhile, Ajay sat at the dining table. In the still house, momentary thunders in the cloudy night sky were as clearly heard as outside.

I alone listened to him, the discussion couldn't be controlled, and it jumped to the main topic of the town, of then. He spoke to me about it opening new details.

Here's what he spoke in his raw language. "The men searched the whole night with their lanterns but couldn't find anybody around the body. The way it has fallen…" he sighed in dread and restarted, "who knows who he was and what was he up to?"

He stopped eating for a minute and while looking down in deep thought, his eyes broadened with dread, spoke, "But I feel he was thrown off."

"And what makes you think so?"

"Ahh… I have lived here for forty-five years, Miss, and I know every spot here. Any rational person wouldn't jump down this cliff at least. Even if the maddest person wants to die, he will not choose to die here."

"What do you mean" I released my arms.

"Stones! Pointed stones and trees down there! He would have been badly torn by the flesh! Everyone knows that down that void lie these…. There are more high cliffs around. I have just come back from there ma'am, it's terrifying to see his expression! Half-open eyes stare at the sky in a horrified unbroken gaze and no more descriptions are required. You know, his eyes didn't shut, and the people couldn't make his head straight, which always tilts down loosely and, and a blackened texture all over his face."

"My God…"

These talks made me walk out of the kitchen. I wished then that I hadn't heard it. But now it got drilled into my head. Though the house worker needn't be blamed.

"If everything which I am thinking is correct; then it is a dreadful end of him," I spoke to myself.

Mrs. A—had come by this time and the worker, after having his dinner, was ready to go. Mrs. A—went to close the gate after he had left. She too had a little talk with him there.

We all entered our room and settled ourselves on our respective beds. I laid on the middle bed, the white blanket over me till my neck and my gaze to the ceiling. I thought everyone was asleep, but it wasn't true.

Mrs. A—said while she gazed at the ceiling, "I asked the man why he had knocked at the garden gate. He replied he never knocked there and instead asked me why he would knock at that gate if there was the main gate?"

She took a turn and said, "Goodnight."

19

This was the end of the series of strange days, but the story begins now. The story behind all of it.

The next morning, I woke up late after a sound sleep. One bed beside me was vacant, the other one still occupied by my sleeping little cousin. Mrs. A—had awakened early, I believed. The morning was a bright one, even though the clouds hadn't faded, but they were quite far. I awakened Ajay, not taking any chance of leaving him alone, and then he followed me down the stairs. As I walked halfway down, not only the shining redness of the hall carpet, shining with the brightest sun rays that have ever entered the hall, struck my eyes but also the noises of doors closing and people talking "slowly" touched my ears. Kind of low commotion it was that was quite unusual for the otherwise silent house.

Three men were sitting on the sofas, with their backs towards the stairs—in a way I couldn't see them. Mrs. A was sitting facing the stairs, in front of a laid table where fruits and breakfast were arranged. She smiled somewhat brightly, looking at me and Ajay, and made a gesture asking to come fast.

Seeing her calling gesture, the three faces turned instantly toward me. These pale, exhausted faces were of Uncle, Arun, and certainly of the doctor.

I smiled, but no one returned it this time and by the time I and Ajay were seated in front of these accomplished gentlemen, and of course, before the lovely breakfast, Uncle said a "Good morning" with a dead nod of his head and a tough expression as if saying to me "Yes you can talk, we are right with our heads."

"Good morning, Uncle!" I said instantly and followed with a good morning to everyone there.

Uncle and Arun were sitting side by side this time.

"How are you both? Doing better?" The doctor asked me and Ajay.

"Certainly," I answered.

"Why don't we eat?" Mrs. A asked.

After which, with no further words, we started eating, so silently as if we were mourning.

"Arun, how are you doing?" I asked at length.

"Fine." He shrugged his shoulders and then asked, "I am released from the hospital, after all. How are you doing?"

"Good," I replied, and then we all started eating again, defending the impressive silence with all our might.

Uncle finally spoke when we had almost done with the breakfast, "Vaanya, first say what do you think of me? I mean, you may think me a clown, I know, but do you really think I was such a lunatic to have left you children alone on that night?"

"Uncle, I think nothing is wrong with you. But didn't you really leave us that night? We were really frightened." I replied at length to the unusual question.

"That's good. Now you must know one thing." He continued, "I was truly appalled seeing what my son was doing in his study, as you showed it to me, and I left the house in anguish, but I wasn't gone!"

"I didn't understand," Ajay said this time.

"I remained in the garden. To see."

"To see what?"

"Ah... you must be thinking that I had always neglected what you told me in case of the strange man who climbed into your window."

"So, is it not true?" I asked, rather perplexed.

"No. I am a lawyer, dear, and how could I take it so lightly? Since the day you said it, I had always been alarmed and aware but unfortunately, I couldn't sight the figure once. I took this opportunity to be in the garden for a while and see if the climber comes again—as somehow it struck me that, I don't know if it was right, that if he was a burglar or something, he would certainly try again in a stormy night such as that, and this was what happened. Though I didn't expect it to happen in the way it did."

I was struck with wordless bafflement.

"What about the painting!" it was as if I had forgotten this question altogether and this reckless exclamation by me was the result.

"Painting! Shaitaan's portrait?" Uncle spoke strangely and continued, "Leave all this, first please say what happened with you both on that night?"

"Uncle, we thought we were all alone. We stayed up till late at night but when you didn't return, we lay on our beds. In the middle of the night, a man broke into our bedroom. I couldn't see him well, but he was high and bulky—what I noticed was that his leg was… I don't remember exactly. He walked in an imbalanced way. Then he somehow found the painting, from under my bed and—"

"How did the painting come under your bed!" Uncle interrupted me and continued "I-I thought there was something terribly strange going on as I couldn't find the painting, where I had kept it safe, in the locked room, the room on the second floor. But then the room was locked. How could you get in and hide the painting in your room? This is preposterous, Vaanya… Why and how?"

I remembered the night when my uncle had come to my room and asked me if someone had come into the house or not and it was only after that he had spoken, "Now all is lost." Was this all related?

"Uncle, I want to clarify something, and I will tell the whole truth. But please tell me, do you know who Vishwakumar is?"

He nodded slightly and an extremely serious expression was shown on his face, but then he looked deep into my eyes with amazement and judgment.

"Please let me explain. I have nothing to do with Vishwakumar or the painting. I even didn't know that it was locked up in the room next to my bedroom, how could I? But Uncle, I-I don't know if I did it wrong or right and I apologize to Arun for my conduct, but when I stepped into Arun's room, I found the painting there."

"Arun's room? How did it come there?" Uncle spoke, even more baffled, and all eyes turned to Arun, who was looking sideways, facing no one and with an expression that was a combination of roughness, disappointment, and guilt to some tiny extent.

"And why did you bring that painting into your room? Vaanya…" The doctor, who was silent for all this while, asked.

"I don't know why," I replied, covering my forehead and eyes with my hand.

"What do you mean?" he asked again, in a gentle and aware tone.

"Doctor, I don't know why I brought that horrifying portrait to my bedroom, a thing that can chill any mortal to the bone. It just happened. Somewhat hypnotizing it was, and as I looked I-I couldn't remove my eyes from it and then I took it into my room…. The face still haunts me at times, comes before my eyes when I close them!"

"Okay, calm down child, no more explanations needed. I understand—" The doctor said and sat back, crossed his legs, and busied himself in lighting his pipe with a very thoughtful expression on his face.

"Arun, will you explain something? How did the painting come into your room?" Uncle asked.

"I-I had the keys," he started speaking at last and made his point which explains to me he was not fully at fault, but partly he was, he continued, "When I saw the signature on that painting, I knew it was, it was made by Vishwakumar and, and the only surviving image of Shaitaan." He spoke no more, and no one urged him to speak anymore. He was appalled as it is and in a weak state.

"So, you, thinking that I didn't know of its value, took the opportunity, and locked it up in your room, Isn't it? Horrible."

"Papa, I thought, and still believe this house is haunted! Do you think what Ajay sees and says is all wrong? I don't think so! I first thought that painting, that horrible face was—was somehow bringing all this negativity or," he sighed hard, "how can someone bear such a black and phantom-like thing to be in the house? I decided to do away with it—it would also fetch huge money and therefore searched for buyers too. What was so wrong with it? I kept it in my room so that when I would return, it would be easy for me to carry it out and exchange it. You never told me about it. That's why I had come that night, to get into my room through the garden window which I had purposely left open and to get that painting easily, but then I saw someone else running with that painting and so I tried to stop him."

"So, you, going in that black car… was it of the painting collectors who wanted to buy it?" I asked.

"Yes…"

"Uncle, Doctor told me of a person whom I had also met on this purpose, some Paul, who lived in this house immediately after Shaitaan's death had also seen a dark figure trying to break in into the house, and he thought it was a ghost after which his mental balance got deteriorated. He told me he had hit the figure badly on his leg and that's why I strongly feel that the climber was the same."

"That may be true!" Uncle replied and continued, "He lost his mind? Then was I lucky that I only lost my sleep and my bravery as I came here and…."

"Yes, you too had sleep problems after coming in this house and it can be connected with my lunatic patient…." The doctor interrupted, but then he spoke no more.

Horrors had pervaded all minds and after this statement, I noticed many eyes turning around to take a look at the house, its large ceilings and locked doors, probably with a different mindset—perhaps to find a couple of eyes staring at us from within the shadows.

The next moment, there was a hard ring on the door. The house servant opened it—two men entered carrying something square-shaped, something big and heavy, but it was covered with a black cloth.

"Keep it there, beside the door itself." Uncle ordered from his position.

The men roughly dragged that thing, tied in the black cloth, over the floor and kept it on the side carelessly.

"Papa, did you also purchase the house for the painting you thought it had? Like this Paul did?" Ajay asked this time, after they had gone, no one moved to look over it.

"No, I didn't know of it before and I didn't buy it for any wrong or greedy motive—but later I must admit, I got to know of the painting and that its value was beyond calculation. I knew it by a book by the same author which had also got misplaced from my room after the painting—probably Arun did that too." He eyed Arun for a moment and then again turned to his little boy and asked, "Will you believe me?"

"Oh, yes!" He replied.

"How did you find it?" the little boy asked again in the most innocent way.

"You want to know it, son? I found it buried in the garden."

"What!" Mrs. A exclaimed.

"Yes, when I was walking, something struck my leg—it was an edge of this frame that was coming out of the loose soil. It was buried carelessly there—in the ground as if done in an immense hurry."

"My God. This means that somebody buried the painting in the garden, then you kept it locked in the room on the second floor, then was taken by Arun and then again into the bedroom of Vaanya, from Arun's room, from where it got stolen!"

No one had anything as a reply.

"Uncle, why did you not want me to go out? It has been sticking around in my mind since."

"That's because I didn't want you to know and burden your mind with the story or gossip about Shaitaan—that goes around all the time in the town. But this happened. Ajay must have told you about the story, right?" He looked at the boy.

"Well, what do you all think is this house really haunted?" Uncle asked this question, a question that he had never asked or addressed.

"Yes, it is." Ajay was the only one to reply, and the other face was in half doubt.

A thought struck me—it was a deep realization that I was turning around in my mind to get it in full. I closed my eyes and remained speechless for a few minutes.

"What is it?" The doctor said slowly and curiously as he singled out me among all the other people who were still talking about these matters and once again everyone was silent.

"I—I am remembering something," I opened my eyes and continued, "Uncle, do you remember Ajay's drawings, which he scribbled? Once awake and the other time half drowsily?"

"I don't remember exactly…"

"Those drawings somewhat, no, perhaps almost matched with the portrait of Shaitaan, which was stolen… Similar expressions. How is it possible if Ajay has never seen the portrait?"

"If it is true then, really, this is—I can't understand how…. Should we believe what he said about the ghost?" Uncle looked extremely puzzled.

All eyes turned to Ajay again and such pressurized he became by the serious looks he endured that he somewhat sank into the sofa and couldn't meet anyone's eyes and just said, "The ghost…"

There was silence for some time.

"There is a second possibility… I think." Mrs. A—who till now had got an understanding suggested exactly what was going in my mind also, "Probably somehow Ajay had seen the portrait itself, in the room at night or something, mistaken it as a ghost! If the painting was so haunting and captivating, it might have stuck to the child's mind and the result was the drawings…"

"Was what he called a ghost his vision or hallucination after seeing the black and white painting? Which I also had at times…? Which means all of it is just…" I replied, and it looked convincing.

"It's unlikely to happen..." Uncle replied slowly.

Silence was there and then Arun supported, "It was locked and then I took it. There was no chance he could see the painting before that…"

"It could happen. It could not." The doctor thoughtfully muttered.

"Where is the painting, by the way?" I whispered to Ajay as I failed to contain my curiosity about it, but my whisper was heard by everybody, owing to the silence.

Now that it was heard, I made an expression to seek the answer from anybody there who could answer it.

"I would...," the doctor started in a very serious and pressing tone, "also like to see the painting."

The next moment four of us were looking deep into the painting, it was the thing bought by two men, covered in black cloth, which lay in front of us all.

"God!" Mrs. A turned away immediately. "I had seen him real." Others also didn't much look at it. Mrs. A—took my little cousin into the other room, as per everyone's agreement, though he also wanted to see the portrait and though he protested.

The painting was torn from the middle. It was found fallen into the void, along with the body. It was destroyed badly, yet the face could be seen.

"This all thing is just about the painting. A psychological trick, perhaps. This might make the painting more valuable. Though it doesn't seem very effective to me, as a man away from the house, the stories, and the darkness, I feel it is scary, but I think it won't come into my dreams. But in your case, hearing the stories repeatedly, being in this isolated house, and seeing this painting in circumstances of mental unrest and under poor light, might have caused you to see it when you close your eyes. Then it might have come into your dreams and when it got mixed with the haunted stories of Shaitaan, the power of this increased and you all thought you were seeing a ghost. All the reason is the overtaxed, overburdened brain, of all of you and the child got affected, mostly. He draws right?"

"Yes, drawing is his hobby..." Uncle answered.

"He also reads a lot of horror books," I added.

"Here is your answer. No point blaming the artist, or the painting, and no point in believing in ghosts—just a psychological coincidence. See, this time, the painting won't affect you. Now it doesn't look scary in the proper light."

"Yes... this time it's not looking scary at all. I wonder how it looks like a perfectly normal person. So can it be that the artist didn't do it purposely, or this was the shape of the face of Shaitaan, and there is nothing in this painting to disturb anybody and whatever happened is just a series of coincidences?"

"It could be... I think you should take all this as a coincidence series and take it lightly. It seems quite laughable. Take it lightly..."

"How did we have similar dreams?"

"Nightmares are similar for people and all of it because of the same stories over repetition that stressed the brain nerves—all science. Maybe the face of this person was such..."

"Yes, under normal light, it looks like an average painting with no brain-affecting genius or trick and far from haunting or scary..." Uncle replied.

"It looks like a traditional, typical painting, likes of which are seen daily in museums..." Uncle continued after a pause.

"So, this is for you..." the doctor stood up triumphantly, "I hope I have solved your problems... Now allow me."

The doctor proudly left us and we all were rather satisfied for the time being, by his idea that all of it was funny and a series of mistakes.

I still wonder how our perception of the painting changed unanimously and suddenly.

"So, no one is to be blamed?" Uncle asked all of us in a calm tone.

"Who is lying dead there?" Arun asked.

"God knows who that climber is, now lying dead. Who was that who knew of this painting?" Uncle said and made a gesture of standing, but soon remembered his injury and didn't.

"I think I know—" I said, "but you won't believe it."

"Who is it?" Uncle spoke partly in a whisper—a curiosity in his tone, and a belief too then leaned forward and then backward again.

"It's, it's none other than candy, Mr. Candy," I replied at length.

"Mr. Candy?" Uncle exclaimed, "He must be now in his shop!"

We stopped further discussions for the time being. But after an hour, the investigator arrived. He wasn't dressed in any uniform—but was dressed in a gray suit, pants, and a hat and carried a leather bag. He came in and first presented his statement:

"So, Mr. Vijay, the valuable painting was in your house's second-floor room. The climber broke into the house to steal it and was successful as the children were alone. Then you, who was giving guard down, tried to stop the climber and then came Arun, who also tried the same, and then a secret service agent who was deployed to monitor the happenings in this house—as recommended by our secret officer. But all was in vain and the climber, ran with the painting, in the night, mistakenly stood at the cliff edge and then was thrown by somebody or fell down by himself. If thrown, we have no evidence to find who threw him down. You all were injured and taken to the hospital the next day."

"Who was this officer who recommended a secret agent to keep track of the events of this house Sir?" I asked.

"Sorry, Miss. Can't say all this to you."

I think I knew who he was.

Then the investigator asked almost everyone for some information. He did so casually, which made none of the witnesses anxious. Arun admitted he had hit Rajesh. The night I had seen the black car in the woods, both had confronted each other there and perhaps both were behind the painting.

"Miss, now you tell…" the investigator asked, and I told whatever I had to say.

"I think the man who is lying dead is Mr. Candy, the Food cabin owner," I said and paused.

"Yes, it's right… the body is of Mr. Candy and he has been identified. Also, the food cabin was a fraud… He never served people there, only had the shop on…" the investigator answered, checking his papers.

This confirmation caused surprise in Uncle and others.

I continued, "Sir, I also know that Mr. Candy is a fake person himself. He is not an old, bearded man. He is a criminal, he is Neelnath."

"What? Why do you think so, according to our records, that criminal is dead months ago?"

"Sir, I had seen the handprint of Neelnath, and Mr. Candy's one matches… Also, I know Neelnath had killed Shaitaan after running from prison as Shaitaan had refused to be part of the deal and then he had done away with Shaitaan's body at the crematorium in his own name and with a fake signature. Thus, he declared himself dead and returned as Mister Candy."

"And why did he return with a forged identity?"

"Perhaps he knew of the last valuable item, the portrait. Perhaps Shaitaan lived his last days in his second and unfinished house and the painting was with him. But Neelnath stole it and hid it the same night when he killed Shaitaan and buried the painting in the garden of our house. As he returned as 'Candy', he couldn't find the painting dug in the ground, so he became desperate. He couldn't find the painting as Uncle found it and locked it up in his room. Then Mr. Candy struck a fake friendship with Uncle to enter the house. He asked me what was there in our house and were all rooms open, questions like that. He almost made friends with everyone in our house except me, who knew his identity. That's why he came to our house, tried to enter my room, and…"

"And... I also think he was the one who had climbed to my window perhaps a couple of times before too, but he could never make it. Almost as if something was resisting him to enter. That night he came again and tried to steal the painting, got success but now is no more alive."

"You know a great deal… Anything more?"

"He also asked and was continuously forcing Uncle to be a part of his business, of the same scandal which Shaitaan had rejected as wanted to set his smuggling route through these old valleys once again. That's why he had sent some crates to Uncle for storage… I think it's the same banned liquor in it."

"Unbelievable… I could have never guessed!" Uncle replied.

"Sir, this is all."

"Miss, I thank you immensely. We will clarify this information probably by evening. You are very brave… you might get an award for this."

"Sir, I also have a request which is of extreme importance to me… will you listen?" I asked.

"We will try. Say."

"I ask a favor. I don't want all of this story to become public. I don't want any award whatever it might be. I want my private identity to remain private—and don't want my findings to be published in dailies, with my name, or in any other way. Whatever I did, I did with no motive, and I want to remain a free individual, not a recognized person in any way—good or bad."

"Oh..." he thought for moments deeply, "It's tough. Though the press is weak here, the death which happened can dominate the headlines for weeks..."

"Sir, please. I really, really request you do anything possible for this." I asked, looking deep into his eyes, and he sighed hard after seeing my requesting look.

"I will certainly try. See the headline the next day. I can't promise anything now. Thank you for your cooperation. Now I have to confirm the facts. Will return in the evening."

"I am, I am... I have lost words. Dear, if you are right then, I was wrong. I-I never guessed this person, having the biggest smile one could have been..." Uncle spoke, but couldn't after some time.

"What she says is true. The man at the crematorium took a bribe and is now arrested... Mr. Candy is no one, he is identified as Neelnath. Also, the crates are full of banned, hazardous beverages."

Hours had passed with the investigator, and soon it was evening. After the investigator had left us, we all, I dare to speak of all, were, as I believe in the same state in which a man believes he is just; a mortal—a meek mortal. Time passed rather quickly, and to all of our astonishment, none of us, even when subjected to such conditions, felt any anguish or distress. I, Ajay, the house worker, and, of course, Mrs. A—were enough for doing the evening work of tea, biscuits, and bread. The only change was in Uncle who looked surprised the whole time and still contemplating—Arun was silent as before, thinking of his fate, which would soon follow—because something bad was still hidden from all of us.

Things in the house looked changed. Things, even the air in the house, looked peaceful as if some unfulfilled work was completed.

The sharp golden rays of the retreating, red sun pierced into the house through slight window openings and from here and there—and when the windows were opened entirely, the beautiful sunshine flooded in, like never.

While we were drinking our tea, the evening had turned calmer and the sun almost retreated, with its beams lighter. After tea, we trooped together to the garden and could persuade Uncle to come with us, but no one could persuade Arun. He was immovable as a rock and when I tried to persuade him and even ask him what the matter with him was, for he looked in shock, he made no answer. Ultimately, I had to leave him alone, thinking he was already this strange and that it was his normal behavior. I was wrong.

All the time we were in the garden, I eyed Uncle. He was totally fine—and I had seen nothing unusual about his behavior. He never talked to me in the local language, his accent never became heavier, and his eyebrows never came closer in a horrendous manner. The beauty in the sky was bewitching, and there was even a natural scent all around and even in the house. I believe I had noticed it so hard for the first time. I and Ajay played for some time. But while running in this play, I at once reached and almost hit the loose boundary fencing. It shook, by the force of my recklessness, and for a moment I stood there to take a breath, while my chin was almost at the top of the fencing. At this moment, my eyes saw something. A man was approaching—that's only what I understood from the momentary glimpse of him, within which the sun ultimately dropped, and the figure was lost from sight. I was taken aback instantly.

"Uncle, someone is coming to our house. Any guest?"

"I don't think so—let's get back, it's getting dark."

"I heard a ring at the gate," Ajay spoke, and we trooped back to the house.

The doorbell was ringing in reality.

I was just a little surprised to see who our unexpected visitor was. It was the temple priest. He stood there still and never entered until Uncle requested him to do so. I soon learned that my uncle had himself implored him to come, which was the most unlikely thing to happen. Even in the short distance which he walked from the gate to the sofa, there was something peculiar, something very noticeable in his way of walking. It was very slow and extremely cautious. He kept on looking around the house even while he sat.

When he was told the complete story in brief and prayed to give an explanation, evidently to solve the matter on the spiritual level, he began:

He turned his face towards Uncle, looked into his eyes deeply, and asked, "Sir, did you really not understand anything?"

There was a pause for a moment while he still kept looking deep into Uncle's eyes. But he didn't reply, kept his head a bit bent all the while.

"You can smell it. Isn't it?" By this time the priest had closed his eyes, and such a conviction was in his words as he spoke further in a little louder voice and for me, quite intimidating too, like a vibration, it flowed "Mr. Vijay, I know, you have yourself seen it, felt it, sometimes. You partly know what has happened here and partly don't. You were and are afraid, too. You deny… lying to yourself. You have felt it."

I held Ajay's hand.

"Am I right?" He opened his eyes and Uncle immediately exclaimed in the most unlikely manner as if words were pulled out of his stomach, though he was comfortable and earnest as he said, "Yes! I didn't believe it. I also felt something here, but what could I have done after purchasing this place?"

"What should we do now? I have done nothing incorrect, and I strongly believe in this." Uncle said.

The priest stood up, walked towards the window, stood there, arms crossed, and said, "No need to do anything, any sort of superstition. Now the work is done, no need to worry."

"You all had similar dreams. You even saw the second house and a scene of killing which you have described." The priest said pointing towards me and continued "The sudden tearing of your dress, your uncle's language changes after wearing those clothes on occasions, the damp, dusty, and pressing smell that stayed in the house and moved through and out of rooms from nowhere, the coincidental sabotage of the climbers attempt and then the pulling down of Candy when he tries to enter your room… all are indications to which I am pointing out. A thing like that, if moves near, can also cause its emotions to enter yours…"

"So, should we leave this house? We will do exactly what you say…" Uncle asked.

"No need. It has nothing to do with you all. Whatever it had to do, it has done. It's no longer here."

Before Uncle could cross the question, "Sir, do not ask more. But remember one thing: his last rites should be done."

He and Uncle talked in solitude for some time, of which I know nothing, but that he had suggested the clothes of Shaitaan be better disposed of in a manner no one could use or sell them. He didn't stay longer.

"There is something more here, isn't it?" The priest asked as he was going out.

"Yes… there is a painting of this man."

"Can I see it?"

The painting was shown.

"A very impressionistic piece of artwork. Rare it looks, has some quality beyond human comprehension, bestowed into it by the artist…"

The painting again looked impressionistic to all of us.

"Destroy the painting Mr. Vijay." The priest told suddenly; his eyes were closed.

"Child, you know something about this, right? Tell your uncle…"

I was stunned for a second after which I said, "Uncle, I have heard that Shaitaan never clicked his photographs. He didn't want the world to see him and keep his face in their memories and that is why this, the only representative of him, also was a personal property that he had kept privately for himself. Probably he lived his last days in his second house and the painting was stolen by Neelnath from there."

"It is already destroyed half… Do not keep such a thing, do not give it to the museum… It is his, do what he must have wanted to do…"

"I do not want any money from this thing," Uncle replied.

So, in front of the priest himself, after the dark, this painting was committed to flames. We watched it burn, bright red, yellow, orange, and gold, dancing flames, lighting up the dark garden. After minutes, light rains started, and we headed into the house. By the fire was extinguished, the rare painting was reduced to ashes… forever locking the secret of Shaitaan's face. The rains were light and blissful, and the priest returned with his umbrella, saying "God bless everyone…"

The head investigator returned by evening and said "Sir, what she says is true. The man at the crematorium took a bribe and is now arrested… Also, the crates are full of banned, hazardous beverages. Whatever she knows is the true story."

He returned without inquiring about the painting and also gave no assurance to me of my request.

Uncle embraced me, and then Ajay followed. Uncle said, "Will you forgive me, dearest? I was completely wrong… I apologize."

His tone was of a person really sorry and emotional, too.

"Uncle, I know you well. Don't ask forgiveness like this. I admire you a lot."

He kissed me on my forehead and said, "You are brilliant and brave, dear."

After he left me, Ajay hugged me tighter, and tears rolled down his cheek. "I learned you are leaving. Don't go."

I kissed his cheek and replied, "I will come back soon here."

This was not meant to happen. Though only a few years have passed; the town, I think will never be the same for me.

I completely forgot about an issue that was making me worry about my name on the headlines, which I really didn't want. I slept the last night over there—the sleep was as divine and as blissful and as comforting and as healing, as I had not had in years. The rains continued easily, hitting my window glass, setting the air in coldness and scent, and I slept peacefully on that silent night.

The next morning, I was awakened by Mrs. A—and Ajay, and both were smiling. It was nine-thirty. As I got down, there was Uncle who said in high spirits, "Dear, here is your breakfast ready, and here is your luggage. Everything for you is done. You need not worry."

"Oh, thank you, Uncle, you surprised me. You look good today!"

"I have disposed of all his costly coats and pants. In fact, I now think they never suited me at all and made me look as funny as a joker. Silly me." Uncle spoke and laughed.

"Don't judge me on that, dear… It was a mistake." He whispered into my ear. I nodded.

After breakfast, we sat talking. The sun was the brightest till that time. The house was in a low commotion, and everything was simply as charming as never.

"We have signed Ajay into the most reputed boarding school, which is near the town itself, they agreed to his admission by a letter that we received in the morning, and also, they agreed to put him in the class in which he should be despite, his study break in the middle. All based on his tests, which he had given a month ago." Uncle spoke in a jolly way and looked at Ajay, who was shy.

"What a surprise!" Mrs. A said.

"Ajay! Congratulations!" I told.

We all clapped for him for a long time. He was leaving the next day.

"Now he would not be involved in overthinking and enjoy with students of his age," I thought and felt happy.

"We are getting the house renovated, which means we are not leaving," Uncle said.

"Keep it up, Uncle…" I said, and we joined in enthusiasm.

Amid all these discussions, I realized what I had forgotten and asked, "Uncle, where is today's newspaper? I want to see it now."

I took half an hour to fetch the newspaper; the job being given to the houseworker. I sat quite tensed—as the investigator had given no assurance and by his words; I had decided that he wouldn't be able to do anything. Four newspapers were bought, which were all for the town and the state.

I hurriedly ran my eyes through them. I sighed hard in relief. Not even a single newspaper had any story about the painting or the death of Neelnath—I wasn't referred to anywhere in any of the dailies. The head investigator was successful in holding the story for investigatory and private reasons. I was relieved and everyone else was, too.

"What about Arun?" I asked.

"He, too, will continue his studies of law in the city. Oh, but he, he… it was a chance that he could be under interrogation for hitting Rajesh, but

Rajesh has returned. He made no complaint against Arun, and the case was ended. Rajesh is truly a great friend. He visited in the morning while you were asleep, he asked for your well-being and then told me the entire story behind his coming to the house."

"Oh, I knew Rajesh wasn't a bad or deceitful person. I was asleep when he came?"

"Yes, dear… we didn't wake you up."

"Oh…" I sighed in a bit of regret and said to myself, "This means I won't meet him ever again."

It was ten thirty, and still, an hour left for me to leave. I sat in nostalgia; in remembrance of the day, I had arrived. My room had been locked and my luggage was down. I ran my eyes through the house, through every corner—as if I was trying to capture it into my memory.

"Vaanya, this is a small gift from my side, with love. A collection of eight unique books on your subject by eight different authors, ordered by me from the town's bookshop—these books are rare. An impressive collection the bookshop has."

"Oh, thank you, Uncle! It is not a small gift!"

"I really hope you like it. It is all."

"It's great, Uncle—I am very, very happy."

Now only half an hour was left for me in the house, and I felt, don't know why my heart beating faster. At this moment, there was a ring at the door.

I opened it and never could have guessed who I saw.

"Rajesh you?"

"Good morning," he said and smiled.

"How are you now? I really thought I won't see you again."

"I am fine—I am good." He spoke standing at the gate and shyly smiled and said nothing more.

"Come in…"

"No. Want to walk one last time before leaving?"

"But I am leaving within fifteen minutes… We cannot go far." I said again in nostalgia.

"Oh, not far, just in the lane—five minutes?"

So, we were out. My first visit with him came to my mind again and again—how old it looked then and how old it looks now. That day, the sun was glaring, and the leaves were shining with it.

"Do not misunderstand me. I will tell you the entire story…" He spoke.

"Yes, say it to me."

"Actually, yes, I was there for the portrait. But my friendship with you was genuine."

"Yes, I know that."

"So, the authorities were behind this famous painting and wanted it for the museum. They had a hint of where it was. That is why I wanted to meet Arun. I had to offer the right price for the painting to him and ensure that the painting legally is transferred to the authorities, and that is why I came that night also, with so much money to persuade Arun. That was my only goal, to do the job I was assigned—and I didn't have any personal benefit involved."

"Oh! Only if Arun would have met you, all this wouldn't have happened."

"Yes... I was the one who deployed that secret service agent to track your house at night, as I expected a danger." He spoke.

"You know, I never misunderstood you. I knew you were a fantastic person and genuine, too."

"I don't want to hide anything from you. If you say I can tell…"

"Don't. No need to go beyond your norms. I have a hint of what you will say. I knew it to some extent since the first day when I had seen the book fall from your pocket. It doesn't make any difference to me. Trust me."

"Oh, thank you Vaanya." He said in happiness, "See how beautiful it is over here and the air has a scent too…"

"Yes… but I wish it rained. It's so, so beautiful when it rains…"

"Now let's return." He said, looking at his watch.

At the gate, I looked at him for the last time.

"Vaanya, just know that you are lovely. I will remember you." These were his last words to me as he looked deep into my eyes and then turned back, waved, and walked.

I couldn't say anything to him in the end—not even a goodbye.

The time was up soon. I walked out of the house. The winds were stronger again and the trees shaking. I took a last look at the house, and the garden, and then walked out. As I was being driven through the lane, I looked at it. I constantly looked at the infinite sky and grasslands. My heart felt heavy as the carriage rolled.

20

Everything was in shades of light and dark blue, black, and white. The sky was cracking with the thunder. Uncle was on the train directing his helper to put in my heavy suitcase. The other luggage was still in my hand. The station was exactly the same as on the day I had come, and that day felt like yesterday. I stood there alone, in the shadeless part of the concrete station. My hair was just a little wet, but still, it was attuned to the flow of the winds. I stood there to have a last look at the lone town and the lone station. It will always be like a dream in my memory, though in reality all of it may be lost.

Soon it started drizzling again. I felt strongly and consciously, the cold drops falling over my face and sliding down my cheeks.

I stepped up onto the train. Mr. Roy was there, doing some change over my seat. The train would set off in a couple of minutes—a couple of trivial minutes?

I sat for the time being on the opposite vacant seat so that I could see from its glassed window my uncle, and my little cousin, who was still there, waiting. Ajay was still waving slowly. I felt overwhelmed with emotion at this moment.

"Good to see you, Ma'am!" Mr. Roy once settled on the seat opposite to mine, said this and looked at me with a big smile on his face.

I leaned back in my seat. I sighed. The train was set in extremely slow motion.

My companion held a newspaper in his hands and started running his eyes through it—once he had one, no one could stop him from reading it.

"Do you believe in ghosts?" He spoke slowly, while his face was behind the paper.

"What—what happened to your voice!" I stood forward in horrified amazement.

The doors of the compartment were locked, the lights were dim; in and out, and no one else was with us. There was a long journey to go like this.

"What scares you so much, Miss? I have a bad throat." He said and cleared his throat heavily.

"Is my voice okay now?"

I felt struck by his question—why did he ask this?

Did I believe in ghosts?

Last time on the train I had avoided reading on this subject—my belief was, in my life, I would have nothing to do with it. When I went to the house and lived, I thought I could explain all of it. Soon I understood human's quest for explaining everything in this world was a dream which would remain unfulfilled ever.

But did I believe in ghosts? Belief is a strong word. I knew I had to make a choice—all have to make it. Well, why do I need an opinion—when facts are not there, and everyone only interprets? Opinions are needed to show to the public—for which I have little care. They aren't needed personally. I had made my choice. I would forever take the position of an "observer" of the phenomena of life and whatever it showed before me—only to observe, without interpreting.

"Mr. Roy, I choose not to care about ghosts or their existence," I replied, but my voice went weak in the end, as Mr. Roy didn't move or remove his paper as he heard my answer.

"Why—why do you ask?" I felt unnerved—because for sure he had no chance of knowing any occurrence at the mansion.

There was silence for seconds and then he replied.

"Oh! See, I didn't ask you. I just mistakenly read aloud the title of a short story from the newspaper."

The train caught speed. The station appeared smaller from far and gradually became invisible. Ajay, after waving, turned and hid his face in Uncle's coat. Uncle was last seen waving to me and then stroking the boy's hair. Drizzling soon turned into rain.

I closed my eyes and saw—how much more there was to see.

~The End~

About the Author

SHASHANK JALAN is (at the time of writing) a college student and simultaneously pursuing professional studies. He also plans to do a postgraduation in Management. He believes his interest in writing and sketching developed in his childhood. Throughout his school days, he wrote many short stories, some of which got published in children's newspapers and magazines. Apart from these, he is interested in philosophy and great personalities' lives.

www.ingramcontent.com/pod-product-compliance
Lightning Source LLC
LaVergne TN
LVHW010542160826
845677LV00013B/2963

* 9 7 8 9 3 9 0 8 8 2 9 2 2 *